Praise for the Zoe Chambers Mystery Series

"I loved *Bridges Burned*. The action starts off with a bang and never lets up. Zoe's on the case, and s... through the mystery's twists and t... vulnerable and relatable. I adore her, a...

New York Times Be...

"New York has McBain, Boston has Parker, now Vance Township, PA ("pop. 5000. Please Drive Carefully.") has Annette Dashofy, and her rural world is just as vivid and compelling as their city noir."
— John Lawton,
Author of the Inspector Troy Series

"I've been awestruck by Annette Dashofy's storytelling for years. Look out world, you're going to love Zoe Chambers."
— Donnell Ann Bell,
Bestselling Author of *Deadly Recall*

"An easy, intriguing read, partially because the townfolks' lives are so scandalously intertwined, but also because author Dashofy has taken pains to create a palette of unforgettable characters."
— *Mystery Scene Magazine*

"Dashofy has done it again. *Bridges Burned* opens with a home erupting in flames. The explosion inflames simmering animosities and ignites a smoldering love that has been held in check too long. A thoroughly engaging read that will take you away."
— Deborah Coonts,
Author of *Lucky Catch*

"Dashofy takes small town politics and long simmering feuds, adds colorful characters, and brings it to a boil in a welcome new series."
— Hallie Ephron,
Author of *There Was an Old Woman*

FAIR GAME

Books in the Zoe Chambers Mystery Series
by Annette Dashofy

FAIR GAME

A ZOE CHAMBERS MYSTERY

ANNETTE DASHOFY

HENERY PRESS

Dedicated to the memory of
Phyllis and Donnie Ryburn

ACKNOWLEDGMENTS

I've known for some time I wanted to set a story at the county fair as a nod to the lifelong friends I made there and to the 4-H leaders who played a huge part in shaping me into the person I am. I apologize for making their fictional counterparts into such sleezy and suspicious characters, but this is a murder mystery after all. I like to think Phyllis and Donnie Ryburn, were they still with us, would have enjoyed the bits and pieces of them that I wove into the tale. I hope so, anyway.

And yes, school bus demolition derby is a real thing at my local county fair.

By way of technical support, I owe a huge debt of thanks to Chris Herndon for her help with the coroner aspects of the book; to Charles Van Keuren for his assistance regarding legal accuracies; and to Kevin Burns for patiently answering all my police procedural questions. Any mistakes in those areas are mine and mine alone.

Thank you to Ramona Long and her Facebook Writing Champions for making sure I show up at the computer every morning to get my pages written. I have no idea how I'd make my deadlines with them holding me accountable.

To my critique partners, Jeff Boarts, Liz Milliron, and Tamara Girardi, thank you for catching my stupid early errors and, like Ramona, prodding me to produce a sizeable submission each and every month. A huge thank you to Erin George for whipping this manuscript into shape and showing me where to trim the fat. You're the best! And to my sharp-eyed proofreaders: Edie Peterson, Anne Slates, Wanda Anglin, and Sheri Bradshaw, thanks for catching the goofs that slip past all the rest of us. Dear readers, if you still find something amiss, please accept my apologies. We really do try our best to provide a typo-free product.

As always, I'm beyond grateful for the support and guidance I've found in Pennwriters and Sisters in Crime, including my Pittsburgh Chapter, National, and the Guppies. You taught me how to be a writer and have been my staunchest cheerleaders since I've been published.

Speaking of published, I want to thank everyone at Henery Press—Kendel, Art, Christina, and Maria. And Stephanie Savage who has once again created an amazing cover. I know I asked a lot this time (school bus demolition derby???) but you really rocked it!

To my readers: THANK YOU THANK YOU THANK YOU for standing by me, for coming out to my events, and mostly for loving Zoe and Pete as much as I do. A special shout to my Facebook street team at Zoe Chambers Mysteries & Friends. If you enjoy the series and want to hang out with some fun and crazy readers and other authors, search us out and join. There's always room for more in "the Clubhouse."

I'd be remiss if I didn't mention my personal support team. Gretchen Smith, Wendy Tyson, Cynthia Kuhn, Meredith Schorr, and Julie Mulhern. You ladies keep me sane. Leta Burns, Terri Watson, and Jeanette Wriston, you three are the sisters of my heart if not my blood. I love you all.

Which brings me to my husband who gives me wings to fly and a soft place to fall when I come back to earth. I couldn't do what I do without Ray Dashofy.

ONE

Vance Township Police Chief Pete Adams shifted his gaze from the report he was working on to the small burgundy velvet box on his desk. He'd been in law enforcement for almost twenty years, half of that in the city of Pittsburgh. He'd faced down crack-heads and killers. Last spring, he'd even taken a bullet.

But nothing he'd ever experienced terrified him as much as what was inside that little velvet box.

The intercom on his desk buzzed followed by his secretary's staticky voice. "Chief, there's a man here who wants to speak with you."

A man. Nancy would've given a name had she known it, so not a regular. She'd come to know nearly everyone who lived in Vance Township, so probably not a resident.

Pete clicked into a different screen on his computer, one that showed the four different security camera views including the vestibule out front. He'd guessed right. He didn't recognize the guy standing at the reception window.

Pete stashed the velvet box in his desk drawer, locked it, and hit the intercom button. "I'll be right out."

Attired in khaki cargo pants and a short-sleeved polo with a company logo on the breast, the stranger stood too tall, his shoulders hiked a little too high. His smile a little too forced. Not someone accustomed to facing law enforcement, and if he was trying to fake being at ease, he was a damned lousy actor.

Pete extended a hand. "Chief Pete Adams. How can I help you?"

"Victor Hewitt," the stranger said, clasping the hand. His mouth tightened, and for a moment Pete thought Hewitt might change his mind and beat a hasty retreat. "I—" He ran his tongue across his lips. "I think I need to report a murder."

* * *

Zoe Chambers tried to remember the last time she'd competed in a horseshow. It had to be close to twenty years ago at the county fair when she'd been a teenager in 4-H. As she stood in the aisle of the Pony Barn at the Monongahela County Fairgrounds in the sweltering August heat, she vacillated between feeling like that eighteen-year-old again and feeling like Methuselah.

Decades ago, the Pony Barn only housed ponies, but in recent years, it also stabled horses during Fair Week. Which started tomorrow, Saturday. Today was the day when everyone hauled in their livestock, entered their produce, and set up their exhibits. In other words, madness.

Behind Zoe, her Quarter Horse gelding paced circles in the stall and snorted his displeasure.

"Yeah," she said to him. "I don't know what we're doing here either."

Patsy Greene, Zoe's second cousin and barn helper at home, bustled in, lugging two bales of hay. "Yes, you do."

"Yes. I do." Zoe took one of the bales and set it in front of Windstar's stall. "You made me come."

"For the gazillionth time. He'd have been a nervous wreck being the only horse left at home."

True. Not including her own horse, Zoe kept three boarders at her money pit farm. The pair of young girls who owned two of the horses were 4-Hers participating in the county roundup held at the fair. Patsy's Arabian mare was the third boarder, and Patsy had decided for some idiotic reason to enter Jazzel in the open halter classes this year. Which would have left Windstar alone in his pasture, whinnying endlessly for his buddies.

Considering his current stall-walking and head-tossing, he wasn't too happy in this strange location either, despite Jazzel's proximity in the next stall.

"I don't know why you're complaining." Patsy thumped her bale on the ground, straightened, and ran her arm across her sweaty forehead. "We've got a nice camper out back. It'll be like a week-long slumber party."

Zoe dug her penknife from her jeans pocket and sliced the twine on the bale. "Last time I spent a week here, I slept on a cot in the barn." She loosened a compressed flake of hay from the bale, slid open the stall door, and tossed it to her edgy gelding. The food did the trick. He stopped pacing and started ripping into the hay.

"Hey, if that's what you prefer, I'll happily keep the camper to myself."

"No, thank you."

As Zoe pocketed her knife, a scuffle and a scream rolled down the barn from the far end of the aisle.

"Catch him!" someone shouted.

She looked toward the commotion expecting to see a loose horse. The animal, however, wasn't loose. Not technically.

A small girl, maybe six or seven years old, was holding onto the end of a lead rope attached to a fat, spotted pony who was struggling to get free. The pinto bumped into buckets, sending them clattering, stumbled into a tack trunk, and wheeled in an attempt to bolt. The little girl held on. Adults and bigger kids scrambled to grab the rope, which only further spooked the pony. It crashed into a wheelbarrow, half jumping, half falling over it. The collision jerked the rope and the girl, who tumbled face-first onto the dirt floor. The lead rope ripped from her hands, and the pony hit the ground, rolled, and clamored to its feet. Free at last, it took off at a dead run toward Zoe and Patsy's end of the barn.

A pair of teens made an unsuccessful grab at the speedy little beast, but it dodged them, leaving only Zoe and Patsy between it and the door. And the rest of the County Fairgrounds.

Side by side, they spread their arms. A two-woman barricade between the wild-eyed charging pony and the great outdoors.

The pony slowed slightly, trying to decide what to do. Then it sped up and churned toward the gap between the two women, committed to getting the heck out of there.

Zoe lunged as it attempted to sail past her, snagged the trailing lead rope in one hand, a fistful of flying mane in the other. Patsy had made a similar move from the other side, grabbing the escapee around its neck. Used to having much bigger horses attempt to drag her, Zoe dug in her heels. Threw her weight back. Water skiing without the water. Or the skis. She was vaguely aware that Patsy had again mirrored her actions.

The pinto may have been able to overpower a small girl. Two women took a bit more effort. Had it been wild and untrained, or just plain rank, it might have continued to battle and would've won. But being a kid's pet and scared, the pony surrendered and stopped at the doors.

Still clinging to the pony and the rope, Zoe got her feet under her, aware of a half dozen adults and older teens surrounding them. Seasoned horsemen, speaking softly, moving slowly, deliberately so as not to set off the jittery beast.

Windstar nickered through the bars on the upper half of his stall. Zoe wondered if he was trying to soothe the pony or saying, *better luck next time, kid.*

A man in a rumpled plaid shirt thudded over to them and took the rope from Zoe. "I've got him," he said, breathing hard.

She looked down the aisle toward the little girl who'd face-planted in her failed attempt to maintain control. A woman was on her knees with the howling child gathered in her arms. Zoe overheard snippets of conversation from the group who'd reclaimed possession of the pony. After hearing someone say, "broken arm," Zoe caught Patsy's eye.

Her cousin gestured to her. *Go.*

Zoe grabbed a duffel bag she'd stashed behind a pair of folded lawn chairs leaning against Windstar's stall and strode down the aisle to the girl. The woman cradling her looked up, tears streaking her face.

Zoe dropped to her knees next to them and offered a comforting smile. "I'm a paramedic. Let me have a look."

"Who's been murdered?" Pete asked.

Victor Hewitt stuffed his hands in his pants pockets. "That's the thing. I don't know. And I don't think it's happened yet. At least I hope it hasn't. That's why I'm here. I want you to stop it."

Pete eyed his secretary who shrugged. To Hewitt, he said, "Come with me."

A few minutes later, they were seated in the station's conference room, Pete at the head of the long table, Hewitt catty-corner from him.

Pete opened his notebook and settled his reading glasses on his nose. "Tell me about this murder you want me to stop."

Hewitt squirmed, trying to get comfortable. "I'm traveling on business and spent last night at the Vance Motel."

Pete knew the place. Small, one-story, outside entrances to about twenty clean and tidy rooms. Situated on what used to be a main route until the four-lane went in, the motel now struggled to make ends meet. But to owner Sandy Giden's credit, she'd refused to rent rooms to riffraff and had kept it family-friendly.

"I was on the verge of falling asleep," Hewitt continued, "when voices from the next room woke me up."

"Shouting?"

He considered the question. "Not really shouting. Loud though. The walls of that place are like tissue paper. At first, I couldn't make out what they were saying. I mean, I was trying to tune them out and go to sleep." Hewitt ran a hand across his mouth. "But then one of them said, 'I want him dead. I'm gonna kill him myself.'"

"Is that exactly what was said?"

"Exactly. I'll never forget it."

"What else?"

"The other guy was quieter. Keeping his voice low. I couldn't hear what he was saying, but it sounded like he was trying to calm the loudmouth down."

"Could you make out anything else?"

"He said it a couple more times. 'I'm gonna kill him,'" Hewitt lowered his head. "Actually, his exact words were, 'I'm gonna kill the son of a bitch for what he's done.' And that was it. I heard the door over there slam, so one of them must have left."

"Did you happen to get up and look out the window?" A description of the man or his vehicle would be nice.

"No. I guess I should have. But I thought, you know, maybe he was drunk and blowing off steam."

"Did he sound drunk?"

"No. Maybe. I don't know."

"And you think he was just blowing off steam?"

"At the time. But then I couldn't fall asleep. The more I thought about it, the more I wondered. You know?"

"Yeah." Pete kept the annoyance from his voice. "You're sure it was two men?"

"Positive."

"And one of them left?"

"I think so."

"Did he come back?"

Hewitt's eyes widened for a moment. "Oh. I don't know. If he did, I didn't hear him."

"When you left this morning, did you see a car that might have belonged to the occupant?"

"No. He—they—must have checked out before I did." Hewitt shifted in his seat. "I honestly didn't know what to do. I thought about minding my own business and not saying anything. But I kept thinking, what if I see a news report about a murder back here. I'd always wonder if I could have stopped it. Then I spotted this place as I was driving by." He waved a hand, indicating the station. "And decided I needed to report what I heard."

Pete collected Hewitt's contact information in case he needed to reach him, thanked him, and sent him on his way. Two men. One loud. Threats of murder. Pete closed his notebook, tucked it and his glasses into his pocket, and headed to the front of the station. Odds were good the guy was simply venting to a friend. Angry. Maybe drunk.

Nancy looked up from her desk as Pete tugged on his VTPD cap. "I'll be back in a bit," he told her. "I'm heading over to the Vance Motel to talk to Sandy Giden."

TWO

The motel sat on a well-manicured knoll. The lawn, green despite the dry summer, showed evidence of a sprinkler system. Hedges, rose bushes, and perennials lined the driveway and edged the currently vacant parking lot. A woman wearing a large straw hat knelt in the wood-bark mulch pulling weeds as Pete eased off the road and up the slight hill.

Sandy Giden climbed to her feet and removed the hat, revealing short-cropped gray hair curling in damp ringlets. She wiped her forehead with a sleeve.

Pete stepped out of his SUV and did his best to ignore the twinge in his left thigh—a ghost that still haunted him from the gunshot and shattered femur he'd suffered months ago. "Doing your own landscaping?" he said.

"Always." She stepped over a plant and onto the pavement. "I can't afford to hire a crew to do it. Besides, I enjoy getting my hands dirty." She swept her gaze across the empty lot. "And I don't have anything else to do at the moment."

"Good. I need some information, and I was hoping you could help me out."

She plopped the hat back on her head, tugged off her gardening gloves, and pointed toward the motel office. "Care for some iced tea?"

"I'd love some."

A couple minutes later, Pete leaned on the registration desk of the clean but outdated lobby and accepted a tall glass from the motel proprietor. "Is this about the argument?" Sandy asked.

He sipped the icy brew and played dumb. "What argument is that?"

"A man who stayed here last night complained about an argument in the next room when he checked out. I can't believe he filed a police report about it."

Pete set the glass down on a cardboard promotional coaster Sandy had provided. "Victor Hewitt?"

"That's him." She folded her arms. "It's my own darned fault. I only have a handful of guests each night. I should space them out, so they aren't right next to each other."

"Why don't you?"

She shrugged. "It's easier for Betsy to clean the rooms when she doesn't have to run from one end of the place to the other."

Made sense. "Did Mr. Hewitt mention what the argument was about?"

"No. Just griped that the walls were too thin, and he could hear every word the men next door were saying."

"Mind telling me who those men were?"

"Only one man was registered. I guess he had a visitor." She scowled. "Why do you want to know?"

Pete hoped she didn't demand a warrant. He took another sip of the tea before answering. "Because according to Hewitt, one of the men was threatening to kill someone."

The color drained from Sandy's cheeks. "Oh my god. Do you think there's something to it?"

"Probably not. You know how it is. People get angry and say things they don't mean, but I thought I should investigate. Just in case."

She raised a finger—*wait a minute*—and ducked behind the counter. "Chief, you know me. I don't rent rooms to anyone I believe might be a problem. I like to think of this place as a family establishment." She retrieved a sheet of paper from a file. "Although, these days I don't get many families. Mostly businessmen who are traveling and need a break from driving." She set the paper on the counter in front of Pete.

"Toby Jones," he read. "From Saint Louis, Missouri."

"Yep."

"And he checked out already?"

"At first light. Rang the bell and got me out of bed to turn in his key."

Which explained why his vehicle was gone by the time Hewitt left. "Did you happen to see his visitor?"

"No, I didn't. Sorry."

"How about your security cameras?"

She huffed. "They quit working six months ago. I haven't had the money to get them fixed."

Pete tapped the registration form. "Can I get a copy of this?"

"Sure." She reclaimed the paper, crossed to a machine in the back corner of the office, and returned a few moments later with the copy. "Here you go." Her gaze shifted over his shoulder. "Hold on a minute." She rounded the desk and headed for the door.

Pete turned to see a woman pushing a housekeeping cart past the windows.

Sandy opened the door. "Betsy, can you come in here for a moment?"

The woman in a dingy white maid's uniform parked her cart against the building and followed Sandy inside. "Is there something wrong?"

Sandy folded her arms. "When you cleaned room one, did you find anything odd?"

The housekeeper eyed Pete before replying to her boss. "What kind of 'odd?'"

Pete fielded the question. "Anything unusual in his trash. Something he left behind. A note, maybe." He didn't expect a potential killer to leave any breadcrumbs to his planned crime, but it didn't hurt to ask.

"No notes." Betsy wrinkled her nose. "No tip either," she muttered. "As for trash, some empty snack bags from the vending machine. An empty bottle of whiskey and a couple of our plastic drinking glasses. That's about it."

"Whiskey?" Sandy huffed. "I won't be renting to Mr. Toby Jones again, I promise you that."

"Do you happen to have his trash bagged separately?" Pete asked.

"Yeah. I can get it for you." Betsy started to turn away.

"I'll walk out with you." He nodded to Sandy. "Thanks for your help."

"Anytime. I hope it comes to nothing though."

"So do I." Pete followed the housekeeper to the door but paused and turned back to Sandy. "Jones was in room one. I gather Hewitt was in room two?"

"Yep. Mr. Jones checked in early yesterday afternoon and I put him down at the end. He'd have had all the privacy in the world if Mr. Hewitt hadn't shown up."

Pete thanked her again and trailed after Betsy.

Toby Jones of St. Louis was likely well out of Vance Township by now and no longer under Pete's jurisdiction. His visitor was another matter. Pete figured the whiskey had a lot to do with the volume of the voices Hewitt had overheard as well as the threats, but Pete kept picturing the genuine concern in Hewitt's eyes. It wouldn't hurt to do a little digging. Not when he might be able to stop a homicide before it happened.

Zoe suspected the little girl suffered from a shoulder dislocation rather than a broken arm. She immobilized the offending limb and sent the child off to the hospital with her mother.

The man in the rumpled shirt had returned the pony to his stall and joined the rest of the gathered crowd as one of the fair's staff drove mother and daughter off in a golf cart. Zoe noticed his hands trembling as he asked, "Is she gonna be all right?"

"I'm sure she will," Zoe said. "They'll do a closed reduction..." She noticed his bewildered expression. "They'll put the shoulder back in its socket. Most likely won't need surgery. She'll be back before evening." Zoe didn't mention she'd be in a brace and wouldn't be handling her pony solo for a while. Which was probably for the best anyway. "Is she your daughter?"

The question startled him. "Huh? No."

"Zoe?" The voice from behind them cut him off from elaborating.

She turned and came face-to-face with a woman sporting a flaming red ponytail flecked with gray and an older version of a very familiar smile. "Diane?"

The woman flung her arms around Zoe. "It's so good to see you."

Zoe returned the affectionate embrace. "I wondered if I'd run into you." A lie. Zoe *knew* she'd run into Diane Garland, her old 4-H leader and pseudo horseshow mom. Diane had been a fixture at every Monongahela County Fair since...forever.

She took Zoe by the shoulders and drew her an arm's distance away. "It's been way too long. You look great."

"So do you."

Diane grasped Zoe's left wrist and held it up, an impish twinkle in her eye. "Still not married?"

Zoe snatched her hand and naked ring finger away. "Nope."

"You need a man in your life, Zoe."

She shoved both hands into her jeans pockets. Diane Garland loved to play matchmaker, pairing kids with the perfect horse and pairing single women friends with suitable bachelors. "I have a man in my life." Zoe thought of Pete back home in Vance Township and wondered if he'd show up at the fairgrounds after work.

A pair of worried creases lined Diane's forehead. "From the look on your face, I'm not sure if that's a good thing or a bad thing."

"It's definitely a good thing." The problems they'd had in recent months were all Zoe's fault. She'd lost faith in her own judgment, but in spite of her doubts, Pete never wavered.

Still, she needed a week away, and the ten miles between the fairgrounds and Vance Township fit the bill nicely.

Diane smiled broadly. "I'm glad. I've always worried about you...being alone."

Her true worries—about Zoe's past poor choices in men—were left unspoken, for which Zoe was grateful.

Diane's attention shifted to the man in the plaid shirt who'd started to walk away. "Jack? Are you okay?"

"Yeah." He didn't sound convincing. "Have you seen Vera?"

Diane looked around. "No. Have you checked the 4-H Barn?"

"I just came from there." He rubbed his ear. "I was looking for her over here when that little girl's pony got away."

Diane studied him, and Zoe recognized the concern in her eyes. Then Diane glanced at Zoe. "Have you met?"

"Not officially." She extended a hand, which he grasped. "Zoe Chambers."

"Jack Palmer."

"Thanks for your help."

"You gals did all the work." He met Diane's troubled gaze. "That pony there got loose from a little girl. Dragged her halfway down the aisle."

"I heard." She touched his arm. "Are you sure you're all right?"

Zoe took a closer look at Jack. He did appear unsteady. Almost fragile. Enough so that she'd assumed he was the worried father of the injured child.

Jack straightened his stooped shoulders. "I'm fine." He pulled out his phone. "I'm gonna try to call Vera again. If you see her, tell her I'm looking for her. Okay?"

"Will do."

He shuffled away, his phone pressed to his ear.

Zoe turned to her old 4-H leader. "What was that all about?"

Diane gazed toward the doorway where he'd exited. "Jack's had a rough year. His daughter was in a bad accident this spring. Poor kid's still in a rehab facility or she'd be here. Jack probably looked at that little girl and saw his own kid getting hurt."

"That's awful." Zoe could well imagine the pain he was going through. "Will his daughter be okay?"

"I hope so."

Zoe waited for a more definitive answer, but none came. "And Vera?"

"His wife. They've been active in our club since they moved here from Beaver County two years ago. After the accident, I thought they'd drop out, but I think they cling to the hope that Cassidy'll be back on her horse one day soon. Letting go of the club would be like giving up on that dream."

Zoe mulled over Diane's use of the word "dream." She clearly didn't believe Cassidy Palmer would be back. And Diane Garland did not give up on kids easily.

The woman shook her head as if clearing away dark thoughts. She turned to face Zoe. "It's great to see you. Are you on standby with the ambulance?"

"Yes and no." Zoe stooped to pick up the duffel bag containing her first aid gear. "I have my horse here, and since I'm going to be around anyway, I'll be spending part of my time on duty."

Diane's eyes brightened the moment Zoe had mentioned her

horse. "You mean you're entered in the show?"

"Yeah. My cousin Patsy talked me into it."

"Well, good for her." Diane caught Zoe's hand and squeezed. "Do you remember Cody DeRosa?"

The name stirred a quagmire of memories. "Sure, I remember him." He'd taken the blue ribbon in every class he entered back then. Zoe'd never beaten him. Never come close. She'd have hated his guts if she hadn't had such a crush on him.

He, on the other hand, never gave her the time of day.

"He's our judge," Diane said, sounding as excited as a kid with an ice cream cone. "All the horse classes all week."

"I thought he moved away?"

"He did. He lives near Columbus, Ohio, now. Owns a big Quarter Horse training facility. Came back just for the fair this year. First time he's been home in over a decade."

"Great," Zoe said, feigning enthusiasm. Maybe he was fat and bald now.

THREE

Nancy looked up from her desk when Pete returned to the station. She wrinkled her nose. "You're bringing trash in here?"

He held up the small bag. "Only a little."

"As long as you don't expect me to go through it."

"Nancy. Have I ever made you dig through trash?"

"Not the physical kind." Her expression warned he shouldn't start asking either.

"Do you have anything I need to deal with?"

She held out a trio of pink notes.

He left the bag in the conference room and scanned the notes as he headed to his office. A request from a woman asking him to talk to her son about cutting class. A report of wayward cattle tearing up someone's yard. And a report of possible marijuana plants being grown on a local farm.

The last one went on top of the pile. Once he settled at his desk and booted up his computer, he placed a call to County Police Detective Wayne Baronick, who headed up the multi-jurisdiction drug task force and left a message about the not-quite-legal crop.

A return call about the cattle revealed they'd already been rounded up and the downed fence had been repaired. Pete set the message from the frustrated mom aside for his next trip out on patrol.

He'd hoped a quick call would put the pre-murder matter to rest, or at least point him in the direction of Toby Jones' visitor. Except when Pete phoned the number Jones had written on his motel registration, the person who answered was female and had never heard of him. Pete thanked her for her time and took a closer look at the handwriting. Had he misread one of the numbers? No. He was certain he hadn't.

He turned to his computer and typed Jones' car license into the DMV. The number was registered to a 2015 Jeep Compass owned by a Shirley Reed from La Grange, Missouri. Not the same phone number as Pete had called. And not the red 2001 Honda Civic Jones had written on the paperwork.

Pete's jaw ached. Instead of quickly dismissing the overheard threat as nothing more than drunken ramblings, he was finding more and more inconsistencies and raising more and more questions.

After another half hour on his computer, he'd located a number of men with the name Toby Jones, none of whom hailed from anywhere in or near St. Louis. No surprise considering everything else about the man had been fake. Pete leaned back in his chair and thought about the bag of motel room garbage in his conference room. How viable was this threat? Was it worth fingerprinting the whiskey bottle and plastic cups for a homicide that hadn't happened and might never happen?

The bells on the front door jingled and a familiar female voice drifted back to him. Nancy didn't bother with the intercom. She didn't need to. A moment later Sylvia Bassi barreled into Pete's office.

"It figures I'd find you in here, gathering wool." She plopped her massive purse on his desk and claimed the visitor's chair across from him.

"I'm not 'gathering wool.' I'm thinking."

"Have you asked her yet?"

He blinked. The burgundy velvet box. "Not yet."

"What the heck are you waiting for? You aren't getting any younger, you know."

Sylvia Bassi, his former police secretary and, as one of the three township supervisors, his current boss, was one of the few people who knew of his plans. Even Zoe, the intended recipient of the piece of jewelry, hadn't a clue.

Which was part of the problem.

Pete shifted in his seat. "It's not the right time."

"And when, pray tell, will the time ever be right?"

He'd rehearsed the moment a thousand times in his head. Dinner at a nice restaurant. Wine. Candlelight. Roses. But between his police duties and her shifts on the ambulance, plus working with the coroner's office, their dates never quite worked out as planned. "Not this weekend or next week. She's camping with Patsy at the fairgrounds." The only way he'd get to see the woman he loved would be to hang out with the horses, cattle, chickens, and goats. Maybe he needed lessons on romance from Old MacDonald. E-I-E-I-O.

Sylvia came forward and planted her arms on his desk, next to the handbag big enough to hide one of those goats. "Trust me on this, Pete. Tomorrow is never promised. Ask her already."

He wasn't sure if Sylvia's fatalistic views were spurred by the loss of her son a year and a half ago or by her heart attack last winter. Speaking of... "You look great. Are you still planning on doing the Mon 5K this fall?"

Her glare faltered, derailed by the flicker of a pleased grin and tinge of pink in her no-longer-plump cheeks. "Thank you. Yes." She cleared her throat and regained her stern matriarchal stance. "And stop changing the subject."

Pete sighed. "The truth is, I'm pretty sure if I proposed right now, she'd turn me down."

"Bullshit."

He tried not to choke. "Excuse me?"

"You heard me fine. That girl loves you. She's not going to turn you down."

"I know she loves me. It's just..." She'd been through hell last spring. He may have been the one who got shot, but Zoe was the one carrying the scars. The kind others couldn't see. But Pete knew they were there.

Sylvia opened her mouth to continue the argument, but Pete's phone rang. Ordinarily, he'd have let Nancy take the call out front. This time, however, he pounced on it. "Vance Township Police. This is Chief Pete Adams."

"Hi, Chief. This is Tiffany. From Parson's Roadhouse?"

The waitress who always sported hair in shades of blue or pink or green. "Yes, Tiffany. What can I do for you?"

"It's probably nothing." She hesitated. "But there's a car in our parking lot that's been here all night. It was there when I first got to work this morning, and I thought maybe someone had too much to drink and took a cab or caught a ride with a buddy. But I looked and it's still there."

Tiffany was right. It was probably nothing. Just like the threats made at the Vance Motel last night were probably nothing. "I'll come by and check it out," he told her.

For one thing, checking out an abandoned vehicle provided a good escape from Sylvia's grilling. For another, Parson's Roadhouse was only about a mile down the road from the Vance Motel. And two probably-nothings that close together on the same day might actually be *something*.

"Look who I found wandering around the fairgrounds," Patsy said.

Inside Windstar's stall, Zoe paused, brush in hand, and rested her arms on her horse's back. She looked at her cousin in the aisle, the word "who" on her lips. But she didn't need to ask. A lanky man with unruly sandy hair and the start of a beard sidled up to Patsy, arm slung around her shoulders. "Oh," Zoe said flatly. "Hi, Shane."

Patsy had met Shane Tolland at the beach during one of her increasingly frequent trips to Florida to visit her newly found family. After six months of long-distance dating, he'd followed her to Pennsylvania, trailing after her like a large scruffy puppy. Considering his constant scratching at the stubble on his face, Zoe thought he might even have fleas.

"What can I do to help?" he asked.

She abandoned grooming her horse and moved to the stall door. "Not a thing. We're all done moving in. Your timing is perfect." As always.

He either didn't catch her sarcasm or didn't care. "Great." He gave Patsy's shoulders a squeeze. "Let's go," he said to her. "You can show me around."

Patsy looked at Zoe. "Do you mind?"

Zoe waved her off. "Have fun."

Patsy stood there a moment, eyeing her. Zoe thought—hoped— she'd blow Shane off and stick around. After all, the only reason Zoe was at the fair was because Patsy had insisted.

But Patsy said, "See you later," and walked off arm-in-arm with her boyfriend.

Zoe turned back to Windstar, who stood with one back leg cocked, head low, eyes at half-mast. At least he'd calmed down enough to nap. She patted his neck and slipped out of the stall.

Soft, rapid footsteps thumping down the aisle drew her attention to a beaming nine-year-old girl racing toward her.

"Aunt Zoe!"

"Lilly." Zoe braced for the collision.

The girl, her niece of the heart but not by blood, flung her arms around Zoe's waist, and Zoe returned the hug. Earl Kolter, Zoe's partner on the county EMS, and his wife, Olivia, approached at a much more sedate pace. Their daughter bounced up and down in delight. "Can I pet Windstar?"

"Yes, but you need to remember. No running in the barn. And no fast movements."

Lilly hung her head. "I'm sorry. I was so excited."

"I know." Zoe gave the girl's ponytail a tug and opened the stall door to let her in.

"Sorry about that." Olivia shook her head. "This child is completely horse crazy."

Zoe chuckled. Last summer, she'd stayed with the Kolter family for a few months. Lilly hadn't been able to understand why Zoe's horse couldn't move in with them too. "She should be in horse heaven around here."

Earl exchanged a look with his wife before turning to Zoe. "We have a favor to ask."

"Oh?"

They exchanged another look. "Lilly's old enough to join 4-H. We were hoping you might introduce her—us—to some of the leaders."

Zoe glanced into the stall to make sure Lilly was heeding the rules Zoe'd drilled into her since her first eager visit to the barn. Like no running around horses. The girl stood quietly next to Windstar, letting him sniff her open palm. Zoe smiled. Another young horse lover for Diane to nurture. "Sure. Let's walk over to the 4-H Barn."

Prying Lilly away from Windstar wasn't too hard once she learned they were going to look at more horses. Olivia kept hold of the girl's hand to corral her enthusiasm. They didn't make it past the goat and sheep pens before Lilly dragged her mother off for a closer look.

"Did you hear?" Earl asked while they waited for his wife and daughter to return. "You're not getting rid of me this week after all."

"What do you mean?"

"I traded my schedule. I'll be working standby with you."

"Why? Not that I don't love having you as my partner, but..."
Being on standby at the fair wasn't usually a prime assignment. For
one thing, it meant temporary duty with the crew out of the Brunswick
garage instead of their regular gang back in Phillipsburg. For another,
Earl lived five minutes from their usual post, and had a twenty-mile
drive to get here. And finally, county fair duty tended to be boring.
Treating a few scrapes and bruises while spending most of the time
doing PR and trying to keep kids from climbing in the ambulance when
no one was looking. "The only reason I volunteered was because I
already have to be here," she said, "and I didn't want to use up my
vacation days."

Earl shrugged. "Looks like I'll be stuck here a lot this week too."

Zoe looked at him. "Why?"

"Aidan and Ryan."

Earl and Olivia's two teenaged sons. "Oh, that's right. I forgot.
They're working on the school bus for the demolition derby."

"Yeah, but that's only tomorrow morning. They intend to be here
all week."

"Oh?"

"They've got the fair bug." He gestured toward his daughter. "Just
not about horses."

Zoe waited for him to fill in the blanks.

"Girls."

"Ah."

"And that." Earl gazed beyond the barns and pens toward the
midway with its carnival rides and games. "They bought full-week
passes with their own money. Aidan said he had a buddy who would
drive them back and forth, but Olivia and I aren't about to let those
boys in a car with a kid who only got his license last Monday. So I get to
chauffeur."

Zoe remembered being the boys' age. Both Earl and his kids were
luckier than they realized.

He misinterpreted the look she gave him. "I know. We could put
the hammer down and say no. But both boys got straight A's in the

final semester. We'd promised them each a reward. Within reason. They've been pondering what they wanted all summer. Since we vetoed matching Corvettes, a week hanging out at the fair turns out to be it."

Zoe watched Olivia and Lilly head toward them. As much as she dragged her feet about being here, she remembered how much fun she'd had as a teenager at the fair. "And they paid for their own passes? You got off cheap, my friend."

FOUR

Parson's Roadhouse sat at the corner of a T intersection. Neither of the roads were heavily traveled and what little traffic passed by was mostly local. Still, the parking lot boasted over a dozen cars and it wasn't noon yet. Pete had no idea which was the abandoned one.

Tiffany, sporting purple hair today, met him the moment he stepped inside. "Thanks for coming, Chief. Like I said, it's probably nothing."

"Don't worry about it." He glanced around at the unmanned bar—too early yet—and the tables, three of which were occupied by early lunch patrons. "How about putting in an order for me, and then you can point out which car has you concerned."

She tugged an order pad and pen from her apron's pocket. "Sure thing. What'll you have?"

"What's the special?"

"Deep-fried haddock sandwich with fries and coleslaw."

"Works for me."

"Eat in or take out?"

"Depends on what I learn when I run the plates on your 'probably nothing' car."

She grinned. "Gotcha."

A couple minutes later, she returned and led him out to the lot and a black Toyota Camry.

"That's it."

Pete thanked her, and she retreated from the baking sunshine into the air-conditioned restaurant.

He strolled to the rear of the vehicle and reached for the two-way clipped to his shoulder. "Vance Base, this is Vance Thirty."

When Nancy responded, he gave her the Pennsylvania plate

number. While he waited, he tugged the brim of his Vance Township PD ball cap lower over his eyes and surveyed the lot. One of the other cars had a smattering of stickers in the rear window. Another had a broken taillight. Still another had a piece of discolored plastic obscuring the license. He bet if he wanted, he could find something to ticket on each and every vehicle there. But he wasn't in the mood. His gaze swept the lot itself. A couple of broken bottles in the gravel provided potential tire hazards. Halfway between him and the road, he spotted a high-heeled shoe and wondered if Cinderella had missed her slipper yet. Closer to the building, a half dozen or so small brown birds flocked around a spilled takeout box, flying off with what was left of the french fries.

His radio staticked to life. "Vance Thirty, this is Vance Base."

"Vance Thirty."

"The license number you gave me," Nancy said, "is registered to a Vera Palmer of 1414 Westview Road, Hancock, Pennsylvania."

The 4-H Barn was a much newer construction than the old Pony Barn but was currently abuzz with the same activities. Parents dragged in tack trunks. Kids decorated the outside of their stalls. Some horses—the ones more seasoned to travel and shows—quietly munched their hay or watched the goings on. Others, like Windstar, were obviously less accustomed to the hubbub and paced or pawed their stalls.

As Zoe and the Kolters strolled down the center of the barn, she noticed Diane Garland stepping from one of the stalls and steered them toward her. "Diane, I want you to meet some friends of mine." Zoe introduced Earl, Olivia, and Lilly and noticed the wide-eyed youngster surveying every horse, every kid, every movement going on in the barn.

Diane noticed too and took over the Kolter family's guided tour.

Zoe watched as her 4-H leader picked out one of the horses and ushered the trio toward it.

"Zoe?"

She turned. The platinum blonde who'd spoken her name wore a thin smile. It took a long moment for Zoe to match this lined, gaunt face with the younger, more rounded version she'd once known. "Merryn?"

"Yeah. I'm surprised to see you here."

Zoe could say the same. She kept the question she wanted to ask—
Why aren't you still in jail?—inside her head and off her lips. Instead,
she lied. "You look great. Love your hair."

The glare Merryn gave her made it clear she knew better. "Do you
have a kid in 4-H too?"

"No." Zoe gestured toward the Kolters and Diane. "Friends of
mine are thinking about letting their daughter join."

Merryn gave an uninterested nod and looked back toward the
barn door. "My boy Luke is around here somewhere. Probably down on
the midway instead of helping me with his horse."

Zoe remembered the boy, a child from one of Merryn's earlier
marriages, and controlled her surprise that he wasn't locked up in
juvie.

"I guess I'd better go drag that boy's sorry ass back here before he
gets in trouble. I'll talk to you later." Merryn stormed away without
waiting for a reply.

Earl, Olivia, and Lilly were talking with a couple of teen girls.
Diane broke away from the group and approached Zoe, a smile on her
face.

"Looks like I have a new 4-Her."

"You know she doesn't have a horse," Zoe said. "I'd let her use
Windstar, but I think his mouth is too soft for a beginner." He would
never hurt the little girl. She, on the other hand, could make his life
miserable.

Diane dismissed her concerns with a blown-out breath. "Not
having a horse has never stopped me from working with kids before.
You know that better than anyone."

True. Diane had loaned or leased ponies and horses to many a kid
over the years. Including Zoe.

"I saw you talking to Merryn Schultz. She didn't happen to
mention Luke, did she?"

"She said he should've been helping with his horse but was
probably down on the midway instead."

Diane rubbed her arms. "Are you busy right now? I have a favor to
ask you."

A rumble of murmurs behind Zoe distracted Diane. The 4-H

leader's attention, as well as Olivia's and that of all the teenaged girls in the barn, was drawn to something behind her.

A man in a silver-belly gray western hat, dark jeans, and spotless cowboy boots swaggered at a leisurely pace toward them. He paused at each stall, gazing in, his movie-star smile bracketed by deep dimples.

Zoe swallowed the knot that rose in her throat. Crap.

The hat concealed whether the man was bald, but Cody DeRosa was definitely *not* fat.

"Sure, I remember Vera," Tiffany said.

Pete sat at one of the tables in the bar, his back to the wall. The haddock, fresh from the fryer, was too hot, so he forked some coleslaw into his mouth.

"She's one of a bunch of women who come in every so often."

He held a hand over his mouth as he chewed. "How often?"

"Maybe once every couple of months."

"Were they here last night?"

"Yep. They came for dinner. They started arriving around six o'clock or so."

Pete swallowed. "Did you see Vera leave?"

Tiffany shook her head, her long purple bangs swishing across her face. "Neither time."

"What do you mean, 'neither time'?"

The waitress used the back of her wrist to brush the wayward bangs aside. "I wasn't the table's server, but I noticed Vera had disappeared at one point. I figured she had to use the restroom, but she didn't come back. At least not until the others had left."

Pete jotted the information on his notepad. "What time did the group leave?"

Tiffany hummed. "I don't know for sure. Like I said, I wasn't their server."

"Who was?"

"Charlene." Before he could ask, Tiffany answered his next question. "She has today off."

He made a note. "You said Vera came back later?"

Tiffany nodded. "I did wait on her then. She was looking for the others, but like I said, they'd left."

"What time was this?" He picked up his fish sandwich and cautiously took a bite.

"A little before ten, I think. Wherever she'd been, she must have been drinking, because she was definitely intoxicated."

"Had she been drinking here?" he asked around the haddock.

"Not that much." Tiffany ran a tongue across her lips. "You'd have to ask Charlene, but I've served this group in the past, and they're always the same. They have dinner, dessert, and one glass of wine. They're pretty strict about it. Don't want to get pulled over for DUI on their way home."

"But Vera appeared intoxicated when she came back?"

"Yes. Very. I was shocked to see her like that. It looked like she'd been crying, and her clothes were all disheveled."

He wiped his mouth with a paper napkin. "Then what?"

"She was upset to find out her friends were already gone and started crying again. I got her a cup of coffee and called Brown's Taxi Service for her. She said she didn't want it, but I called anyway."

Pete inhaled. "That's it then. She took the taxi home and simply hasn't come back to get her car yet."

Tiffany shook her head and her purple bangs dropped across her face again. "No. We were busy last night, and I didn't see her leave, but the taxi driver came in looking for her. She was gone. I figured she must have driven herself home. I hated the idea of it, but what else could I do?"

"You did fine. Is she married?"

"I think so. She wears a ring. But I don't know her or any of her friends that well, so I couldn't tell you her husband's name."

Pete skimmed back to the page where he'd scrawled Vera Palmer's contact information after Nancy had given it to him. "I'll call her. She probably caught a ride with someone and is home nursing a hangover."

Tiffany smiled weakly. "I hope so. You'll let me know?"

"Absolutely."

The waitress scurried off toward a pair of men in work uniforms who'd claimed a table close to the door. Pete took another bite of his sandwich and pulled out his phone. Once he'd chewed and swallowed, he punched in the number Nancy had given him. It rang. And a recording answered. "You've reached the Palmer residence. At the tone, please leave a message."

He didn't. Being requested to call the local cops tended to freak people out, and there was probably no reason for concern. Vera Palmer's husband hadn't reported her missing.

Pete dragged a fry through the puddle of ketchup on his plate and studied the address in his notes. Hancock was a small town on the northern edge of the county. Not his jurisdiction. But the abandoned car and the drunken and disheveled woman who owned it bugged the hell out of him. Once again, the phrase *probably nothing* echoed in his mind. This time he wanted to quash the "probably" part.

He wiped his greasy fingers on the paper napkin, pulled out his phone, and keyed in the station's number. When Nancy answered, he said, "Call County and request a wellness check at that address you gave me for Vera Palmer."

With the exception of a few lines on his tanned face, Cody DeRosa hadn't changed much since the last time Zoe had seen him. She'd been in her final year as a 4-Her—eighteen years old and a wild child—right here on these same fairgrounds. He'd beaten her out for a chance to qualify for State, same as he had the last three years. Her competitive side had been bruised, but not as badly as her ego when she'd tried every move she knew to catch his eye—and failed.

He spotted her, smiled, and approached.

"Hello, Diane." He extended a hand toward the 4-H leader.

Okay, so he'd spotted Diane, not Zoe. Knowing that Pete, at least, had eyes only for her helped her ego absorb yet another blow.

"It's so good to see you again," Diane said. "I can't tell you how pleased I was to hear you'd be judging the horseshow this year."

"Happy to do it. It's been ages since I've been back to my old stomping grounds." He released Diane's hand and turned to Zoe, bumping his hat up off his forehead with one thumb, revealing a shock of dark hair. Not bald either. "Hello there."

His tone and the glint in his eye reminded her of a hungry wolf, but Zoe could tell he had no idea who she was.

"You remember Zoe Chambers, don't you?" Diane said. "You were in 4-H together."

"Of course, I remember Zoe."

Of course, he did not.

He reached out and took her hand. "You look incredible."

Her cheeks warmed in spite of her determination to resist his charms. "Thanks." She tried to pull her hand free, but he held tight.

"Do you have a horse in the show?" he asked.

"Yeah." With her free hand, she gestured in the general direction of the Pony Barn. "I'll be in the open classes."

"Excellent. We'll have to get together later and reminisce about old times."

She tried again to retrieve her hand and again failed. Inside her head, she pointed out to him that they had no old times about which to reminisce. "That'd be great." No, it wouldn't. Maybe she could bring Pete along.

"Excellent. I'll track you down later." Cody released her hand and swaggered away, pausing to speak with Olivia. Zoe noticed Earl sizing up the cowboy.

"He's still an insatiable flirt," Diane said. "He can't seem to help himself."

"Didn't I hear he got married?"

"Twice. But neither marriage lasted long. Both women thought they could tame him." Diane shook her head. "Didn't happen."

Cody apparently realized Olivia was off-limits. He nodded to Earl and made his way toward the far door as Patsy and Shane strolled in. Zoe watched the introduction and flirtation routine begin anew.

Olivia and Lilly continued to chat with the girls, but Earl, phone in hand, moved toward Zoe and Diane. "The boys are ignoring my texts and calls. I bet they're scouting out the games on the midway, so I'm gonna take a walk and track them down." From the tone of his voice, he had some stern words for his sons once he found them.

Diane touched Zoe's arm. "That reminds me. The favor I mentioned? Could you keep an eye out for Luke, and if you see him, tell him to get back here? I'd asked Vera to ride herd on him, but she must've gotten tied up helping someone else."

"Sure," Zoe said. "But I'm not sure I'll recognize him. It's been a few years."

Diane wrinkled her nose. "You'll know him. He hasn't changed much except for getting taller."

Zoe wondered if the hadn't-changed-much comment referred to his rebellious streak as well as his appearance.

Diane must have read the question in Zoe's eyes. "If there's trouble anywhere on these fairgrounds, you can count on Luke Holmes being in the middle of it."

"Terrific." Zoe looked at Earl. "Mind if I go with you? If you're looking for two boys, and I'm looking for one, we might as well look for them together."

"I don't mind at all. You might keep me from banging their heads together."

Diane eyed Cody, who was working his charm on Patsy while Shane's expression darkened at his every word. "Speaking of banging heads, I best make sure our judge doesn't get beaten up by a jealous husband."

"Boyfriend," Zoe corrected under her breath, although the distinction apparently didn't matter to Cody.

FIVE

While Pete waited to hear from County, he headed back out to the Roadhouse's sweltering parking lot and Vera Palmer's black Camry.

Probably nothing.

One of the woman's friends *probably* came back and gave her a lift home. Palmer *probably* had an early appointment somewhere and planned to pick up her car later. There was *probably* nothing to require a police presence.

So why was his gut nagging him? It wasn't the coleslaw.

Pete circled the Camry, noting the dented rear passenger door. Rust showed through the spot of missing paint. Old damage. Otherwise, the car appeared well cared for. When he came around to the driver's side, a glint of sunshine reflected off something under the car. He knelt for a closer look. Keys.

His unease kicked up a notch. He pulled a pair of black Nitrile gloves from his hip pocket and wiggled his fingers into them before reaching under the vehicle. He came up with a ring holding a Toyota fob and several generic keys. Pete stood and pressed the button on the fob. The Camry's locks gave a soft but audible click. He tried the door. It opened. Inside, the front seats were clear. He glanced into the backseat. A cardboard box held a stack of folders and papers. On top of the stack, a program for the county fair. Pete's thoughts flashed to Zoe.

Until he spotted the gray leather wallet on the driver's floor mat.

He resisted the urge to pick it up. Not now. If his gut spoke the truth and something wasn't right here, he'd need to first photograph everything as he found it. He closed the door and surveyed the area again.

That shoe.

Pete strode across the lot to stand over it. It was one of those shiny leather high-heeled numbers that women somehow managed to walk in. Beige. He looked around. Only one. Had the wearer flung it at someone in a fit of anger? He didn't spot a second shoe, but something else nearer the road caught the sun. And his eye. He crossed to it and dropped to one knee.

A small gold cylinder. Lipstick. And it wasn't alone. A half-used roll of breath mints and a small tube of hand cream also lay on the ground, dusted with a fine layer of dirt but not mashed into the gravel as they would've been if they'd been there any length of time.

Pete took out his phone and snapped a couple of photos before standing and gazing back toward the Roadhouse, Vera Palmer's car, and the shoe. Connecting the dots created a relatively straight line to where he currently stood. A childhood tale involving breadcrumbs whispered in his memory. He looked toward the road. A couple of residences with large yards sat across the straight stretch forming the top of the T intersection. Perhaps Vera had knocked on one of their doors. He turned his back toward the Camry, extending the invisible line created by the car, shoe, and lipstick.

Guard rails edged the road coming down the hill from the state game lands, ending several yards shy of the stop sign. A tangle of vines and brambles created an impassable barricade between the pavement and the creek beyond. No way the woman could have gone that direction.

But...

Was that a dirty beige handbag lying under the guard rail? Pete checked for traffic and crossed the road.

The handbag was coated with road dust, just like the lipstick, breath mints, and hand lotion. It'd been dropped over the railing, the rest of its contents spilled in the weeds. And it matched the shoe.

A car rounded the bend above him and slowed as it approached the stop sign. Pete raised a hand to wave at the driver who shot him a curious glance. Once the car had passed, made a complete stop—probably for Pete's benefit—and turned right, Pete picked his way down the hill toward the intersection and the end of the guard rail.

The babbling of the creek beyond the brambles grew louder, but he barely heard it over the rumblings inside his head.

Rumblings that fell silent when he spotted a bare foot protruding from the tangle of wild rose bushes...a foot attached to a leg and the rest of a woman's body enveloped in vines.

Leaving the Kolter females with the horses, and the flirtatious judge in the care of the 4-H leader, Zoe and Earl headed down the hill to the midway. None of the games, rides, or food trailers were open for business, so the area was devoid of patrons. But like a traveling circus, activity buzzed everywhere. Workers arranged prizes inside the portable booths. A miniature rollercoaster rumbled around the track, riderless.

"There." Earl pointed down the row of temporary and transient stands housing various games of chance in the process of being set up. A trio of boys, two of whom were Kolters, stood at one of the counters talking to whomever was inside. Earl strode toward them.

Zoe jogged to keep up.

"Hey," Earl barked in his authoritative dad voice.

All three boys' heads snapped toward them, and the man inside the shed leaned over the counter, looking in Earl's direction.

"When I call or text, you answer."

Aidan and Ryan Kolter made a simultaneous show of looking at their phones with wide, surprised eyes. "We didn't hear them," Aidan, the older of the pair, said.

Zoe didn't believe him, so she knew Earl wasn't buying the innocent act. The third boy struck a tough-guy pose, one hip cocked against the counter. His tightly tucked lower lip gave away the presence of snuff. Diane had been right. Even though Zoe hadn't seen the kid in years, she recognized Merryn's son.

"Hey, Luke," Zoe said. "Diane sent me to find you."

He gave a bored eye roll.

"And," Zoe added, "your mother's looking for you."

His cool-dude façade cracked. "Where is she?"

"She *was* at the 4-H Barn, but last I saw her, she was headed down here."

The remainder of the mask crumbled. He glanced at the guy in the booth and then at Earl's sons. "I gotta go. Catch you later." He darted between the booth and the corn dog trailer next to it.

The Kolter boys' echoes of "Later" trailed after him. Earl, arms crossed, glowered at his sons. "If you two want this week of roaming the fair to actually happen, you darned well better answer your phones when your mother or I call."

Ryan, the younger boy, made a pained face. "Aw, Dad..."

Earl's laser-sharp glare stopped him mid-whine.

Aidan crossed his arms, mirroring his father's stance. "We earned this week. If you're gonna keep tabs on our every move—"

The man inside the booth had been perched on the edge of a stool, but came forward, one hand raised at Aidan. "Your father's right. Bad things can happen around here, and your folks want to know you're safe."

Zoe looked at the guy. He seemed a little older than her thirty-seven years, clean-shaven, and wore his brown hair short. If it wasn't for his snug polo shirt emblazoned with the amusement company's logo, she'd have pegged him as a 4-H parent rather than a carny.

"Thank you," Earl said to him.

Aidan's bravado faded against the tag-team reprimand.

The carny extended a hand to Earl. "Trent Crosby. You have two good kids here."

Zoe's partner introduced himself then gestured at her. "And this is my coworker. Zoe Chambers."

Crosby nodded politely. To Earl, he said, "I'll keep an eye out for your boys this week." He shifted his gaze to Aidan and Ryan. "And you two. Mind your parents. No ignoring phone calls or texts."

They murmured stereo "yes, sirs" aimed at their feet.

Raised angry voices from behind the row of food trailers and game booths drew Zoe's attention, especially since they came from the direction Luke had gone. She followed his path. Behind her, she heard Earl order his boys not to move and knew he was on her heels.

It hadn't taken long for police units from assorted local jurisdictions to converge on the intersection. Pete called in his off-duty officers, Seth Metzger and Kevin Piacenza. His newest officer, Abby Baronick, lived outside of the township and had farther to travel but was on her way. Pennsylvania State Police arrived and were helping with traffic control, not that there was a lot. Mostly incoming Roadhouse patrons, a few of whom were miffed at the inconvenience of having to park on the far side of the restaurant.

The county officers who'd been in charge of Vera Palmer's wellness check had called Pete minutes after he'd discovered the body and reported what he already knew. Vera was not at home. No one was. Those officers, upon learning of Pete's find, joined several other county units at the death scene.

By the time Coroner Franklin Marshall showed up, yellow police tape cordoned off the entire east side of the parking lot.

Pete had already photographed the car, the shoe, the lipstick and breath mints, and the handbag and was looking through the latter item's contents when the coroner, lugging his kit, approached him. "Tell me about the deceased," Marshall said.

Pete pinched the victim's driver's license between his gloved fingers. "Forty-one-year-old female. Name on the ID is Vera Palmer." He relayed what Tiffany had told him earlier.

Marshall gazed at what could be seen of the woman in the brambles. "You didn't touch the body, did you?"

"You know me better than that. I didn't even have to check for a pulse." The grayish tint to her skin and the opaque coating over her opened but unseeing eyes told Pete all he needed to know. "I had my men clear away enough of the foliage to gain access to her, but nothing more."

"Did you get your photographs of the body?"

"Yep. Before and after we hacked at the vines. Sketched the scene too. She's all yours."

Marshall's chuckle said what he was thinking better than words could have. As county coroner, the body was "all his" with or without Pete's permission.

Pete watched as Marshall took his own set of photographs to document the body's positioning, condition, as well as its immediate surroundings.

"One shoe is missing," he said.

Pete aimed a thumb over his shoulder. "It's in the parking lot. I don't know how women walk in those things sober, but as drunk as she was, she must have stumbled and lost it."

The coroner looked at the deceased woman's feet and gave a noncommittal hum. "The shoe she's still wearing is missing the heel."

"Oh?" Pete moved closer.

Marshall fingered a tendril of the clingy brambles and lifted it clear. The woman's left foot—the one Pete had first spotted—was bare, the sole abraded and dirty from crossing the parking lot and road. Her right foot was protected by a worse-for-wear beige pump that looked more like a slipper. A match for the one he'd found earlier sans the heel.

Pete raised his own camera and snapped pictures of the woman's feet. Then, while Marshall moved to the victim's head to begin his physical examination, Pete pulled out his notebook and pen. *Second shoe missing the heel*, he scribbled.

"The body's in the rigid stage of rigor," Marshall said.

"She's been dead at least twelve hours, then." Pete added a notation. "Probably left the bar like the waitress said, staggered over here from the lot, fell into the weeds, and died." He wondered exactly how intoxicated Vera Palmer had to have been to end up ensnared in a thicket of wild rose vines. Had she struggled to free herself? Pete knew from personal experience how nasty these brambles could be. He'd suffered many scrapes and many torn and snagged pairs of hunting pants while traipsing through the southwestern Pennsylvanian woods.

"At least twelve hours," Marshall echoed in agreement. After going over the back of the woman's body, he motioned to Pete. "Help me turn her."

The vines weren't cooperative, but the two men managed to log roll the victim onto her back, and Pete got his first clear look at her.

He already knew from her driver's license that Vera Palmer had been an attractive woman but the bruise-like livor over half of her face didn't do a thing for her.

"After what you told me about her heavy intoxication," the coroner said, "I thought she might've been hit by a car as she stumbled across the road."

"The thought crossed my mind too." Pete glanced at the road and its berm. "No blood though."

"No sign of injury either." Marshall checked for obvious fractures or wounds. "At least so far." He raised a hand and yelled to his assistant. "Gene! Bring the cot." Marshall looked at Pete. "I'll know more after the autopsy and toxicology reports. But for now, it appears the poor woman quite literally drank herself to death."

SIX

Two boys, one of them Luke, and a teen girl in tight ripped jeans and a crop top that left little to the imagination were facing off behind the row of trailers and stands. The girl stood back, hands planted on her thin hips. The two boys were going toe-to-toe. The second kid jabbed Luke in the chest with a finger. Once. Twice. Before he could poke him a third time, Luke shoved the kid, sending the boy sprawling on the gravel. Zoe managed only one step toward them before the boy rebounded and launched toward Luke with a tackle worthy of the Steelers' offensive line. Both boys slammed the ground, Luke on the receiving end of a pummeling.

Zoe charged toward the fight, aware of Earl right behind her. She grabbed the boy by the back of his collar at the same time that Jack Palmer in his rumpled plaid shirt appeared and snagged the kid's arm—the one he'd drawn back in a fist, ready to land another blow. They hauled him up and off Luke. From the corner of her eye, Zoe spotted Earl and the carny guy subdue Luke before he retaliated on his captive opponent.

With both boys on their feet and corralled by adults, their attempts to kick each other's asses seemed all for show. Or, Zoe presumed, for the benefit of the girl with the bare midriff.

The carny guy gave Luke a shake. "What's going on here?"

Luke made a lunge at the other boy, but Earl and the carny guy held onto him. "He's messin' with my girl."

"She's *my* girl," the other boy said, punctuating the statement by spitting out a name not suitable for polite company.

Jack snapped the boy around to face him. "Watch your mouth,

son. There are women present."

A screech from down the row interrupted any equally impolite response. Zoe half turned and spotted Merryn barreling toward them, her face a deep crimson. "Lukas Edward Holmes," she huffed. "What did I tell you about getting into fights?"

Zoe recalled a few skirmishes involving Merryn and various other girls back when she'd been Luke's age. She wondered if what Merryn had told her son might've included how to win one.

"He started it."

The boy strained against Zoe and Jack. "Only 'cause you was hittin' on my girl."

"I'm not your girl." Bare Midriff finally spoke up. She glared at Luke. "I'm not your girl either. I'm my own girl."

Zoe nodded her approval.

Merryn brushed past the rest of them to grab a fistful of her son's shirt. "I don't care who started it." She said something else in a raspy whisper that Zoe couldn't hear. To Earl, Merryn said, "I've got him now. Thanks."

Earl released the teen, and Merryn marched him off in the direction of the Pony Barn.

With no one left to fight, the other boy wiggled free from Zoe.

Jack gave the kid a light backhand on his shoulder. "Take a walk and cool off."

The kid grumbled and reached for Bare Midriff. She stepped back, throwing her arms up in a *don't touch me* gesture, spun on one sequined-sneakered sole, and strutted her teenaged backside away from the group. Deflated, the kid slumped off, headed the other way.

Zoe moved to Earl's side. "What did Merryn whisper to Luke?"

Earl made a sour face. "She asked him if he wanted to spend all winter locked up in juvie."

"I guess he didn't." Zoe looked around. "Where'd the carny guy go?"

Earl tipped his head toward the game booth. "Once everything was under control, he said he needed to get back to his post. Which reminds me. My boys better be where I left them."

The phone in Zoe's pocket sang out the tune "I Fought the Law."

"That's Pete," Earl said. "You answer it. I'm gonna check on Aidan and Ryan."

She dug it out and swiped the green button. "Hey. What're you up to?"

There was silence on the line for a beat too long, and she thought for a moment the call had been dropped. But then Pete's voice replied, "Hi." He sounded odd. Tense. "Do you happen to know a man named Jack Palmer?"

She lifted her gaze to the guy in the rumpled plaid shirt, who was currently ambling away from her. "Yeah. Why?"

Another pause. "Do you know his wife?"

Zoe didn't like the sound of this. "Vera?"

"You do know her then."

"Not really. What's going on?"

"Do you know where Jack Palmer is right now?"

"I'm looking at him."

Zoe heard Pete tell someone, "He's at the fairgrounds." Then a tired sigh drifted through the phone. "I'm sending county police there to talk to him. You may want to stay close. He's going to need a friend."

Pete had seen Tiffany deal with a party of twenty demanding and ungrateful diners without losing her composure. Today, however, her fingers trembled as they rested on her lips, and her other arm wrapped around herself as if trying to hold everything together.

She stood outside the Roadhouse watching him go through Vera Palmer's glove compartment. "I can't believe she's dead." Tiffany's quivering voice gave evidence that she was indeed failing in the holding-it-together department. "I can't believe she left here last night, walked out there, and..." The quivering voice fractured. "...died." She struggled to regain her equilibrium. "I was the last person to see her. I should have done something. Stopped her from leaving. Made her wait for the taxi."

"Hindsight is twenty-twenty. You had no way of knowing." He shut the glove compartment's door, having found only the car's instruction manual, insurance and registration, and a few fast food napkins. Not what he was looking for. He backed out of the passenger seat and looked at the purple-haired waitress. "Did you happen to notice whether Vera had a cell phone on her?"

Tiffany didn't seem to hear him. "I never ever serve alcohol to someone who's over-intoxicated. It's our policy. We don't wanna be responsible for anyone getting into an accident because we let them leave here drunk."

He peeled off his gloves, approached, and put a hand on her shoulder, a move that brought her eyes up to meet his. "Did you serve her alcohol?"

"No. And I'm sure Charlene only served her the one glass of wine with dinner. And that was hours before..." Tiffany gestured across the parking lot toward the patch of brambles.

"Then you didn't do anything wrong. None of this was your fault. She left and got drunk somewhere else." He gave the waitress a comforting smile and gently squeezed her shoulder. "Now, did you see whether or not she had a cell phone with her?"

Tiffany blinked. Her eyes shifted as she searched her memory. Then she nodded. "At dinner. Yeah. I stopped to refill water glasses and remember seeing it on the table."

"How about later? When she came back. Did she have it then?"

Tiffany caught her lip between her teeth and thought about it. "I don't know. I'm sorry."

Pete patted her shoulder. "That's okay."

Her eyes welled. "I'm really so, so sorry. If I'd have done more, she'd still be alive. I should've called an ambulance instead of a taxi, I—"

Pete silenced her with a wave of his hand. "You did everything you could've done. More than most would have. Cut yourself a break, okay?" He gave her another smile.

This time, Tiffany smiled back, although it wasn't very convincing.

The rumble of a diesel motor drew his attention back to the parking lot. The state cops at the edge of the lot had waved through a flatbed truck from the local towing company. Once Pete got the Camry to the township garage, he'd do a thorough search for the phone. For now, he was about done here. The body had been removed to the county morgue. Vera's personal belongings had been photographed, inventoried, and collected into evidence bags in the back of his SUV. As soon as Franklin Marshall declared the death accidental, everything would be returned to her next of kin. Until then, he'd keep them in the evidence room back at the station.

Just in case.

Zoe was glad Diane Garland had managed to call in a favor and secure an unoccupied food booth at the fairground's new exhibit hall. With the two women standing by, a pair of uniformed county police officers broke the news to Jack Palmer.

His face went white. "Dead?" His eyes welled. "How? Was she in an accident?"

"It doesn't appear so," one of the cops said.

The other one added, "We're still trying to put the pieces together."

Jack's knees buckled, and the cops eased him into a nearby folding chair. He covered his face with both hands, doubled over, and moaned, "No, no, no, no."

Zoe glanced at Diane whose face lost all trace of its tan. "Oh, poor Jack," the 4-H leader had whispered when Zoe told her why they needed a quiet spot. "First his daughter, and now this."

With one cop on a knee next to him and the other standing at his side, Jack looked decades older and much smaller than he had only a few minutes ago.

He sobbed for what must have been fifteen minutes and then sat, his elbows on his knees, his head heavy in his hands, for a while longer before the cop kneeling by him cleared his throat. "We need to ask you a few questions. If you're up to it."

"Can't you give him some time to process this?" Diane asked.

Jack inhaled and, with what appeared to be a superhuman effort, straightened. "No. It's fine." He sounded like his vocal cords had been hit with forty-grit sandpaper.

"When was the last time you saw your wife?" the cop asked.

Jack swallowed and wiped his eyes with both hands. "Last night. She was leaving the house to have dinner with a bunch of her friends. They get together about once a month."

"You didn't see her after that?"

"No."

"Did she call or text you?"

Jack pulled out his phone. The one Zoe'd seen him on several times that morning. He stared at it. "No. I've been trying to reach her all day, but she hasn't answered." The way he said it, he sounded like he still hoped she might.

"You didn't find it odd that she didn't come home last night?"

"No. Maybe." He lowered his face, burying it once again in his hands.

The room fell silent except for his choked sobs and the muffled conversations and clanging of equipment sifting through the block walls as food vendors set up in the next space.

"Take your time, sir," the standing cop said.

After another few minutes, Jack sniffed and lifted his head. Diane stepped forward and handed him a tissue.

He thanked her and blew his nose. After another moment, he looked at the cop kneeling beside him. "Sometimes they...the girls and Vera...go to a movie or a concert after dinner. She...Vera...has been under a lot of stress lately. We both have. Because of our daughter's health. She needed some time to unwind. Kick back. You know? So I didn't worry when she wasn't home by the time I went to bed."

"What about this morning?"

"I overslept. I figured she'd come in late and crashed on the sofa. She'd do that, you know. So she wouldn't wake me." He gave a feeble grin. "Or if I was snoring real loud." The grin faded. "We were supposed to be at the fairgrounds early, so I figured she'd gotten up and left to come here. I thought she would've left me a note or something, but—" His voice broke. "I came here to find her but couldn't. And she wasn't answering her phone."

Zoe thought of the worry she'd seen in Jack's eyes that morning. *Have you seen Vera?* No one had.

Because she was already dead.

The county cop asked Jack for the names and contact info of his wife's girlfriends. "I only know a couple of them, and I don't have their numbers," he said, "but they should be in Vera's phone."

The cops exchanged a glance. The one who was standing said, "We haven't been able to locate it."

This produced a reaction from Jack. "What d'ya mean? She always has her phone on her. Always. In case someone needs to reach us about our daughter."

"It wasn't on her—" The kneeling cop stopped before completing the sentence. *It wasn't on her body.* He ran his tongue over his lips. "It wasn't in her purse or in her car."

Jack's eyes shifted. He shook his head. "That's not right. She wouldn't walk off without it. I know she wouldn't."

The standing officer patted his shoulder. "We'll find it. Heck, they may have already located it and not told us yet."

Jack seemed appeased.

"One last question," the kneeling cop said. "Where were you yesterday evening?"

"I was at home." Jack turned to look at him, puzzled. "Are you saying—you think she was murdered?"

"No, no. Actually, right now it looks like an accidental death."

"But you said it wasn't an accident."

"It wasn't a *traffic* accident." The kneeling cop looked to his partner for help but received none. He met Jack's questioning gaze. "It would appear your wife was intoxicated and wandered away from her car. She was found in some underbrush across the road from Parson's Roadhouse."

"Intoxicated?" Jack looked away from the cops. Away from all of them. Zoe could only imagine the horror he was picturing in his mind. "No. That can't be right. Our daughter isn't well and might need us at any time. Vera wouldn't let herself be impaired." Tears in his eyes, he met the cop's gaze again. "She would never have gotten drunk."

The cops exchanged looks again. "Has she ever used drugs? Been on medications?"

"No. Never." Jack wiped a hand across his face. "Look. I know it sounds like a cliché, but Vera wouldn't even take an aspirin."

Zoe studied the agony on his face. She imagined herself in his shoes. Being told something had happened to Pete. In her case, the possibility was real. She'd witnessed the hazards of his job firsthand. But if a pair of uniforms tried to tell her he'd died as a result of being impaired by drugs or alcohol, she'd react the same as Jack.

She touched Diane's arm and whispered in her ear. "I'll be back in a minute." Then she stepped out into the wide, covered food court area, where fairgrounds workers were busy setting up picnic tables, and dug her phone from her hip pocket. She keyed in a number and listened to it ring. When the call connected, she said, "Franklin? It's Zoe. I want to assist when you do Vera Palmer's autopsy."

SEVEN

Vera Palmer's autopsy was scheduled for that evening, and Pete decided to attend. He hadn't expected to find Zoe there but couldn't help but smile when he saw her, decked out in what she referred to as butcher-shop chic.

Until recently, Doc Abercrombie, the forensic pathologist used by the county, and Franklin Marshall had taken fiendish pleasure in demanding Zoe take a hands-on role with autopsies. Once she'd gained some tolerance for the stomach-curdling odors involved, they'd let her off the hook, allowing her to stand back and observe.

Her face lit up when she spotted him too, and he thought of that little velvet box back in his desk drawer. Maybe, in spite of his trepidation, she might just say yes.

He crossed to her, resisting the urge to wrap an arm around her, autopsy garb or not. "Hey."

"Hey yourself," she said with that damned sexy grin of hers. "I'm surprised to see you here."

Marshall nodded a greeting. "Are you expecting us to find something out of the ordinary?"

Pete gave him a noncommittal shrug. "I'm keeping an open mind."

"As should we all." The coroner scanned his notes. "Forty-one-year-old white female. Married. One child. Self-employed accountant. Nonsmoker. No history of alcohol or substance abuse." He lifted his gaze to the woman on the stainless-steel table, shook his head, and directed his next question to her. "What happened to bring you here?"

Vera Palmer's body had already been washed and photographed. Pete, Zoe, and Franklin stood around the table and watched as Doc and his assistant made note of the tiny punctures and pricks on her skin, a result of the thorny wild rose bushes.

Pete leaned closer to Zoe's ear and whispered, "Why aren't you at the fair?"

"Vera's husband said a few things that made me want to be here for this."

"What things?"

"The county cops said she'd been under the influence, but Jack insisted she would never have gotten drunk."

Pete recalled Tiffany's assertion that the victim never had more than one glass of wine. Yet, Vera had clearly become intoxicated elsewhere. "Maybe he didn't know what his wife did when she was out with her girlfriends."

"I thought of that too. Except they have a young daughter who's in a physical rehab facility and isn't doing well. Jack said Vera would never get drunk, because the daughter could need them at a moment's notice."

Pete kept his gaze on the body. A daughter in rehab might be reason to stay sober. Or might be reason to tie one on. The need to escape one's responsibilities for a few hours could be a powerful motivation to veer from the usual code of conduct.

After several long moments of listening to Doc and Franklin record their findings, Zoe pointed toward the body. "I realize what's been bugging me."

"What's that?" Pete asked.

"All those pinprick marks from the wild roses? They're *only* pinpricks. No scrapes or tears. She didn't struggle once she fell into them."

Marshall turned to them. "Good observation. She must have lost consciousness before or as she fell into the underbrush."

Pete had imagined the poor woman, trapped by the thorny vines, flailing to get free until she finally succumbed. At least that was one vision he could expunge from his mind.

The autopsy progressed with no surprises. Zoe turned her usual shade of green when they opened up the abdomen, but she set her jaw and toughed it out without bolting.

The bone saw created a whole other set of foul stenches when the autopsy assistant used it to cut through the skull. Zoe brought an arm up to her face, breathing into the crook of her elbow.

Pete nudged her. "Are we having fun yet?"

She shot him a glare. He chuckled.

A few minutes later, Doc Abercrombie bent over the body and announced, "There's your COD."

Pete, Zoe, and Marshall leaned in for a closer look. The pathologist gently lifted the victim's brain from the opened skull.

Pete had been to enough autopsies to know what a normal brain looked like. There wasn't usually this much blood.

"Subdural hemorrhage," Marshall said flatly.

"Yes." Doc placed the brain into the stainless-steel pan of the scale. "There's a small bleed at the base of the skull."

"So she didn't die because she was drunk," Zoe said, sounding vindicated.

Doc shrugged. "Yes and no."

Marshall folded his arms. "We see it all the time. A drunk falls and hits his head. The bleed in the brain is the cause of death but being intoxicated is the cause of the fall."

Zoe looked at Pete. From the expression on her face, she was thinking the same thing he was.

"The problem with your theory," Pete said, "is that Vera Palmer fell into a patch of brambles. They may have poked and jabbed her, but they also cushioned her fall. There was nothing there to strike her head on."

By the time Zoe got back to the fairgrounds, the activity of the day—but not the suffocating heat—had died down. The exhibit halls' doors were locked as judges examined produce, canned goods, artwork, and crafts, awarding the first of the fair's ribbons. The livestock settled into their temporary homes.

Word of Vera Palmer's death had reached the Pony Barn, and what might have been a festive evening anticipating the week ahead instead turned somber. Walking down the aisle, Zoe spotted the little girl from that morning, her arm immobilized in a sling. The child's mom met Zoe's eyes and gave her a tight, sad smile.

At the end of the row, Windstar and Jazzel had calmed down.

Patsy's Arabian mare picked at the hay in her stall. Windstar dozed with one hind leg cocked and his lower lip drooping. His hay net had been filled and his water bucket topped off. Zoe silently thanked Patsy, who was nowhere to be seen.

They had borrowed a small camper, which was parked in the leveled off field above the barn, and Zoe wondered if Patsy had already retired to her bed. Zoe also wondered if she was alone or with Shane. If that was the case, Zoe had no interest in interrupting.

Instead of heading to the makeshift campground, she strolled to the doorway and leaned a shoulder against the frame, gazing down the hill at the fairgrounds sloping away from her. Directly below the Pony Barn sat the enclosed show arena. A few kids hung out with their 4-H projects on the paved apron leading into it. Sheep. A pair of Jersey cows. A few horses. The teens and their animals getting used to the structure. Farther down the hill, a display of tractors and farm equipment had been set up on a grassy area. Below that, the big commercial exhibit halls and the midway with its rides and games sat idle. Zoe wondered if Earl's boys would be back tomorrow for their week of freedom from parental demands.

Her train of thought carried her from the fairgrounds across town to the morgue where Vera Palmer lay in the cooler, her parental duties now piled onto her husband. Zoe had only recently met him but couldn't get his overwhelming grief out of her mind. He firmly believed his beloved wife would not have risked being unable to respond to the needs of their child. Was Jack with his daughter tonight? Was he breaking the news to her right now that her mom wouldn't be coming to see her anymore?

An unexpected swell of sadness blocked Zoe's throat. Warmed her eyes. She had been that little girl. Not injured in an accident but destroyed by the sudden loss of her father.

Zoe swept a hand across her face. Maybe she'd talk to Diane tomorrow. Find out where Cassidy Palmer was rehabbing and go spend some time with her.

"Oh, good," came a familiar voice from behind her. "I was hoping I'd find you here."

Zoe spun to face Rose Bassi, her childhood best friend.

Rose looked very much like a cowgirl in boots, jeans, and a snug tank top that hugged her curves in all the right places. She must have noticed Zoe's damp eyes. "Are you okay?"

Zoe ignored the question. "Oh my god." She threw her arms around Rose in a crushing hug. "What are you doing here?"

Rose returned her embrace. "Aren't I allowed to come home for a visit?"

"Of course, you are. But you didn't say anything about it on the phone last week."

"I wanted to surprise everyone."

"You succeeded." Zoe took Rose by the shoulders and held her at arm's distance. Her red hair was longer than it had been since Zoe last saw her. However, the biggest transformation was the relaxed smile that reached beyond her lips and eyes. "Are the kids with you, or did you leave them out west?"

"They're both here. I dropped them off at Sylvia's." Rose's late husband had been Sylvia Bassi's son. "When we heard you were here at the fair, Allison pleaded to come with me, but Grandma wouldn't hear of it."

Zoe pictured sixteen-year-old Allison and her older brother Logan as she'd seen them last November in New Mexico. Both kids had fallen in love with the southwest and become more at home there than here in Pennsylvania. Rose had been slower to adapt, although looking at her now, Zoe had to admit she'd been completely indoctrinated to the wardrobe if not the lifestyle.

Rose stuffed both hands into the front pockets of her jeans. "How's everything with you?" The corner of her mouth curled into a wicked grin. "And Pete?"

"We just had a Friday night date."

The grin blossomed into an eager smile. "Oh?"

"At the morgue."

The smile fizzled. "Oh."

Zoe gave an abbreviated version of the day's events but left out the part about her doubts regarding Vera Palmer's intoxication.

Rose shook her head sadly. "That poor man. I know exactly what he's going through."

Zoe winced. Maybe she shouldn't have brought up Vera's death. It had been only a year and a half since Rose lost her husband under tragic and unexpected circumstances. "I'm sorry. I didn't mean to open old wounds."

"You didn't. I'm fine. I mean, you know I'll love Ted forever, but I'm...okay." Her smile was back. "Better than okay."

Zoe suspected she knew the source of this particular smile. "How is Detective Morales?" While Rose's kids had fallen in love with New Mexico, Rose had fallen in love with one of San Juan County's finest.

"Miguel is just fine." She dragged out the last word and made it sound erotic.

Zoe held up both hands in a *stop* gesture. "Say no more. I get the message."

"In fact, Miguel is the reason I came home."

"Oh?"

The biggest smile yet lit Rose's face. "He asked me to marry him." She pulled her left hand from her jeans pocket and extended it to Zoe, displaying a turquoise band spouting a dazzling diamond. "And I said yes."

The next morning, Pete had the station to himself. His weekend officer, Nate Williamson, was out cruising the township. Since Saturday was typically Pete's day off, he left the Out-on-Patrol sign hanging on the door and headed to the rear of the building where Vera Palmer's car was secured in the evidence garage.

Last night's autopsy had provided no answers. Toxicology reports could take weeks, but Pete wasn't willing to wait. No matter what they revealed, something didn't feel right. If Vera was indeed under the influence of alcohol, where had she gotten it? Not at Parson's Roadhouse. Of that Pete was sure. Or maybe the culprit wasn't alcohol but drugs. Same question. Where had she gone to get it? Or had someone slipped something into her drink? And how had she sustained that blow to the back of her head when he'd found her face-down in the scratchy but cushioning bed of brambles?

It all came back to one question. Where had she been between visits to Parson's Roadhouse?

Pete checked his watch. Still too early to head over there and talk to the woman who'd waited on the group's table. One of Vera's friends was bound to know where she'd gone. Hopefully the waitress could provide him with at least some of their names.

Which brought his attention back to the black Camry.

He'd documented the wallet he'd found into evidence yesterday. Nothing suspicious there. Fifty dollars in cash. A few reward and credit cards. A driver's license. He'd also stashed the box from the backseat in the evidence room. But a quick search of the car hadn't turned up Vera's missing phone.

Pete let himself into the smaller evidence room to retrieve the key fob and then returned to click open the car. He pulled out his notebook and thumbed through it to find Vera's number, which he keyed into his own phone. When he pressed send, her voicemail immediately picked up. He swore and jammed his cell and his notebook back into his pocket before donning a new pair of gloves and climbing into the driver's seat.

The cup holders were empty. The center console storage compartment held some charger cables and an EZ Pass but no phone. He leaned over and popped open the glove box even though he'd already searched it. There wasn't anything in it he hadn't seen there yesterday. Running his hand between the seat and the console revealed nothing.

He climbed out and squatted to look under the seat. An empty plastic water bottle had rolled under it. He reached in and felt around. Nothing. His search of the backseat, under the passenger seat, and under the floor mats was equally unproductive.

He locked the garage, returned to the evidence room, and moved the box he'd found in Vera's backseat from the shelf to the table. Time for a thorough inventory.

He'd already noted the fair program that topped the box. Beneath it was a stack of file folders containing copies of 4-H project records— information about the kids' horses, what they fed the animals, veterinary and blacksmith reports, expenses. The financial stuff took him aback. How on earth could anyone afford to keep a horse if this is what everything cost?

How could Zoe afford to keep *her* horse if this is what it cost?

Pete shook his head and skimmed through the rest of the members' paperwork. Next was a folder of the club's expenditures and income, including membership dues, bake sales, and concession stand sales from a couple of horseshows over the summer.

The last folder at the bottom of the box contained flyers from those horseshows and a few others.

Zoe had mentioned Vera and her husband were active in the 4-H club. She must have been the keeper of the records, none of which answered any of his questions.

He'd finished returning the contents to the box and the box to the shelf when the buzzer on the station's entrance blasted.

Pete locked the evidence room and headed down the hall to the front door. He swept aside the closed vertical blinds to discover Sylvia looking impatient. But there was a glimmer in her eyes too.

He punched the security code, and she breezed through the door almost bulldozing over him. "Why in heaven's name do you have the door locked?"

"Because it's my day off. I'm not really here."

She eyed him up and down. "Really? So what's this? An apparition?"

Pete noted the time. The Roadhouse employees would be arriving to prepare for the lunch crowd. He didn't have time to banter with his former secretary. "What do you need?"

The corners of Sylvia's eyes crinkled mischievously. "Have you talked to Zoe?"

Now he was worried. Sylvia had something up her sleeve. And it involved Zoe. "Yeah. At the autopsy last night."

"But not since then?"

"No. Why?"

"I have company. Rose and the kids are home for a visit."

"Oh." That explained Sylvia's flushed cheeks. It did not explain why she looked like she was about to bubble over.

"Rose and Miguel got engaged."

"Miguel? Morales?"

Sylvia's eyes narrowed in annoyance. "Now how many Miguels do you know who would propose to my daughter-in-law?"

She had a point. "How do you feel about that?"

"I'm thrilled. He's a good man. The kids are crazy about him. And Rose is happier than she's been since Ted..." Sylvia still had trouble saying the word "died." She lowered her eyes briefly, but when they came up again, the smile was back. "They're planning to get married two weeks from today."

"Wow. That's fast."

"It won't be anything big or fancy. They've both been down that road before. Miguel doesn't have any family except for his daughter." Sylvia's expression turned grim. "Rose's mother's been in failing health, you know. No way could Bert make the trip out to New Mexico." Sylvia brightened, and the mischievous twinkle was back. "I had this fabulous idea. It's perfect."

The way she was looking at Pete made him feel like a lamb being eyeballed by a coyote. Whatever her perfect idea was, he knew he wasn't going to like it.

"You already have the ring in your desk drawer." Sylvia beamed. "You and Zoe could make it a double wedding."

EIGHT

The gates to the Monongahela County Fair opened at nine on Saturday morning. By ten, the grounds teamed with folks, old, young, and everyone in between. Zoe thought the early birds might be there to beat the heat but knew the steaming August weather wouldn't deter many. Besides, she and Patsy had sweated their way through the entire night in that tin can on wheels. The next time her cousin borrowed a camper, Zoe intended to make sure the air conditioner worked.

Once they'd fed Windstar and Jazzel and refilled water buckets, Zoe and Patsy joined the bulk of the fairgoers checking out the exhibit halls, reopened this morning after last night's judging.

Patsy turned away from the display of Best of Show winners to face Zoe. "Do you want to tell me what's bothering you? Besides the whole autopsy thing."

"What do you mean?"

"You haven't said more than five words since you came back to the camper last night. And those were directed at Windstar this morning." Patsy held two fingers. "Move over." A third finger. "Whoa. Easy, boy." She finished off with a full hand. "Five."

Zoe couldn't argue with Patsy's math. But the list of what was bugging her might take both hands.

And possibly a foot.

She settled on one. "Rose is in town."

Patsy lowered her hand. "Really?" Her puzzled expression told Zoe she had no idea why this bothered her.

Zoe wasn't so sure either. "She's engaged."

"Really?" Patsy repeated, happier this time. "That's terrific." She again looked perplexed. "Isn't it?"

Zoe sighed. "I guess."

"Her first husband's been gone almost two years, right?"

"A year and a half. But it's not Ted. To be honest, he'd want this for her. Miguel's a great guy." He reminded Zoe of Pete.

"Then what?"

She didn't have a good answer. When Rose had stuck that ring in Zoe's face last night, she'd given all the appropriate responses. Squeal of delight. Hugs. Gushing. But deep down, she'd felt...what? Envious? No. She'd felt...hollow.

Pete had already proposed to Zoe once. She'd put him off. Even now, she wasn't sure marrying him was a good idea. She loved him. She couldn't imagine her life without him. She remembered vividly the terror she'd felt when she'd seen him bleeding and in shock from a gunshot wound four months ago. So why was the idea of marriage equally terrifying?

Patsy broke through Zoe's ruminations. "Oh my god. You're jealous."

"No," Zoe said quickly. Too quickly?

"Rose has a rock on her hand and you don't."

Zoe blew a raspberry and walked away from the Best of Show display and from her cousin.

Patsy followed her. "That's it. You wish it was you."

Zoe spun to face her. "No. I don't." The words were out before she'd had a chance to self-edit them.

Her cousin's teasing grin melted into a look of shock. "You don't want to marry Pete?"

"No. Yes." Which was the correct answer to that question? "I don't know." The air in the hall suddenly felt devoid of oxygen. She turned away and headed toward the entrance.

Patsy kept up stride-for-stride. "For heaven's sake, why not?"

Zoe shouldered through the glass door. Instead of finding breathing room outside, she felt trapped in a suffocating web of heat and humidity.

Patsy caught her arm, forced Zoe to look at her, and silently demanded an answer.

"I don't *not* want to marry him. I'm just..." What? How could she explain to Patsy what she couldn't explain to herself? How seeing him shot and nearly die had thrown her world as she knew it into a freefall.

Pete was a cop. A hero. She loved him for that, but it also meant that she could lose him at any given moment. Plus, she still grieved the man who *had* died that night. A man she had no right to grieve. It was a loss she couldn't talk about. Not to Patsy. Not to Pete. Not to anyone.

But if Zoe was truly honest with herself, the events of last spring were only partially responsible for her reluctance. No, the real obstacle to her dreams of a life with Pete went back decades—to a diagnosis in a doctor's office confirming the one thing she was incapable of giving him.

Patsy waited, still holding Zoe's arm, for an answer.

"I'm not ready." The truth, but only a tiny portion of it.

Patsy released her, apparently accepting the reply but not happy with it. "What's it gonna take for you to *be* ready?"

Zoe faked a grin and shrugged.

Patsy rolled her eyes. "You're hopeless."

"And hungry." It seemed like a good time to change the subject. Zoe aimed a thumb over her shoulder toward the hall they'd come from. "All those cakes and pies in there and not a sample to be found."

The topic of food succeeded in directing Patsy's attention elsewhere. "It's not fair. They should have to bake enough to let everyone have a taste."

Zoe wasn't about to discuss the impossible logistics of such a task. Instead, she looked around. To their right, the midway, which wouldn't open for business for another hour or so. In front of them, the commercial exhibit hall filled with home improvement companies and politicians. Around to their left, a row of food vendors including the slot where she'd witnessed Jack Palmer's world collapse on him yesterday.

Her appetite disappeared.

"Zoe, Zoe!"

Diane jogged unevenly toward them through the midway booths and trailers, waving. Zoe waited. By the time the 4-H leader reached them, she was out of breath, sweat glistening on her forehead. She bent over, braced her hands on her thighs.

"You didn't have to run," Zoe told her. "I'd rather not start the day treating a heart attack."

Diane gave her a dirty look. "Not funny."

"I didn't intend it to be."

"I wanted...to ask...what you found out...at the autopsy last night. Was Vera really drunk?"

"We won't know anything for certain until the toxicology reports come back."

Diane straightened. "How long does that take?"

A booming voice replied before Zoe could. "Too long."

The voice belonged to a man approaching from the commercial hall. He looked vaguely familiar, although she was positive she'd never met him before. Despite temperatures nearing ninety, he wore a suit and tie in contrast to the jeans and t-shirts worn by everyone else. A campaign button graced his lapel. Zoe couldn't make it out until he came closer.

Davis for Coroner.

That's why he looked familiar. She'd seen his picture on billboards.

He extended a hand to Diane. "Dr. Charles Davis. I'm running for Monongahela County Coroner in the upcoming election."

After the 4-H leader had shaken his hand, he offered it to Zoe, then Patsy. Had there been a baby in their midst, Zoe felt certain he'd have kissed it.

"I couldn't help overhearing your conversation," he said.

His ears were probably attuned to pick the word "autopsy" out of a conversation anywhere within a quarter-mile radius.

"The county currently outsources all the important work of death investigation." He stressed *important.* "If I'm elected, the county won't have to pay for an outside forensic pathologist to perform autopsies. I intend to use the money I save to upgrade the morgue, building a new facility that will include our own lab. The wait for toxicology reports will be cut drastically."

Doc Abercrombie must have been making a pile of money if his county paycheck was the equivalent of a new building and forensic lab. Zoe wondered if Dr. Davis knew she was part of the current coroner's office that he was planning to dismantle. She didn't have to wonder long.

He fixed her with hard dark eyes. "You're one of Coroner Marshall's deputies, aren't you?" He sounded as if the words tasted bitter on his tongue.

"I am."

His expression appeared equally contemptuous as he gave her a once over, taking in her barn sneakers, dusty jeans, and Pittsburgh Steelers t-shirt. She wished she would've encountered him later, after she'd cleaned up and gotten into her EMS uniform.

"What training do you have?" he asked, sounding as though he doubted she'd graduated eighth grade.

"I've been a paramedic for almost fifteen years, and I've taken the coroner's Basic Education Course and kept up with the continuing education requirements every year. I've aced the exam each time."

"None of which qualifies you as a real investigator."

Zoe forced her clenched fists to relax. Davis' smug expression told her he knew he'd struck a nerve. The fact she let his assessment bother her pissed her off even more.

"I can't believe the DA manages to get any convictions on the forensic evidence your department handles. Or mishandles." Davis sniffed. "Well, I suppose if you went back to college and got your degree, I'd consider hiring you."

She made a mental note to pick up additional *Re-elect Franklin Marshall* signs to post around the county. "You haven't won the election yet."

Davis gave her a slow smile. "I will." With a knowing wink, he turned and sauntered back toward the commercial exhibit hall, pausing at the doorway to shake hands with more constituents.

"Wow," Diane said.

Patsy gave a short laugh. "Yeah. Wow. What a jerk."

Zoe didn't reply. Something about that wink and the confidence of those two words—*I will*—gave her that walking-over-a-grave sensation.

Diane shook her head and faced Zoe. "At the risk of summoning the demon again, did you find anything in Vera's autopsy to contradict the cops' theory that she was drunk?"

Zoe blinked. She'd lain awake last night in the sweltering tin-can camper thinking about that very question. Or more precisely, how much of what she and Pete had discussed should be shared. "Not really. Franklin said Vera suffered a head injury consistent with a fall occurring as a result of intoxication." All true.

"So he says her death was an accident?" Diane asked.

"He ruled the manner of death as undetermined pending toxicology." At Diane's raised eyebrow, Zoe shrugged. "It's standard procedure."

It also gave Pete—and her—the greenlight to keep investigating.

Diane gazed across the midway toward the 4-H Barn. "It's darned tragic. Poor Cassidy. And poor Jack. Vera was the glue that held them together. She never left her daughter's bedside in those first weeks after the accident. And even when the doctors gave them the lousy prognosis for recovery, Vera never gave up hope. Neither did Jack, but I think he drew his strength and faith from his wife. Now?" Diane shook her head. "I don't know."

"It sounds like she was under a lot of pressure," Patsy said. "If it was me, I'd go out and get hammered too."

Zoe looked at her cousin.

Patsy shrugged. "Well, I would. So sue me."

"Vera wasn't like that." Diane rubbed her arms. "At least, I didn't think she was." She glanced toward the barn again. "I better get back. Oh." She turned to Zoe. "Will you still keep an eye on Luke? Like I said before, I'd originally asked Vera for help but..."

"Keep an eye on him? You want me to follow him around?"

"No, of course not. Just...I don't know. If you see him acting like he's getting into trouble, tell him to get back to the barn."

Not exactly how Zoe had hoped to spend her week at the fair. Babysitting a juvenile delinquent. "I'm not sure he'll listen to me. What about his mother?"

Diane rolled her eyes. "I'll ask someone else to keep tabs on *her*."

"That isn't what I mean, and you know it."

"Yeah, I know. But Merryn is precisely the reason I need someone to watch out for Luke. I still hold out hope for *him*." Diane fluttered a hand in farewell and walked away.

"Who are Luke and Merryn?" Patsy asked once Diane had disappeared into the jumble of midway attractions.

"A 4-H kid and his mother." Zoe's mind had already slipped back to Dr. Charles Davis and his comment about her qualifications.

"I figured that much. But why does she need you to keep tabs on them?"

Zoe barely heard her cousin's question. Instead, she pictured Davis' smirk. His words, "None of which qualifies you as a real investigator," echoed in her ears. Maybe it was time for her to prove him wrong.

Patsy jabbed Zoe's shoulder.

"Ow."

"You didn't hear a thing I said, did you?"

"Sure I did," Zoe lied.

Patsy huffed. "Never mind. Are you still hungry?"

Zoe looked around. "Yeah. Let's grab something to eat. Then let's check in with the gang at the 4-H Barn."

NINE

For the second day in a row, Pete arrived at Parson's Roadhouse before they opened for lunch.

Tiffany unlocked the door to let him in. "Anything new on Vera Palmer?"

"Not really." He looked beyond the empty bar toward the dining room and kitchen. "Is the waitress who served her and her friends here?"

"Charlene? Yeah. Do you want to talk to her?"

"Please."

Tiffany disappeared down the short hallway between the bar and the restaurant. Pete took a seat at one of the bar tables, his back to the corner, and took out his notebook and his reading glasses. He recognized the woman who appeared from the direction Tiffany had gone. She'd waited on him several times in the past. Efficient but quiet and generally unsmiling. Today was no different.

She approached his table with a cup of coffee, which she placed in front of him.

"Thank you." He half-stood and gestured for her to take a seat across from him. "Charlene?"

"Yes, sir." She sat, her spine rigid, her hands resting in her lap.

"I understand you served Vera Palmer and her friends on Thursday evening?"

"Yes, sir."

"Do you happen to recall how much Mrs. Palmer had to drink?"

"Yes, sir. Only one glass of wine. Pinot noir. Her usual."

"Did any of her friends have more than their usual?"

"No, sir." Her gaze lowered. "Zinfandel, Chardonnay, two Pinot Gris, and a Merlot." Her head shifted slightly with each wine listed, as if she was looking around the table at each customer.

"You remember everyone's orders or just this group?"

Charlene's eyes met his and her mouth twitched into a fleeting smile. "I'm good at what I do. I rarely need to write down orders. And I've served this particular group a number of times. They always order the same drinks and mostly the same entrees."

Pete was impressed. Perhaps the waitress' photographic memory would come in handy. "Did you notice anything different about Mrs. Palmer this time?"

Charlene scowled. "Different? She ordered the New England scrod with a baked potato, sour cream, no butter. And a dinner salad. Sometimes she orders broasted chicken with fries. But it's usually one or the other."

"How did she behave? Did you notice if she acted differently?"

The question puzzled her. "No, sir. I never pay attention to how a patron acts. Unless they're especially rude. These women weren't. Rude, I mean. I left them alone except to see if they needed refills on water or coffee."

So much for the photographic memory. "Did you notice what time Mrs. Palmer left?"

"She asked for her check a little before nine, I think." Charlene's eyes widened. "If you're looking for things out of the ordinary, that would be it. Normally, they all leave at the same time."

"Did you notice when she returned?"

"No. I didn't see her again."

Pete scanned his notes. According to Tiffany's statement, Vera had returned around ten. "Do you have any idea why she left early or where she went?"

"No, sir."

Other than the details of Vera Palmer's last meal and the time she'd left, Pete had learned nothing new. "Any chance you can give me the names of Mrs. Palmer's friends?"

Charlene gestured over her shoulder. "When Mrs. Palmer was found dead, we went through Thursday's credit card receipts and put hers and her friends' aside. Do you want them?"

"That would be a big help. Thank you."

He sipped his coffee while he waited for Charlene to return with the receipts. He wasn't sure how much help they'd be. No addresses. No phone numbers. Just names.

Charlene hurried back into the bar, clutching a handful of paper slips, which she held out to him. "Is there anything else I can do for you? Because if not, we're about to open, and I need to finish setting up my tables."

Pete thanked and excused her. Once he was alone, he filed through the receipts, making notes. Vera's was on top and matched what Charlene had told him. The timestamp on it read 8:57. Pete set it aside. The other five receipts were timestamped in a cluster, a half hour later. No other early departures. He jotted down the five names and didn't recognize the first four. Then he spotted the final one.

Olivia Kolter.

Everyone who stabled horses in the 4-H Barn knew Vera and adored her. Zoe heard over and over what a lovely woman Vera was. "Poor Jack," they all said. He lived and breathed for his wife and child.

And, to a person, no one believed Vera would allow herself to be impaired.

After an hour of chatting with parents, kids, and 4-H leaders, Zoe hadn't discovered anything new.

"Maybe Dr. Davis was right," Zoe grumbled to Patsy. "Maybe I am unqualified to be an investigator."

Patsy blew out a noisy puff of air. "Or maybe Vera really wasn't the type to get falling-down drunk."

As they wandered toward the end of the barn, Zoe checked her watch. "I better look in on Windstar and then get a shower. I have to be on duty soon."

They'd almost reached the doorway when Cody DeRosa in his cowboy hat sauntered in surrounded by a trio of preteen girls. He spotted Zoe and Patsy and stopped. "Hello, ladies."

Patsy murmured a greeting. Zoe looked at her. Was she blushing?

The girls stopped, waiting for him.

"You go on," he told them. "Get your horses out. I'll be along in a moment."

They thanked him and hurried off, giggling and whispering

among themselves.

Cody swept his hat off and ran his fingers through a full head of dark hair that showed a hint of silver. "They're having problems getting their horses to square up for the Grooming and Showmanship class. I said I'd help them out."

"That's nice of you." Zoe thought back to her early days in the show ring, working with a borrowed horse that refused to stand with all four feet flat and aligned to best show its conformation in front of the judge.

He shrugged. "I'm a trainer, and I love working with kids." He grinned, and those killer dimples framed his mouth. The same dimples that had melted Zoe's heart all those years ago. "And if I do a bad job of teaching them, I'll know when I see them in the show ring on Wednesday."

The dimples apparently had an effect on Patsy too. She tipped her head at a flirtatious angle. "Will you go easy when judging them if their horses don't cooperate after you've worked with them?"

He held Patsy's gaze, the dimples deepening. "No, ma'am. I don't play favorites. Not inside the ring, anyway."

Zoe fought the urge to roll her eyes.

"*Hey.*" The sharp voice and clomping footsteps came from behind her.

She spun to see a very unhappy Shane Tolland storming their way, fists clenched. Patsy hadn't pried her eyes away from Cody, so Zoe elbowed her.

Patsy gave a whiny "ow" but cut it short when she spotted her boyfriend, apparently ready to take a swing at the horseshow judge.

Cody didn't appear at all concerned, although the dimples had vanished. He placed the hat back on his not-bald head and gave the brim a tug to seat it firmly. "Well, ladies, I have a training session to get to." His gaze lingered on Patsy then shifted and settled on Zoe. "I'd love to buy you both dinner one evening this week. The food around here isn't fancy, but it's good."

Shane seethed but kept his fists to himself.

Cody finally acknowledged Shane by touching a finger to his hat's brim as he walked past him.

Shane glared after him. "That's twice I've had to run that snake away from my woman." He turned to aim the glare at Patsy. "If I catch him bothering you again, he's gonna regret the day he met me."

Zoe wanted to point out that Cody hadn't exactly been "run off" either time. And if Shane did decide to press the point with his fists, Zoe's money would be on Cody.

"He wasn't bothering me," Patsy said. "He's friendly with everyone."

Especially women, Zoe thought.

Patsy caught Shane's arm and pressed against him. "Zoe's on her way back to the Pony Barn. Why don't you and I see what's going on down at the grandstand?"

Zoe watched them walk away, as if Cody had been completely forgotten. She had a feeling such was not the case. With a shake of her head, she left one barn, threading her way through the crowds and up the hill toward another. Halfway there, "I Fought the Law" burst from her phone.

"Hey," she said.

"Hey yourself." Pete's voice warmed her, but she noticed an edge to it as well.

"What's up?"

"I don't suppose you've seen Earl around today, have you?"

"Not yet. We're both on standby with the ambulance here but not until three o'clock."

There was a pause. Then Pete asked, "I don't suppose you know where I can find his wife, do you?"

Following Zoe's instructions, Pete had no problem tracking down Olivia Kolter.

A horde of teens and adults armed with an array of spray cans—probably leftovers discovered in parents' storage sheds and garages—swarmed a dozen or so school buses parked around the far side of the fairgrounds' racetrack.

The kids laughed and spray-painted the buses—and each other—in their various school colors. But there were splashes of every other color in the spectrum, which supported Pete's theory about the kids cleaning out their parents' stashes of half-used paint.

Graffiti at its finest. And most legal.

Pete found Olivia near the rear of one of the buses, pointing at a makeshift mural-in-progress and offering guidance to the wannabe artists, two of whom were her sons.

She didn't notice Pete's approach. He stood behind her and folded his arms. "All this work and it's going to be trashed in a few days."

Olivia spun. "Oh. Hi, Pete. Well, you know how it is. School bus demolition derby is only partly about who has the last bus still moving. The paint jobs are a matter of school pride. Whoever wins gets to pick next year's theme."

Pete had to confess, he'd never witnessed a school bus demo derby. It sounded like fun. With Zoe at the fair, he might have to make a point to attend this year. But the school bus wasn't his reason for being here today. "Could I borrow you for a few minutes? I need to ask you some questions."

Olivia's eyes widened. "Is Earl okay?"

"He's fine. I wanted to talk to you about Vera Palmer."

Olivia's face softened from panic to sadness. "Of course." She barked a few last orders at the graffiti artists and then gestured for Pete to follow her to the shade of a maple tree and a trio of coolers. She opened one and reached in. "Would you like a bottle of cold water?"

He accepted and thanked her. Once he'd unscrewed the cap and chugged half the contents, he twisted the lid back on and set the bottle in the grass at his feet. After drying the condensation from his fingers on his shirt, he pulled out his notebook. "I gather you've heard about Vera."

Olivia pressed the cold bottle against her throat. "Yeah. I was shocked. We'd had dinner together that evening."

Pete didn't mention that he already knew as much. "Were you two close?"

"Not really. We have a mutual friend in our little dinner group. I only knew Vera through her. Still, I was horrified to hear the news. What happened?"

"That's what I'm trying to figure out. Was she acting strangely that night?"

Olivia pondered the question. "Not really. Other than leaving early, but I assumed it had to do with her daughter. Her little girl's in a rehab facility after being severely injured a while ago. I felt so badly for her. Vera changed after the accident. But then again, as a mother, I can't imagine something like that *not* changing you."

"What made you think Vera left because of her daughter?"

Olivia shrugged. "Why else? She was always checking her phone when we were together. You know, fretting over whether Cassie was okay. It was the same way on Thursday. One ear on the conversation, one eye on her phone. Except this time, she must have gotten a text from the facility, because she got upset and said she had to leave."

"Did she say the text was about her daughter?"

Olivia caught her lip between her teeth. "It's funny. I thought she did, but now that you mention it, maybe not. Maybe I just assumed that's why she left. No. No, I don't think she said what the text was about."

"But the text upset her?"

"Yes. We asked what was wrong, but she would only say she had to go."

Pete jotted a note. "Do you happen to know what rehab hospital the girl is in?"

"No, I'm sorry. Like I said, she and I weren't close. But I bet some of the other gals know. Especially Nell McDonald. She's the mutual friend I told you about. And she and Vera used to be neighbors."

"Do you have a phone number or address for Nell?"

Olivia extracted her phone from her back pocket. "I don't think I have an address, but I know I have her number."

TEN

Zoe didn't know exactly how hot it was and didn't want to. The humidity left her feeling like she needed gills. Squirming her damp body into her Monongahela County EMS uniform after showering in the cinder block building near the Pony Barn left her sweatier than she'd been before the attempt to clean up.

Standing at the rear of the ambulance while keeping watch over the wide-eyed kids gazing through the open back doors, Zoe made a mental note. Never again.

But there was a perk. They were manning one of the newly purchased EMS trucks. The county wanted to show off its shiny fresh-off-the-assembly-line unit to the fairgoers.

Earl had positioned himself at the side of the vehicle with both the front patient compartment and passenger cab doors open. He chatted with a young family, touting the financial benefits of subscribing to the ambulance service as well as answering their questions about the equipment and capabilities of Medic Ten.

"Can I go for a ride in it?" one of the youngsters at the rear doors asked Zoe.

She glanced at the boy, who was probably nine or ten years old. "Only if you get hurt."

A little girl, the boy's younger sister, Zoe guessed, stood on one leg and held the other one to show off a SpongeBob bandage. "I scraped my knee this morning," she said with a hopeful lilt in her voice.

Zoe closed her eyes. She'd walked right into that one. Opening her eyes again, she forced a smile. "Looks like someone already treated you."

"What if my rabbit bites me?" another kid asked.

"You come by. I'll give you a—" Zoe was going to say Band-Aid but pictured the whole lot of them showing up with everything from a skinned elbow to a mosquito bite, requesting Band-Aids. "I'll give you a tetanus shot."

This brought a round of *ewwws* and sent the kids scurrying off to look at the goat pens.

"You are shameless."

She turned to find Pete grinning at her. "I've only been here for twenty minutes and have been asked six times to let them run the siren."

"Only six?" Unlike Zoe, Pete was not in uniform. Instead, he wore a gray polo shirt and blue jeans—a pair of Wranglers that she'd bought him. They fit a little tighter than all of his others, which was precisely why she'd chosen them. He moved closer, slipped an arm around her waist, and whispered in her ear. "I missed you last night."

Her cheeks warmed. "You saw me at the autopsy."

He stepped back and chuckled. "That's not quite the same."

"No, it's not."

Earl spotted Pete and waved.

"Did you tell him I talked to his wife?" Pete whispered to Zoe.

"No. I guess you tracked her down then?"

Earl approached them, having handed out a brochure to the family before they moved on. "Tracked who down?"

Zoe allowed Pete to field this one.

"Olivia," he said. "Did you know the dead woman we found across the road from Parson's was a friend of hers?"

"I know she was acquainted with her. Olivia was stunned to hear about Vera. But I don't think they were close friends."

"Yeah, that's what she told me."

Earl crossed his arms. "You talked to Olivia?"

"I'm trying to retrace Vera Palmer's last few hours to see how she got into the condition she was in."

"Was Olivia able to help?" Zoe asked.

"She gave me the name and number of a woman who apparently knew Vera well. Unfortunately, I only got Nell McDonald's voicemail, and she hasn't called me back."

Earl nodded. "Sounds like Nell. Olivia is always complaining that she's hard to reach."

Pete grunted. He looked at Zoe. "Have you seen Vera's husband around?"

"Not since yesterday when we broke the news to him. I'd be more surprised if he was here, all things considered. He has funeral arrangements to make and a daughter who now fully relies on him."

"Which is why I haven't bothered him yet."

"But you think he might know something?" Zoe pictured Jack Palmer, heartbroken and sobbing.

Pete gazed into the distance. "He might have an idea of where his wife would've gone and why."

Zoe knew Pete was visualizing something other than the fairgrounds. She reached over to touch his arm. "Have you located Vera's phone yet?"

"No," he said. "I haven't. I sent Nate to make one more sweep of the area where we found her body. If he comes up empty, I plan to get a warrant for her cell records."

Earl's gaze drifted beyond Pete. "Looks like we have a customer."

Zoe turned and spotted Diane hobbling toward them from the direction of the 4-H Barn. Zoe jogged to meet her. "What happened? Are you okay?"

"Nothing happened." Diane took Zoe's arm as a cane and continued the rest of the way to the EMS truck. "And I'm not okay. I don't suppose you folks can dispense pain-killers without doctor's orders, can you?"

Earl looked at her. "What kind of painkillers?"

Diane took a seat on the rear bumper with a grunt. "The stronger the better," she said with a humorless laugh.

"What's wrong?" Zoe asked.

"Oh, it's my damned hip. I need to have a replacement, but my crappy insurance coverage won't pay for it. They say it isn't bad enough." Diane let out a growl. "They'd think differently if they had to live in this body."

"Were you limping like this yesterday?" Zoe hadn't noticed it.

"No." Diane wiped a sweaty gray curl from her forehead. "I'd taken my pills before I left home. Problem is, I walked off and left them on my kitchen counter. I hate to drive all the way back home."

Earl braced a hand on the framework of the ambulance's back

doors. "We have packets of aspirin and regular strength acetaminophen."

Diane chuffed a laugh. "Regular strength doesn't put a dent in the pain." She lifted her face, looking past Zoe. "Hey, Luke," she called.

The teen, who had been ambling toward them, came to an abrupt stop. He looked like a cornered horse trying to decide if there was any hope of escape if he made a break for it.

"Luke," Diane called again, her tone lower, hinting at dire consequences for the boy if he tried to bolt.

His shoulders slouched, and he shuffled over to the ambulance. "What's up?"

"Take my Tempo down to Doyle's Pharmacy and pick up a bottle of extra strength acetaminophen. The keys are under the driver's side floor mat." She dug in her jeans pocket and pulled out a twenty-dollar bill. "Straight there. Straight back. No side excursions. And no passengers. Got it?"

"Got it. The car parked in its usual spot?"

"Of course."

After Luke had taken off at a lope, Zoe turned to Diane. "The Tempo? You still have that car?"

"Unfortunately. I never lock it in the hopes that someone'll steal the thing, but so far it's always right where I left it."

Zoe spotted Pete's raised eyebrow. "Her Ford Tempo is older than my truck. And it was nothing but an old beater when I was in 4-H." She looked at Diane. "Remember the time we packed five of us in it and drove all the way to the State Show in Harrisburg? And the muffler started to fall off?"

Diane nodded. "We tied it back up with baling twine."

Zoe laughed at the memory. "Except the baling twine burnt through. We almost caught the whole car on fire."

Diane smiled, shaking her head. "And that isn't even the worst thing that's happened to it."

Zoe realized Pete had no idea who this woman was and apologized before introducing them.

"Chief of Police?" Diane flushed. "Is it illegal to admit to leaving your car unlocked in the hopes of having it stolen?"

"It's not illegal. It's not advisable either."

She shrugged. "I wouldn't even know what to do with a nicer car. I bring it here every year and get a parking pass to keep it on the fairgrounds rather than out in the lot. That way if anyone needs to borrow it..." She gestured in the direction Luke had vanished. "Or if I need one of the older kids to run an errand for me, I don't have to worry about it getting dented."

"Or catching on fire?" Pete said with his lopsided grin.

"Exactly." She struggled to stand. Earl and Zoe both caught an arm to assist. "Thanks." Diane squinted toward the 4-H Barn. "Is it just me or is that thing getting farther away by the year?"

Earl offered her his arm. "I'll walk you back."

She waved him off. "Don't be silly. I'll be fine."

He shook his head. "It's part of my job. Besides, I have some questions about Lilly joining the club." He glanced at Zoe and Pete and winked. "And those two want to be alone for a few minutes."

"Well, in that case..." Diane accepted his arm. "Let's not get in the way of the lovebirds."

Zoe watched her partner escort her former 4-H leader back toward the barn. Pete rested a hand on Zoe's shoulder, giving it a gentle squeeze and drawing her against him. She'd been living under his roof for a few months shy of a year now, but his touch still sent bursts of electricity sizzling through her.

"You heard them," Pete whispered into her hair. "We're lovebirds."

She leaned into him for a moment, wishing they weren't surrounded by hundreds of fair-goers. One child with his mom and dad pointed their way. Was it the EMS truck that excited him? Or was he asking his parents about those two people snuggling in public?

"Hey, break it up, you two." The comment hadn't come from either the mother or the father. Sylvia stood at the corner of the ambulance, fists planted firmly on her hips. The scowl on her face didn't match the twinkle in her eyes.

Zoe eased away from Pete, but he kept a gentle grip on her shoulder.

Sylvia shot a questioning look at Pete. "Do you have any news you'd like to share?"

Zoe looked up at him. Was he...blushing?

"No," he said quickly.

"What's going on?" Zoe asked. "What news?"

He released her shoulder and rammed both hands into his jeans pockets. "Nothing."

He shot a glare and a quick headshake at Sylvia. There was most definitely something going on. But Sylvia plastered an exaggerated innocent expression on her face, and Pete's set jaw told Zoe he wasn't about to share.

"Have you seen Rose and my grandkids yet?" Sylvia asked.

Okay. The subject had officially been dropped. "No," Zoe said. "They're here?"

Sylvia gazed toward the grandstand. "I bet they headed straight to the main attraction. Whatever that happens to be today."

Zoe searched the passersby on the off chance she might spy her best friend. "Tractor pulls. They started with pedal-powered, then they're doing lawn tractor. Later they'll have the big boys."

Sylvia wrinkled her nose. "Those big ones are too noisy. But maybe I can still catch the pedal power." She reached over and slapped Pete on the back. "Carry on," she told him with a wink. She started to walk away, then turned and called back to them. "If you spot the kids, tell them I'll be at the grandstand."

Once Sylvia had merged with the crowd, Zoe faced Pete. "What was that all about?"

He suddenly become very interested in the new EMS truck's patient compartment. "Nothing. I don't know what you mean."

"Which is it?" she asked. "Is it nothing or you don't know what I mean?"

He looked at her and grinned. "Both."

Secrecy between Sylvia and Pete was never good, and Zoe had a strong suspicion that it had to do with her, which made it even worse.

His expression turned serious. "Have you learned anything new about Vera Palmer?"

Zoe knew full well his attempt at changing the subject was geared at steering her away from Sylvia's comment. But his misdirection worked. "Not much. I've been asking around. Everyone loved her. No one has ever seen her take a drink or even an aspirin."

Pete stared into the distance.

"What?" Zoe asked. "Did you learn anything different?"

"Not about Vera's drinking habits."

"What then?"

"Olivia said Vera got a text while they were having dinner and left immediately."

"What was it about?"

Pete shook his head. "She didn't know. But I have a feeling that text will fill in a lot of the blanks."

Blanks. Zoe started ticking them off. "Where she went. Who she met. What happened to make her get drunk."

"Yeah."

But something about Pete's tone sounded off. "What am I missing?" Zoe asked.

He brought his eyes back to meet hers. "You said she wouldn't take an aspirin."

"Right."

"Voluntarily."

The word sunk into Zoe's brain. "You mean...you think someone slipped her a mickey?"

He didn't have to say yes. She could read it in his face.

Pete lifted his chin and gazed toward the midway. Zoe assumed, like her, he was picturing an endless array of shadowy scenarios involving the time between Vera's stops at the Roadhouse. The autopsy had revealed no evidence of sexual assault, so at least that nightmare was off the table. Why else would someone have drugged her? *If* she'd been drugged. The toxicology report would answer some of their questions, but it would take weeks to get back. Someone out there knew what had happened.

Pete's voice cut through her thoughts. "What do you think about Rose and Miguel?"

Zoe blinked. "You mean their engagement?"

Pete didn't reply but looked at her quizzically.

"I..." She stretched the one word out for as long as she could, hoping a good response would present itself. Her earlier conversation on the same subject with Patsy didn't seem appropriate in this instance.

And Pete continued to wait.

"I'm happy for them, of course."

"Well, I knew that much."

Then what was he asking?

"Sylvia said the wedding's in two weeks."

"Yeah." Zoe huffed a nervous laugh. "I don't know why they're in such a rush. Unless Rose is pregnant." The words came out before the thought sunk in. Could Rose be pregnant? Again?

The possibility sucked the air out of the entire fairgrounds and sent Zoe spiraling back to Rose's first two pregnancies. She and Zoe had been promiscuous as teens. Neither of them had fathers, and a psychologist wouldn't have to search far to come up with the diagnosis that both girls had been seeking to fill the masculine voids in their lives. Rose had paid the price by having two kids while still a teen and without a husband.

Until Ted had come along.

Back then, Zoe had considered herself lucky to have dodged that particular bullet, only learning much later that luck had nothing to do with it.

ELEVEN

Sunday morning, Pete was having no luck. Nell McDonald had yet to respond to any of the three messages he'd left her. He'd finally tracked down the three other women who had dined with Vera, Olivia, and Nell, but none of them knew who had texted Vera, and she didn't tell them where she was going.

They all agreed, if Vera had told anyone, it would've been Nell.

He'd had more success with his warrant for Vera's cell phone records. A judge who owed Pete a favor had been willing to sign off on the affidavit even on a weekend. Now Pete waited for the service provider to get around to sending the requested data.

Which brought him back to his first question. Where was Nell McDonald?

Pete faced his computer and pulled up a popular social media site. He wouldn't be caught dead on one of these things, but they'd become great resources for law enforcement. Stupid criminals loved to boast about their illegal deeds, even posting photos of themselves in the midst of committing crimes.

Equally stupid honest people posted photos of their expensive toys and their vacation trips. Nell McDonald fell into the latter category. Her cover photo showed a stately buff brick house on a rambling professionally landscaped lawn. Her most recent post, dated yesterday morning, was a selfie with a statue of Franco Harris making the Immaculate Reception in the background. Pete recognized it from his last trip out of the Pittsburgh International Airport. Nell's caption read, *On my way to Maui. If you need to reach me, too bad. Going off the grid.*

That answered one question.

It only took him a few seconds to come up with his next move. He pulled out his phone and scrolled through his contacts.

Less than a minute later, a groggy voice picked up with a gruff, "What?"

Pete glanced at his watch. A few minutes after nine a.m. What time did that make it in Maui? "Hey, Chuck. Did I wake you?"

A pause. "Petey?" Chuck Delano followed with a string of ear-stinging curses. "Did you wake me? Hell yes, you woke me. It's three o'clock in the goddamn morning. What do you want?" Chuck had been Pete's partner at the Pittsburgh Bureau of Police until a gunshot wound taken in the line of duty ended Delano's career as a cop. He'd relocated to Hawaii and found a cushy career in hotel security.

"I'm looking for a woman—"

"You mean that girl of yours finally dumped you? Good for her."

Pete took a long breath and started again. "I'm looking for a woman who may have information on an investigation I'm working. She's vacationing in Maui and has apparently decided to go unplugged. I need you to track her down and have her call me."

The silence on the end of the line lasted so long Pete thought they'd been disconnected, but then Chuck blew a noisy growl across the Pacific Ocean and into Pete's ear. "You know, if you hadn't saved my life, I'd tell you what you could go do to yourself."

"Yeah, I know. And I appreciate your help with this."

There was the sound of shuffling in the background. Pete pictured his old buddy sitting up in bed and fumbling for a pen and paper. "Give me a name and anything else you got."

"Nell McDonald." Pete spelled her last name and passed along the home address he'd been able to track down.

"Any idea where she's staying?"

"Sorry. But from the looks of her social media page, she's not going to be slumming it."

Chuck snorted a short laugh. "This is Maui. No one who comes here is slumming it. I'll check my contacts. *At a decent hour.*"

Pete thanked him and was about to hang up.

"Hey, Petey."

"Yeah?"

"When are you and that girl of yours gonna move out here? I can still find you a job."

"Goodbye, Chuck." Pete ended the call with his former partner's words echoing in his head.

He slid open his desk drawer. There sat the burgundy box. Maui would be a great place for a honeymoon. But the look on Zoe's face yesterday when he'd mentioned Rose and Miguel's upcoming nuptials hadn't been encouraging.

Pete wasn't sure what he'd expected from Zoe. He knew she was skittish where marriage was concerned. He'd asked her to marry him once before, months ago, and she'd put him off without actually saying no. It had been a spur of the moment proposal. Sincere. But impulsive. This time, he wanted to get it right. He wanted to hear a definitive and enthusiastic *yes* from the woman he loved.

But yesterday afternoon, the mention of Rose's engagement had evoked an unexpected reaction. Zoe's discomfort had been palpable. He should have dropped the subject. Instead, he'd let it sit there between them. And then Zoe's comment about the betrothed couple rushing into things had triggered something—Pete wished he knew what—that turned her face the same sickly pallor as autopsies used to. For a long moment, he'd thought she was going to burst into tears. A young family had shown up then, interested in the ambulance, and Zoe shifted into tour-guide mode.

"Hey, Chief." Officer Nate Williamson stood in the office doorway, taking up much of the space.

Pete had been so focused on the burgundy box and his thoughts of Zoe, he'd missed the jingling bells on the front entrance signaling the new arrival. "Nate." Pete closed the drawer and hoped his officer hadn't seen its contents. "Come in."

Nate approached the desk and lowered his muscular frame into the chair across from Pete.

"What have you got?" Pete asked.

"Not much." The officer leaned back, crossing an ankle over his knee. "A woman out on Conklin Lane reported her horse had been stolen, but while I was taking her statement, a neighbor came walking down the road leading said horse, which had apparently decided the grass was greener somewhere else."

Pete eyed the wannabe comedian.

"Sorry. It's been a long shift. I responded to a drunk and

disorderly at Rodeo's Bar. Called the guy's wife to come and escort him home." Nate went on to list a half dozen more minor incidents that had occurred in the township overnight.

"Anything new on Vera Palmer or her missing phone?"

"Nothing. I did like you asked and went back out to the Roadhouse. Searched both sides of the road, through the weeds, even across the intersection. No phone. I talked to the people who live in the houses across the intersection, but they said cars come and go all the time, and they don't pay any attention. I also questioned the entire Saturday night staff. A couple of the waitresses had been on duty Thursday evening, but no one knew anything about our victim. No one noticed her leave the parking lot, so..."

Nate's words trailed off. Pete filled in the blank. "So no one saw which direction she went."

"Right."

"She damned well didn't vanish into thin air. And aliens didn't snatch her."

Nate stared at him.

Pete climbed to his feet and moved around his desk to the faded county map tacked to one wall. With the advent of GPS and phone apps, he and his officers rarely resorted to the paper dinosaurs anymore. He located the intersection on which Parson's Roadhouse sat and placed a finger there. "Vera Palmer left at nine. Returned around ten. One hour. How far could she have gone in one hour?"

Nate rose and stepped to Pete's side. "Half hour out, half hour back. If she stayed on the local roads, even speeding, she couldn't go over fifty-five miles an hour. So, twenty-seven, maybe twenty-eight miles?"

"And she didn't go straight there and straight back. She stayed where she went long enough to get drunk or drugged."

"Or both."

"Unless one of her friends at Parson's had slipped something into her drink there."

Nate looked at him. "You think that's possible?"

"Anything's possible until we definitively rule it out. But no, I don't think it's probable."

Nate faced the map again. "What do you think then? Twenty-mile radius?"

"Maybe. No more than twenty-five." Pete consulted the mileage scale in the corner of the map and created makeshift radius around the Roadhouse. The amount of area encompassed in the circle made him swear.

"Not a lot of help," Nate muttered.

The officer had a knack for understatement. Two townships in addition to Vance. Almost a dozen small villages plus the borough of Phillipsburg. "Even if we tighten the circle by five or even ten miles, there's too much territory."

"And too many bars."

"Not to mention the private residences she could have visited." Pete let his hand drop to his side. "Okay, I'm outta here."

"What do you want me to do about the missing phone?"

"I doubt it's going to turn up now. We'll have to wait until her service provider responds to our warrant."

Nate scowled. "Why'd we need a warrant? She's deceased. A dead woman has no privacy to protect."

"That's true. But the phone captures conversations and photos involving other living individuals who would have an expectation of privacy. I want our asses covered in case this turns into more than an accidental death."

"Good point." Nate followed Pete into the hallway. "Are you going to be at the fair?"

Pete grunted. "That's the plan."

But he took a detour.

He didn't expect to hear from Maui anytime soon, but there was still one person who might have some idea of where she went on Thursday night.

With the draft horse classes well underway in the covered arena directly below the Pony Barn, Patsy suggested she and Zoe take Jazzel and Windstar down to the outdoor show ring at the grandstand. "Hitch classes don't start there until noon," Patsy said, studying the fair schedule of events. "We can get the horses out of their stalls and ride for at least an hour before we get kicked out." She cast a cautious glance in the direction of the indoor show arena. "And Cody DeRosa will be tied up with his judging duties."

Zoe snickered as she grabbed her saddle. "What's the matter? Cody's a good-looking guy. I thought you were enjoying his attention."

"Well, yeah." Patsy's scowl was a little too forced. "Shane can't stand it. If Cody doesn't back off, I'm afraid Shane might pop him before the week's over."

"Shane's not around today. What he wouldn't know, wouldn't hurt anyone." Zoe meant it to sound like a joke, even though she thought Cody might very well be an improvement over Patsy's current boyfriend.

Patsy rolled her eyes and hefted her own saddle off its stand. "Shane would know. I don't understand how, but he always seems to know when another man is paying attention to me."

Another reason for Zoe to dislike him.

"Besides, Cody's just a flirt." Patsy lugged her saddle into Jazzel's stall. "He doesn't mean anything by it."

Zoe wasn't so sure. He may not have serious aspirations toward any of the women he ogled, but if Patsy—or Zoe or any of the others for that matter—seemed willing, he wouldn't object to slipping off for a literal roll in the hay.

Twenty minutes later, they'd led the horses through the sparse Sunday morning crowds to the dirt racetrack below the grandstand. They weren't alone in their plan to take advantage of the currently event-free venue. Three standardbreds jogged around the track with their sulkies and drivers. About a dozen riders claimed the show ring situated in the infield and a few more shared the track with the racehorses.

Zoe looped the lead rope around her saddle horn, gathered the reins, and swung onto Windstar's back. Patsy mounted beside her. "Racetrack or show ring?"

Having been stalled for longer than they were accustomed, both horses fidgeted as one of the sulkies passed by.

Patsy snugged up on her reins. "As much fun as a good gallop would be, I'm afraid Jazz might buck me off."

Zoe had to agree. "The show ring it is then."

They waited for the track to clear before crossing to the infield and the ring.

After about ten minutes of snorting and prancing, Windstar settled down to an easy jog. Zoe searched the riders for Patsy and spotted her still battling with the Arabian mare who clearly disagreed with the decision to skip the full-speed gallop around the track.

Zoe hadn't noticed a rider moving alongside her. "Nice horse," he said.

She turned her head. "Cody? I thought you were judging the show."

"Nope. Only the light horses and ponies. And the 4-H show, of course." He rode a gorgeous palomino, silver covering his saddle and bridle. "I don't know enough about the heavy breeds to qualify as a judge."

Zoe caught herself admiring the ease with which he sat the horse, hips rocking side to side in unison with the animal's smooth gait. Cody DeRosa truly appeared to have been born in the saddle.

"You like?" he asked.

She met his eyes, realizing he'd been watching her watch him and was enjoying her attention.

"He's a nice-looking horse," she said, meaning it and hoping Cody believed the palomino was all she'd been admiring.

He smirked. "Yes, he is. And so is yours."

The fact that his gaze never slipped lower than Zoe's chest wasn't lost on her.

"Seriously. He is," Cody said, sounding almost apologetic. "Have you had him long?"

"All his life. I bought his dam when she was in foal."

"Do you still have her?"

"No." Zoe wasn't about to go into that sad story. "Just him."

This time, Cody really did give Windstar a closer look before meeting Zoe's eyes. "What are you doing later?" He seemed earnest, not flirtatious.

"I'm on duty."

He gave her a questioning look.

"With the ambulance." She gestured up the hill. "I'm on standby beginning at three."

"Oh." He sounded disappointed. "Not every day, though, I hope."

"Almost. I'm off tomorrow because of the horseshow, but I'm on call every other day this week."

Cody nodded thoughtfully. "Good. Tomorrow then. After the show. I'm buying you dinner."

He flashed his dimpled smile and brought his heels in on his horse's sides, loping off before she could argue.

She reined up, watching him ride away.

"What's he doing here?" Patsy asked, drawing alongside her.

Zoe opened her mouth to say, "asking me out," but instead she said, "Exercising his horse. Same as us."

Patsy choked a sarcastic laugh. "Right. Come on. Let's make a lap or two around the racetrack to take the edge off." She spun Jazzel and cantered toward the gate.

Zoe kept her gaze on Cody a moment longer, wondering what he was up to. In spite of the smile he'd given her, she suspected he had something other than seduction on his mind.

"Zoe," Patsy yelled. "Come on."

Zoe watched him ride up alongside a pair of 4-Hers and start to chat. She wheeled Windstar and booted him into an easy lope. "Right behind you."

TWELVE

The address Pete had for Jack and Vera Palmer in the small town of Hancock led him to a gray single-story house that looked to be an updated vintage 1950s style. A white wraparound porch decorated with wilted hanging baskets must've been part of the update. The brown lawn with patches of green weeds was indicative of the lack of rain this summer. Similar-looking homes flanked the narrow lot. From the driveway, Pete spotted a small barnlike structure behind the house.

He climbed out of his vehicle and followed the sidewalk to the front door. Pressing the doorbell produced a muffled tone from inside, but nothing else. He knocked. Still nothing.

He headed back to the driveway but instead of returning to his car, he strolled toward the makeshift barn. It appeared to be a do-it-yourself project. The horizontally divided half doors stood open, and a well-fed copper-colored horse dozed in the shade of an old oak, swishing its tail against buzzing flies.

"No one's home," a voice called from the next yard.

Pete turned to find a balding man, mid-sixties, observing him.

"If you're planning to take advantage and rob the place, you should know we have a pretty active neighborhood watch."

Pete realized he wasn't in uniform. He did, however, have his badge and ID in his pocket. He pulled it out as he approached. "Pete Adams. Chief of Police, Vance Township."

The man gave him an embarrassed grin. "Sorry." He held out a hand. "Miles Koskey."

Pete grasped it. "No need to apologize. Neighbors watching out for each other makes my job easier."

Koskey nodded. "Well, you know, thieves troll the newspapers and prey on families who've lost loved ones." He crossed his arms.

"Vance Township? You're out of your jurisdiction. This is Crossroads Township."

"I'm aware of that. Mrs. Palmer's body was found in Vance." Pete didn't mention he'd been the one to find her.

"Ah. Yes, I suppose that's right. You here to talk to Jack?"

"I am. You say he's not home?"

"Afraid not. He and his wife always visit little Cassidy on Sunday mornings. Now it's only him."

Pete removed his ball cap and wiped the sweat beading on his forehead with a bandana. Maybe he'd found someone who could provide some answers. "Sounds like you know them well."

Koskey shrugged. "Not especially. They've only lived here a couple of years, and all of us in this neighborhood try to mind our own business." He paused. "Unless we think someone's looking to break in."

"But you're aware of their comings and goings. Enough to know Jack's visiting his daughter."

Koskey thought about it. "I suppose so."

"Do you have any idea where Vera Palmer had planned to go on Thursday evening?"

"Nope. I saw her car pulling out. But where she was going? Not a clue."

"Do you think any of your other neighbors might know?"

"Possibly. But like I said, we all try to mind our own business."

What Pete needed was one busybody. He pocketed his bandana and settled his hat on his head. Something Earl's wife had told him came to mind. "Tell me, Mr. Koskey, do you know what rehab facility the Palmers' daughter is in?"

"Sorry. Just that it's supposed to be a good one in Pittsburgh."

Pete thanked him for his time. As Koskey walked back to his own house, Pete headed toward one on the opposite side of the Palmers' home. If he learned nothing else today, at least he could eliminate the possibility that Vera had gone to see her daughter between stops at the Roadhouse. Pittsburgh was thirty miles east, well out of the twenty-mile radius.

A massive tent with a small stage had been set up about a hundred yards below the spot where the EMS truck was parked. A flamboyant dark-haired young man dressed in black satin, despite the heat, performed magic tricks. Zoe and Earl currently boasted a bigger crowd thanks to a screaming six-year-old boy.

"They should post signs." The boy's mother hovered over the child as Zoe examined his arm. "They should warn people that these animals are dangerous."

Zoe raised her gaze to Earl and could tell he was struggling to maintain a passive face.

The boy's parents had already told their story. Little Johnny had been running ahead of them through the beef barn. He'd been excited about seeing all the animals. Other kids were playing in the barn too, so it must be safe. Suddenly, one of those vicious cows kicked him.

The owner of the offending steer, a fifteen-year-old girl, stood nearby, her hand pressed to her mouth with tears brimming. The girl's father, a lifelong farmer, draped a protective arm around her shoulders.

"There are signs," the farmer said, pointing at a large notice tacked to the side of the nearby goat shed. Similar posted statements, assigning the liability of risk of injury to anyone who entered, were plastered at every entrance to every barn on the grounds. "And those other kids you mentioned are the cattlemen's children who know better than to run over and pull on a steer's tail."

Little Johnny's mother, who wore white shorts and high-heeled sandals, abandoned her post next to the boy and stormed toward the farmer. She showed no fear of creating a scene in front of a crowd of onlookers. If anything, she seemed to feed off the attention.

The wailing child's arm didn't appear broken. He wiggled his fingers and had a firm grip on Zoe's left hand. A red welt promised to bloom into a lovely bruise, though. Zoe thumbed tears from his soft cheeks and assured him everything would be okay.

Earl pounded on a single-use ice pack to break the plastic core, then shook it to mix the chemicals. He handed it to Zoe as the boy's mother chided the farmer for bringing dangerous animals to a public venue. "I'm going to call security," Earl whispered.

Zoe looked up at her partner, but her gaze was drawn beyond him. "Don't bother. The cavalry has arrived."

Even out of uniform, Pete exuded a sense of authority that parted the crowd, allowing him through. "What seems to be the problem here?" He held up his badge, which drew the woman in white away from the farmer.

The boy's mother started her tirade all over for Pete's benefit. The child's wailing, after an initial chirp when Zoe applied the ice pack, dwindled to a few sniffles. Zoe smiled at him, and he gave her a damp smile back.

"How's that feel?" she asked.

"Cold."

She heard Earl chuckle behind her.

Ten minutes later, after hearing from both sides, including a tidbit from the farmer about how the mother had been glued to her cell phone instead of keeping an eye on her child, Pete managed to mediate a truce. When the woman noticed Little Johnny not only wasn't crying anymore but seemed fascinated by the stethoscope Zoe had plugged into his ears, she decided to drop the threats to sue the farmer, the fair board, and the entire county. In exchange, the farmer agreed to hang signs by his fair entries about the risk of animals kicking. The woman in white and her son and husband walked away, hand in hand, with a promise to make an appointment with the boy's pediatrician first thing tomorrow morning.

As the crowd dispersed, some to take in the rest of the magic show, Zoe turned her full attention to Pete. "Thanks. Your timing was perfect."

"Just doing my job, ma'am," he said with that sexy lopsided grin of his.

"I'd about given up on seeing you today. You didn't stick around very long yesterday."

The grin faded. "You were busy." He tipped his head in the direction Little Johnny and his parents had gone. "Looks like you're still busy."

"Oh, no," she said, drawing out the words and rolling her eyes. "Jumpy animals, clueless city people who don't know how to act around livestock, kids climbing on the tractors and equipment on display? What could possibly go wrong?"

As if answering Zoe's rhetorical question, Merryn barreled up the hill in full steamroller mode, heading directly toward them. "Zoe," she huffed, "where's Luke?"

"I have no idea. I've been on duty."

The answer didn't appease her. "You're supposed to be helping me keep an eye on him."

Diane had asked her to watch out for the boy, but Zoe didn't realize Merryn was aware of the assignment. Nor did Zoe realize they expected her to be a twenty-four-seven babysitter.

Earl came around the ambulance. "I saw him with my boys down on the midway not too long ago."

Merryn's face flushed to deep crimson. "What? I told him to stay away from—" She must have heard her words growing louder or noticed passersby staring and bit off her rant. "Luke is not to go anywhere near the midway." To Earl, she said, "And if your sons are hanging around there, I don't want Luke near them either."

Earl's expression darkened. "My kids know to stay out of trouble."

"Not if they're hanging out with that bunch of thieves, they don't." Merryn jabbed Zoe's shoulder—hard—with one finger. "You need to keep a closer eye on him. I know Diane asked you to since Vera died."

Pete had been standing by, arms crossed, a silent observer, until the mention of the dead woman. "You knew Vera?" he asked.

Merryn spun and appeared ready to spew an angry response, but one look at him silenced her. She shifted from tornado to sunshine in a heartbeat, even going so far as reaching up to primp her disheveled platinum hair. "Yes, I knew her. She was a good friend of mine. Poor dear. And who are you?"

Zoe thought about how Merryn had batted her eyelashes at Jack on Friday, before they'd known his wife was dead. Some friend.

Pete extended a hand, which Merryn quickly grasped. "Vance Township Chief of Police Pete Adams."

She snatched her hand back as if he'd electrocuted her. "Police?"

"I'm investigating Vera Palmer's death. If you knew her well, I'd like to ask you a few questions."

"Actually, I didn't know her *that* well. And I certainly don't know anything about her death. I have my own problems." Merryn turned her laser glare on Zoe again. "You find my son and tell him to get his ass back to the barn. His horse's stall is filthy." With that, she wheeled and stormed away.

"Wow," Pete said after a pause.

Zoe watched Merryn march down the hill. "You have no idea."

"What's her story?"

The last person Zoe wanted to discuss was Merryn Schultz. "Cliffs Notes version, she and I were in 4-H together. She's always been rough around the edges—"

Earl snorted.

Zoe shot him a dirty look. "She's been married two or three times and has frequent flyer miles in jail and rehab."

Zoe noticed Merryn stop and turn. Even with the distance, Zoe could see her posture turn coquettish before sauntering over to Cody DeRosa.

"Drugs?" Pete asked.

Zoe blinked, bringing her attention back to their conversation. "Plus who knows what else. I haven't seen her in years."

"And Luke? Is that the kid I met yesterday?"

"Yeah." Her gaze drifted back to Merryn, who clung to Cody's arm and whispered into his ear. "Her son from her first husband. He's been in and out of juvie, but I get the feeling Diane still has hope for him."

"I guess so. She trusted him with her car."

As Zoe watched, Cody ducked out of Merryn's grip and held up a palm to her, signaling *stop*.

"It's not much of a car." Zoe turned back to Pete. "Diane's the one who asked me to help keep tabs on him."

"I was going to ask why this Merryn woman couldn't watch out for her own son, but I've kinda figured it out." Pete's gaze drifted toward the 4-H Barn. Zoe knew what he was thinking. He wanted to talk to Diane Garland.

Before Zoe had a chance to say anything more, Earl swore. She followed his gaze and spotted Cody, who'd brushed off Merryn and was striding toward them, dimples and all.

"Medic, Medic," he said in mock agony. "I have a boo-boo. Can the pretty ambulance lady kiss it and make it all better?"

So there was one person she wanted to discuss less than Merryn.

Ignoring Pete and Earl, the cowboy zeroed in on Zoe with a flirtatious intensity that made her take a step back. "Sorry," she said. "I don't have a license to dispense medical kisses. I can give you a Band-Aid though."

He chuckled. "I was only kidding about being hurt. Not about the kiss, though."

Her face and neck warmed. She risked a glance at Pete, who looked about as unhappy as she'd expected. "Cody DeRosa, this is my...boyfriend." She hated that word. *Boyfriend* didn't seem appropriate for a man well into his forties. "Pete Adams. He's Vance Township's Chief of Police."

"Police? Oh, no," Cody said with the same mocking tone he'd used about his *boo-boo*. "Are you here to arrest me?"

"Maybe." There was no humor in Pete's tone, only a low, menacing promise.

His tone wasn't lost on Cody, whose smile vanished. "Are you here in an official capacity? Or simply enjoying the county fair?"

Pete's gaze fixed on Zoe. "I'm here visiting my girl."

Her cheeks warmed again, pleasantly this time.

He turned back to Cody. "I'm also investigating Vera Palmer's death."

"Oh." Cody struck a casual pose with one hip cocked and his hands shoved into his jeans pockets. "Terrible thing. But I thought it was an accident."

"It may have been." Pete crossed his arms. "Did you know Vera?"

"Not really. Only what Diane has told me about her. You know how it is sometimes. You hear so much about someone, you feel like you know them when you've never met." Cody glanced at his watch. "Oh, dear. I'm late for a meeting." He placed a hand lightly on the back of Zoe's neck. "I'm looking forward to our dinner tomorrow."

He leaned in close enough that she smelled his leathery aftershave mingled with a hint of horse sweat—a combination she imagined was nearly irresistible to most horsewomen. At another time in her life, the seductive touch and the earthy scent might have made her swoon too. But at the moment, all she could feel was Pete's gaze on her.

Cody trailed his fingers down her back as he moved away. "Nice meeting you, Chief." He swaggered off into the crowd.

Zoe knew her face was glowing red as she raised her eyes to Pete and Earl. Her partner's lethal gaze followed the retreating cowboy.

Pete's was locked on her.

"Who," he asked, "was that?"

Earl responded before she had a chance to. "God's gift to women. At least *he* thinks so."

But Pete, wearing his best poker face, continued to watch Zoe.

She cleared her throat. "Another fellow 4-Her. He's the horseshow judge this year."

The stony expression shifted slightly. "Old friends, huh?"

"No," she stuttered. "And I'm not having dinner with him either."

Pete didn't look relieved.

Earl nudged him. "He pulled the whole touchy-feely routine on Olivia too. If you wanna slug him, I'll hold him down for you."

A hint of a cockeyed grin crossed Pete's lips, and he huffed a short laugh. "I may take you up on the offer. Later."

Freed from the grip of those icy blue eyes, Zoe exhaled and watched him scan the fairgrounds.

"I'm going to take a walk through the midway and see if I can find that boy," he said.

She'd almost forgotten about Merryn's tirade. "Luke?"

"Yeah."

"He's probably hanging out with my kids," Earl said. "Make sure they're staying out of trouble too, while you're at it."

"Will do." He met Zoe's eyes briefly before walking away.

Unlike Cody, Pete didn't touch her. And the absence of that simple gesture left her feeling sucker punched.

THIRTEEN

Heat waves shimmered over the pavement as Pete trudged down the hill to the rows of carnival games surrounded by rides. He'd come to the fair to spend time with Zoe. Instead, here he was, searching for a wayward teen, while Zoe was making dinner dates with what Pete could only imagine was an old flame. A horseman no less. The guy probably owned a farm somewhere, the kind of place Zoe dreamed of. The kind of place she'd feel perfectly at home in.

The kind of place she deserved.

But Cody DeRosa? According to Earl, the guy hit on every female he encountered. *God's gift to women*, Earl had said. Well, not Pete's woman. No damned way.

As he entered the row of game and food trailers, the crowds thickened and grew younger, consisting mostly of twentysomething boys and couples mingled with teens and pre-teens. Pete had seen this Luke kid once. Would he be able to spot the boy among the hordes?

It didn't take long to find out. Pete located Earl's sons shoulder to shoulder at one of the booths. Luke stood next to them. All three kids were laughing along with the man running the game. Hardly the picture of delinquent youths.

Pete walked up behind the trio, placing a hand on each of the Kolter boys' shoulders.

They turned toward him. "Chief Adams," the older one said with a note of surprise.

Pete kept his smile relaxed. "Boys."

Luke pivoted toward him too, his expression wary.

Earl's older son gave Pete a put-upon teenager glower. "Did our dad ask you to check up on us?"

"He wanted me to make sure you weren't getting into trouble. And from what I see, you aren't."

The guy manning the booth leaned against the counter. "You can tell their father he's got a pair of well-behaved boys here. He should be proud."

Pete noticed the third kid slowly edging away and reached over to clamp a firm but gentle hand on his arm. "Your name's Luke, right?"

"Yeah." His response sounded more like a question than an answer. "You a cop?"

"Afraid so." Pete maintained the light grip on Luke's arm. He had a feeling the kid would try to bolt if given half a chance. "Your mother wants you back at the barn. Something about a dirty stall."

"My mother sent the cops after me? Seriously?"

"Actually, she sent Zoe, but she's busy right now, so you got me instead."

Luke let out a growling sigh of disgust. "I'm not doin' anything wrong. You can't arrest me."

The man at the counter straightened. "Luke," he said, an authoritative tone to his voice. "You best go tend to your chores."

The teen looked at the guy, pleading.

But the man shook his head and pointed in the direction of the barns. "You know the rules. Go."

Luke's shoulders sagged. He glanced at the Kolter boys, said, "I'll see you later," and turned away.

Pete released him but fell into step alongside.

Luke sneered. "You don't have to march me back to my mommy."

"I'm not. I'm headed that way myself."

"Why?"

"I want to talk to Diane Garland."

"Oh."

Luke seemed to relax, apparently convinced Pete wasn't there to haul him off to juvie. Taking advantage of the lowered barriers, Pete said, "I gather Vera Palmer was supposed to keep tabs on you this week."

"I guess." The kid shoved his hands into his pockets and kept his head lowered, watching the ground in front of him.

Pete weighed his next question, not wanting to bring the barriers back up. "Did you like Mrs. Palmer?"

Luke gave a bored, one-shouldered shrug in response.

"I bet it's a drag, having an adult assigned as a babysitter."

That got a reaction. "Nobody babysits me. I do whatever I want."

"Your mother doesn't seem to agree."

"My mother's a—" He stopped walking and pressed his mouth closed. Facing Pete, he said, "If anyone needs a babysitter, it's her. I can't wait to get away from her, and she knows it."

Pete sensed the boy wanted to say more, but he turned and continued toward the barn, his pace faster. Pete had to lengthen his stride to keep up. "I could use your help."

Luke shot him a skeptical glance. "*My* help?"

"I'm trying to find out what happened to Mrs. Palmer."

"How should I know?"

Pete raised a hand, gesturing him to calm down. "I thought you might be able to tell me who around here knew her well."

"Diane and her were tight. And she got along with the other parents."

"Anyone in particular?"

"I dunno."

"Did she get along with your mom?"

Luke snorted. "Right." His voice dripped with sarcasm. "My mom doesn't get along with anyone. Except men." He reconsidered his comment. "And then she only gets along with them until they get to know her. Or make the mistake of marryin' her."

They climbed the last stretch to a green structure baring a sign that read 4-H Horse Barn. As the road leveled out near the entrance, Luke stopped and faced Pete. "Look. Mrs. Palmer was all right. But I don't know who she hung out with. Other than Diane. And Mr. Palmer."

Pete squinted into the barn. "Except Mr. Palmer isn't here right now."

Luke made that typical teen face that said grownups were clueless. "Yeah, he is. I saw him down by one of the food booths a little while ago."

Zoe spotted him wandering up the hill from the direction of the big exhibit hall. Even though his shirt was now pale blue and crisp, he somehow seemed more rumpled than he had two days ago. "Jack?" He looked around, searching.

Zoe waved to catch his attention, but he still looked puzzled. She walked over to him. "You probably don't remember me, but—"

Recognition sparked in his eyes. "You helped the girl with the runaway pony the other day."

She extended a hand, which he grasped, and introduced herself. "I was there when the cops talked to you too."

"Right." His voice grew faint. "Right."

"I'm surprised to see you back here."

His eyes turned downcast. "I didn't have anywhere else to go. It's too quiet at home. I spent all morning with my daughter." He paused, on the verge of saying more but reconsidering. "I made arrangements to hold a memorial service next week so Vera's friends from here could attend."

"That's sweet." Zoe glanced around, hoping to spot Pete. He'd been wanting to speak with Jack, and now would be the perfect opportunity. Except Pete was off in search of Luke. Under different circumstances, she'd have eagerly seized the chance to question a witness, but Jack Palmer wasn't a witness. He was a grieving husband with a daughter to care for. Every one of the questions forming in Zoe's mind felt harsh and unfeeling. She knew the pain of loss. But maybe that made her the perfect person to do the asking. "How are you holding up?"

He laughed, a short, choked, damp laugh that carried no humor. "I'm not."

Zoe nodded sympathetically. "I know. I lost my dad when I was eight, but I still feel the loss." She thought of a more recent loss only four months ago. Equally painful, but with a mountain of guilt heaped on top. "I've...lost others I've loved deeply too."

Jack gave her a doubtful look.

"I mean...if you wanted to talk...about Vera...you could talk to me. I kinda know what you're going through."

"Really?" He blinked, and his flooded eyes overflowed. Embarrassed, he wiped a hand across his face. "You know what it's like to lose the person you love more than life?"

An image of Pete bleeding from a gunshot wound flashed across

Zoe's mind. That night, she'd almost lost him. But not quite.

Jack must have read her answer in her face. "No. And have you ever had a child...a beautiful energetic daughter who could no longer walk? Could no longer do anything that didn't involve wheelchairs and being carried?" He grew more devastated with each sentence. "No. So you've never had to tell your daughter that her mom wouldn't be coming to visit her anymore." His voice cracked, and he no longer tried to wipe away the torrent of tears.

Her own eyes filled. Jack was right. "I'm sorry," she whispered.

They stood in silence, surrounded by fair goers passing by. Zoe sensed their eyes on the pair, but she kept her gaze on Jack. After a few long moments, he drew a raspy inhalation and looked down. "No," he said softly. "I'm the one who's sorry. I didn't mean to go off on you like that." He smudged his face with a hand. "I know you were only being kind."

She looked at the ground, unable to force words from her throat. So much for being the perfect person to question him. Instead, she'd been the least perfect person on the face of the earth.

Jack touched her arm, and she lifted her gaze to him. He smiled weakly. "As a matter of fact, I could use someone to talk to."

After asking around the 4-H Barn, a pair of teen girls told Pete that Diane was in the tack room and pointed the way.

The door to the room stood open. Pete found the woman with her back to him, bent over a card table, riffling through a stack of papers.

He cleared his throat. "Excuse me."

She straightened and wheeled, her face flushed. "Oh." She pressed a hand to her chest. "You scared the poop outta me."

"Sorry."

She waved off his apology. "It's okay. I didn't hear you coming. You're Zoe's gentleman friend. Pete Adams, right?"

"Yes, ma'am."

"What can I do for you?"

"I hoped we could talk for a few minutes." When Diane looked puzzled, he added, "About Vera Palmer."

"Oh." Diane shot a glance over her shoulder at the papers on the table behind her. "Sure." Facing Pete, she smiled and gestured toward the aisleway outside the tack room. "Let's have a seat."

He stepped back to allow her to pass before he followed her to some battered lawn chairs parked outside one of the stalls. "I see you're walking better."

"Yes, I am." She sat and gestured to the chair next to her. "Thank goodness for modern medicine."

Pete eyed the flimsy aluminum frame and shredded webbing and pictured himself sprawled on the aisleway's dirt floor. Not very dignified for a law enforcement officer. Especially one who was still healing from a shattered femur. He decided to stand. "I understand you and Vera Palmer were close."

Diane nodded thoughtfully. "She was a wonderful woman. A good mother. Always willing to lend a hand."

He glanced down the aisle where Luke shoveled dirty bedding into a wheelbarrow. "Like keeping tabs on a troubled teen?"

"Exactly. And anything else I asked of her. I wish I had a dozen more 4-H parents like that."

"When was the last time you saw her?"

Diane brought a hand to her face, tapping her lips with one finger. "Let me think. Last weekend. Saturday. We had a practice session for the kids who'd never shown at the fair before. Vera and Jack came to help."

"Was she acting unusual?"

"How do you mean?"

Pete shrugged. "Nervous. Upset. Worried. Anything out of the ordinary."

Diane considered the question. "Not that I noticed." She met Pete's gaze. "Why do you ask? Her death was an accident. Wasn't it?"

He gave her a relaxed smile. "Probably. I'm just trying to fill in some blanks."

Diane didn't match his smile. "Oh."

"Vera was having dinner with friends at Parson's Roadhouse the night she died, but she left at one point. When she returned, she appeared to be under the influence. I'm trying to find out where she was during that hour."

Diane stared at him. "I have no idea. She and I were friends because of 4-H, but I didn't socialize with her beyond that." Shifting in her chair, she said, "I gotta tell you, I find it difficult to believe that she got drunk. That wasn't...*her.*"

"Maybe she wasn't drunk. And maybe she didn't get that way on her own."

Diane scowled. "I don't understand."

"Maybe someone slipped her something."

Diane's lips moved, silently repeating his last three words. After several moments, she asked, "Who would do that?"

"I was hoping you might be able to tell me."

"I'm sorry. I don't—I can't imagine."

"Was there anyone who disliked Vera? Or anyone Vera disliked?"

"No." Diane gazed past Pete for a moment before coming back to him. "Honestly, I can't think of a soul."

"Is there anyone you can think of who might know something?"

She shook her head.

"Anyone in 4-H Vera was especially friendly with?"

Diane continued to shake her head. "No. I mean, she was friendly with everyone, but I never noticed her getting buddy-buddy with any of them."

Pete again looked at Luke who wheeled his load of manure toward the door. "What about Luke's mother?"

Diane choked. "Merryn? No. Merryn doesn't hang out with other women."

Pete remembered what Luke had said. "What about Vera's husband? Did Merryn hang out with him?"

The implication widened Diane's eyes. "No way. Jack loves his wife. *Loved* his wife. He never gave Merryn the time of day."

Pete pictured the woman he'd met only a half hour ago. Claiming she was good friends with Vera. Playing the seductress with Pete.

Until learning he was a cop.

Luke had said his mother only liked men. Perhaps she'd liked Jack even if he didn't reciprocate.

Pete dug a business card from his pocket. "Thank you for your time. If you think of anything or hear of anything that might be of help, please call me."

The woman pushed up from the chair, winced, and took the card.

"I will."

Pete noticed her look past him—toward the tack room—yet again. "I'm sorry I interrupted you."

She waved a dismissive hand. "Not a problem. The paperwork's never completely done."

"Amen to that." He touched the brim of his ball cap. "I'll let you get back to it."

As he headed toward the stall Luke had been mucking out, Pete's phone vibrated in his pocket. He pulled it out, and the screen indicated a text from Zoe. He tapped the icon.

I'm at the 4-H Dairy Bar with Jack Palmer.

Dairy Bar? Or did she mean barn? Pete tapped out a reply. *On my way.*

Luke entered the barn from the far end with an empty wheelbarrow. The kid's expression soured when he saw Pete. "Now what d'ya want? I haven't gotten into any trouble between here and the manure pile."

"Do you know where I could find your mother?"

Luke snorted. "Seriously, man? I try hard to stay as far away from her as I can. So no. I have no idea where she is."

"You mentioned she likes men."

"Yeah. A lot."

"Anyone in particular?"

"Nope. As long as they're breathing and she hasn't already been married to 'em, she's hot for 'em."

"How about Jack Palmer?"

"What about him?"

"Was your mom hot for him?"

Luke's eyes shifted. "Maybe." He stuttered. "But no more than anyone else. And he never...I mean...he doesn't respond to her." Luke lowered his gaze. "Not like most." He kept his head down but glanced around the barn. "I gotta get back to work."

"Go right ahead. Oh, is there a 4-H dairy bar on the fairgrounds?"

Luke gave a tip of his head. "Right by the side entrance gate. You can't miss it."

On Pete's way out, a backwards look revealed Luke busy mucking the stall once again. Diane was nowhere to be seen.

FOURTEEN

Zoe took a seat at the end of one of the picnic tables set up between the rows of food booths operated by various charities and local small businesses. Jack Palmer sat across from her. They'd both ordered milkshakes—strawberry for him, chocolate for her.

"Vera never liked milkshakes." Tears gleamed along the lower edges of his eyes, revealing the sorrow lurking behind the lightness of his words. "Can you imagine? She said they were too sweet."

"I didn't think there was such a thing as too sweet."

He tried to smile but failed. "I can't believe she's gone. I keep looking around, expecting to see her, and then I remember—"

Zoe sipped on the straw, waiting for Jack to compose himself.

"I caught myself sending her a text earlier. I'm so used to always being in touch with her. It doesn't seem real that she's not...*here*...anymore."

Zoe struggled for words. Something comforting. But she'd tried that already with the reverse effect. After several long moments of silence, she decided to simply start him talking. "How long were you married?"

"We had our fifteenth anniversary this summer."

"Wow. Did you have a big party?"

Jack shook his head. "With Cassie in the shape she's in, we didn't feel much like celebrating."

"How is your daughter?"

"Not well." His lips parted as if wanting to say more, but he closed them and continued to stare at his yet untouched milkshake.

Zoe hesitated, then asked the question she really wanted the answer to. "What happened to her?"

Jack's face slowly contorted into the image of total devastation.

He buried it in his hands. He made no sound, but his shoulders jerked in sobbing convulsions.

Aware that others around them were looking, Zoe scooted around the end of the picnic table to sit next to him and draped an arm around his shoulders. "I'm sorry."

A muffled, agonized moan escaped through his hands along with a few unintelligible words. The only thing she could make out was "all my fault."

A shadow fell over them. She looked up to find Pete with concerned furrows lining his brow. She glanced toward the seat she'd vacated. He took the hint, lowering onto the picnic bench opposite her and Jack.

Minutes passed before the widower composed himself enough to lift his face.

Zoe made the introductions and hoped Pete could read her mind. Go easy on the guy.

Jack sat straighter, clearing his throat. "You're the cop who's been leaving me messages."

"I am."

Jack gave a quick nod. "I apologize for not getting back to you." He dug out his phone and placed it on the table in front of him. "You should see the number of texts and voicemails I have on this thing. I simply haven't had the energy to respond to them."

"I understand," Pete said. "Do you think you're up to talking to me now?"

No, Zoe thought.

But Jack took a deep breath and blew it out. "You're working on Vera's case?"

"Yes."

"Then absolutely. I don't believe what I've been told—that she got drunk. I want to know what really happened to my wife."

"So do I, Mr. Palmer." Pete glanced at Zoe but directed his question to Jack. "Is there somewhere around here we can speak in private?"

Zoe had given Pete the key to the camper she was calling home this week after texting Patsy to make sure she wasn't using it.

The travel trailer was small, cramped, and cluttered. A table flanked by bench seats obviously served as a bed but had been reinstated to its primary purpose. Pete shoved aside a rolled sleeping bag, squeezed in next to it, and gestured for Jack to take the other seat.

With his notebook open on the table, Pete studied the man. Pale. Gaunt. Eyes sunken and red from crying. "I'm sorry for your loss."

Jack mouthed the words "thank you."

"When was the last time you saw your wife?"

"Thursday evening before she left home to meet her friends for dinner."

"At Parson's?"

"Yes."

"Did you talk to her later that evening? On the phone or by text?"

Jack looked like an invisible thousand-pound weight settled on top of him. "No."

"Is that odd?"

"Not really. I mean, not hearing from her Thursday evening wasn't odd." He paused deep in thought. "She's been under a lot of stress lately. We both have. I wanted her to go out and have a good time with the girls. When I didn't hear from her, I assumed they'd gone to a movie afterwards."

"Did they do that a lot? Go to a movie after dinner, I mean?"

"Not a lot but sometimes. I went to bed and figured she'd be there next to me when I woke up." Jack's eyes filled. "She wasn't."

So far, Jack's story matched what Pete had read in the report from the county police. "Mr. Palmer, is there anywhere your wife might have gone by herself after leaving the Roadhouse?"

The question startled him. "By herself?"

Pete turned a page in the notebook. "According to the restaurant staff and the women who were dining with your wife, she received a text message and left early."

Jack frowned. Clearly, this was news to him.

"She returned roughly an hour later, showing signs of intoxication."

"No. That's not right. She wouldn't get drunk."

Pete gave Jack a moment before adding, "Perhaps someone

slipped her something."

Jack met Pete's gaze, his eyes wide. "Someone drugged Vera?"

"It's a theory."

The widower covered his mouth with one hand. His stunned eyes lowered, and Pete could only imagine what he was picturing. A minute passed, and then another. Finally, Jack looked at Pete. "Why would anyone do such a thing?"

"I was hoping you could tell me."

"I don't...I can't..."

This wasn't getting anywhere. Pete glanced around the camper, his gaze settling on the refrigerator. In the tight quarters, he only had to reach over to open it. A small carton of milk, bottles of water, cans of assorted soda pop, and a six-pack of Budweiser. Pete pointed at the selection. "Can I get you a beer?" He wasn't sure if it was Zoe's or Patsy's, but he figured he'd replace whatever he took.

Jack stared blankly at the fridge. "Water would be good."

Pete pulled out two and passed one across the table. Once Jack had taken a long draw on the bottle, Pete said, "Tell me about your wife."

"What about her?"

"Just...tell me about her."

Jack looked at him, puzzled.

"Learning about her might give me some insight into what happened that night."

Jack didn't seem convinced, but he set the water bottle down and wiped his mouth with the back of his hand. Leaning back, his gaze drifted somewhere far from the inside of the small camper. A hint of a smile played across his lips. "She was the most beautiful woman on the face of the planet. I never did figure out what she saw in me, but I wanted to become the man I saw reflected in her eyes. Sometimes I think she saved my life." He fell silent. Pete thought he was going to have to prompt him, but Jack heaved a sigh and continued. "Then she gave me a daughter as beautiful and smart as Vera was. I wanted to give Cassie the moon and the stars."

As much as Pete longed to ask what had happened to the girl, he had a feeling Jack still wasn't ready to go there. Though Pete already knew the answer, he asked, "What did your wife do for a living?"

The diversion worked. Jack sniffed. "She was an accountant. She used to work in a bank. That's where I met her." The memory brought a faraway smile. "It was love at first sight. For me anyway. I had to work at it to get her to go out with me on that first date. I think I asked four or five times before she said yes. By then, I was shocked. I'd pretty much given up. But I kept on asking."

Jack fell silent. Pete let him enjoy his memories of happier days. Would he have to ask Zoe that many times to get her to accept his proposal?

"By our third date, we were inseparable. She quit the bank when we got married. She was old-fashioned that way. Wanted to take care of me and our home. And later, Cassie."

Jack again grew quiet, his expression turning serious.

"What is it?" Pete asked

Jack flinched as if he'd forgotten he wasn't alone. "Nothing really." He reached up and rubbed his ear. "After Vera quit the bank, she started working out of our home as an accountant. To keep her hand in the business world. You know? Not full time or anything. Only a few clients. Friends mostly, who had small businesses of their own." His gaze drifted away.

After several long quiet moments, Pete prompted him. "And?"

Jack shook his head. "I'm sure it's nothing. But about a month ago, I had a feeling she was working on something that upset her."

"Upset her how?"

"She was...distracted. At first, I thought she was just worried about Cassie. But when I asked her, she assured me that wasn't it."

"Did she say what 'it' was?"

"No. And that's what was so odd. We talked about everything. She wasn't one to keep things from me." Jack's eye twitched. "I think it was something work-related that upset her. You know, something confidential? Something she couldn't share with me."

"Why didn't you mention this sooner?"

Jack shrugged apologetically. "For one thing, I'd forgotten about it. Besides, whatever it was, Vera must've gotten it straightened out."

"Straightened out?"

"Yeah. One day, she was unbelievably stressed. The next day, she seemed...I dunno...calm. Determined. But calm."

"As if she'd come to a decision?"

"Exactly. She acted like she'd figured out how to handle whatever it was, so there was nothing else to worry about."

Interesting. "When was this?" Pete asked.

"Like I said. About a month ago."

"And how long ago did she seem to resolve the matter?"

Jack pondered the question. "Maybe two weeks."

Pete scribbled in his notebook.

"You don't think this has anything to do with her death, do you?"

Pete met and held his gaze. "It might. You said your wife worked out of your home?"

"Yeah. She converted our third bedroom into an office."

"Would you mind if I come over and take a look around?"

Jack lifted his chin. "Not at all. If you think it might help, by all means."

Pete picked up his water bottle to take a long drink.

Jack placed one hand flat on the table between them. "Chief Adams, I want to thank you."

He swallowed. "I haven't done anything yet."

"Yes, but you're trying. I got the impression those cops from county were convinced my wife was a drunk. She wasn't. Someone killed her." Jack's eyes welled again. "And you're the only one who's seriously investigating her death. Please. Find out who murdered my wife."

After sending Pete and Jack off to chat, Zoe stayed where she was and finished her milkshake.

She couldn't get Jack's sorrowful eyes out of her mind. In her years with the EMS, she'd encountered more pain and grief than she cared to admit as well as experiencing it herself. She'd seen Jack's look of devastation before. In the eyes of the woman injured in a crash that had killed her husband on impact. In the eyes of the mother whose child had fallen unnoticed into the pool and been under too long to be resuscitated. In the eyes of the man cradling his son's mangled body after the boy had been hit by a car while riding his bike.

In her own eyes staring at her reflection in the mirror.

She drained the last of the sweet chocolate, deposited the empty cup and Jack's untouched one in the trash, and fired off a text to Earl to let him know she was taking the long way back. He responded, *Take your time. Nothing going on here.*

Pete had whispered to her that he'd tracked Luke down in the midway and deposited him at the barn. She decided to make sure he was still there.

Zoe found the teen slouched on a tack trunk outside a stall, tapping on his phone's screen. He spotted her approach and pocketed the device. "You didn't have to send the cops after me."

She started to tell him she hadn't but decided on a different angle. "Seems like it worked."

Luke made a face like he'd sucked on a sour lemon. "I'm not a kid."

"No, you're not. You're almost a man. Start acting like it."

"Who the hell are you to talk to me like that?"

Zoe aimed a finger at him. "That is what I'm talking about. A real man wouldn't cuss out the people who care and are trying to keep him safe."

He choked a laugh. "*You?*"

She didn't reply.

"Or you mean my mother?" He said it as if the word tasted worse than that sour lemon.

"I meant Diane. I'm trying to keep an eye on you because she asked me to. And because she seems to think you're worth saving."

The mention of Diane leeched away some of the bitterness from his face. He lowered his head, staring at the darkened phone screen.

"In spite of your mother." The words slipped out before Zoe could contain them.

But they drew a snide smile from the teen. "You know my mother?"

"I did. A long time ago."

Luke kept his face lowered and nodded. "Did Diane think she was worth saving too?"

"Diane thinks all kids are worth saving. At least until they prove her wrong."

The teen snickered and raised his face, meeting Zoe's gaze. "I guess you're right about that."

Zoe crossed her arms. "Are *you* worth it?"

His eyes shifted. "I dunno."

She'd expected another smartass reply. The hint of self-doubt caught her off guard. "You don't have to follow in your mother's footsteps, you know."

He huffed a short laugh.

"Have you given any thought to what you want to do with your life?"

"College is out of the question. Mother never bothered to put any money aside. And I don't have the grades for a scholarship."

Another surprising answer. The kid had indeed given thought to his future. "What would you study?"

"Veterinary Science."

"Really?"

His face darkened. "What? You think I'm too stupid to be a vet?"

"Not at all. It's what I wanted to be when I was your age."

He gazed at her, searching for a sign that she was BSing him. "You serious?"

"Yep." Zoe gestured for him to move over, and when he did, she joined him on the tack trunk. "My mother and I don't have a very good relationship either. My dad died when I was eight. Mother remarried and moved to Florida. I stayed behind."

"How old were you?"

"Fifteen."

Now she had his full attention. "Really? You've been on your own since you were fifteen?"

"Not exactly. I stayed with my best friend and her mom."

"And your mother allowed it?"

Zoe let her head drop back against the bars covering the top portion of the stall and her mind drop back into her distant past. "Allow? I think she was relieved. She didn't know what to do with me, and when I said I wanted to finish high school here, she jumped at the excuse to hand me over to someone else."

"Huh." Luke pondered her words. "I wish I had somewhere else to go."

"Do you ever see your father?"

"No," Luke said, the bitterness seeping back into his voice. "My mom forbids it."

"I'm sorry."

He looked at her. "You mean that, don't you?"

"Yeah, I mean it. I'll never see my dad again. If he was alive and out there somewhere..." Zoe let the thought trail off. Trying to recapture a part of her father, even in the form of a missing sibling, had cost her dearly.

"So what happened?" Luke's words cut through her memories.

For a moment, she thought he was asking about last spring. "What?"

"You said you wanted to be a vet." He motioned at her EMS uniform. "I guess you changed your mind."

"Oh. Kinda. I had it changed for me. I started college but had to drop out." She saw the question in his eyes. "Money."

"Ah. But you're a—a—"

"Paramedic. Yeah. I took night classes."

"Huh," he said. "I never thought of that."

Zoe's phone buzzed in her pocket. She checked it to find a text from Earl. *Could use some help here.* She texted back, *On my way,* and jumped down from the tack trunk. "Gotta go. Duty calls."

"Hey," Luke said. "Thanks."

She dug a small notepad from her pocket, jotted her number on a page, ripped it out, and handed the sheet to him. "If you ever want to talk."

He looked at the paper. "Thanks."

"Do us all a favor and stay away from the midway."

He grinned at her with a mischievous glint in his eyes. "I can't promise that."

Zoe groaned. "You're hopeless."

"No, I'm not." He pointed down the aisle. "Just ask Diane. There she is now."

FIFTEEN

Jack had been ready to meet Pete back at the Palmers' house immediately after leaving Zoe's camper. But Pete had one more person he wanted to talk to at the fairgrounds first.

No one at the 4-H Barn had seen Merryn lately. Nor did anyone know where she might be.

Pete strolled toward the grandstand where large horses were hitched to a variety of carts, buggies, and carriages and were being driven around a show ring in the racetrack's infield. He parked himself at the rail, away from the crowd watching the competition, and surveyed the onlookers.

No Merryn.

He looped back through the midway, complete with its bells and whistles from the games, screams from the rides, and the scent of grilled onions and peppers drifting from the food trailers. He made passes through a couple of exhibit halls, one with produce, home-canned goods, and artwork and the other filled with commercial booths promoting roofing companies, cosmetic vendors, and politicians.

No Merryn.

The endless walking took a toll on his still-healing leg, the ache driving him to lower onto a bench next to an elderly couple. Pete silently cursed the bullet—and the shooter—who'd robbed him of his stamina. The couple gave him a sympathetic smile, making Pete realize he was gritting his teeth. He manufactured a reassuring grin for their benefit and refocused on his task. Merryn.

He was beginning to understand why the 4-H leader had assigned first Vera then Zoe to keep watch over Luke.

Pete climbed to his feet and was about to head back up the hill toward the dairy barns when he spotted the bleached blonde ambling into the fairgrounds through the side gate. She didn't notice him and headed toward the row of food concessions where he'd found Zoe talking to Jack earlier. Pete angled toward her, cutting her off.

"Hello again, Merryn," he said.

She stopped and squinted up at him through bloodshot eyes. Her lips curled into what he imagined she believed to be a seductive smile. "Well, hello there, handsome." She swayed as if fighting a breeze and reached toward him, catching his arm for support. "Have we met?"

Pete noticed her unsteady stance and her half-mast eyelids, but the dead giveaway was the distinct aromas of cannabis and beer wafting from her. "Earlier today when you were talking to Zoe Chambers."

Merryn appeared to struggle with the memory.

He helped her. "Pete Adams. Vance Township Chief of Police."

Her reaction matched her earlier one, only slower. "Oh." She withdrew her hand from his arm and swayed back so far Pete thought she was gonna fall on her ass. He reached to catch her, but she dodged his grasp. "Don't touch me."

"Okay." He held up both hands, showing her that he was keeping them to himself. "I've been looking for you."

"I haven't been doin' nothin'."

He knew exactly what she'd been doing, but busting her for smoking weed wasn't the way to garner her cooperation. "I wanted to talk to you for a few minutes."

She eyed him. "About what? My boy in trouble again?"

"Nope. I just saw Luke. He's helping some kids up in the barn."

"Oh, good. Well, I'm busy."

Pete glanced at the food booths. "I'll buy you a burger."

This sparked her interest. She looked at the row of food booths, ran her tongue over her lips, and brought her gaze back to Pete. "I'd rather have a pizza."

Five minutes later, they sat across from each other at one of the picnic tables, a box containing a large pepperoni pizza open in front of Merryn as she devoured her first slice. Pete had a feeling she'd stab him with a fork if he tried to claim one for himself.

"I was hoping you could answer a few questions."

She glared at him over a slice dripping with grease. "What about?"

"Where were you Thursday evening?"

"Whoa. Why d'ya wanna know? What d'ya suspect I did?"

"I'm simply trying to clear you."

"Of what?"

Pete grinned at her. "Of anything that happened Thursday evening."

Her frown told him she didn't find him amusing. "Thursday evening," she echoed. She chewed and thought at the same time. In her condition, multitasking might be beyond her capabilities. After several moments, she shrugged. "I can't remember. Hell, I can't remember what I had for breakfast this mornin'."

"Do you remember Vera Palmer?"

"Sure, I do."

"What can you tell me about her?"

"Why? She broke some law or somethin'?"

Pete studied Merryn. She genuinely seemed clueless. "She's dead."

Merryn stopped chewing. "Seriously?"

"You didn't know?"

She started chewing again. "That makes Jack a widower, right?" She sounded a little too eager.

"How well did you know Vera?"

Merryn shrugged and took another huge bite from the pizza. "Pretty well, I guess," she said, clearly not concerned about talking with her mouth full. "Didn't like her much."

"Oh? Why not?"

"She was too hoity-toity for my taste. Thought she was smarter than me. Rude. Ya know?"

"So you never socialized with her?"

Merryn stumbled over the word. "Sosh...shoshial...socialized? Hell no. She wouldn't give me the time of day."

"Do you know any of her hangouts? Places she liked to frequent?"

Merryn snorted. "Are you deaf? No. I don't know nothin' about where she went or who she socialized with." This time she enunciated the word slowly but still slurred it.

Pete let her eat in silence, rethinking his strategy...and remembering his conversation with Luke. "What can you tell me about

Jack?"

"Jack?"

"Palmer."

"Oh." Merryn chewed and thought. Multitasking again. "Jack and me. We go way back." Emphasis on *way*.

"How long have you known him?"

More chewing and thinking. "I don't know. A long time. I've always thought he and I should have gotten together. Instead of..." She appeared to struggle with her memory. "Instead of him and Vera. Me and Jack? We'd be good together. Better'n *them*." A frighteningly predatory smile crossed her lips. "I need to track him down. Now that stuffy ol' Vera's out of the way, I'm sure he needs some consoling."

Poor Jack, Pete thought. *Run, Jack.*

Diane stood outside what Zoe knew was the 4-H Barn's tack room, a hand on her head as if she had a monster headache.

"Are you okay?" Zoe asked.

"Huh?" Diane looked up. "Oh. Zoe." She lowered her hand and forced a smile. "Yes, I'm fine. I'm just missing some paperwork."

"What kind of paperwork?"

"The kids' project books. The County Extension Office needs to verify all the county roundup participants have put in the work required to be eligible to compete."

Zoe glanced into the tack room. A folding table had been set up and held several stacks of papers and folders. Boxes on the floor held more. "Can I help you look?"

Diane gave her a weary smile. "Thank you, dear. No. I've already searched through all my 4-H materials here." Her hand went back to her head. "The kids submitted them to me at the last meeting. I know I had them all boxed up, but I can't find *that* box."

"How soon do you need them?"

"I was supposed to take them into the Extension Office last week, but I couldn't find them. You know how it is. I kept expecting they'd turn up somewhere. The 4-H horseshow's on Wednesday. As long as I can show our extension agent that I have the reports in my possession, everything will be fine."

"And if you can't?"

The strain on Diane's face said she'd been trying not to think about it. "If I don't have those project books in my hands by the start of the show, none of our kids will be permitted to compete."

Jack Palmer welcomed Pete into his modest home and invited him to tear the place apart if it would help with the investigation.

Pete had assured him "tearing the place apart" wouldn't be necessary, but standing in the doorway to Vera's office made him reconsider. The small room looked more like a storage closet with a desk. Overflowing plastic milkcrates sat on the floor along the periphery. Stacks of papers and accounting books covered the surface of a table. More papers and notebooks leaned in precarious piles atop her desk.

"Have you had a break in?" Pete asked.

Jack chuckled from behind him. "Looks that way, doesn't it? No. It's always like this."

The rest of the house, as far as Pete had seen, was tidy. Uncluttered. Vera apparently saved her slob tendencies for her office.

"The funny thing," Jack said, "is she knew where everything was. If a client asked for one particular form she'd been working on, she'd reach into that mess and pull it out. I nagged her once to organize the place." He squeezed past Pete into the room and opened the closet door. Shelves inside were filled with storage bins containing an old coffee pot, empty bags from the grocery store, some leather and nylon pieces of equipment similar to stuff he'd seen in Zoe's barn, and an assortment of other stray items. "I bought her shelving and these bins to help with the effort. She tried to neaten the place up but always complained she couldn't find anything afterward. So I gave up and let her handle her business however it worked for her."

Vera might've been able to find anything she wanted in this mess, but Pete had doubts he'd be as lucky. He took a deep breath and knelt to tackle the first pile on the right. This could take the rest of the afternoon and well into the evening.

Jack left the room and returned with a stool from the kitchen island and a cup of coffee, which he offered to Pete. He disappeared again only to return with a second cup before perching on the stool. "Do you mind?" Jack asked. "If you'd rather work alone, I can go find something to do."

Pete sipped the coffee—good stuff—he wondered what brand Jack used—and then set the cup on the floor since there weren't any clear spots on the desk or table. "No, that's fine. This way we can talk. And you can answer questions about anything I find."

"I thought that too."

Jack appeared to have gotten a grip since their conversation in the camper. "Do you feel up to talking more about Thursday night?" Pete asked.

"I think so."

Pete kept sorting through the pile of papers. "For starters, where were you that night?"

"Here. At home. Alone." He smiled sadly. "Sorry. I guess I don't have an alibi."

"Anyone see you? Did you order pizza? Make any phone calls?"

"No. I didn't know I'd..." His voice trailed off, but Pete understood. He didn't know he'd need an alibi for the murder of his wife.

"Have you given any more thought to where Vera might've gone when she left the Roadhouse?"

"No. I mean, yes. I've been racking my brain, but I can't think of who would've texted her. Or who would've wanted to harm her. It occurred to me, though...can't you get that kind of information from the cell phone company?"

"I've already put in a request."

"But they'll give the information to you, right?" Jack sounded eager. "We might know something tomorrow?"

Pete hated to disappoint the guy, but it never happened that fast. "Maybe not tomorrow, but soon."

Jack nodded, his jaw set. "Good."

Pete moved on to a second pile. And a new topic. "How well do you know Merryn..." What was her last name?

"Merryn Schultz?" Jack asked.

That was it. "Yeah. She told me the two of you go way back."

Jack looked like he'd taken a bite of something truly disgusting.

"Her definition of 'way back' must be a lot different than mine."

"How well do you know her?"

"Not very. But that's still *too* well. You know?"

Pete chuckled. "I've met her."

"Did she proposition you?"

"It didn't get that far. She found out I was a cop and cooled off pretty fast."

"You're lucky." Jack grew thoughtful. "You know those pesky gnats that swarm around your face? Merryn Schultz is like that with men."

"So I've gathered. Did she act that way when your wife was around?"

"Not quite as bad, but yes."

"Vera couldn't have been happy about it."

Jack's laugh carried a sharp edge. "No. She wasn't."

Pete paused in his sorting. "Did Vera ever confront her about it?"

"Vera wasn't the jealous type. She knew I wasn't interested in any other women. Especially the likes of Merryn. But yeah. About a month ago, Merryn was being very—*affectionate*—and was getting on my last nerve. I think Vera did it because Merryn wasn't paying any attention when I kept brushing her off." Jack smiled sadly. "My wife came to my rescue. Kinda pitiful, isn't it?"

"What did she do?"

"Vera shoved her. Told her to back off."

Pete had a mental image of Zoe doing the same thing if Merryn had continued to flirt with him. "Did she? Back off, I mean?"

"Yeah. Sorta. Merryn stopped for the moment. But I saw the two of them arguing later that day."

"About you?"

"I guess. I didn't hear what was said, but they were toe-to-toe and in each other's faces. When I asked Vera about it, she told me they'd reached an 'understanding.'"

"An understanding, huh?"

"Yeah." Jack chuckled. "Like Merryn understood if she didn't keep her hands to herself, my wife was gonna open a can of whoop ass on her."

Pete snorted. "I think I'd have liked your wife."

Jack's smile twisted into the same agonized grimace Pete had seen earlier. "Most people did."

Most people, Pete thought. But not Merryn Schultz.

SIXTEEN

Pete had gone through Vera's home office, checked every file, every stray sheet of paper, and found nothing. With Jack's blessing, he'd brought her laptop back to the station.

Monday morning, Pete was back in uniform and back in his office. He placed a call to his newest officer, Abby Baronick, and asked her to come in early. In the four months since she'd joined the Vance Township Police Department, she'd proven to have a talent for all things computer related. Maybe she could dig around in Vera's laptop and figure out what had concerned her in the weeks prior to her death.

He struggled to focus on his weekend officers' reports and the phone messages demanding his attention. Vera Palmer seemed to cry out from the grave insisting he discover her secrets.

He made his last call to a local businessman with questions about security systems, tossed the pink sticky note in the trash, and leaned back in his chair. With his immediate duties tackled, he shifted his focus to Vera, selected a pen from the chipped mug on his desk, and started doodling on a legal pad.

Merryn Schultz had a temper, a history of incarceration and drugs, and a tendency to change her story whenever it suited her. Not to mention the drugs weren't strictly in her past. She'd been smoking marijuana yesterday and was possibly on more than weed. With access to drugs, she had the means. Merryn might not be guilty of premeditated murder, but Pete could picture her slipping something to Vera out of spite. Plus, she had no alibi.

But, why would Vera agree to meet her? And where?

On the topic of no alibis, Jack didn't have one either. But Pete didn't believe he was a good enough actor to fake the raw grief that overcame him whenever Vera was mentioned. Jack Palmer loved his wife and his child intensely and would have given his own life to save either of them.

Bells jingled from the front of the station and female voices drifted back to him. A few moments later, Officer Abby Baronick appeared in his doorway.

Pete stood and rounded his desk. "Thanks for coming in early."

"No problem. You mentioned Vera Palmer's computer?"

He brushed past Abby and motioned for her to follow him. "Her laptop. I need you to go through it and see what you can find."

"Is there anything in particular I should be looking for?"

Pete told her about Vera's accounting business. "Her husband mentioned something she was working on roughly a month ago had upset her. Apparently, she'd resolved the issue, but I want to know what and who had worried her."

Abby trailed Pete into the evidence room. "Maybe whoever caused the problems didn't care for how she resolved the issue."

"Exactly what I was thinking." He picked up Vera's laptop from the shelf and handed it to Abby. "If you find anything unusual, I want to know immediately."

By eight a.m., the temperature was already pushing eighty with high humidity and no breeze. Because she'd been on duty the previous night, Zoe put off bathing Windstar until early morning, and she wasn't sure he'd dry in time for his class. She sweat-scrapered as much moisture from his sorrel coat as she could and covered him with a stable sheet to keep the dust from undoing her efforts. She planned to grab a shower, but the line at the cinderblock building was out the door.

No doubt she'd be clammy again five minutes after showering, so it didn't matter. Everyone on the fairgrounds smelled like livestock anyway.

Patsy appeared in the Pony Barn's doorway adjusting a navy-blue scarf knotted at her throat. It was a perfect complement to her glittery blue blouse and navy pants, hat, and boots. "You better get dressed."

Zoe glanced at her watch. Almost a quarter of nine. "Crap." The show started in fifteen minutes, and the first breed class was hers. American Quarter Horse. Why couldn't the fair organizers skip the

AQHA breed title and list it later, under Q? At least they'd run through mares and stallions before getting to Windstar's gelding category. "Why are you in your show clothes already? Arabians won't be in the ring for a while yet."

"Because I want to watch the show." Patsy snapped her fingers at Zoe and made a shoo motion.

"I'm going. I'm going."

The tiny camper felt like a sauna. Zoe clicked the button on the air conditioner, hoping it might decide to work. No such luck. She stripped from her soggy barn jeans and t-shirt and struggled into the outfit Patsy had insisted she buy. A curve-hugging burgundy western blouse, to which she'd pinned her entry number, and black show pants. She already owned black boots and a black hat, which had cut back on the bill at the western shop.

By the time she returned to the barn, she wished she'd opted for brown. Dust coated her legs from the knees down. How did anyone manage to walk into a show ring looking spotless?

She stripped the stable sheet from her horse and gave him a quick once-over with a soft brush and a towel. Dabbed a coat of polish on his hoofs. Baby-oiled his muzzle and the inside of his ears.

Patsy, breathless, appeared in the doorway. "Get moving. Your class is next."

When Zoe and Windstar arrived at the entrance to the ring where her fellow competitors gathered, she discovered the class before hers had just entered the arena. With a little time to kill, she located a vacant spot of shade around the corner of the show ring and squatted, her back against the steel structure. Windstar found a patch of grass and grazed. She had to admit, her horse looked good. The sun glistened off his coppery coat and flaxen mane and tail.

"He really is gorgeous," someone said.

Zoe looked up to find Diane watching from the corner of the enclosed arena. "Thanks." As her former 4-H leader approached, Zoe asked. "Did you find the kids' project books?"

Diane's smile faded. "Not yet."

"What are you gonna do?"

"I'm gonna go home this evening, after the show." She tipped her head, indicating the one going on at the moment. "I'll tear my house apart. I know I had them. And an entire box of paperwork doesn't walk off on its own. I'll find it." Her words carried more conviction than her face.

Zoe wanted to ask what she planned to do if she didn't find them, but before she had the chance, she spotted three generations of Bassi women headed her way—Sylvia, Rose, and sixteen-year-old Allison.

"Aunt Zoe!" The teen hurried toward her without breaking into a run. Zoe had been harping on her about moving slowly around horses since the girl was a toddler. It seemed the lessons had stuck.

"Hey, kiddo." Zoe pushed up to stand and caught Allison in a hug. Zoe hadn't seen her since last November in New Mexico. "What are you doing here?"

"We came to watch you win the trophy," Sylvia said.

"There's no trophy. The most I can hope for is a Grand Champion Gelding ribbon."

"You'll win it." Allison cast an appreciative gaze at Windstar. "He looks awesome."

"See?" Diane nudged Zoe. "I told you. I'll let you visit with your company. Good luck."

Zoe thanked her and watched Diane amble away, still favoring her hip slightly.

"There was something I meant to ask you the other day," Rose said.

"Oh? What?"

Rose gave her a broad smile. "Would you be my maid of honor?"

Zoe didn't have to think about it. "Yes, of course I will."

Rose and Allison squealed and crushed her in a two-sided hug.

The ringmaster's shout carried over the crowd of waiting horses and handlers. "Geldings aged four and up, in the ring, please."

"Oops. That's me." Zoe brushed off the seat of her pants. "Gotta go."

Allison kissed the white stripe on Windstar's face. "For luck."

Zoe headed for the massive doorway into the arena, merging with the other entrants. Eight of them. She wondered how many places they pinned. Seven? Being the only one to not get a ribbon would suck. She eyed the other horses. Two of the geldings acted like they'd never been out of their own pasture before, fidgeting and prancing circles around their handlers. One of them was being shown in a faded nylon halter instead of the leather ones the others wore. Three of the remaining horses looked like old pros. Zoe intentionally guided Windstar, who was alert and nervous but not flighty, toward those horses as the ringmaster waved them into the ring.

She glanced at Cody, who looked ultra-professional in his silver belly Stetson and western-cut jacket over dark jeans. He didn't seem at all bothered by the heat. Unlike Zoe, who hoped the sweat forming on her forehead didn't find its way into her eyes.

The handlers and their horses walked around the ring with Cody and his clipboard in the center watching. After the second lap, Cody nodded to the ringmaster, who ordered them to line up.

Zoe wasn't sure if it was the heat threatening to choke her or the nerves. How long had it been since she'd done this? And why the hell had she let Patsy talk her into it this time?

The eight entrants lined up side by side, facing the bleacher seats, which held a good-sized crowd. The Bassis were in there somewhere. Patsy too. But Zoe didn't have the luxury of diverting her attention to look for them.

The horse in the nylon halter refused to stand quietly. Zoe had managed to position herself and Windstar well away from the rambunctious animal, who kept dragging his handler in circles. The horse next to him tried to sidestep out of his way. The horse next to that one pinned his ears and struck out with one hind foot.

Windstar flicked a wary ear in the direction of the melee but kept the other one aimed at Zoe who cooed to him. "Easy, boy. Whoa, fella."

She shot a glance at his feet, glad to see he'd remembered the lessons from back home and stood nicely squared. Now, if he'd only stay that way when Cody got to them.

Cody started at the other end of the row with the uncooperative horses. He stayed well clear of their hooves and, Zoe noticed, gave each handler ample opportunity to gain some control rather than merely dismissing them.

By the time Cody arrived at the exhibitor next to Zoe, Windstar had grown bored and cocked one back ankle. She jiggled the lead chain and applied pressure on one shoulder to wake him up. It worked. He planted the foot solid on the ground. Zoe whispered a silent prayer that he didn't decide to cock the other one. At least for a few more minutes.

Cody turned to her. She almost expected him to flash his dimples at her. But he didn't. He gave her a cool nod and shifted his full attention to the horse.

Zoe recalled the long-ago coaching Diane had given her. Stand tall. Keep one eye on your horse, the other on the judge. Don't block his view at any time. Be confident.

Cody made his loop around Windstar, jotted his notes on his clipboard, and moved on to the final horse in the class.

Zoe exhaled.

A few minutes later, Cody and the ringmaster conferred at the announcer's table. The ringmaster gathered the ribbons and headed toward the door. The PA system crackled to life.

"First place and the blue ribbon goes to entry number four fifty-eight. Bars Heritage owned and shown by Whitney Cameron."

The crowd applauded and a few whoops went up, echoing under the steel roof. The jittery horse at the end reared, nearly knocking his handler off her feet.

"Second place and the red ribbon goes to entry number five nineteen. Dudes Poco Windstar owned and shown by Zoe Chambers."

Allison's squeal of delight rose above the applause.

Zoe's knees weakened. She leaned against Windstar, patted his neck, and then gathered herself and led him toward the door and the ringmaster. And her red ribbon.

With her prize clutched in her hand, Zoe led her horse to the doorway. And Cody. She hadn't noticed his move to the entrance, but she spotted his approach. He stepped in front of her, dimples at full bloom.

"Dinner tonight. I'll meet you at your stall at six."

She sputtered. "I can't."

If he heard, he ignored her. "I have a business proposition for you. See you then."

"Business—?"

But he was gone, headed back to his judging duties.

The next class was attempting to enter the ring, and Zoe was impeding their progress. "Come on, Windy," she said to her horse and maneuvered through the crowd, feeling very much like she was headed the wrong way on a one-way street.

As much as she'd disliked being in one of the early categories, having the rest of the day free was a definite perk. She stashed Windstar in his stall, removed his show halter, and tossed him a flake of hay. "Relax, big guy. You done good."

After depositing some congratulatory carrots into his feed bin, tying the ribbon to his stall door, and returning her hat to its box, Zoe headed to the arena as a spectator. The Bassis had saved her a seat in the bleachers.

Allison gave her a hug. "You did great."

Sylvia sniffed. "You were robbed."

"No, I wasn't."

As the Appaloosa classes progressed through the categories, Zoe watched Cody DeRosa at work. There was none of the flirting, no joking, no dimples. In fact, his poker face while studying each animal's conformation rivaled Pete's at their Saturday night card games. She watched for signs of favoritism but found none. His selections for ribbons were spot-on. And she admired the way he gave the younger kids every opportunity to set up their horses to the best advantage.

Cody might be a womanizer outside the ring, but inside it, he was a total professional.

Zoe excused herself from the Bassi women's company as the final Appaloosa category entered the ring. She'd spotted Patsy bringing Jazzel down from the barn and wanted to wish her well.

What she hadn't noticed was Shane's hovering presence. As she approached them through the sea of waiting horses and handlers, she became aware Patsy's boyfriend was not pleased.

"He has to look at me," Patsy was saying once Zoe grew close enough to overhear the conversation. "He's the judge."

"He's judging your damned horse, not you."

Patsy's expression darkened at the disparaging remark about her mare. "He has to judge how well I present Jazzel."

Zoe closed the distance and blurted a too perky, "Hi there," hoping to defuse the blossoming argument.

But Shane turned on her. "I saw him panting after you when you finished your class. Like a damned dog in heat."

"Shane." Patsy's tone lowered into the threatening range.

"He's hot for every female on these fairgrounds." Shane continued to direct his rant at Zoe, his words growing steadily louder. "Your cop may not care about other men hitting on you, but I won't have him making moves on my woman."

"*Shane.*" Patsy's face had turned crimson.

If anything good came from this week at the fair, Zoe thought, it might be the end of Patsy and Shane's relationship.

The final Appaloosa class had been pinned and the horses and handlers started pouring out of the arena. Zoe noticed Cody trailing them, speaking with a youngster. From the body language he used, she could tell he was advising the kid about how to control his animal.

"*Shane!*"

The panic in Patsy's voice snapped Zoe's attention away from the judge and the kid.

Shane stormed through the departing show entrants, fists clenched, his back a mass of knotted muscles, visible through his snug t-shirt.

The kid's eyes widened and his grip on his lead shank tightened. The reaction caused Cody to turn toward whatever had scared the child—Shane. Others saw him coming too and scrambled out of the way.

Shane slammed the judge, both hands driving into Cody's chest sending him reeling backwards. He stumbled and went down, flat on his back into the dirt. A rumble of gasps with a few screams rose from the bleachers. Shane continued to steamroll toward Cody, who was sprawled and shocked motionless.

Zoe saw Shane draw back with one balled fist ready to drive down on the cowboy's face.

But the ringmaster appeared out of nowhere, hooked Shane's cocked arm with his own while using one leg to trip him. Off balance, Shane went down next to Cody.

Men—fathers, farmers, horse owners—appeared from the crowd, some pinning Shane, others helping Cody up.

Patsy covered her face, mortified   .

Zoe draped an arm around her cousin's shoulders and caught Jazzel's lead shank with her other hand. "It's okay," she whispered.

"No." Patsy moaned into her hands. "No, it's not okay. Not at all."

SEVENTEEN

Pete listened on the phone while Zoe told him about her second-place ribbon as well as the excitement surrounding her cousin's class.

"I'm sorry to hear that," he said when she reported that Patsy only received fourth place. Out of four. "Do you think DeRosa held her boyfriend's attack against her?"

Abby appeared at Pete's door, the laptop tucked under her arm.

Zoe's soft laugh filtered through the phone's earpiece. "Who could blame him? But honestly, no. I think it had more to do with Jazzel flaking out in the ring, kicking at the horse next to her and coming darned close to taking a chunk out of Cody's arm when he walked in front of her. Plus, there were some gorgeous mares in that class."

Abby gave Pete a raised eyebrow.

Pete held up an index finger and mouthed *one minute*. "How's Patsy taking it all?"

"She locked herself in the camper after telling Shane to go to hell. I'm glad I had a chance to change out of my fancy show clothes before she barricaded the doors."

"Is she going to be all right?"

"I'll give her another hour to get over her temper tantrum and then go peek in the windows."

Abby leaned against the door jamb.

He took the hint. "I have to get back to work. Congratulations on your ribbon."

She thanked him, and he ended the call.

Pete turned his full attention to his waiting officer. "What have you got?"

Abby pushed away from the jamb and entered the office. "Not as much as we'd hoped." She opened the laptop and placed it in front of him.

The screensaver revealed a smiling little girl on a fat fuzzy pony. Pete recognized Cassidy from the framed photos on Vera's office walls back at the Palmers' house. This was a much younger version. And so adorable, it ripped at Pete's soul. He rarely thought about the unborn child he and his ex-wife had lost, but for some reason, Cassidy Palmer unearthed the long-buried ache.

Abby came around his desk and leaned over his shoulder to finger the laptop's mouse pad. Cassidy vanished, and a spreadsheet appeared. Pete swallowed, forcing the ache back into the recesses of his memory.

"Vera has everything password protected, and she doesn't use those apps that autofill it on her own machine. Makes it tricky. Her accounting software was easy to unlock. She used her daughter's name and birthday." Abby clicked through several files. "She has about a dozen clients from what I've found. Mostly small businesses. One local charity. The rest are individuals."

"Did you find anything hinky?"

"Not so far. I've been going through them, entry by entry. Everything adds up. No red flags on any of the tax returns she's filed for her clients. There aren't that many, but she's been doing this for a number of years, so it'll take me a while to get through them all."

Finding out Vera Palmer was an honest accountant with an honest clientele wasn't helpful. "Did you find anything that might've concerned her?"

"Not yet. I've gone through the most recent entries on all the files." Abby straightened and crossed her arms. "Nothing."

Pete scanned the open file. As Abby said, it looked normal. He clicked through the dozen or so spreadsheets for Vera's assorted clients, taking note of the names. Some he recognized. Some he didn't.

And one nagged at him. "Hang on a minute," he told Abby and picked up his phone, punching in the last number from which he'd received a call.

"Miss me already?" Zoe's suggestive tone stirred a completely un-businesslike reaction in him.

He shifted in his chair. "Always." Aware that Abby stood at his shoulder, he cleared his throat. And his mind. "Hey, what's Patsy's boyfriend's last name?"

"Shane?"

"Yeah."

"Tolland." She spelled it. "Why?"

Pete gazed at the accounting records in front of him. "Because he's one of Vera Palmer's clients."

Zoe strolled back to the fairgrounds main gate after walking the Bassis to their car and exchanging goodbye hugs.

The remainder of the horseshow had gone off without incident. Cody dusted himself off and completed his judging duties as if nothing had happened, although Zoe thought she detected a limp developing as the day went on.

Patsy remained in the camper. She did, however, unlock the door when Zoe knocked to check on her, locking it again when Zoe left. If Patsy was laying low to avoid Shane, she needn't have bothered. He'd slunk away after the shoving episode and hadn't been seen the rest of the day.

Until now.

As Zoe approached the fair gate, she spotted a familiar Ford Tempo jacked up with its trunk open. Diane stood back and watched as Jack Palmer and Shane Tolland worked on a rear tire.

Pete had mentioned Shane was one of Vera's clients. Now might be a good time to find out how much he knew about his late accountant.

"Can you believe it?" Diane said when she noticed Zoe. "I was out running a few errands and made it back this far before the darned tire blew."

"This car?" Zoe snickered. "Of course, I believe it."

Shane muscled the old tire off and rolled it to Jack, who let it drop flat to the ground and picked up and handed the replacement to Shane. "I hope your spare has air in it," Jack said.

Diane rubbed her arms. "You and me both."

Shane hoisted the tire onto the hub, jiggled it until the rim lined with the lug bolts, and slid it on. After he'd screwed on the lug nuts, he released the jack.

They stood around staring at the bulging sidewalls.

"Darn it," Diane muttered.

"It's better than the other one." Shane aimed the tire iron at the less-flat flat.

Jack slapped Shane on the back. "Come on. We'll run it down to the Fast Fill and put air in it. That should hold Diane for a while."

Diane looked doubtful. "Thanks, guys."

Zoe took a step toward them. "Hey, Shane, I wanted to talk to you for a minute."

Shane glared at her. "No, thanks. Your cousin's already said enough."

"It's not about that."

Ignoring her, he heaved the flatter flat into the trunk and tossed the tire iron on top of it before slamming the lid. To Jack, he said, "I need to get out of here for a while anyway."

Zoe stood next to the 4-H leader and watched the men drive off in a cloud of dust. Diane waved a hand and coughed. "Come on. Let's get back to the barn."

As they showed their wristband passes to the man at the gate, Diane congratulated Zoe on her second place. "I hope you didn't feel slighted, not winning the blue."

"Not at all. Whitney Cameron had the nicer horse by far."

Diane gave her a look. "I wouldn't say 'by far,' but when your family owns one of the biggest Quarter Horse breeding facilities in the state, it almost doesn't seem right to compete at the county level. Heck, they clean up at Nationals every year."

"I'm not upset about it. Really. I like Whitney. Her horse might be worth fifteen grand, but she acts like she's a backyard owner with a herd of scrub ponies."

"True." Diane glanced at her watch. "It's after six. I heard you have a date with our judge."

"You heard?" Zoe wondered who'd been feeding the fairgrounds' grapevine. It didn't matter. She'd already made up her mind to join her cousin locked in the camper. At least until Cody had gotten the message that she didn't intend to take him up on whatever proposition he had in mind. "I was planning to blow him off."

A strange look crossed Diane's face. Zoe noticed her gaze dart over her shoulder. And realized her "date" was standing right behind her. Crap.

"Planning to blow me off, huh?"

She turned, her face warm. "Hi, Cody. Sorry."

"My day just keeps getting shittier by the moment." The dimples belied his downtrodden appearance. "Come on, Zoe. Give a guy a break."

"Look, I—"

"If you'll excuse me," Diane said. "I have to make sure my kids haven't destroyed anything." She hobbled away.

Zoe made a mental note that she owed Diane. And not in a good way.

Cody leaned toward her. "I hope you're hungry."

"As I was saying, I'm not interested in going on a dinner date with you."

"It's not a 'dinner date.'" He made a don't-be-ridiculous face. "I'm only buying you a meal. At the fair. If it was a date, we'd get all dressed up, and I'd take you to Romano's."

"You do realize I'm seeing someone."

"The cop, right?"

"Yeah."

"Well, I'm not about to get on *his* bad side. I've already been flattened by one jealous boyfriend today. That fills my quota." Cody tipped his head and flashed his dimples. "We both have to eat. And I hate to eat alone."

Zoe suspected that would never happen. If he sat down by himself, women and girls would appear out of the woodwork, vying for his attention.

"Besides, I was serious earlier when I said I have a business proposition for you. Business. Nothing more."

She wasn't going to win this debate.

He must have recognized her capitulation. "Come on. The ladies from Elm Grove Presbyterian Church make a mean fried chicken dinner."

Five minutes later, Zoe found herself inside the makeshift dining room the church had set up at the end of one exhibit hall. A heavy paper plate in front of her was piled with golden chicken and a mound of fries, accompanied by a Styrofoam container of slaw. She inhaled the mouthwatering aroma wafting from her meal and ripped open the clear plastic packet containing a fork and knife. Cody pulled up the chair across from her and sat down to an identical plate and container. He placed two tall cardboard cups of iced tea between them.

He took a sip. "I know you're here under protest, so let me get down to business."

"Good." Zoe picked up a crispy chicken leg and took a bite.

"I want to buy your horse."

She choked. Grabbed a napkin and pressed it to her mouth. Windstar? The horse she'd raised from birth? From *before* birth? She'd sat in the stall with his dam the night he'd been foaled. She'd broke him to halter and later to saddle. Granted, she didn't have time to ride as much as she wanted.

After managing to chew and swallow, she said, "You're kidding, right?"

"I don't kid about horses. Ever. Is he well broke?"

"Very."

"I assumed as much. In the ring this morning, he was nervous, but he never flipped out, even though there were some high-strung animals not far from him. Gave me the impression that he's bomb proof."

"Kinda." She kept studying Cody, expecting him to crack a joke.

"He's what? Thirteen years old?"

"Yeah."

"And he goes back to Samson T Dude on his top line?"

Referring to Windstar's bloodlines on his sire's side. A tidbit of information Cody could not have discovered by reading the cardboard sign tacked on Windstar's stall in the Pony Barn. Zoe placed the napkin on the table and pinned it beneath her palm as if it might fly away in the same way her thoughts were spinning out of control. "What's this all about? Why are you interested in buying my horse?"

Cody leaned back, folding his arms across his chest. "I don't know if you're aware that I run a training facility out in Ohio. I take in horses that have behavioral issues as well as youngsters who haven't been handled enough. I also work with their owners."

"Windstar doesn't have any behavioral issues."

"Exactly. I'm always on the lookout for a horse I can use to pony

the rank ones. Or that I can stick a green rider on and know he's safe."
Cody grinned. "It helps if the horse is a looker. Wouldn't help my
reputation to have an ewe-necked, sway-backed broom-tail in my
stable."

Zoe thought of the second-place ribbon. "Did you make this offer
to Whitney Cameron?"

Cody chuckled and came forward, picking up a piece of chicken. "I
can't afford Whitney's horse."

Which clarified the picture for Zoe. Cody had done his homework.
He knew Windstar's age and bloodlines. He probably also knew about
Zoe's financial struggles and figured he could lowball an offer and have
her jump at it. "But you think you can afford mine."

He took a big bite from a thigh, studying the piece as he chewed.

Zoe waited while he took what seemed like ages to swallow.

When he finally did, he made a point of wiping his mouth and
fixing her with a hard stare. "Seventy-five hundred."

She stuttered. "Seventy...seventy-five? Hundred? Seven thousand
five hundred?"

He held her gaze without replying.

She melted against the back of the chair. She'd never entertained
the idea of selling her horse. She'd always assumed she'd own him until
he died.

Granted, times had been tough. Losing her home on the Kroll's
farm over a year ago and then having to vacate their barn last winter
had made horse ownership a challenge. Now, thanks to her mother,
she owned a farm of her own—which created a multitude of new
headaches. The house wasn't quite livable yet in spite of all the work
that had been done this spring and summer. And even if it were, what
about Pete? She'd been living with him in the little village of Dillard for
almost a year, a situation which pleased him immensely. But she
missed living out in the country. She dreamed of moving into her
house—with Pete and her cats. Expanding the barn to allow more
boarders. Having friends out for dinners and picnics with nothing but
pastures and woods and hillsides around them.

The problem with her dream was Pete. He'd grown up in the city.
To him, Dillard was rural. She thought of the old TV show and its
catchy theme song. *Green Acres* but in reverse. Pete was the one

resisting farm living.

Windstar was always her anchor. Her excuse. Pete knew how much she loved that horse and would never ask her to sell him. They'd fixed up her barn well before doing any work on her house, because a home for the horses...hers and Patsy's...took top priority.

For months, Zoe existed in limbo. Living with the man she loved in town while half of her heart and all of her dreams resided out on the farm.

If she sold Windstar, there would be no need for the farm. Patsy would buy it in a heartbeat. Of that, Zoe was certain. She'd be free to move in—permanently—with Pete. In town. He would be ecstatic.

"You don't have to make up your mind right this minute."

Zoe blinked.

Cody still watched her, a hint of the dimples showing. "I know you've had him all his life, and the decision isn't an easy one. But I can assure you he'd have a good home." A suggestive grin and his dimples blossomed. "And you'd be welcome to come out and visit him anytime you'd like."

Yeah. That wasn't gonna happen. "How soon do you need an answer?" She couldn't believe she was considering the offer.

Cody picked up another piece of chicken. "I'm here until after the 4-H show. I plan to drive home Friday morning. I'd much prefer to take him with me as opposed to hiring someone else to haul him back to Ohio."

Zoe counted. Three days to make a decision that would alter her life.

EIGHTEEN

Pete didn't make it to the fairgrounds until almost seven o'clock Monday evening, along with just about every other resident of Monongahela County. Probably half of Allegheny and Fayette County's populations too. Along with the hordes, he funneled through the gate, glad he'd texted Zoe, who'd told him to meet her by her horse's stall. He'd never have found her in this throng otherwise. A mega-decibel roar arose from the direction of the grandstand. If the noise was any indication, they were launching rockets into outer space.

The crowd thinned as he trudged up the hill toward the Pony Barn. Dark clouds gathered overhead, and the air was thicker with humidity than it had been earlier, if that was even possible. Pete hadn't checked the program to see what drew the masses tonight, but he feared whatever was going on at the grandstand might be washed out before the evening ended.

True to her word, Zoe waited for him at the end of the barn.

"Hey." He strode to her and slipped an arm around her waist, brushing her cheek with a safe-for-public-viewing kiss.

She leaned into him, much as she always did. But he sensed a hint of resistance.

"You okay?"

"Yeah." She smiled, but it didn't reflect in her eyes.

Something wasn't right. "How's Patsy?"

"She finally came out of the camper long enough to take care of her horse." Zoe gestured to the next stall. "But then she left without saying much. I think she went to watch the modified tractor pulls."

"Is that what's drawing the crowds tonight?"

"Yeah. They already had the normal tractors compete over the weekend. Tonight, it's the souped-up beasts."

Which explained the deafening rumble he'd heard when he entered the grounds. "I hope she took hearing protection."

Zoe reached into her jeans pocket and pulled out two small plastic bags. Earplugs. "I thought you might want to get the full fair experience."

As they made their way back down the hill, Pete took her hand in his. "Did you have dinner yet?"

She tensed. Not a lot. No one else would've noticed. But he knew this woman and felt the subtle change all the way to her fingers. "Yeah," she said.

He waited for her to say more. When she didn't, he asked, "Anything good? Because I haven't eaten, and I'm starved." The moment he said it, he remembered the conversation yesterday. That guy in the cowboy hat and boots. Cody DeRosa. *I'm looking forward to our dinner tomorrow.* Zoe had insisted otherwise. But he'd seemed...persistent.

"There's food everywhere. You can get whatever you like," she said. They'd reached the intersection in the pavement with the midway straight ahead and the road to the grandstand bearing right before she spoke again. "Have you talked to Shane Tolland yet?"

All right. Dinner was a bad topic. "No. I was hoping he'd be around here this evening."

"Last I saw him, he and Jack Palmer were driving off in Diane's car about an hour ago."

"Oh?"

She told him about the flat tire and spare that needed air. "I haven't seen either of them since then. But I haven't been looking either."

"Did they act like they knew each other or were friends?"

"Shane and Jack? It was hard to tell. I mean, they were working together to change the tire, but they weren't behaving like old friends or anything." She bumped Pete with her shoulder. "You guys don't get all chatty like we gals do." Her easy smile was back.

"True."

The migrating crowds grew thicker and the eardrum-busting roar crescendoed making conversation a challenge. By the time Pete and Zoe had reached the highest point on the road with the grandstand seats built into the hillside below them, his leg started to ache, and the current competitor had completed his pull. The tractor's noise level dropped to a rumbling idle.

Zoe eyed Pete. "Your leg's bothering you."

"Don't worry about it. I'm fine."

She didn't appear to buy his lie but held out one of the packages of earplugs to him. "We can sit up here. Unless you want a closer look."

He wanted a closer look, but at the crowd. Not the behemoths with tires that cost more than the national debt of some fair-sized countries. Accepting the small plastic pouch, he pointed downward. "Let's walk around. Maybe we'll run into Tolland."

She glanced at his leg, no doubt recalling that night as she'd fought to keep him from bleeding out. Bringing her eyes back to meet his, she managed a grin. "On patrol it is then."

He tore into the bag but held onto the orange foam earplugs as they continued along the road down to where the competitors' crews and supporters mingled with the hardcore fans who clearly didn't care about hearing loss.

A woman stopped Zoe. An old friend if the way they hugged was any indication. Pete surveyed the crowd, searching for Tolland's scruffy face. He'd only met Patsy's new boyfriend—former boyfriend, perhaps—once at Zoe's farm. The guy reminded Pete of the tall skinny kid in the cartoon about the mystery-solving dog.

Someone jabbed Pete in the ribs. He turned, coming face-to-face with Monongahela County Police Detective Wayne Baronick—Vance Township Officer Abby Baronick's brother—wearing his veneered smile. "Fancy meeting you here."

"You're out of uniform, Detective." Pete gestured at Baronick's jeans and crisp white shirt, a change from his usual suit and tie.

"I'm undercover."

"If that's the case, you're too clean."

"I'm undercover as a spectator, not a farmer."

"Ah."

Baronick grew serious. "Have you learned anything about Vera Palmer's homicide?"

"I didn't think you were working that case."

The detective looked over the crowd. "I'm not. I've been tied up with the drug taskforce. Besides, there's no real evidence that Vera's death wasn't an accident."

"True."

Baronick's gaze came back to Pete. "But your notorious gut thinks otherwise?"

"I don't like unanswered questions. And that's all I've been getting on this one."

"If there's anything I can do to help—"

"As a matter of fact." Pete crossed his arms. "How familiar are you with Merryn Schultz?"

Baronick huffed a laugh. "Everyone on the taskforce knows Merryn. She's a frequent visitor to the county jail. Why? Is she one of your unanswered questions?"

"No. I have her number. But according to the victim's husband, Merryn and Vera had a confrontation a month or so ago."

"Merryn's had her share of confrontations with wives over the years. I bet she was trying to get cozy with the husband."

"Still is."

"That's Merryn, all right."

"And she was under the influence of something when I spoke to her yesterday."

Baronick looked at him. "'Something?'"

"Alcohol. Drugs. Both. I don't know. I didn't run a tox screen on her."

"Wouldn't surprise me if she was using again."

"What about her son?"

"Luke? What about him?"

Before Pete could respond, one of the monster tractors revved, blasting flames from its dual smokestacks and overpowering any conversation for a half mile. The beast roared down the track towing a weighted sled and spitting fire. The stench of diesel drifted toward them.

As soon as the tractor reached the end of its run and throttled down to a dull rumble, Zoe tucked a hand into the crook of Pete's elbow and pressed against him. "Hey, Wayne." She wagged a finger at his attire. "I thought you only wore jeans on Sunday."

"He's undercover," Pete said.

"Oh." She scanned the spectators. "Any sign of Shane?"

"Who?" Baronick asked.

"One of my unanswered questions." Pete said.

Zoe gave him a quizzical look before replying to the detective. "My cousin Patsy's boyfriend. And one of Vera Palmer's accounting clients."

Baronick raised an eyebrow. "Disgruntled customer?"

Pete raised an eyebrow back.

"That's one of your questions. Got it." Baronick adjusted his collar. "You kids have fun. I'm gonna keep doing what I was doing."

"Undercover," Pete said.

Baronick touched his nose. "Bingo. You're catching on."

As the detective strolled into the crowd, Zoe faced Pete. "You two are getting along remarkably well these days."

"I get along with him just fine as long as he doesn't try to muscle in on my case."

"He's not interested in Vera's homicide?"

"Not until we prove it wasn't accidental." Another space-age-looking tractor moved into position, this one sporting four smokestacks, although they didn't appear to be rigged as flame throwers. Pete took Zoe's hand and squeezed it. "I don't see Tolland down here. Let's make a pass through the grandstand and then get out of here."

"Good idea."

They climbed the concrete steps to the first row of open-air bleacher seats. Pete led the way along the front of them, scanning the crowd above for one scraggly man.

Halfway across, Zoe tugged the back of Pete's shirt. "Do you see him?"

"No. You?"

"No."

Dammit.

They made their way to the end closest to the midway without a glimpse of Tolland, but Pete knew they could easily have missed him. Rather than climb the steps up to the road, Pete took the stairs down toward the racetrack, glancing back to make sure Zoe hadn't stopped to chat with yet another old friend. She was looking at the spectators gathered on the track rail below, watching the monster tractors continue to spew smoke, noise, and sometimes flames.

Even with the ear protection, Pete suspected he'd be half deaf for days. How those guys driving the beasts had any hearing left amazed him.

He'd almost reached the bottom step when Zoe tapped him hard on the shoulder. He turned to see her focused on one spot in the crowd. "Do you see him?" he shouted above the roar.

She shook her head, pointed, and mouthed—or yelled and he couldn't hear—the word, "*Look.*"

He followed her gaze.

Wayne Baronick stood talking to Merryn who clung to Jack Palmer's arm despite his attempt to put distance between them. Baronick reached over and put a hand on Merryn's shoulder. She shrugged him off, but the detective renewed his grip, and this time he appeared determined to hold on. Taking a big step away, she wrested free. At the same time, Jack side-stepped, breaking her grasp on his arm. Even from the distance, Pete could see Merryn's displeasure as she wheeled and retreated. Baronick made a halfhearted attempt to catch her, but Jack said something to him—let her go, perhaps—and the two men continued to chat.

The latest competitor ran out of muscle and throttled down to a still-deafening rumble.

Pete felt Zoe press against him from behind. "Did you see that?" she shouted through his earplugs.

He nodded and thought of Luke's comment about his mother. *As long as they're breathing, and she hasn't already been married to 'em, she's hot for 'em.* Considering how she reacted to Pete and Baronick, he should add cops to the list of men who didn't appeal to Merryn Schultz.

NINETEEN

Zoe sat outside Windstar's stall in one of the molded plastic lawn chairs she'd brought from her front porch and reveled in the relative quiet. The Pony Barn was mostly void of humans at the moment, and even though her ears still hummed from the noise of the modified tractors, she could hear the soft horsey sounds of munching with an occasional snort. Darkness had brought cooler air. While the roar of diesel engines continued to drift up the hill, Zoe embraced the peace.

Patsy appeared in the barn's doorway and shuffled over to claim the second lawn chair. The harsh light of the overhead bare bulb did little to improve her glum expression.

"Have you seen Shane?" Zoe asked.

Patsy turned to her. "Seriously? You *had* to mention his name."

"Only because Pete and I have been all over these fairgrounds looking for him to no avail."

"Pete? What does Pete want with him?"

"It seems he knew Vera Palmer."

"Really?"

"He never mentioned to you that she was his accountant?"

Patsy continued to glare. "How many of your old boyfriends shared the names of their bookkeepers with you?"

"Good point. Sorry I brought him up."

Patsy sat back in the chair. After several long moments of silence, she said, "No, I haven't seen him. Not since this morning when he decked the judge. Who then took it out on me."

"I don't think Cody held Shane's behavior against you."

Patsy shifted to face her. "Whose side are you on?"

Zoe considered mentioning Jazzel's poor manners but decided against it. "Forget I said anything."

Patsy relaxed, and they let the silence settle around them again.

But another topic had been festering in Zoe's mind for hours. "Cody wants to buy Windstar."

She'd expected Patsy to either leap or fall out of the chair. Instead, Zoe wondered if she'd fallen asleep and hadn't heard. But then Patsy sat up and turned toward her. Slowly. Deliberately. "That son of a bitch."

"Excuse me?"

"Are you gonna do it?"

Zoe wanted to say no. Of course not. She'd never sell Windstar. Wouldn't even consider it. Instead, she said, "I don't know."

Patsy flopped back, closed her eyes, and swore.

"I didn't say I was. I said I don't know."

"But you're thinking about it."

"Well...yeah."

Patsy swore again.

"How many years do you think it's gonna take to make my house livable?"

"It's almost there now. You have electricity and water."

Which was part of the problem. The memories from last spring of how she'd been given that gift. Of who'd been responsible for the repairs. And why. If Patsy didn't want to talk about Shane, Zoe most definitely didn't want to broach the subject of what had happened to her brother. "I don't have appliances or furniture. I need new windows and probably a new roof. The house is little more than a shell."

"So you're gonna sell your horse to pay for fixing up your house?"

"No." She said it too fast. And knew the rest of the equation had just added up for Patsy.

"You're gonna get rid of the farm and stay with Pete."

"I...don't know."

From the far end of the barn, the slow muffled *clomp, clomp, clomp* of cowboy boots on hard-packed dirt drew Zoe's attention.

Cody approached them, his thumbs hooked in the front pockets of his Wranglers. His hat threw his face into shadows cast by the row of lights set into the ceiling. But Zoe recognized his swagger.

So did Patsy. "Oh, great," she muttered.

"Good evening, ladies." He stopped in front of them.

"Why aren't you out picking up girls?" Patsy asked. "Or aren't tractor-pull bunnies your thing?"

"Not really." He looked around, crossed the aisle to borrow a chair, and planted it facing them. "I prefer horsewomen."

"We're not interested." Patsy shot a look at Zoe, who wasn't sure if her cousin was asking a silent question or giving her a silent order.

"I know. I just wanted to hang out for a few minutes." He sat, crossed a booted ankle over one knee, and removed his hat, setting it brim up in his lap.

Without the brim shading his face, the bare lightbulb shone on the bruise coloring one eye. Zoe looked at her cousin whose opened mouth indicated she was thinking the same thing.

Patsy stuttered. "Did—Did Shane do...?" She aimed a finger at Cody's face. "I'm so sorry."

He lowered his face. "Don't worry about it. I'm fine."

"Oh my god." Patsy's voice sailed into the shrill range. "He gave you a black eye."

"I'm fine. Really." Before Patsy could sputter more apologies, Cody turned his asymmetrical gaze on Zoe. "Have you given any more thought to my offer?"

It was Zoe's turn to stutter. "I thought you were giving me until the end of the week for an answer."

"I am. But if you're leaning toward turning me down, I wanted a chance to plead my case." He glanced over her shoulder at Windstar's stall. "He'll have a good home. I can promise you that. And you could come out to Ohio to visit and ride him anytime you want."

She studied him, searching for some sign of a leer surrounding the invitation. Maybe the pain or the swelling around his eye limited his capability to smirk, but she spotted no hint of impropriety. "I appreciate that. And I know you'd give him a good home." Probably better than what she could provide.

He toyed with his hat's brim. "Then you're accepting my offer?"

"I didn't say that."

"Look. I'll be honest with you. Something's come up. I'm going to have to leave as soon as I finish judging the show, and I'd like to have this settled well before that. You know. Ownership transfer. Checks written. Transportation arranged." His smile looked fatigued. "Buying a horse isn't like buying a pair of boots."

Zoe sensed steam radiating from Patsy. "How much is he paying you to give up the only life you know?" she asked.

Zoe looked at her, about to tell her she was exaggerating. But was she? Without a horse, would Zoe even recognize herself? She'd always worn the title of "horsewoman" like a badge of honor, since the first moment her father had plopped her tiny butt onto the saddle of a pony at a local fireman's festival. From that moment on, there had been more pony rides followed by more borrowed and leased horses than she could count. She'd bought her first horse, Windstar's dam, at an auction shortly before the mare had dropped the foal in a stall with Zoe watching. The mare died a tragic death a short time later, leaving Windstar an orphan. Zoe had raised him. Trained him. Broke him to ride.

If she sold him now, what would she be? No longer a horsewoman.

But if she kept him—and the farm—what would happen to her and Pete? She knew he'd never be happy out there even if she found the means to make the place livable, let alone comfortable. The farm and her horse would continue to be a wedge between her and the man she loved.

Not that it would be the only one.

Cody resettled his hat on his head, once more throwing his face into shadows. He stood. "I can see you haven't made up your mind. It's a big decision. But let me know as soon as you can. Okay?"

"Yeah. I will."

He placed his borrowed chair back where he found it, looked at Patsy, and touched the brim of his hat with one finger.

She said nothing, and the receding *clomp, clomp, clomp* of his boots followed him out the way he'd come. Once he'd gone, Zoe waited for Patsy to rant, shout, or otherwise throw a fit. Instead, she remained still and silent for at least a full minute, maybe two. Then she stood without meeting Zoe's gaze, turned, and stalked out of the barn.

Zoe took a breath. Exhaled. And wondered if selling her horse also meant losing yet another family member.

*   *   *

When Pete arrived at the station the next morning, his graveyard shift officer, Seth Metzger, leaned in the doorway to Nancy's office, holding several sheets of paper. He stepped out of Pete's way, clearing a path to the Mr. Coffee.

"What have you got there?" Pete asked as he poured a cup.

"Vera's cell phone records."

Pete paused, mid-sip. "That was fast."

"It's only a partial report. They said the rest would take another week or so."

"At least it's a start." He collected his daily stack of pink sticky notes from his secretary and carried them and his mug past Seth. Tipping his head toward the rear of the building, Pete headed for his office with Seth on his heels.

Pete slid into his chair as his young officer took the one across from him and set the papers between them.

"Have you looked at them yet?" Pete asked.

"I scanned them quick. There are phone numbers, dates, and times. But no content of the texts. And no cell tower information. I guess that's the stuff they said they'd send later."

Pete set his mug on the build-up of coffee stain rings and placed the pink notes next to his phone before picking up the report. He skimmed through the columns of numbers and codes, trying to make sense of it. Why was it that every time he'd had to get these things, the company redesigned them to make the needed information harder to decipher? What he wanted was the numbers she'd texted Thursday night while having dinner with the girls.

After several minutes of searching, he figured out why he was having so much trouble. There had been no texts exchanged that night. He flipped a page. No phone calls made or received either.

Pete looked at Seth. From the officer's expression, he'd seen that much already. "Why do I get the impression you've more than 'scanned them quick?'"

Seth shrugged. "I didn't go through each and every number listed. But I did check the night Mrs. Palmer died."

"Did you check anything else?"

"There were a bunch of incoming unanswered calls beginning Friday morning. A few texts too. All from the same number."

"Whose number?"

"That's the 'quick' part of my scan. I didn't check it yet."

"Probably the husband." Pete sipped his coffee. "Anything else?"

"Nope. Sorry. If the report had come in earlier, I'd have started tracing the numbers."

"Don't worry about it. Anything else happen overnight I should be aware of?"

"It was a quiet night. Everyone must have been at the fair."

If they were, the entire township was deaf this morning. Pete's ears still buzzed from the monster tractors, and he'd been wearing earplugs.

Seth pointed at the tray on the desk. "My report's in there."

"Thanks." Pete checked his watch. "It's after eight. Go home and get some sleep."

After booting his computer and dealing with the stack of pink notes, Pete turned his full attention to the list of numbers Vera had been in contact with in the days prior to her death. With a highlighter, he marked those that repeated. He turned to his PC and opened the reverse directory.

It didn't take long to verify that the number from Friday morning belonged to Jack. His number cropped up a few times every day, incoming and outgoing calls and texts to and from his wife. Pete had to work a little longer to track down the other repeating calls. Best friend Nell McDonald's number showed up a dozen times with the last call— an incoming one— placed Thursday afternoon.

On a whim, Pete picked up his phone and punched in the number. It went to voicemail without ringing. Slightly envious of anyone who could go on vacation and shut off their phones, he identified himself and asked her to call back, stating it was urgent.

He'd no sooner returned the phone to its cradle when it rang. He let Nancy take the call and continued to type numbers into the reverse directory.

The most frequently called number belonged to Children's Rehab

Institute in Pittsburgh. No surprise.

His intercom buzzed. "Call for you, Chief. Line one."

Pete started to tell her to take a message, but instead he asked, "Who is it?"

"Says his name is Cody DeRosa."

Mr. God's Gift to Women. "Thanks, Nancy. I've got it." He punched the blinking light and picked up, identifying himself.

"Chief Adams, this is Cody DeRosa. We met at the fair the other day."

"I remember." Pete tried to control his annoyance but wasn't sure he succeeded.

"I really need to talk to you."

"Okay. Talk."

"Not over the phone."

DeRosa's tone stirred Pete's curiosity. There was none of the arrogance of Sunday's encounter. If anything, he sounded frightened. "Can you give me some idea of what this is about?"

A pause. "I'd really rather save it until I can meet with you in person. Are you coming to the fair tonight to see Zoe?"

So the guy really was aware of their relationship. "Yeah."

"Good. I'll give you my phone number. Text me when you get there and tell me where you want to meet."

Pete jotted the number in his notebook. "I plan to be there by six."

"I'll see you then. And thanks."

DeRosa ended the call, leaving Pete perplexed. What the hell did Zoe's old "friend" from 4-H want to talk to him about that couldn't be discussed over the phone? Maybe the guy had seen too many cloak-and-dagger spy movies.

Pete shook his head and returned to the list of Vera's calls and texts, typing the frequently used numbers into the reverse directory. Like the Children's Rehab Institute, most weren't surprising. The remainder of the repeat calls were to or from her dinner companion friends, the 4-H leader, or assorted names matching her client list.

The one number he didn't find was Shane Tolland's. No calls. No texts. If he was responsible for Vera's stress a month ago, they hadn't communicated about it through her cell phone.

Pete turned his search to the few random calls and texts. Most belonged to local businesses—a car dealer's service department, an office supply store, a pizza shop.

There was one long distance number, a call placed by Vera two days before her death. He typed it in and clicked search. The name that popped up stopped Pete cold. According to the reverse directory, the number belonged to one Cody DeRosa.

TWENTY

"Tonight's the big night." Earl stepped down from the driver's side of Medic Ten's cab as Zoe slid from the passenger seat.

She slammed the door and looked around. They'd relocated the truck to the racetrack's infield, well clear of the area where the local districts' school buses would compete, but close enough for a fast response time. "Are the boys excited about the demo derby?"

Earl circled to her side and leaned back against the ambulance, crossing his arms. "Yeah. But honestly, I think Olivia's even more excited than they are."

She noticed the glint in her partner's eyes. "I think you might be more excited than all of them."

He broke into a broad smile. "Maybe. Probably. This is the first year I've gotten to see it. I hear it's a riot."

"It's fun. Different, you know? Slower paced than your normal demolition derby. But way louder." She thought back to the last time she'd been at the fair for the annual event celebrating the rivalry between local high schools in a way no sporting contest could. How long ago had it been? Five years? Six?

Dust rose from the expanse of bare ground where the competition would be held as two more dented and decorated yellow buses lumbered in. The display on the ambulance's dashboard had read 4:47 p.m. and ninety-one degrees, although with the humidity, it felt over a hundred. Zoe looked skyward. Billowing gray clouds crowded out the blue as they had the last three afternoons, teasing sweaty fair-goers with rain that hadn't fallen. If the heavens fulfilled their promise today, the derby could be taking place in a mud bog.

For the sake of the high school bands scheduled to perform first, Zoe hoped the rain held off.

A familiar young voice cut through the hubbub. "Daddy! Aunt Zoe!" Lilly raced toward them with her mother trailing.

Earl scooped her up and planted a kiss on his daughter's cheek. "Hey, Lills. What trouble have you and your mom been getting into?"

"Diane's been showing us ponies."

Olivia caught up and rolled her eyes. "I fear we've created a monster."

"I could've told you that," Zoe said. "Horses are like crack to little girls."

Earl tipped his head in her direction. "Big ones too."

"Guilty as charged."

Cody's offer floated to the surface of her mind again. Could she give up her horse? The farm? Dilapidated though it may be. How long before she grew uncomfortable living in town? She'd already suffered pangs of claustrophobia at Pete's house.

She loved Pete. But her biggest fear of all was growing resentful of him if she gave up her first passion.

No. Her biggest fear was of him growing resentful of her for not being able to give him what she knew he wanted.

"Where are the boys?" Earl asked his wife.

"Where do you think? If horses are crack to little girls, carnival games are the addiction of choice for our teenaged sons. We were on our way over here when we ran into that kid from the 4-H group. Luke? They all took off for the midway."

Earl set Lilly back on her feet. "Better than real drugs."

"True." Zoe gazed down the length of the track toward the colorful lights decorating the rides. "But Luke's mother ordered him to stay clear of there."

Olivia raised her hands in surrender. "I didn't know. Besides, I have enough to deal with keeping control over my own offspring." She grew serious. "Speaking of drugs, you don't think that Luke kid is…?"

Merryn's intoxicated behavior two days ago came to mind. "I honestly don't know," Zoe said. "But I do know your kids well enough to trust they wouldn't fall into that trap."

Olivia's brow furrowed. "I hope you're right." She and her husband exchanged a look—one of those wordless conversations Zoe had seen with other married couples. "Lilly, you want to stay with your dad and Zoe? I'm going to take a walk."

Lilly caught her mother's hand. "Where're you goin'?"

"*Not* back to the horse barn."

"Oh. Okay." Lilly summarily dismissed Olivia and turned back to her father. "Can I sit in the ambulance?"

Olivia and Earl exchanged another one of those looks before she headed off to make sure her sons weren't being lured into the narcotics trade.

He reached up to unlatch the rear doors of the truck. "You can sit on the jumpseat, but don't touch anything." To Zoe, he said, "We have more company."

She followed his gaze and spotted the Bassi clan—Rose, Allison, Logan, and Sylvia—crossing the racetrack and heading their way. Logan reached her first and drew her into a hug.

"Hey, kiddo." An unexpected knot tightened in Zoe's chest. "Good heavens, how tall are you now?"

He released her, grinning. "Six-three."

"Good lord." She looked at Rose. "What are you feeding him out in New Mexico?"

"Hatch green chiles," he said.

Zoe narrowed her eyes at him. "Green chiles won't make you grow that much."

Rose huffed a laugh. "They will when you make them into chile rellenos. And eat three of them in one sitting."

Zoe poked him in his rock-hard abs. "At some point, eating like that isn't gonna make you taller anymore."

He draped a lanky arm over her shoulder. "I'll worry about that when the time comes."

"How's Patsy doing?" Rose asked.

Before Zoe could answer, Allison rubbed her hands together. "If I had two cute guys fighting over me, I'd be doing great."

Logan chuckled. "Yeah, like that would ever happen."

"Shut up."

"Make me."

Rose groaned. "Stop it. Both of you."

"Some things never change," Zoe said with a laugh.

"What about Patsy?" Rose repeated.

Zoe rubbed her eyes, hoping they thought it was the dust making them water. "Patsy isn't speaking to me or to Shane."

"For heaven's sake, why?"

Sylvia fielded her question. "Because Shane acted like an ass yesterday."

Rose glared at her mother-in-law. "I knew that much." Turning back to Zoe, Rose asked, "But why isn't she speaking to you?"

Rather than delve into the topic of Cody and Windstar, Zoe shrugged. "Hard to tell."

Sylvia nudged Logan and Allison. "Come on, you two. I have no intention of standing out here in the heat for the next three hours. Let's go find something to eat. I'm buying."

Logan stepped away from Zoe. "Gram said the magic words. Mom? You comin'?"

Rose shooed him with a flip of her wrist. "I had a salad before we left." After the trio had headed back across the track, she grinned at Zoe. "I'm eating salad for every meal until the wedding if I'm gonna fit in my dress."

The *rat-a-tat-tat* of drums reverberated from the far end of the track. Zoe pointed. "The Battle of the Bands is getting ready to start."

Rose followed her gaze. "Great. You have just enough time to tell me why Patsy isn't speaking to you."

Pete checked his phone in case he'd missed the vibration signaling a new text. There was none. Dammit. DeRosa was the one who insisted they meet. Now he wasn't responding to the message Pete had sent him twenty minutes ago as he'd pulled into the fairground's parking lot.

When he lifted his gaze from his phone, he pulled up short to keep from plowing into Sylvia holding a cardboard container of fries.

"Don't you know better than to walk and text at the same time?"

Deciding the best defense was a good offense, he pointed at the fries. "That's not on your heart-healthy diet."

She scowled. Started to reply. Stopped. And started again. "These are for Logan."

"Liar."

Busted, she glowered at him. "I eat good ninety percent of the time. It's the fair for cryin' out loud."

"If that's the case, why are you eating french fries instead of funnel cake?"

From her guilty twinge, Pete surmised she'd either already had some or planned to before the night was over. She lifted her chin. "Why haven't you given Zoe that ring yet?"

Apparently, he wasn't the only one using the good-offense tactic. "The time hasn't been right."

"If you wait for the perfect moment to present itself, you'll die a lonely old bachelor. Just do it already."

A litany of excuses piled up inside his brain, jockeying for position...and he realized how lame they all sounded. For the first time in his life, he was grateful to spot Wayne Baronick walking up behind Sylvia.

Baronick gave Sylvia his patented blinding smile. "Good evening, Mrs. Bassi."

She shot him the same dirty look she'd given Pete a moment ago. "It *was*." Turning the look back on Pete, she said, "I'm not done with you." With a sniff, she wheeled and lumbered toward the grandstand.

Baronick watched her go. "I don't know what I ever did to her."

"Besides accusing her grandson of murder? I can't imagine."

"That was a couple years ago."

"She holds a grudge."

"So it would seem." Baronick brought his gaze back to Pete, gesturing to the phone he still held. "Expecting a call?"

He glanced down at the screen. No missed texts. "Someone asked to meet with me here."

"Something to do with the Palmer case?"

Pete thought of the call log from Vera's cell provider. "You could say that. By the way, I saw you chatting with Merryn Schultz last night. Learn anything?"

"That she likes me slightly less than Sylvia does."

"You have that effect on women."

Baronick snorted a laugh. "What about you? Did you find the unanswered question you were looking for?"

"Shane Tolland?" Pete scanned the swarms of folks heading in the same direction Sylvia had gone. "No. I'm still looking for him."

A crash of cymbals followed by the unmistakable rapid-fire beat of drums and the blare of tubas and trumpets wafted from the direction of the grandstand.

Baronick tipped his head toward it. "The high school marching band competition is well underway. I noticed Zoe and her ambulance are parked near the track this evening. You planning to join her?"

Pete had hoped to meet with DeRosa first. "Eventually. I'm going to make a pass around the horse barns looking for this guy who wants to talk."

"And your unanswered question?"

"Him too."

"Good luck. I'm sure we'll run into each other before the evening's over."

Pete watched the detective amble away, then looked at his phone. Again. Still nothing. He typed in, *I'm at the fairgrounds waiting to hear from you.* Pocketing the device, he started up the hill toward the Pony Barn.

Pete's patrol of the fairgrounds proved unfruitful. No Cody DeRosa. No Shane Tolland.

No text.

He did spot Merryn's son strolling through the midway with Earl's two boys. All three acknowledged him with a wave. Luke's appeared hesitant. Pete nodded to him. *Yes, I see you. Yes, I know your mother doesn't want you here. No, I'm not going to bust your chops over it.* The kid understood and gave him an appreciative grin.

By the time Pete shoehorned his way through the crowd—a pickpocket's dream—to the grandstand, the bands had completed their performances and were accepting their trophies. As Baronick had said, Zoe, Earl, and the EMS truck sat next to the track on the infield, at the ready to treat any injuries from this school bus demolition derby thing. Far from being all business, they had the rear of the rig open. Zoe and Rose sat on the edge of it, feet resting on the back bumper. Earl, his wife, and their daughter relaxed in folding lawn chairs set up next to the truck. Everyone was munching on either popcorn or nachos.

"Are you guys on standby or having a tailgate party?" Pete asked.

Zoe looked up from her popcorn and smiled. "I was afraid you were gonna miss the derby."

"It's all everyone's been talking about for the last two weeks. I wouldn't dare miss it." He leaned over to kiss her, glad to see her relaxed and—hopefully—happy to see him.

Rose slid closer to one side. Zoe scooted to the center of the doorway and patted the space they'd made. "Have a seat."

The storm clouds that threatened earlier had cleared, leaving a mostly blue sky. The sun had already dropped behind the hill, casting them in long shadows. It might turn out to be a nice evening for some entertainment.

Pete looked toward the end of the infield where he counted six graffitied school buses parked. Five more waited on the track for the second heat. Men and a few women scurried around the mostly yellow behemoths, some checking under the hoods, some climbing into the drivers' seats. One roared to life followed by another.

"Gentlemen, start your engines," Earl said.

Pete claimed the seat next to Zoe. "Olivia, aren't your boys going to watch their bus compete?"

"Oh, yeah. They'll be here. Like you said. They wouldn't dare miss it. Not after all the time we've put into our artwork."

"Artwork?" He studied the buses. Most of the "artwork" consisted of spray paint. Football players' names and numbers. Cartoonish renditions of school mascots. A few mild insults aimed at their opponents.

"Self-expression," Olivia said. "One kid's artwork is another man's graffiti. At least this way, they aren't vandalizing private property."

She had a valid point.

Over the next fifteen minutes or so, the rest of the drivers climbed into their rigs and the ground crews cleared out. The two Kolter boys jogged across the track to join the party and stretched out on a blanket their mother tossed onto the ground.

"Where's your friend?" Pete asked.

"Luke?" the older boy said. "I dunno."

"We asked him if he wanted to watch with us," the younger Kolter added, "but he said he had something better to do."

Pete hoped his "something better" involved staying clear of the midway. He checked his phone again.

Zoe nudged him. "You expecting a call?"

"No." He debated how much to share with her. "A text. Your friend Cody DeRosa called me earlier asking to meet here."

"What about?"

"He didn't say."

She grew pensive, gazing into the distance, but Pete had a feeling she wasn't looking at the buses or the lights of the midway. After a few moments, she said, "I think I might know."

"Oh?" Had DeRosa told her about his phone call to Vera?

"I told you about Shane blowing up at him during the horseshow yesterday."

"Yeah?"

"Well, Cody showed up last night with the start of a shiner."

"A black eye? I thought you said Shane only shoved him."

"He did. During the show. I have a feeling they had a rematch and things got more physical later on."

Pete mulled over a mental image of the two men going at it. Over Patsy? Or something else? Both knew Vera Palmer. "Have you seen Shane lately?"

"Not since yesterday when he helped Jack change Diane's flat."

"Not at all today?"

"No." Zoe rattled the almost empty popcorn box. "The only reason he was here at all was because of Patsy, and she's furious with him." Zoe paused, as if she wanted to say more.

But didn't.

TWENTY-ONE

Zoe had forgotten how noisy—and how much fun—school bus demo derby could be. Motors with many miles in their past—and not many more in their futures—roared as the graffitied yellow monstrosities lurched and careened into each other with grinding metallic explosions.

The Phillipsburg Blue Demons' entry was one of the first to drop out of the running when a bus from a cross-county rival thundered backwards into its front end. No amount of Olivia's students' artwork could save it from the crippling blow. With its engine laid bare, the Blue Demons' entry wheezed and choked. And died in a belch of smoke.

Adding insult to injury, another bus slammed into the disabled one from behind.

"I guess we now have a minibus," Aidan Kolter yelled over the racket.

"No," his younger brother said. "A compact."

"It's compacted, all right," Earl said before giving his wife's shoulder a consolation squeeze.

She feigned weeping into her hands. "All our hard work."

The remaining buses continued to rumble and crash into each other. Large, slow-moving bumper cars.

Zoe noticed Pete checking his phone for the third time. Why had Cody asked to meet with him? Did he want to file charges against Shane for assaulting him? It made sense. Except why wouldn't Cody contact the Brunswick City Police? Or Monongahela County Police? The fight had taken place here on the fairgrounds. At least she assumed so. And that placed it well out of Pete's jurisdiction.

Unless the black eye had nothing to do with the call.

Zoe hadn't mentioned Cody's offer to Pete yet. He'd probably be thrilled. Sell the horse. Put the farm on the market. Trade in her twenty-something-year-old truck for a more sensible car.

Sensible. All of it made perfect sense. Windstar would have a great home. She'd be freed from the financial burden of her money pit. And she wouldn't need a three-quarter-ton gas-guzzling pickup anymore. Her life would be different. But change wasn't necessarily bad.

Life with Pete definitely wasn't bad. Nor was the seventy-five hundred dollars Cody was willing to pay.

Zoe drew a long breath of diesel-infused night air. Tomorrow, she'd talk to Cody and accept his offer. She shot a glance at Pete who was again checking his phone. He'd be overjoyed with her news.

But she wanted to be the one to tell him. Not Cody.

A cheer went up from the grandstand. Zoe looked up to see what she'd missed. Only one bus continued to limp along, the others, crippled, mashed, and smoking. Mangled scraps of fenders, hoods, and bumpers lay scattered in the dirt. The announcer encouraged a round of applause for their winner, the Fort Franklin School District.

Tractors, bulldozers, and front loaders moved in to begin clearing the debris even before all the prizes had been handed out.

Rose hopped down from the back of the EMS truck. "Well, that was fun." She pulled out her phone and thumbed a text. "Now I need to track down my family."

"There's no rush," Zoe said. "It's gonna take you at least an hour to get to your car and out of the lot." She aimed a finger at the emptying grandstand. "Everyone's heading the same direction."

Olivia stretched. "You're right. We might as well hang out a little longer."

The boys scrambled to their feet. "Can we go play some games?"

"No. I don't want to have to round you up again. As soon as the crowd thins, we're going home."

Rose gave Zoe a hug. "Logan says he, Allison, and their grandma will meet me at the food court, so I'm outta here. Talk to you tomorrow."

Pete stuffed his phone back in his pocket. "I guess I should head home too. I have cats to feed." He winked at her.

"How are Jade and Merlin?" At least her tabbies didn't care where they lived as long as they got fed and had their litter boxes cleaned.

"They miss sleeping with you." Pete slipped an arm around her waist, drew her close, and whispered into her hair, "So do I."

The rush of heat didn't stop at her cheeks. "The feeling's mutual."

A frantic shout rose above the machinery noise surrounding the wrecked school buses.

Zoe stepped away from Pete and turned toward the activity. "That doesn't sound good."

More raised voices joined the first, and one by one, the tractors and bulldozers fell silent.

Earl came around to the rear of the ambulance to shut the patient compartment doors. "I bet someone got cut on some of the scrap metal. Better get ready to stop some bleeding."

The workers, who'd been clearing debris, scurried toward a single bus.

Zoe headed for the passenger door. "Let's drive over there and see what's going on."

"I'll meet you there." Pete had taken two steps in the direction of the melee when a man in bibbed overalls appeared, jogging toward the ambulance and waving.

"Help!"

Zoe leapt into the truck's cab. Earl climbed into the driver's seat. From her window, she spotted Olivia gathering the kids, blankets, and chairs.

Earl wheeled Medic Ten around and flipped on the emergency lights. He slowed as they drew alongside Pete, who'd broken into an uneven lope. Zoe powered down her window. "Climb in!"

He waved them on.

Tough guy. Too proud to admit he was hurting.

Earl slowed again as they approached the guy in the bibs.

"What's the problem?" Zoe called to him.

He flailed an arm toward the buses and the cleanup crew who had gathered around one of them. "Back of...Maple Grove...bus," he replied, struggling to catch his breath. "A man...*dead.*"

* * *

The heavy machinery had fallen quiet and all the workers milled around the rear of one badly mangled school bus. Pete phoned in a report of a dead body to county dispatch and placed a request for backup. He strode toward the group. "Police. Clear the area."

Zoe and Earl were ahead of him, elbowing their way through the crowd.

"Move aside. Please." Pete waded into the sea of looky-loos. "*Police.* Clear the rear of the bus. But please don't leave the area." Backup better show up soon. He needed to make sure any potential witnesses—or worse—stuck around.

The onlookers reluctantly stepped back, allowing Zoe, Earl, and Pete access.

The Maple Grove School District's bus had taken a hard hit—probably several hard hits—to the back end, driving what was left of the emergency entrance forward, halfway to the rear axle. The last few men standing at what would have been the back bumper, if it hadn't been ripped off by another bus, parted.

At first glance, Pete saw nothing but a jumble of bench seats, ripped from their moorings. Then he spotted a cowboy boot protruding from the wreckage.

Climbing in through the jagged metal would be challenging at best. He'd have to circle around to the passenger door. Except when he looked toward it, he spotted a pair of curious onlookers standing inside the front of the bus, peering in Pete's direction. Dammit. Where was the crowd control he'd requested?

"Get out of the bus," he ordered. He turned to Earl, who stood behind him with Zoe. "I need to get in there. Keep everyone back while I go through the front."

Zoe edged in front of Earl. "No," she said. "I'm the one who needs to go in there."

Pete gave her a look he hoped said *ain't no way.*

"I'm the deputy coroner. And the paramedic. We assume he's dead, but what if he's still alive? Besides, you need to stay out here to control the scene."

Dammit. He hated when she made sense.

"Give me a leg up," Zoe said.

He looked at the mangled steel and then at her. "Seriously?

"Seriously." She raised one bent knee.

He'd boosted her onto her horse's bare back a number of times. But never a bus. Especially a wrecked one. "Be careful of the sharp edges." He leaned down, cupped her shin in both hands, and hoisted her.

She landed lightly on the exposed frame of the bus and picked her way through the gaping emergency doorway and around the pile of seats. Earl nudged Pete aside and reached in to set a large duffel and a Maglite on the floor. She picked up and clicked on the flashlight, aiming the beacon toward the body. Moving deliberately, Zoe reached down, and Pete knew she was checking for a pulse. Balancing the big flashlight on one of the bus seats beside her, she slipped a penlight from the pocket of her tactical trousers and leaned over the body. A flick of the tiny beam as she checked his pupils.

Even in the shadows, Pete saw her muscles tighten.

Seconds ticked off. She straightened but kept her back to him as she dug in the duffel, coming up with a blood oxygen meter. Pete had seen her and other paramedics use the finger clip gizmos as the final indicator of life or death.

She again bent over the victim. Moments later, she sat up. No sense of urgency. No rushing to begin resuscitation efforts. But she didn't face them or say anything.

"Zoe?" Pete said.

Her shoulders rose and fell, and he heard her exhale.

She half-turned, not quite looking at him. "He's deceased," she said, her voice husky.

"Do you know who it is?"

She lifted her gaze to meet his. "It's Cody DeRosa."

Zoe didn't recognize him at first. Not until she'd leaned down and hit his lifeless eyes with her penlight. Even then it took a moment. His face looked like it had taken the brunt of the impact, leaving the black eye as the least of his injuries. She hadn't yet examined his head but could tell it wasn't right. The term "compressed skull fracture" flitted through her mind.

"You gonna be okay?" Pete's question filtered through the noise inside her head.

She balanced on an unsteady, tilted vinyl bench seat gazing down at Cody's misshapen body sprawled on the floor beneath her. "Yeah."

"Do you want me to call Franklin?" Earl asked.

She swallowed. "Please. And get my camera."

Earl ducked away. Pete leaned in as much as he could without touching the ripped steel. "You should come out of there."

The whoop and wail of sirens in the distance signaled backup was on the way.

"No." She looked down at Cody again. "I'll stay in here until Franklin arrives. As soon as Earl brings my camera, I can start taking pictures."

"Do you want me in there to help?"

More of her death scene investigation classes—and Franklin's griping—echoed in her brain. "No. The more people, the more contamination."

Pete glanced around. "I think that ship's sailed."

"Not in here. Not yet."

"*Move away from the bus,*" Wayne Baronick's familiar voice boomed from outside.

For a moment, she thought he meant Pete, but a glance out of the glassless window revealed the workers continued to press in, some on tiptoes, trying to get a glimpse.

Wayne appeared next to Pete. "What do we have?"

"Deceased male," Pete said.

"Got an ID?"

"Cody DeRosa." Pete gestured at Zoe. "An old friend of hers."

Wayne caught her gaze. "I'm sorry."

From his expression, he was more curious about the "old friend" comment than anything else. But she was grateful he didn't ask.

Wayne turned and surveyed the scene. "We are never gonna find any useable evidence around here."

"You think?" Pete said, oozing sarcasm. He tipped his head toward the crowd. "We need to make sure no one leaves before we have a chance to talk to them. Find out what they've seen."

They moved away from the door to discuss a plan of action, leaving Zoe alone with the body. Cody's body.

Along with the damage to his skull, the rest of his body had clearly sustained considerable trauma. Even through his filthy jeans and dusty, rumpled jacket, she spotted at least two fractures. An arm bent at a spot where there wasn't a joint. A leg torqued at an unnatural angle.

What had happened to him? Was the damage done by the bus-against-bus collisions? What had he been doing in here? Hiding? Caught unaware? Could Cody's death be nothing more than a tragic accident? Possibly.

Or was that what his killer had hoped everyone would believe? Had he been killed elsewhere and placed in the bus to camouflage the crime?

Definitely more likely.

She looked at the gaping hole where the emergency door had been and thought of Pete giving her a boost to get in. No way could Shane—or anyone else—hoist a body in that way even prior to the destruction caused by the derby. She turned toward the front and closed her eyes against the image that cropped up.

Shane dragging the limp body of Cody DeRosa. The bunching of his jacket around his armpits was consistent with having been dragged by his boots.

Except how had Shane—or anyone—dragged a dead body into the bus without being seen? Cody wasn't a small man.

She opened her eyes and shone the light on the dark shimmer coating Cody's head and face and pooled on the floor. No. If he'd already been dead when he was dumped, there wouldn't be this volume of blood, even with the violent hits the bus had taken.

Somehow, Cody had walked onto the bus alive. With his killer. And only one of them walked off.

Earl returned, lugging the evidence-collection bag Franklin had given her. "Here you go."

She shook her head to chase the image away and stretched to take the bag from her partner. "Did you reach Franklin?"

"He's on his way."

"Good." She set the bag next to her, dug out the camera, and aimed the Maglite at it to check the settings and turn on the flash.

She'd spotted the pond of blood when she'd first climbed in the bus and had avoided stepping in it. Now she swept the light around to see where she *could* step...what she could touch...without disturbing the evidence.

The beam revealed a smear of crimson in the aisle. She looked closer. No footprints. The killer had dragged Cody—dead or dying—from the front of the bus but hadn't walked through the blood to get back out. Either he'd climbed over the seats or jumped from the rear emergency door. In order to avoid adding her own boot prints to the scene, she had the same two choices.

"What do you need?" Earl asked.

"Out. Without contaminating the crime scene." And without being sliced open by the sharp edges.

He held up his arms. "Jump."

The potential outcomes flitted through her mind. Both of them sprawled on the ground with her hemorrhaging from having severed a limb. She looked toward the front of the bus. "No. I'm gonna climb over the seats."

"Suit yourself."

At least the seatbacks were padded. She slung the evidence bag's strap over her shoulder and shone the flashlight on each bench before swinging a leg over. Paused every few seats to take stock of her surroundings. The blood smear on the floor seemed to grow thicker as she neared the front. About six rows from the driver's seat, she stopped when the beam revealed spatter on the front of the seat back. She looked down at her boot planted on the bench. And on more spatter.

"Crap," she muttered. So much for not leaving any part of herself on the crime scene. Before advancing farther, she shot a photo of her foot. She counted and jotted a note. Seven rows from the front on the side opposite the driver's seat.

She raised the beam. The seats across the row were also speckled with blood. And perched brim-down, a silver belly cowboy hat. She raised the light to the ceiling. A burst of spatter stood out against the white paint. Without moving her foot, she leaned toward the aisle and shined the Maglite on the floor.

The smear ended—or began—here in a shimmering thick puddle.

Zoe lifted her camera and fired off a series of shots. First, a wider-angle view of the front for orientation purposes. Then she zoomed in on the floor. The ceiling. The seat across from her. With Cody's hat.

Brim down.

She thought about the old adage about always placing a cowboy hat brim up, so the luck wouldn't run out.

Right here on this spot, Cody DeRosa's luck had done just that.

TWENTY-TWO

Pete and Baronick corralled the cleanup crew and drivers next to another mangled bus. It occurred to Pete that they should check it for a body too. But until backup arrived, the best they could do was control and contain.

The phrase *herding cats* came to mind.

The sirens grew louder. He looked toward the road fronting the fairgrounds where a steady stream of head- and taillights snaked from the parking lot. Vehicles filled with tired and happy families who had no idea that watching a man die had been included in the evening's entertainment.

A trio of squad cars roared into view, slowed, and made the turn through the front gate. The going would be slow the rest of the way as they negotiated the dwindling crowds still lined up to play the midway's carnival games.

"Help's on the way," Baronick said.

Hopefully someone in this group of workers had seen something. Even if they weren't aware of it. The area immediately surrounding the bus had been trampled by the onlookers gawking at DeRosa's body. Not to mention the havoc the colliding vehicles wreaked on this end of the infield. Physical evidence would be impossible to find. Unless Zoe discovered something inside.

Another emergency vehicle, a dark van, trailed the squad cars through the front gate. Pete recognized it as the County Coroner's meat wagon.

The rumble of a different kind of motor drew Pete's attention away from the approaching red and blue strobes. A dark-colored four-wheeled utility vehicle bounced toward them, coming from the direction of the grandstand. In the hazy glow of the overhead lights,

Pete made out three men—security guards—crammed in the thing. "We can put these guys on crowd control."

A flash from inside the bus caught Pete's attention. Zoe was photographing the interior.

Baronick elbowed Pete. "She's handy to have around."

"You'll get no argument from me."

The cruisers, two from county and one from the City of Brunswick, rolled across the racetrack and through the gap in the infield rail, braking to a stop and raising a cloud of dust. The coroner's van parked beside them.

On the other side of the bus containing Cody DeRosa, the UTV rumbled to a stop, and two security guards in ill-fitting uniforms stepped out. The third guy, wearing a suit and tie, climbed out awkwardly, as if he'd never ridden in such a contraption before. He reached into the bed and pulled out some kind of bag.

Pete directed the two rent-a-cops toward the workers, ordering them to keep the group contained and to keep them from talking amongst themselves any more than they already had. Eyewitness statements were unreliable enough when they hadn't been diluted by what they'd overheard others say.

Baronick handled the county and city cops, setting up a plan to pull the workers and bus drivers aside one at a time and take their statements.

Pete limped over to them. The jog across the uneven ground hadn't done his leg any favors. "Ask if they took any photos before and during the derby. We'll need those."

Baronick raised his voice, aiming it at the group. "Which one of you drove this bus?" He pointed to their crime scene on wheels.

One scrawny arm rose.

The detective waved at the guy as if motioning traffic to keep moving. "You're with me."

Franklin Marshall trudged toward them, toting a larger version of the duffel Zoe used. "Where's the body?"

Pete fell into step beside him. "In the bus. With Zoe."

"Anyone else go near him?"

"Depends on your definition of 'near.' Zoe's the only one who's been inside with him." Pete glanced toward Baronick and the bus driver. "As far as we know."

"Good."

"You should use the front door." Pete had no intention of giving Marshall a leg up.

The coroner looked toward the bus and pulled up short. "Son of a bitch."

Pete followed his gaze.

Zoe stood in the front doorway, her arms crossed. The man in the suit who'd ridden in with the security guards stood outside. Neither looked happy.

Marshall launched forward. "What the hell are you doing here, Davis?"

The man in the suit turned, his chest puffed. "That's *Doctor* Davis, *Mister* Marshall. And I'm here to make sure you and your wannabe detective don't muck up the investigation."

Zoe had spotted Dr. Davis' approach and clambered over the front rows of bus seats as quickly as she could without destroying any more blood evidence. At the door, she blocked the pathologist's entry, never before so grateful to see Franklin arrive.

He and Dr. Davis stood toe-to-toe, one cool and defiant, the other defensive and furious.

She caught Pete looking at her and read the question on his face. She gave him a nod. Yep. *That* Dr. Davis. The one whose political signs outnumbered Franklin's by a wide margin. The one who'd been in the local news for months touting the need for a true medical examiner to bring Monongahela County out of the dark ages.

The one who, if elected, would put her out of her second job as deputy coroner. A job for which she'd developed an affinity. Maybe even a passion.

"You do realize your being here risks contaminating the crime scene," Franklin told his political adversary. "My crime scene."

"I'm only here to help." Dr. Davis straightened his already perfect tie. "I'm sure the victim, were he able, would want a professional around to make sure his death would be thoroughly and efficiently investigated."

"And it will be. As soon as you get the hell outta here."

"How can you say it will be when you have a rank amateur in there with the body?" He aimed a raised hand toward Zoe.

Rank amateur?

"Zoe Chambers is more than qualified."

She made a mental note to thank Franklin as soon as the interloper left.

"Because she's had a few hours of training? And how many hours have you had, Mr. Marshall? Would you like to know how many years of formal education I've had to earn my degree?"

Franklin took another step closer to Davis. For a moment, Zoe feared Franklin was going to deck the guy, in spite of the fact that Davis outweighed him by at least fifty pounds.

Davis must have thought the same thing. He took a step back.

"Until the good people of this county vote you into office, your degree means nothing here. I'm the elected coroner. She's my deputy. And you, sir, are impeding our investigation. Now, must I ask this law enforcement officer here to have you removed?" Franklin gestured over his shoulder to Pete. "Or do you prefer to leave of your own volition?"

The artificial lighting gave everyone the same grayish coloring, but Zoe would have bet Dr. Davis glowed crimson.

His thin lips pressed into an even thinner line. "You're a fool, Marshall. I could provide a level of professional assistance you'd not receive from anyone else."

The two men glared at each other in silence. Davis probably expected Franklin to change his mind. *Oh, of course you're right. Please take over our case because we're totally inept.*

Didn't happen.

Pete edged closer to stand behind Franklin.

Davis' eyes flitted from the coroner to the cop. To the coroner. "Fine." Back to the cop. "Could you ask my chauffeurs to give me a ride back to the exhibit hall?"

Pete placed his hands on his hips in the same take-charge stance Zoe had seen a million times. "If you mean the security police, they're busy."

Davis looked like he wanted to kick something. A rock. A puppy. Instead, he wheeled and stormed off toward the grandstand.

Franklin's thin shoulders sagged. He turned to Pete. "Thank you."

"Just doing my job."

The coroner shrank even more. "Yes, but your job may have you working with that man on a daily basis in the very near future."

Pete left Marshall and Zoe to process the body in the bus and joined Baronick, who was barking orders to the growing legion of law enforcement. Cruisers from additional local jurisdictions joined the first responders, and the numbers of red and blue strobes expanded along the racetrack and into the infield with more arriving by the minute. Flashes of distant lightning joined the emergency beacons. Pete hoped the storm went around them. The crime scene unit already had their work cut out for them without a downpour turning the dirt infield into a muddy quagmire.

"Where do you need me?" Pete asked Baronick.

"Wanna join me while I question the driver?"

"I thought you'd already talked to him."

"Nah. I only put him on ice until I could rally my troops."

Baronick led the way to a City of Brunswick Interceptor where one of the city uniforms had been assigned to sequester the bus driver. The detective opened the back door of the sedan and motioned for the guy to step out. He reminded Pete of a scarecrow. Bibbed overalls hanging on bone-thin shoulders. A shock of straw-like hair sticking out from under a John Deere ball cap.

"What's your name?" Baronick asked.

"Bob Widmer," he said and spelled his last name.

"And you were driving the bus where the body was found?"

Even in the shadows cast by the overhead lighting, Pete could see the guy's Adam's apple rise and fall. "Yes, sir."

"Why were you driving that particular bus?"

"I work for Maple Grove School District as a bus driver. A couple of us wanted to do it, but I've done regular demolition derbies before, so they picked me." He lowered his head. "I wish like hell they'd picked someone else."

"Did you know Cody DeRosa?"

Bob's head came up. "Is that the dead guy?"

Baronick didn't answer.

Bob must have taken the silence as a yes. "No. I never heard of him before."

Pete believed him.

"When you got on the bus this evening, did you check it?" Baronick asked. "Do a walk-through to make sure it was empty?"

The driver's eyes glistened. "No. I wish I had. But, I mean, who in their right mind hides in the back of a demo derby bus?"

"You didn't notice him in the rearview mirror?"

Bob shook his head.

Pete crossed his arms. "You didn't notice the blood when you first got on the bus?"

"Blood?" Bob's eyes widened. "You mean...he was dead...before the derby?"

Pete didn't reply. Neither did Baronick.

Bob's narrow shoulders sagged. His gaze darted from the two cops to the ground and back. "I was driving around with a dead guy the whole time?"

Baronick leaned a hip against the car's front fender. "That's what we're trying to find out."

Bob shook his head so hard Pete's neck hurt. "I didn't see a thing. I swear. I didn't notice any blood. But I wasn't looking for it either. It was already getting dark before I got ready to drive the bus." He pointed upward toward the halogens. "And those things didn't exactly light up the inside."

"You didn't have interior lights?"

His laugh was almost a sob. "They don't work." He looked around toward the other mangled buses. "These derby buses are pretty well stripped down."

Pete tapped his pen on his notebook. "What time did you arrive here at the fairgrounds?"

Bob thought about it a moment, his face relaxing. "A little after two."

"Did you happen to check the interior of the bus then? When it was still daylight?"

Bob's face brightened. "Yes. And I can tell you for sure there wasn't anyone on it then. Dead or alive."

"Who else was around when you arrived?"

Bob's unfocused eyes shifted over Pete's shoulder. "A couple of the other drivers. A few bus mechanics. Oh, and there were some kids riding horses over in the show ring. A couple of parents watching them." The driver half-turned and looked toward the mass of police vehicles with their emergency lights creating constantly changing patterns of blue and red across the grounds. "There was a man and woman over there having a big fight."

Pete followed Bob's gaze. "Over where?"

"Across the track. Between it and the rides. I remember thinking it was funny. The woman was reading the guy the riot act, screeching so loud I could hear her over all the other sounds."

"What was she yelling about?"

"Oh, hell, I don't know. I was over here. Too far away to make out what she said."

"Could you recognize them?" Baronick asked. "Was the man our victim?"

Bob scowled. "I dunno. He had his back to me. And besides, I never saw the dead guy."

Before the detective could ask his next question, Pete held up his pen and aimed it toward the midway. "Was the man wearing a cowboy hat?"

"No. I'd remember that."

Baronick looked annoyed. "Probably has nothing to do with our homicide."

"Probably." But on a hunch, Pete asked, "What'd the woman look like?"

"Kinda average, I guess. White-blonde hair. I remember that. But otherwise, I wasn't paying attention. Just noticed because she was so loud." Bob glanced from Pete to Baronick. "And like you said, it didn't have anything to do with this. Right?"

"Right." Except Pete couldn't shake the image of a very blonde Merryn Schultz in full rant mode. He caught Baronick's gaze, and from his expression, suspected he'd made the same connection.

The detective tapped a note into his phone as he picked up the interview. "Were you in or around your bus the whole time?"

"No. Me and some of the other guys took off to check out the fair."

He gave a nervous chuckle. "Reckoned we got in for free. Might as well take advantage, you know?"

"Did you lock your bus?"

Bob choked a laugh. "What the hell was there to steal?"

"I take that as a 'no.'" Baronick looked at Pete.

There might not have been anything of value to steal. But a wide-open bus, hours from demolition, made a perfect place to hide a body and cover a murder.

Pete and Baronick turned Bob loose with their business cards tucked in his wallet and orders to contact them if he thought of anything else.

"We need to put out a call for photos." Pete gazed at the assembled potential witnesses, some being interviewed by various officers, others waiting their turns.

"I was thinking the same thing. And not just these guys. Everyone who was in attendance tonight."

"I bet there were a lot of students and parents milling around the buses, taking pictures of the paint jobs. Probably posting on social media."

"I'll get in touch with the schools and have one of my men check out Instagram and Snapchat." Baronick squinted up at the lights. "Don't suppose they have security cameras around this place."

"I've seen them over in the new exhibit halls. Not over here."

"Figures."

"I spotted a reporter and photographer from the newspaper on the grounds earlier. I bet they got some shots."

Baronick tapped a note into his phone. "I'll call the paper."

Pete thought of the near capacity crowd watching the school buses. Before that, the Battle of the Bands. Mostly high school kids and their families. Viewing the action on the screens of their phones. Somewhere out there, someone had to have captured an image of Cody DeRosa.

And his killer.

TWENTY-THREE

Zoe stood shoulder to shoulder with Wayne, watching Franklin and Doc Abercrombie dissect Cody DeRosa. The external examination had confirmed what she already suspected. Fractures of the ulna and radius bones of both arms, the tibia of his right leg. The autopsy revealed multiple compressed fractures of his skull along with several broken ribs.

"Did anyone get the number of the bus that hit this guy?" Doc asked.

"I think there were several," Franklin replied dryly.

Zoe nudged Wayne with an elbow. "Any leads?"

"Not yet. The Brunswick newspaper's supposed to email me the photos their guy shot yesterday. We've put out a call on social media for anyone who attended the band competition or the demo derby last night to send us their pictures."

She looked at him. "Do you realize how many photos you're gonna have to sort through?"

"That's why I'm assigning three of our rookies to the job."

"You're evil." Zoe turned her gaze back to the body on the stainless-steel table and remembered the rapscallion with the dimples. Remembered him years ago as her competitor and crush. Always in a cowboy hat. Always smiling. Always flirting. Had that flirting gotten him killed?

"What?" Wayne said.

She blinked. "Huh?"

"The look on your face. Do you know who might've wanted him dead?"

"When did you start reading minds?"

"Doesn't take any psychic skills in this case. You were friends with the guy."

"Not really."

Wayne hiked an eyebrow.

"Acquaintances is more like it."

"You're avoiding the question. Who might have wanted to kill your 'acquaintance?'"

She hadn't seen Shane since he and Jack changed Diane's flat tire. As of earlier this morning, neither had Patsy.

"Well?" Baronick said. "You've still got that look on your face."

"Cody pissed off a lot of people. Especially husbands and boyfriends."

"Like Pete?"

She glared at the detective. "Cody liked to flirt."

"With you?"

She wasn't about to play this game. "With most women."

"Who in particular were you thinking about just now? And don't try to deny it."

Patsy was going to kill her for throwing her boyfriend—ex-boyfriend—under the not-so-proverbial bus. "Shane Tolland."

"Vera Palmer's disgruntled customer?"

"I don't know about disgruntled. But a client. Yeah."

"And you said he dates your cousin."

"Did. Past tense." Zoe told Wayne about the shoving incident at the show ring two days ago. "Then Cody showed up later with a black eye."

"Courtesy of Tolland?"

"That would be my guess."

Wayne fell silent. He dug out his phone and tapped in a note. "Anyone else take offense at DeRosa paying too much attention to their girl? Besides Pete, I mean."

Zoe still refused to fall prey to Wayne's trap. "Not to the point of punching him, let alone killing him."

"Okay. Let's look at the other side of the coin. Were there any women who might resent his attention to *other* women?"

The question pulled Zoe up short. "You mean someone he was seeing?"

Wayne shrugged. "Maybe. Or a woman who wanted to be his one-

and-only and didn't appreciate his wandering eye."

"You think a woman might have done this?"

He shrugged again. "Why not?"

"Someone dragged him from near the front of the bus all the way to the rear. He's not a small guy. I don't think a woman would have the strength."

Wayne looked at her askance. "Who is it who keeps telling me she kicks a thousand-pound horse's ass and could take me down with no problem?"

She recognized her own words and winced.

"We're talking about a fairground full of farmgirls who wrestle with horses and cows," Wayne said, "not about a bunch of princesses who're afraid of breaking a fingernail."

He had a point. Zoe rolled the last several days—her encounters with Cody—over in her mind. And landed on the one woman she'd seen hang on the cowboy's arm, only to have him shrug her off. "I can't imagine she'd do this." Zoe nodded at the body.

"Let me be the judge. Who?"

"Merryn Schultz. The three of us—her, Cody, and me—were all in 4-H together when we were kids."

Deep furrows creased Baronick's forehead. "And she had her sights set on him?"

"She had her sights set on just about everyone." Zoe eyed the detective. "Everyone who wasn't a cop. I saw you talking to her and Jack the other night."

"Yeah. I'm *acquainted* with her." Baronick grinned, apparently pleased to again throw Zoe's words back at her. His grin faded. "About her and DeRosa. Was there any special connection between them that you're aware of?"

"Not really."

"Did they date back in their 4-H days?"

"I don't remember. Probably. They ran with a different group than I did. Both had really good horses. They took turns winning. It's very likely they dated."

Baronick thumbed another note into his phone. "Anyone else?"

"Nope. Sorry."

Zoe gazed at Doc's and Franklin's backs but sensed Baronick's eyes on her.

"What about you?" he asked.

"What do you mean? I didn't kill him." She shot him a smug look. "I was on duty and have witnesses."

"I didn't mean that. Did you and the victim date back in the day?"

"No." Even to her own ears, she said it too fast. She caught the questioning look he was giving her. "No," she repeated. And she wasn't about to admit she'd wanted to. She refused to meet Wayne's gaze but knew he was still watching her.

"Why do I get the feeling there's more than you're telling me?" he said.

She pictured Cody at dinner Monday evening. The dimples. The business proposition. Then later in the barn with the black eye. And something he'd said. "He offered to buy my horse."

"And you turned him down?"

"No. I didn't."

"Really?" Wayne's shocked tone drew the attention of Franklin and Doc.

Zoe motioned to them. *Never mind.* Once they returned to their autopsy, she said, "I didn't accept either. I was thinking about it."

"I'm...shocked."

"You aren't the only one."

"Pete?"

"I haven't mentioned it to him yet."

"Who then?"

"Patsy. But here's the thing. Cody made the offer Monday evening at dinner. Then he came to the barn later—which is when I noticed the black eye—and told me something had come up and he needed to leave earlier than planned."

"Did he say what?"

"No. I didn't think anything of it at the time. But now..."

Wayne fell silent, and for a minute or two, the only sounds were Franklin's and Doc's low murmurs.

The detective tapped something into his phone. "How did your cousin react to you thinking about selling your horse?"

"Not well. She hasn't said more than five words to me since she found out."

Wayne made a noise in his throat.

Zoe looked at him. "What?"

"Nothing."

She didn't believe him, but before she could prod, Franklin turned to them. "Well, Detective, even without Dr. Davis' *expertise,*" he said with more than a note of bitter sarcasm, "I can tell you this. You definitely have a homicide to investigate."

Pete's thigh ached worse than usual, a sign, he'd learned in recent months, of changing weather. Perhaps today, they'd finally get rain.

In the Vance Township Police Station's conference room, he drew an angry vertical slash down the center of the whiteboard. On the left side, he scrawled Vera Palmer. On the right, Cody DeRosa. Two totally unrelated deaths?

No damned way.

The bells on the front door jangled. Through the open door, he heard Nancy direct the visitor in his direction. A moment later, Baronick strode in, a cup of Starbucks in each hand.

Pete was making progress in his attempts to train the detective.

Baronick handed one of the cups to Pete and lowered into a chair. "Cause of death was multiple blunt-force trauma to DeRosa's skull." Baronick leaned back, crossed an ankle over one knee, and took a long hit from his own cup.

"Nothing earth shattering there." Pete inhaled the aroma and sipped.

"According to Doc Abercrombie, both arms were broken perimortem. The rest of the injuries occurred post mortem."

"Still not surprising. Zoe told me about the blood trail inside the bus. Any insights about the murder weapon?"

"Some kind of pipe. Franklin said probably heavy. The killer delivered four blows to the skull. The injuries to the arms were made by the same weapon."

"Defensive wounds."

"Yep. Someone used DeRosa for some serious batting practice." Baronick tipped his head toward the whiteboard. "You think there's a link?"

"Don't you?" Pete didn't wait for a response. He scribbled the words *horses and 4-H* under Vera's name and drew an arrow to DeRosa's half of the board.

"That's a pretty broad connection. If you're reaching that far, you might as well add that they both died of head injuries."

"All right." Pete scrawled *head injuries* with another arrow.

"I was kidding."

He ignored the detective and started adding to Vera's list. *Phone call to DeRosa.* He drew an arrow and under DeRosa's name wrote *Lied about not knowing Vera.*

"What's that about?"

"He told me he'd never met Vera Palmer. If that's true, why'd she call him two days before her death?"

Baronick didn't have an answer, so Pete returned to the board. Under Vera's name, he added *Last seen at Parson's Roadhouse.* Next, he listed names. *Jack Palmer, husband.* The women who dined with Vera the night she died. He marked a star next to Nell McDonald and made a mental note to call Chuck in Maui and find out if he'd had any luck tracking down Vera's best friend.

Pete added Merryn Schultz and her son, Luke Holmes, to the list with an arrow.

"Merryn, I get." Baronick squinted at the board. "Sort of. But why the kid?"

"Vera was supposed to keep an eye on him this week. Maybe he resented it." Pete wasn't convinced, but until he ruled these people out, he intended to keep them on his radar. "And why only 'sort of' for Merryn?" He held up one finger. "She had the hots for Vera's husband and for DeRosa." Pete held up a second finger. "Neither man exhibited any interest in her." A third finger. "She changes her stories more than she changes her socks." A fourth finger. "Jack Palmer told me Vera and Merryn had a confrontation about a month ago." Pete added his thumb. "And she has access to drugs. I have no problem imagining her slipping something into Vera's drink."

"No argument there. What I can't see is her beating the crap out of DeRosa."

"Crime of passion?" Pete shrugged. "She stays. So does the link."

"Fine. Why link the kid to both victims?"

"4-H. Horses."

Baronick shook his head.

Pete added one more name. Shane Tolland. With an arrow.

The detective shifted in his chair, sitting taller. "You might want to put a star next to that one. I heard he gave our second victim a shiner."

"Yeah." Pete gazed at the name. "DeRosa called me yesterday."

"You neglected to tell me that."

"We were busy. I knew about the black eye and assumed he wanted to file a complaint, although I wasn't sure why he contacted *me* about it."

"You were looking for Tolland the other night. Did you ever find him?"

"Nope. He hasn't returned any of my phone calls, and he's not posted on any of his social media pages either." Seemed like everyone who might have answers had vanished. "Maybe he's with Nell McDonald in Maui," Pete said under his breath.

"What?"

"Nothing."

Baronick uncrossed his legs. "I have one problem with Tolland as DeRosa's killer."

"Oh?"

"We believe DeRosa was alive when he got on the bus. Why the hell would he willingly go anywhere alone with someone who'd already assaulted him?"

A genuine concern, but it only made Pete question the "willingly" and "alone" part of the scenario.

Baronick pushed up from the chair, crossing to Pete's side. He held out a palm and wiggled his fingers.

Pete handed him the marker. "You have something you'd like to add?"

"Yeah." Baronick stepped over to DeRosa's side of the board.

Pete couldn't see what he wrote until he stepped out of the way.

Patsy Greene.

"Zoe's cousin? You're kidding."

The detective didn't show any signs of humor.

"Why?"

"She's upset."

"About the fight between her boyfriend and DeRosa? She's upset with Tolland. Not DeRosa."

"That's not it." Baronick grew pensive. Pete thought he was going to have to prod the detective, but Baronick inhaled and said, "DeRosa offered to buy Zoe's horse."

The statement swirled in Pete's brain like sugar in a glass of iced tea. Not dissolving. Not making sense. Spinning. And drifting to settle in the base of his skull. "She said no, right?"

Baronick shook his head. "She was thinking about it. Pretty seriously if I'm any judge. And Patsy wasn't pleased."

No, she wouldn't be. If Zoe was thinking about selling her horse, she was also thinking about selling that money pit of a farm her mother had given her. And if she was thinking about selling the farm, she must be planning to stay with him. Permanently. Pete's gaze drifted to the hall, but his mind made it all the way to his office, his desk, and the little burgundy box in the drawer. Zoe making her home with him was exactly what he wanted.

But not at the cost of giving up a part of herself.

Baronick's hand on Pete's shoulder jarred him back to the conference room. "You okay?"

"I'm fine."

"Because you got awfully pale there for a minute."

"I said I'm fine." He looked at Patsy's name on the whiteboard. "You can take her off. She's not a murderer."

Baronick capped the pen. "She stays. You get to add your choices to the suspect list. I get to add mine."

A knock at the open conference room door drew Pete's attention. Nancy stood in the hallway. "Pete? You have a call from Maui. A Nell McDonald? She said you wanted to talk to her."

TWENTY-FOUR

After the chill of the county morgue, the oppressive heat and humidity pressed down all the harder on Zoe when she returned to the fairgrounds.

A check on Windstar revealed plenty of hay and fresh water, evidence that while Patsy was nowhere to be seen, she'd been around recently—and wasn't taking her anger out on Zoe's horse.

She needed to get down to the grandstand show ring. Would the 4-H competition be held this morning as planned? Or would Cody's death and subsequent loss of their judge force a postponement?

Zoe slipped into the stall and draped an arm over her horse's back, resting her forehead on his soft, warm hide. She inhaled his horsey scent, still mingled with the smell of the shampoo she'd used on him two days ago. He shifted his feet, and the muscles on which her cheek rested rippled.

In that moment, she knew. Even if Cody was still alive, she would never part with Windstar.

Leaving him with a pat on the neck, Zoe headed for the 4-H Barn.

The place buzzed with activity as if nothing had happened. Parents and older 4-Hers hustled in and out of stalls, braiding manes, currying coats to a high shine, painting hoofs with black or clear polish.

Zoe checked the tack room for Diane but found it unoccupied. A leader from another club pointed toward the grandstand.

From the crest of the hill behind the bleacher seats, the scene below appeared the same as any other horseshow day at the county fair. The school buses had been dragged to the weeds well beyond the racetrack. Otherwise, no trace of last night's crime scene remained.

The first classes of the day were Grooming and Showmanship—halter classes, similar to the one Zoe had earned her red ribbon in, except the focus wasn't on the horse's conformation. Instead the 4-Her was being judged on how well he or she groomed and presented the animal. And themselves.

Most kids hated this class. Too much work and no riding. While the organization didn't require participation in G and S, Diane did. Any kid who belonged to her club and wanted to show their horse in any other class, had to enter this one.

The junior divisions were up first, so the 4-Hers milling around outside the ring were the younger ones, wearing their finest show clothes, their horses and ponies immaculate. No ratty blue jeans and t-shirts in this class. And no dirty nylon halters or cotton lead ropes either.

Zoe found Diane inside the announcer's booth, which didn't surprise her. What did was finding Patsy there wearing the same outfit in which she'd shown Jazzel two days ago. They both looked up when Zoe rapped on the doorframe. "What's going on?" She directed the question at her cousin.

But Diane, whose lined face and wide eyes hinted at an overabundance of caffeine, was the one who replied. "Good. I'm glad you're here. Patsy's agreed to judge Grooming and Showmanship. Can you help run the timers later for the game classes? And help judge tomorrow's Western classes?" The words tumbled out, further bolstering Zoe's suspicion that Diane had imbibed way too much coffee.

"Uh—"

Diane rubbed her arms as she bent over the show program. "I need to find someone to judge the English classes this afternoon."

Zoe looked at Patsy, who met her gaze without smiling.

"Well?" Diane asked, her tone demanding.

"Uh—" Zoe swallowed. "I'm not qualified."

"You're all I've got." The 4-H leader's voice rose a panicked octave. Her expression morphed from frantic to grief-stricken. "Cody's dead." She reached for the desk as her knees buckled.

Zoe and Patsy sandwiched her between them and eased her into a dented metal folding chair.

"Don't worry," Patsy told Diane. "We've got this."

The 4-H leader slumped over the desk, braced her elbows on it and buried her face in her hands.

Patsy motioned Zoe toward the door. "She's taking this really hard," Patsy said once they were outside.

Zoe checked her watch. Five to nine. The smaller kids gathered with their horses around the gate, nerves showing on their young faces, entry numbers pinned to the backs of their spotless shirts. She sighed. "While you're judging the showmanship classes, I'll try to track down someone qualified to handle the English classes."

"And you'll run the timers for the game classes?"

"Unless I can coerce someone else into doing it."

Patsy lifted her face, looking toward the ringmaster who gestured for her. "I have to get this show on the road." She met Zoe's gaze and tipped her head toward Diane. "Keep an eye on her. She's been freaking out over losing all the paperwork for the club and now this."

Zoe watched her cousin stride toward the gate.

The PA system crackled to life. Diane's ragged voice echoed overhead. "The Monongahela County 4-H Roundup begins in five minutes. First up, Junior Grooming and Showmanship. Contestants should be at the gate and ready to go."

Zoe stepped inside as Diane clicked off the microphone and wanted to ask about the lost project reports. She'd assumed Diane would've found them by now. But one glance at the woman's pale face changed her mind. "Are you gonna be okay?"

"I have to be."

Zoe pulled a second chair next to Diane's and lowered into it, placing a hand on top of her 4-H leader's wrist—a trick she'd developed to surreptitiously check an anxious patient's pulse. "Surely someone else can announce the show."

Diane gave her an unconvincing smile. "I always announce the show. You know that. And right now, I need the distraction."

The pulse under Zoe's fingertips was rapid. Too rapid. She wished she had a blood pressure cuff and a stethoscope nearby, but she and Earl had returned the EMS truck to its parking spot on the hillside after last night's excitement. "All right. I'm gonna track someone down to help with this afternoon's judging." She pointed at the microphone. "But you page me if you need anything."

"Will do." Diane shooed her toward the door and pulled a small

CD player close to the microphone. "I have work to do." She clicked the mic. "Will everyone please stand for the National Anthem."

Having been summarily dismissed, and after "The Star-Spangled Banner" finished playing over the PA, Zoe wandered to the concession stand to buy three bottles of water—one for her and two to leave with Diane. While she waited to pay for her purchase, she placed a call to the EOC and asked the dispatcher to contact whomever was on standby with the EMS truck to make a non-emergency trip to the announcer's booth. Diane would be furious with her, but not as furious as Zoe'd be with herself if the woman keeled over with a heart attack.

After delivering the water, Zoe made a lap around the show ring in quest of a substitute judge. She either didn't recognize or only vaguely recognized most of the parents, 4-Hers, and observers lining the fence. One man in a polo shirt bearing the amusement company's logo stood at the end of the ring closest to the midway. He spotted her and gave a nod.

The carny guy who'd been talking to Earl's boys and Luke last Friday—what was his name? She nodded back.

A half hour later, Zoe completed the loop having had no success at filling Cody's judging shoes.

The junior divisions of Grooming and Showmanship continued. She paused to watch.

"Hi, Aunt Zoe."

She turned as Lilly approached and could tell the girl struggled to not run. "Hey, kiddo. Are you learning what to do when you're out there next year?"

Olivia followed her daughter, smiling and shaking her head.

"Yeah." Lilly hooked her fingers over the vinyl fencing next to Zoe. "It doesn't look too hard."

"I have a feeling it's harder than you think," Olivia said. She pointed into the ring. "Isn't that your cousin?"

"Yep. The guy in the bus last night?" Zoe took a long sip from her half-empty water bottle. "He was supposed to be the judge."

"Oh, no."

Zoe had to admit, Patsy appeared professional and well-suited to the role. "We're scrambling to find fill-ins," Zoe said. "Patsy was in 4-H in Washington County when she was younger and was on the judging team. She knows her stuff."

A piercing squawk drifted from a cluster of older kids gathered near the gate for the senior division. Zoe scanned the group for the source. She almost didn't recognize Luke as the well-groomed young man talking to Merryn. Or more accurately, being yelled at by Merryn. Aidan and Ryan stood behind Luke, backing away from the force of her bluster.

"What in heaven's name...?" Olivia had caught sight of the commotion and appeared torn between rushing to protect her male offspring and staying with her youngest.

Zoe touched Olivia's arm. "Stay with Lilly. I'll go deal with Merryn."

"Tell the boys to get their butts over here."

As Zoe circled the arena, closing the distance between her and the brouhaha, she caught a glimpse of movement. The carny guy stormed toward Merryn and Luke from the opposite direction.

Merryn's shrill words grew clearer as Zoe neared. "You stupid shit. You don't listen to a word I say. I told you to stay clear of that place."

By the time Zoe reached them, other parents and 4-H leaders had converged on the mother and son, attempting—and failing—to direct her away while comforting Luke. The poor kid appeared on the verge of tears. Not something any seventeen-year old wanted his friends and competitors to witness.

Zoe put a hand on each of the Kolter boys' shoulders. "Your mom wants you."

Aidan gestured at Luke. "But we want—"

"I know. Let the grownups deal with his mother first. Then you can support your buddy."

The boys thought about it and agreed.

Merryn hadn't noticed the carny guy's approach and wheeled when he grabbed her arm. Zoe couldn't see her face but saw her stiffen. "You," Merryn snarled and flung a sizzling string of epithets at him.

Zoe elbowed her way through the crowd to Luke's side. "Are you okay?"

"Hell no." He shoved his horse's lead shank at her and bolted.

Carny Guy gripped Merryn by both arms and gave her a rough

shake. "Look what you're doing," he said.

She twisted and flailed. "Get your hands off me." Unable to squirm free, she swore. And kneed him.

He gasped and doubled over.

Merryn continued to produce every swear word Zoe had ever heard as well as a few creative ones. "If you ever come near me or my kid again, I'll kill you, you bastard."

Pete left Baronick in the conference room with the whiteboard and crossed the hall to his office, intent on not limping in front of the detective. Shutting the door, he braced a hand on his desk as he circled it, picked up his phone, and hit the blinking button for line one.

"Ms. McDonald? This is Chief Pete Adams from Vance Township."

The response from the other end sounded annoyed. "A security guard from another hotel contacted me and told me to get in touch with you. What's this about?"

"I'm sorry to bother you. I wanted to speak with you about your friend, Vera Palmer."

The line went silent and stayed that way. "Hello?" Pete said.

"I'm here," the woman replied, the annoyance replaced by something more like trepidation. "Vera? What about her?"

"I'm sorry to be the one to tell you, but she died last Thursday night."

More silence. Then a sob. And a squeaked, "What?"

Muffled noises crossed the airwaves. Pete waited, picturing her covering the phone's receiver while ripping tissues from a box.

After several long moments, the line cleared. Nell McDonald, while still shaken, sounded stronger. "That can't be. We had dinner together Thursday night. Are you sure you have the right person?"

"Did Vera leave the restaurant at approximately nine o'clock?"

An intake of breath. "Yes."

"Did you speak with her again after that?"

"No."

Pete let it sink in.

"You mean...?"

"Her body was found the next day."

"Oh my god. What happened?"

"That's what I'm hoping you can help me with. Do you know where she was going when she left Parson's?"

"No, I don't. She kept looking at her phone. Then she excused herself and said she'd talk to me later."

"But she didn't?"

"No. I had an early flight out Friday morning. I figured she got home late and knew I'd be turning in early, so she didn't disturb me."

"Why did you assume she'd be out late? Where did you think she went?"

There was a pause. "I told you. I don't know."

"I heard you. But I asked where you *think* she went." When Nell still didn't reply, Pete said, "Everyone I've talked to said you were Vera's best friend. If she'd confided in anyone, it would be you. I'm asking. As her friend. If you were to venture a guess, where would she have gone?"

"Can't you check her phone to see who was texting her?"

"We did. There weren't any texts in or out."

"Oh. Well..." Nell dragged the word out. "I honestly don't know where she went. But I know something had been bothering her, and she'd intended to confront the person on Friday."

Pete froze, his hand on his pen. "Do you know what was bothering her?"

A pause. "Not in detail."

"Tell me what you do know."

A transpacific, transcontinental sigh breathed into his ear. "Vera had discovered discrepancies in the records of the 4-II club her daughter was involved in. She was really upset about it. She liked the woman. A lot. Said she'd really helped Cassie before the accident and had been a godsend since. But Vera was good at what she did. And she'd double- and triple-checked the numbers. She'd planned to confront the woman at the county fair Friday morning."

The seed of a monster headache sprouted inside Pete's forehead. "Do you know the woman's name?"

"Yes. It's Diane. Diane Garland."

TWENTY-FIVE

Zoe walked Luke's horse back to the 4-H Barn. As suspected, she found the boy sitting in the corner of his stall, hugging his knees, his face lowered. "Hey," she said softly.

He looked up, battling to keep his jaw set. A shimmer of tears edged his eyes betraying his tough guy mask.

"I brought you a friend." She held out the lead shank.

The mask crumbled. "Thanks."

Luke made no move to get up, so Zoe led the horse into the stall. It lowered its face to sniff the boy, and he reached up to stroke its soft muzzle. "I guess I screwed that up."

"What do you mean?"

"Bailing on Showmanship. Now Diane won't let me show in my other classes tomorrow." He swept an arm across his eyes. "I really thought I had a chance to make it to state."

Zoe stepped around the horse to sit beside the teen. "I don't think for a minute that *you* screwed up anything. Neither does Diane."

"You talked to her?"

"Briefly. Under the circumstances, she's waiving her rule."

Luke's face brightened. But then he looked down. "What about my mother?"

"Security was talking to her when I left."

"She's drunk. Again."

Zoe didn't respond.

"It's my fault."

She looked at him. "No. It's not. You didn't force her to pick up a bottle." Or a joint. Or a needle. Zoe wasn't sure how deep Merryn's addictions ran.

"Maybe not. But I drove her to it."

"You can't carry that burden."

Luke lifted his head but didn't meet Zoe's eyes. "In this case, I can. She told me to stay away from the midway. But I didn't. I couldn't."

The ache in his voice puzzled Zoe. "Why?"

Luke met her gaze, making no further attempt to stem the tears. "Because...that guy? The one who worked the games?"

"The one..." She almost said *the one your mom kneed?* But instead, said, "The one who tried to stop your mom down there?"

"Yeah." Luke swallowed. "He's my dad."

The ache in his leg almost forgotten, Pete stormed into the conference room the moment he ended the call and crossed to the whiteboard.

Baronick looked up from his phone. "What's going on?"

Pete picked up the marker and added Diane Garland's name with an arrow.

"Who?" Baronick asked.

"Zoe's former 4-H leader.

"Wow. You're really reaching now."

"She'd been in recent contact with both victims prior to their deaths." Pete crooked a finger at him and strode back into the hall and to the evidence room in the rear of the building with the detective trailing.

"Do you wanna tell me what this is all about?" Baronick asked as Pete unlocked the door.

Without answering, he retrieved the box he'd found in Vera's car and set it on the table in the middle of the room. He lifted out the stacks of individual project records and set them aside. The file he wanted stared up at him from the bottom of the box. He removed the folder and showed it to Baronick. "Vera's husband told me she'd been upset about something about a month prior to her death. She never told him why, but he thought it had to do with her work. According to him, she seemed calmer after a couple of weeks. As though she'd solved the problem or come to a decision about how to handle it."

Baronick took the folder and flipped it open.

"That phone call I had was from Vera's best friend who confirmed that something was off with her." Pete nodded at the folder. "This."

"You sure?"

"Vera discovered discrepancies in the 4-H club's financials. She'd intended to confront Diane Garland Friday morning."

Baronick's gaze snapped up to meet his. "Friday morning?"

"Uh-huh."

"And Vera Palmer died under mysterious circumstances Thursday night."

"Uh-huh."

The detective scanned the report. "I wish like hell I understood what I was looking at."

Pete crossed his arms. "It happens I know who to call to help with that."

Abby Baronick arrived at the station a half hour later, wearing a Vance Township PD t-shirt and faded jeans. She took one look at her brother and groaned. "You didn't tell me *he* was gonna be here."

Pete fixed her with a stern parental glare. "Can't you two play nice for an afternoon?"

She lifted her chin. "I can if he can."

Baronick choked a sarcastic laugh.

Pete knew from experience the older sibling was the bigger pain in the ass. "You could leave now for the fairgrounds. We'll call you when we find any incriminating evidence to support Nell McDonald's claim."

"I'll wait."

"Then behave." Pete handed the folder to Abby. "You never found anything questionable on Vera's laptop, right?"

"Right." Abby squinted at the handwritten numbers in the file.

"Was this 4-H club the charity you mentioned?"

"No, it wasn't."

"I want you to take a fresh look at Vera's computer. See if you can find anything that matches these." Pete tapped the folder in Abby's hands.

"On it, Chief." She brushed past them, heading for the evidence room and the laptop.

Pete eyed Baronick. "I was serious about you leaving now for the fairgrounds."

"You're trying to get rid of me."

"Yep."

The detective glared at him in mock disdain. "I can take a hint. Besides, I have work to do." He put a hand on the front door. "Call me if my sister finds anything useful."

Pete stopped in his office to refill his coffee cup and found the pot empty. He carried the glass pot to the restroom, dumped the dregs down the sink, and filled it with water. Back in his office, he poured the water in the top, loaded the basket with a fresh filter, and scooped in the Maxwell House.

Once he'd filled his cup with the steaming brew, he headed to the rear of the station. Abby sat at her desk in the bull pen with Vera's laptop open in front of her.

"I found something."

"Already?" Pete grabbed a chair from Officer Seth Metzger's empty cubicle and slid it next to hers. "That was fast."

"I already knew how to get into her accounting files this time." She turned the laptop toward him and pointed at a column on the screen. "See this?"

He leaned in for a closer look. "Yeah."

Abby held up one of the paper spreadsheets from the folder and set a finger next to a similar column. "This," she said, "is supposed to match."

He looked from one set of numbers to another and back. "They don't."

"No. They don't."

"Wait." Pete put on his reading glasses for a closer inspection of the computer. "You showed me this two days ago, and I didn't notice a folder for Diane Garland or Golden Spurs 4-H Club."

"That's because it wasn't with her regular clients. Vera had a subfolder titled 'audits.' This was the only file in it." Abby swiveled her chair back and forth. "Maybe she was running the audit on her own."

"Maybe." He studied the columns of handwritten numbers, comparing each to the computerized version. "There isn't a huge difference. Maybe Diane Garland is lousy at math."

"Or she's smart enough to only fudge the numbers a little at a time." Abby flipped a page and tapped the mousepad. After a moment of intense scrutiny, she nodded. "This one's off too. Not a lot." She looked up at Pete. "Give me an hour and I should be able to tell you whether this woman is a really bad bookkeeper or a really crooked one."

Zoe stood inside the show ring and tugged her ball cap lower over her eyes against the late morning sun breaking through the clouds. The 4-H dress code for game riders was more relaxed than for other classes. Patsy, however, had forced Zoe to swap shirts with her in the restroom so she'd "look more professional."

The ring crew took over the arena with measuring tapes and large plastic barrels to set up the cloverleaf pattern. Two of the guys worked on the placement of the timer and its electric eye. All Zoe needed to do was sit with her clipboard, note the entrant's back number, and jot down the digital read-out of their time.

While the men finished setting up, she scanned the assorted kids, parents, and club leaders scattered around the area surrounding the show ring. No Merryn. No Carny Guy.

Luke's confession set on her heart like a rock. The kid had a father who wanted to see him. Spend time with him. Yet Merryn forbade it. Zoe had plenty of experience with crazy mothers, but even Kimberly wouldn't go so far as keeping Zoe from her father had he still been alive.

The PA crackled to life, and Diane's voice blasted through it, announcing the run order for the entire class, concluding with, "Number 482, be at the gate. Six-twelve on deck." The PA clicked off.

Zoe gazed toward the announcer's booth. A tall man in dark blue jeans and gray shirt stood at the window conversing with someone inside. Probably Diane. Zoe recognized him as the Monongahela County extension agent, the guy from Penn State University who oversaw the 4-H clubs and their activities. From where she sat, he didn't look happy.

She remembered how frantic Diane had been to find that box of missing reports. *"If I don't have those project books in my hands by the start of the show, none of our kids will be able to compete,"* she'd said.

"Are they putting you to work?"

Zoe wheeled to find Wayne, once again in his usual suit and tie, resting his arms on the fence. "Last night's victim was supposed to be today's judge. We're scrambling to fill in."

Wayne raised a skeptical eyebrow. "You're judging?"

"Only the game classes."

"The what?"

"Cloverleaf barrels, pole bending, and keyhole. They're timed events." She pointed at the timer perched on a tripod. "All I have to do is keep track of numbers. I guess they figure since my patients' lives depend on me being able to track their vitals, I'm qualified for the position."

Wayne chuckled. "You got me there." He looked toward the freshly smoothed expanse of dirt at the far end of the racetrack's infield. "They made short work of cleaning up the school bus debris once we cleared the scene."

"Had to. With all these horses showing today, they couldn't risk the liability of leaving anything lying around where the animals or the kids could get hurt." Zoe studied his face. "Any word on the investigation?"

"Into DeRosa's death? That's one of the things I'm working on today."

"One of the things?" she echoed. "What else?"

Instead of answering, Wayne turned to look toward the announcer's booth, the gate, and the competitors gathering around it. "You're friends with Diane Garland, right?"

"Yeah. Why?"

"What do you know about her?"

Zoe eyed him. Wayne Baronick didn't ask casual questions about anyone. Ever. "Why do you want to know?"

"Just curious."

"Yeah. Right. I'm not buying that. What's going on?"

"Can't you tell me a little about the woman without getting paranoid?"

"I'm not paranoid. And you aren't 'just curious.'"

He glared at her. "How long have you known her?" Now, he sounded like he was interrogating her instead of pretending to carry on a casual conversation.

"Since I was thirteen or fourteen."

Her answer appeared to surprise him. "I didn't realize you knew her that long."

"She was more of a mother to me when I was a kid than Kimberly was. Why the questions?"

He opened his mouth, paused, and closed it again. "Never mind. Is Diane around?"

Zoe looked toward the announcer stand. The extension agent was gone. "She's—"

The static from the PA system interrupted. "This is your final call for cloverleaf barrels," a familiar voice blasted. "Number 482, be ready at the gate." The PA clicked off. The voice may have been familiar, but it wasn't Diane's.

Why the hell was Patsy manning the microphone?

The ringmaster strode over to Zoe. "We're ready to start when you are."

"Let's do it."

He touched the brim of his hat and jogged toward the gate.

She looked at Wayne. "Diane was in the announcer's stand last I saw her."

"Thanks."

Zoe watched him walk away and wondered what a county detective would want with her old 4-H leader. But her questions—and any answers—would have to wait. A high-strung buckskin danced through the gate, and Zoe signaled for the rider to make his run.

TWENTY-SIX

Abby showed up in the doorway to Pete's office in well under the requested hour.

"Well?" he asked.

"I estimate Diane's siphoned off a little over six hundred dollars from the 4-H club's treasury over the last five years. And that's as far back as these records go. Could be more."

He lowered his foot from the guest chair and leaned back. "That's a lot of accounting errors."

"I doubt any of it was done in error. Vera's computer records show cash received that isn't listed in Diane's paperwork. Vera also shows several small cash draws not included in Diane's math. None of it alone would send up any red flags. But when you add it up?" Abby let the question hang.

Pete did some quick math. The discrepancy averaged out to only a hundred and twenty a year. A pittance to most. But to a small group of farm kids in a 4-H club? "I wonder where Vera got her numbers."

Abby shrugged. "A second set of books?"

He pulled out his notebook and flipped through the pages. "I searched Vera's home office and didn't find anything. But I didn't know what I was looking for either."

"Do you want me to get a warrant?"

"We won't need one if her husband's still agreeable." Pete found Jack's number and punched it into his phone. As the ringback tone hummed in Pete's ear, he looked at Abby. "Would you be willing to go over there and do the search? You know what you're looking for better than I do."

"No problem."

The call connected. "Hello?" He sounded distant. Sleepy.

"Jack? This is Chief Adams."

A pause. "Oh. Chief. Hello."

"Would it be all right for one of my officers to look through your wife's office again? We may have a break in the case."

Jack's voice cleared. "Really? You have a suspect?"

Pete hedged his bet. "Let's say we have a person of interest who may become a suspect depending on what Officer Baronick finds in Vera's papers."

"Absolutely. Send him over. I'll be waiting."

"Her," Pete corrected. "Officer Abby Baronick."

"Oh. Fine. Fine. I'll be waiting. And Chief?"

"Yes?"

"Thanks again. You don't know how grateful I am that someone's taking Vera's death seriously."

Pete ended the call and keyed in another number. "While you're doing that, I'm going to update your brother. He might be able to use his Baronick charm on Diane and get some answers."

Abby mimed gagging and retreated into the hallway. "I'll let you know the minute I find anything."

Pete chuckled. "You do that."

By the time the final contestant in the last game class made his run, dark clouds once again crowded out the sun but did nothing to cut the humidity. Zoe watched the lanky teen rider on an equally lanky horse gallop full out across the finish line and jotted down the reading from the digital timer. She scanned the list and noted the top seven times, filling in the back numbers in order. Before she was through, the ring crew had already dismantled the raised keyhole pattern. A John Deere farm tractor with a rake attachment waited at the gate to even out the show ring's surface in preparation for the first of the Saddle Seat classes.

Zoe handed her completed judge's card to the ringmaster. "Where'd Diane go?" she asked.

"Beats me," he said and walked away before Zoe could ask if they'd found a judge for the rest of the classes. It wasn't going to be her. She'd ridden hunt seat one time—poorly—and had never attempted saddle seat. She preferred a nice heavy-duty western saddle and a smooth-jogging Quarter Horse to the minimalist slips of leather they called saddles and posting trots of the hunters and high-stepping Saddlebreds and gaited breeds.

Zoe shuffled toward the gate. She hadn't seen Wayne since his inquiry about Diane, who never returned to her announcer's duties. Zoe found Patsy and the ringmaster huddled over the paper Zoe had turned in. Patsy clicked the button on the microphone, waking the outside speakers. "In Raised Keyhole, senior division, first prize and the blue ribbon goes to number three-one-one, Tiffany Cox of Golden Spurs..."

Three of the top seven spots went to Golden Spurs' riders. Diane would be proud. Had she been around.

Once Patsy finished reading off winners, she flipped the switch on the mic and gave Zoe a look of exasperation. "This wasn't how I planned to spend my day. Where the hell—" She flinched and glanced around, apparently concerned about young ears. "Where the heck is Diane?"

"I was hoping you knew."

"She told me to take over. That she'd be back in a few minutes." Patsy looked at her phone. "It's been two hours."

"Did Wayne Baronick stop here looking for her?"

"Yeah. I told him the same thing. That she said she'd be right back. So he waited a little bit. Then he got a phone call. Told me I should plan to finish out the day for her and took off."

None of this sounded good.

"On a brighter note, I found a replacement judge for this afternoon," Patsy said. "A former 4-Her who used to show English and who has judging team experience agreed to fill in."

"Good." Zoe gazed toward the hillside above the grandstand bleachers. "I'm gonna go find out what happened to Diane. Do you need anything from the concession stand?"

"Nope. The ring crew's been taking care of me."

Zoe left the horseshow behind and hiked up the hill. By the time she reached the 4-H Barn, Patsy's fancy show shirt clung to Zoe's back and sweat tickled her belly.

Inside the barn, the first ribbons from the show hung on the fronts of stalls. But the atmosphere lacked the normal celebratory buzz. A few kids went about their chores in silence or whispered to each other in hushed tones.

Luke stepped out of his horse's stall, spotted Zoe, and ducked away.

"Hey," she called. "Luke."

He froze and did a slow pivot to face her.

"You okay?"

"If you're looking for my mom, I haven't seen her. And I'd rather keep it that way."

Merryn was on Zoe's list. So was Luke's carny guy father, but first things first. "Actually, I'm looking for Diane. Have you seen her?"

His gaze darted to the far end of the barn. "Is she in some kinda trouble?"

"Why would you think that?"

"I've never seen her cry before."

Diane was crying? "Where is she?"

Luke tipped his head. "Down there. In the tack room. And she's not alone."

Before Zoe could ask anything else, he spun and trudged away in the head-down, slouched posture of one used to dodging emotional bullets.

She trailed after him, noticing the kid picked up his pace as he passed the tack room and didn't so much as glance toward it. Hear no evil. See no evil.

Zoe had no such aversion.

The tack room door was ajar. She knocked but pushed it open without waiting for an invitation. Diane slumped in a folding chair, her elbows braced on the card table, her head in her hands. Wayne sat catty-corner from her. The extension agent stood across from her, arms folded. She lifted her tear-streaked face as Zoe entered.

"What's wrong?" Zoe demanded, looking from Diane to the agent, settling on Wayne with an accusatory glare.

Diane took a sobbing breath and looked helplessly at the man towering over her.

Zoe shifted her full attention on him. "Well?"

"I'm afraid none of the Golden Spurs members' results here will count toward qualifying for District or State." He shook his head. "I'm already bending the rules by even permitting them to compete. I'm flat out breaking them by letting the kids keep their ribbons and premiums."

Zoe looked at Diane. "This is about the project reports?"

Her eyes flooded. "Yes. I swear I don't know what happened to them. I've torn my house and my car apart. And we searched everything in this room. Again." She shook her head. "They're gone."

Zoe spotted a fleeting twitch in Wayne's jaw. A miniscule narrowing of his eyes. He caught her watching him, and his poker face kicked in. "I'm sure they'll show up."

Good cop. Bad cop. Only the bad cop was an extension agent for Penn State, who shrugged. "Perhaps. But I should have had them in my hands prior to the start of the show. I'm truly sorry." He shot a glance at the detective, tipped his head to Zoe, and left.

Diane buried her face in her hands again. Her muffled sobs escaped into the room.

Zoe pushed the door shut and dragged another chair over to sit opposite Wayne. "The kids will understand," she said, not believing her own lie.

Diane hiccupped and lifted her head to fix Zoe with a look she'd seen too many times before. Diane wasn't buying her lie either. "The kids will be heartbroken. Especially the ones who are in their last year. This is their final chance to make it to District and State. And what about the ones who've never qualified before but do well here? They've finally earned their shot and are going to miss it because of me."

She was right. The 4-Hers loved Diane and would eventually forgive her. Maybe. But their pain and their parents' outrage would be an epic disaster for the club.

Wayne's jaw worked as if he had something stuck in his teeth. "What if these reports were to show up?" he asked. "Soon."

"You heard the man. He needed to see them before the start of the county roundup."

"But what if...hypothetically...they'd been taken?"

"Taken?" Diane looked puzzled. "You mean stolen?"

"Not necessarily. More like borrowed."

"Who on God's green earth would borrow 4-H project books?"

Zoe eyed the detective who avoided her gaze. "Wayne?"

He risked a glance at her.

It was more than enough to convince her he knew exactly where the missing project books were. "Wayne," she said again. "What aren't you telling us?"

He sat taller and took a deep inhalation. The guilty-little-boy look dissolved to one of professional law officer. He faced Diane. "Vera Palmer."

"What?" Zoe said.

"Vera?" Diane said, her voice brittle. "What do you mean? What about Vera?"

Wayne didn't blink. "Can you explain why your box of 4-H project books was found in Vera Palmer's backseat?"

"*What?*" Zoe repeated.

Diane's mouth hung open, frozen in a confused "O." But her eyes shifted, reflecting the layers of confusion that must be whirring through her brain until a flash of something—fear?—drew a twitch. And closed her mouth. "I have no idea." She looked at Wayne, her face emotionless. "Where are they now?"

"In the evidence locker at the Vance Township Police Station."

Vance Township? Pete hadn't mentioned any of this to Zoe. Not that they'd had much time to talk lately. She quelled her racing mind. He had no way of knowing what those reports were or the impact they had on the 4-H club.

"Thank heavens," Diane said, although she didn't sound relieved. "What do I need to do to get them back?"

Wayne shook his head. "I'm afraid they're evidence in Vera's homicide investigation."

Diane stuttered. "But they don't—didn't belong to her. I'm not sure how or why she had them, but they're mine. Or the 4-H kids'. And they need to be turned in." She leaned toward him. "You heard the man. If he doesn't get them, the kids will be banned from going to District. To State. Those project books don't have anything to do with Vera's death."

Zoe reached over and touched Diane's hand. "I'll talk to Pete—"

Wayne brought a palm down on the table, stopping Zoe before she could make a promise she already knew she might not be able to keep.

"I'm afraid there's nothing Pete or anyone else can do."

Zoe caught the warning look he shot at her. What the hell was going on?

He turned his gaze back to Diane. "I need to ask you. Where were you last Thursday evening?"

Abby's phone call had been brief. "Got it. I'm on my way back to the station."

Pete met her as she came through the front door carrying a brown evidence bag. "That didn't take long."

Abby looked smug. "I completely understood her filing system and went right to it."

"You call that a filing system?"

"Worked for me. And for Vera, apparently."

He pointed at the bag. "Well?"

"Come on. I'll show you." Abby hustled into the hallway. She started past the conference room but froze at the door. "Can I use the table in here? So I can spread stuff out?"

"Absolutely. I'll get the laptop and spreadsheets from the evidence room."

"Thanks."

Two minutes later, Pete watched as Abby arranged the items on the conference table and booted up the computer. She reached into the bag and retrieved a stack of ledgers. The kind office supply stores sold to folks who didn't use or trust computers.

"There are two sets for each of the last five years," Abby said. She divided them into pairs and laid them out in chronological order. Then she sorted the handwritten spreadsheets and placed each with the corresponding ledger.

Pete stood back as she started with the earliest sets of records, opening the ledgers and tracing her finger down the pages, stopping every so often to compare numbers to the duplicate copies.

This could take a while. He moved to the whiteboard, scanning the notes he and Baronick had added that morning.

Patsy. No way. Even if Zoe sold her horse and sold the farm, Patsy would likely be the buyer of the property.

Zoe without her horse. Without a farm. As much as he loved having her under his roof, the image he always carried of her involved the outdoors. Wisps of hay tangled in her honey-colored hair. The smile that always brightened the moment she arrived at the barn and saw Windstar. The smile that became blinding the moment she climbed into the saddle.

He looked for the marker. Not in the tray where it was supposed to be. He remembered scrawling the star next to Diane's name and tossing the marker. Stepping back, he scanned the floor, and there it was. Next to a plastic trash bag. He bent down to retrieve the marker and realized the bag was the one he'd collected almost a week ago at the Vance Motel.

The murder threat. Nothing had come of it. Vera was the only homicide in the township, and the guy who'd stopped to report it said he overheard "I want *him* dead. I'm gonna kill *him* myself." Him. Not her.

Pete reached for the bag. He should toss it in the dumpster.

Abby tapped one of the ledgers to grab his attention. "This is it all right. It'll take me a while to go through everything, but I can already tell you Diane Garland kept two sets of books. One set's in pencil and appears to be the accurate one. She used the separate spreadsheets to calculate the differences once she siphoned off cash payments or withdrew cash from the club's account." Abby rested a finger on another ledger. "The second set of books are in ink. I'm guessing these are the ones she intended for public viewing and for audits."

"Do you know how much money we're talking about?"

"Close to my original estimate. Not a lot by legal standards. I'd guess it's gonna come down as a first-degree misdemeanor rather than a felony. But we're talking about a kid's club, right?"

"Right." Any amount would be a lot when the bulk of their income came from bake sales. And when the dollar amount ended up costing Vera Palmer her life.

TWENTY-SEVEN

"Thursday evening?" Diane sounded baffled. As the realization sank in, the color drained from her cheeks.

Zoe stared at Wayne, convinced he'd lost his mind. "What? You think Diane killed Vera over a box of project books?"

He didn't look away from the 4-H leader. "That wasn't the motive, was it, Diane?"

She turned her wide-eyed gaze on Zoe. Made a couple false starts at speaking before slumping like a balloon losing its air.

Wayne's phone rang. He held up a finger, silencing Zoe, and answered. "Yeah." He listened, his focus never shifting from Diane. "Uh-huh."

Zoe tried to read his face, but he masked his expressions better than she'd ever seen.

"You don't say."

The mask shifted, enough that she didn't like what she glimpsed in his eyes. She'd seen that predatory gleam before.

"Thanks. Keep me posted." He ended the call and set the phone on the table. "Now. About last Thursday."

"No." Zoe gripped Diane's wrist. "Don't answer any of his questions until you get a lawyer."

His gaze swung to Zoe. The mask dropped away. "You can leave."

"I want her to stay," Diane said.

Zoe looked at her. The balloon had re-inflated.

"I didn't kill Vera. I don't need a lawyer. Thursday night I was at home getting ready for this." Diane gestured to the general surroundings. Zoe knew she meant the fair.

"Ready?" Wayne's lips twitched. "Like packing."

"Yes. Exactly."

"And probably loading your car."

"Yes."

"With the stuff you needed to bring with you."

Diane appeared to know where he was going. She lowered her face. "Yes."

"Like the box of project reports?"

She didn't look up. Didn't reply.

He waited. When she showed no intention of answering him, he shrugged. "So you were at home getting ready to come to the fair. Was anyone else there helping?"

"No."

"Did anyone see you?"

"No."

"Is there anyone who can vouch that you were at home and not out in Vance Township?"

"No. But there isn't a soul who can tell you I *was* in Vance. Because I wasn't."

Zoe opened her mouth to remind Diane about shutting up until she had a lawyer.

"Fair enough." He leaned back in his chair and crossed his arms. "Let me ask you something else. Do you have any idea what else was in that box of project records *besides* project records?"

Zoe stared at him. "What are you talking about?"

Diane placed her hand over Zoe's. She looked at her old and trusted friend. Diane stared at the table, but Zoe had a feeling she was seeing something else. Her eyes glazed. As Zoe watched, the woman appeared to age a decade.

Diane swallowed, and when she spoke, her words were little more than a whisper. "Maybe I do need that lawyer."

Pete left Abby to crunch numbers and carried the bag of motel trash down the hallway, intending to deposit it in the dumpster out back. But he paused when he passed the doorway to his miniscule lab. His small department didn't have the budget for most forensic gadgets and gizmos, however he'd dug in his heels when he'd first moved here from the Pittsburgh Bureau of Police and managed to come up with funding for a fingerprint lab.

He looked at the whiskey bottle. Hell, he might as well put the matter of the unsubstantiated threat to rest once and for all. He unlocked the door, flipped on the lights, and booted up the IAFIS computer terminal.

Over the next half hour, Pete managed to develop and lift a trio of promising latent prints. Satisfied with his work, he labeled the backs of each lift card before scanning them into the computer and pressing send.

The process took longer than they showed on TV, nor were the results as definitive. Pete packed away his powder and brush and left the computer to get a fresh cup of coffee and check on Abby.

"How's it going?" he asked.

She leaned back and skimmed the ponytail elastic from her hair. "I'm still finding discrepancies throughout. What I can't figure out is why in the world would she keep both sets of books. This woman has given us a perfect paper trail."

Pete leaned a shoulder against the conference room's door jamb. "Some criminals are stupid. Lucky for us."

Abby considered his answer. "Maybe. But I have a hard time thinking of her as a criminal. I mean, the grand total is going to be considerable for a kid's club to lose. But she's embezzled such tiny amounts over such a long period of time." Abby shook her head.

Pete thought about it and the woman he'd met. Zoe cared deeply for Diane Garland. Was Zoe's judgment once again impaired? Or was there more going on than he knew? "Maybe," he mused, "on some level she wants to be caught."

"That's what I've been thinking." Abby ran her fingers through her hair and once again bound it into a ragged ponytail.

"What's your current total?"

"Of how much she's syphoned off?" Abby checked a sheet of paper at her elbow. "Three hundred and eighty-two dollars. That's in a little over two years so far."

"Keep at it."

He left her and headed to the lab to discover IAFIS had kicked out a list consisting of a handful of potential matches. He took a seat at the computer and pulled up each of the records indicated. The remainder of the work—his favorite part—required him to study the prints he'd lifted from the bottle and compare them with the prints in the system.

It didn't take long to eliminate several of the possible matches. However, one criminal file matched two of Pete's prints. He lifted a magnifier to his eye for a better look. Satisfied, he typed in the number attached to the file to pull up more information.

"And the winner is…"

The mugshot looked vaguely familiar. The name didn't mean a thing. Trent Crosby. He printed out the information from IAFIS, closed up the lab, and headed back to his office. Logging into the police database, he typed the name.

The results stilled Pete's breath. Trent Crosby had a long and varied rap sheet with everything from drunk and disorderly to aggravated assault. And his fingerprints were on a whiskey bottle from a room at the Vance Motel. A room from which threats of murder had been overheard. Was Crosby the visitor?

Pete scanned Crosby's last known address. Illinois. What was he doing here? The entry next to last known place of employment gave Pete his answer. Crosby worked for the amusement company that was currently operating at the county fair.

Wayne stepped out of the tack room office to talk on his phone, leaving Zoe and Diane alone.

"What's going on?" Zoe demanded. "I feel like I'm the only one here in the dark."

Diane had regained her composure. "Because you are." She smiled weakly. "I'm so sorry."

Zoe's throat closed. "You killed Vera?"

"No. Good heavens, no. I would never."

"Then what?"

Diane leaned back, her eyes rolling upward to the cobwebby ceiling. "You're going to find out anyway." She swallowed. Hard. "I've been taking money from the club."

This answer didn't rest on Zoe's mind any easier than homicide. "You stole? From Golden Spurs?"

"It sounds horrible when you put it like that."

Stunned, Zoe tried to process this latest development. "Why? How?"

"I wish I could give you some altruistic reason like I was giving it to the kids who needed financial help. But the fact is, I've done so much of that in the past...given money from my savings to help families buy feed for their ponies...that when I needed that money for myself, I ran through what little was left pretty fast." She shifted in the chair and winced. "There were repairs to the car. I had to sell my other one."

"You mean you're driving that old beater as your everyday car?"

"Yeah. I needed cash, and the Tempo wasn't worth anything."

"What did you need so much money for?"

"Meds. Doctor bills." Diane lowered her eyes. "My hip. I have lousy health insurance. It won't pay for surgery. It barely touches the pain meds I need to function. A few years ago, I was collecting dues and some of it was cash. And it just happened to be enough to cover my prescription that month. I told myself I was borrowing the money and would pay it back."

"But you didn't."

"No. After that, it got easier to keep cash payments. It was never a lot."

Zoe rolled Diane's plight over in her mind. "Why didn't you say anything? The kids and their parents adore you. They'd have given you money. Hell, they'd have done a fund-raiser to help you out."

The 4-H leader's eyes welled. "You're right. I should have. But I kept track of every penny and always thought I'd come up with the money somehow to pay it all back."

"What's this all have to do with Vera Palmer?"

Diane stood, stretched, and limped to a rack holding a show saddle. "There's been talk of the club being overdue for an audit. Vera volunteered to do it, her being an accountant and all. I've been frantically re-working all the books. She'd been bugging me about getting the stuff to her, and I kept putting her off." Diane leaned on the saddle. "If I was to venture a guess, she found the financial reports when she was at my house a few weeks ago and slipped them into her car—along with the project books—when I wasn't looking."

Zoe let the confession sink in. Vera had been suspicious of Diane, enough so to take what turned out to be evidence of her crimes. A few weeks later, Vera turned up dead, a victim of intoxication. Or being drugged.

And Diane was in possession of strong painkillers.

Zoe's throat closed. Had she once again been so trusting, so gullible, as to not see a killer right in front of her?

The door swung open, and Wayne strode in. "All right. Where were we? Oh, yeah. You want a lawyer."

Diane hobbled back to the table and placed both hands on it. "No."

Wayne's eyes widened in surprise. "No?"

"No," she repeated. "I'll waive my right to an attorney and confess to embezzlement. On one condition."

Wayne crossed his arms. "What's that?"

"You release the project books. They have nothing to do with the money I took. I don't know if the extension office will accept them now, but it's the only shot at getting my kids to district competition."

Wayne thought about it. Nodded. "I think I can arrange that. But what about Vera Palmer?"

Diane slumped into the chair and met Zoe's gaze, responding to her instead of the detective. "I swear to you. I had nothing to do with Vera's death."

Pete checked in with Abby, who continued to add up the nickels and dimes that Diane Garland had funneled from the 4-H account. "I'm going to follow up on another angle," he told the officer.

"I'll call if I stumble across anything interesting," she replied.

By the time he reached the Vance Motel, black clouds simmered overhead. A wave of moisture-laden air hit him when he stepped out of his Explorer, bolstering his aching thigh's weather forecast that this evening might be the one to break the drought.

He glanced at the empty parking lot and toward the room at the end of the row. The one where murder had been threatened almost a week ago.

Sandy Giden sat behind the front counter and looked up as Pete entered. "Well, hello, Chief. What brings you back?" She took off her glasses. "Oh, no. Don't tell me the guy who stayed here really did kill someone."

"I'm not sure." Pete pulled up Trent Crosby's mug shot on his phone. "I think this may be the guy who visited your guest. Take a look and see if he looks familiar."

She took the phone from him and put the glasses back on. "That's Toby Jones. The man who rented the room."

"You sure?"

"Yes, I'm sure." She returned Pete's phone. "What's he done?"

"He registered under a fake identity for starters. But he has a rap sheet longer than your driveway, so that's not surprising."

"Who is he?"

"Trent Crosby."

Sandy pursed her lips. "Nope. Sorry. The name doesn't mean a thing."

"No need to apologize. At least now we know who stayed here." Pete tucked the phone in his pocket. "Have you remembered anything about his visitor?"

"Afraid not. I wish I could be more help. Should I keep an eye out for him in case he comes back?"

"If you see him, definitely give me a call." But Pete knew where to find Trent Crosby. And he intended to speak to him before he had a chance to pay another visit to Vance Township.

TWENTY-EIGHT

Zoe gauged the temperature had to be in the nineties with a hundred and ten percent humidity. Black clouds boiled overhead, once again threatening a deluge.

She rolled the sleeves of Patsy's fancy horseshow shirt up as far as she could and untucked the tails from her jeans, flapping the fabric to stir up a breeze. Leaving Diane with Wayne, Zoe had exactly fifteen minutes before she had to be on duty. Fifteen minutes to check on Windstar and Jazzel, grab a shower, and change into her uniform. But instead of heading toward the Pony Barn, she detoured to the midway.

The carny guy, Luke's father, handed a large stuffed giraffe over the counter to an excited teen girl. She and her friends giggled as they left the booth with their prize.

"Ten dollars gets you four darts. Five dollars gets you two," he said to Zoe. "Care to try your luck?"

"Not right now. We met the other day. My name's Zoe Chambers. I'm a friend of Luke's."

His huckster smile froze. "Who?"

"Your son."

The smile melted. "Who told you?"

"Luke. Like I said. We're friends."

"When you were here before, you were ordering him back to the barn for his mother. I figured you were her friend, not his."

Zoe shrugged. "Merryn and I were in 4-H when we were Luke's age. But I know what it's like to not have your father around, so I understand where he's coming from."

The guy crossed his arms and studied Zoe. "You aren't friends with Merryn?"

"Diane Garland asked me to keep tabs on Luke. I think because

Merryn's not up to the task."

He sniffed. "That's for damned sure."

"I'm sorry. I can't remember your name."

"Trent Crosby. Are you here to ask why I'm not in my kid's life?"

"Not really. Merryn doesn't want you around him. That's pretty clear."

"Merryn," he said, oozing disgust. "She's been in and out of AA and NA for as long as I've known her. Mostly out. And she's definitely out right now."

"Yeah. I kinda got that."

"I suppose you've seen her fawning over every man whose path she crosses too."

"It's hard to miss." Zoe studied his face. "I know she doesn't want you near Luke. But considering what a train wreck she is, why haven't you tried to get custody?"

His eyes turned cold. "What makes you think I haven't?"

Zoe paused, her mouth open. She closed it. True. She knew nothing about their relationship. "I'm sorry. I guess I was making assumptions."

"Yeah, I guess you were." His expression softened. "Look. I know you mean well. Merryn never told me she was pregnant. I travel a lot, and she didn't try very hard to find me. Instead, she married some other guy and lied to him and Luke. It's that guy's name on the birth certificate. His name that my boy carries. Luke was ten before I knew he existed. And Merryn's done her best to turn him against me." Crosby waved a hand, indicating his booth. "This is the first opportunity I've had to spend any time with him. And Merryn went into a full-blown meltdown when she learned I was here."

"Yeah. I saw you and her this morning."

He winced at what had to be a painful memory.

The brewing storm kicked up a sudden breeze, swirling dust down the midway and flapping the canvas edging the booth. Zoe checked her watch. She had exactly two minutes to look in on the horses, get a shower, and change.

"I have to get to work." She met Crosby's gaze. "I want you to know, Luke's turned out to be a good kid. He wants to be a veterinarian." She looked at the game booth. Merryn couldn't afford to send the boy to college, and his father didn't appear financially solvent either. "I hope he can find a way to make that happen."

Crosby's face turned stony. "Yeah."

A trio of teens clambered up to the counter cutting off any further conversation.

Without a thank you or a goodbye, Crosby turned to flash his smile at the kids. "Care to try your luck?"

Pete stepped out of the air-conditioned motel lobby into the oppressive heat and looked skyward. The clouds had thickened and darkened even more in the time he'd been inside. He pulled out his phone and keyed in Baronick's number. As it rang, instead of climbing into his vehicle, Pete limped down the sidewalk toward the room Crosby had occupied.

"Pete," the detective said, "I was about to call you."

"Oh?"

"I'm waiting on an arrest warrant for Diane Garland."

The news startled Pete. "For murder?"

"Well, no. She denies having anything to do with Vera Palmer's death. But she confessed to theft from her 4-H club."

"Considering the evidence your sister has dug up, it's a wise move."

"She did have one condition."

"I don't think she has any grounds for making demands."

But once Baronick explained about the project books Pete had found in Vera's car, he mulled it over. She'd obviously intended to return the books on Friday had she not died Thursday night. The same person responsible for her death was also to blame for the kids missing their chance to progress to the state level.

"It may not matter at this point," Baronick said. "The county extension guy insisted it was too late. They should have been turned in before the show. But I thought I'd stop in their office once I'm done here and have a chat with him. Explain the meaning of extenuating circumstances, you know."

Pete stopped in front of the door to what had been Crosby's room. "Let me know. If he's willing to look the other way for the sake of these kids, maybe we can too."

"What you mean 'we,' Pale Face?" Baronick asked, using the worse Tonto accent Pete had ever heard. "You're the one with the books logged into his evidence locker."

Pete turned his back on the motel door and gazed across the parking lot. A gust of wind sent a paper cup rattling across the pavement. "I have something else here. It may have nothing to do with any of this, but you know how I hate coincidences."

Baronick turned serious. "What?"

Pete told him about the man who'd stopped at his station Friday morning to report a homicide that hadn't happened yet. The raised voices and threats coming through the thin walls of the Vance Motel. The whiskey bottle Pete had nearly forgotten and the prints he'd lifted from it. "The guy's name is Trent Crosby. Heard of him?"

"Can't say that I have. You do realize people make drunken threats all the time."

"Which is why I hadn't paid closer attention to this particular threat until now. But the Vance Motel is only a mile from where I found Vera's body."

The line fell silent, followed by Baronick's "Huh."

"And Trent Crosby? He's currently employed by the amusement company at the Monongahela County Fair."

"Son of a bitch," Baronick muttered. "The only thing I hate more than a coincidence is two coincidences."

"Exactly."

"I'll look into him as soon as I deal with the 4-H tough guy."

"Keep me posted." Pete ended the call and looked down. Cigarette butts, the wrapper from a fast-food burger, and a mashed aluminum pop can littered the lot, blown against the yellow-painted curb at his feet. Crosby's car would have been parked here. His guest's vehicle would have been in the next space. But no. The guy—what was his name?—who'd filed the report would've parked there.

Driven by his gut, Pete stepped off the sidewalk and hobbled across the lot toward the landscaping on the far side. Had the spaces facing the motel been filled, a visitor might have parked over there.

More litter, swept by the breeze, gathered against the curb. A few scraps of paper clung to the shrubs edging the lot. What the hell did he think he was going to find?

Pete shook his head, the phrase *wild goose chase* flashing through his mind.

Another gust, stronger this time, scattered the trash, herding it like cattle toward some far corral. Overhead, a flash of lightning split the sky. He needed to get back to his vehicle. But one bit of debris hadn't blown away with the rest. He looked. Squinted. Moved closer. And squatted.

A beige heel from a woman's shoe rested again the curb.

The feathers from those wild geese tickled the space behind Pete's breastbone. He swiped his phone to bring up the camera app as a low rumble of thunder vibrated the air. After snapping some quick photos, he dug in his pocket for the pair of Nitrile gloves he kept there. Wiggled his fingers into them and picked up the heel.

He'd seen the shoe matching it less than a week ago. On Vera Palmer's foot.

Lightning lit the sky again.

Pete scanned the pavement. If he'd had time, he'd have started collecting every bit of trash and debris. Something he should have done last week, but kicking himself for discounting the reported homicide threat and the coincidence of Vera's body found not far from here wasn't going to accomplish anything.

The drumroll of thunder followed closer this time. What was the calculation he'd learned as a kid? Five seconds between the flash and the thunder for every mile? If true, the storm was nearly on top of him. The fact that the ground shook from the percussion supported his estimate.

He expanded his visual search to the mulch and the shrubs bordering the parking lot.

The first fat raindrop splatted him square between his shoulder blades. More, as big as quarters, struck the concrete in slow succession. In a matter of the next minute or two, all remaining evidence of Vera's presence would be obliterated.

Pete spotted something dark under one of the shrubs. Darker than the mulch. Darker than the shadows. He stood and moved closer. Knelt. He snapped a quick series of photos before reaching beneath the shrub. His gloved fingers closed around a thin piece of plastic.

The back of a cell phone.

A third flash of lightning sizzled, raising the hairs on the back of his neck as thunder crashed. No longer a base drum, but an explosion as a tree a mere hundred yards away burst into flame and smoke.

Pete flinched but didn't move. The lightning had reflected off two other objects in the mulch beyond the shrub. The raindrops went from splat...splat...splat to a downpour in an instant. He scooped up the rest of the phone and its battery, tucked them in his trouser pocket, and, ignoring the pain, bolted across the lot to his SUV.

By the time he slid behind the wheel, his uniform shirt clung to the Kevlar he wore beneath it. He removed his drenched ball cap and tossed it on the passenger seat. And he retrieved the items he'd collected from his pocket, holding them in his hands.

A phone in pieces. Vera's phone. The battery removed. The heel from her shoe.

He clipped the battery into the phone and snapped on the back. Pressed the power button. Nothing. With any luck, charging the battery would bring it back to life.

Pete gazed through his rain-streaked windshield to the hotel room in which Trent Crosby had stayed the night Vera died.

Whatever had happened to her—whatever drugs or alcohol had been introduced into her system—happened here.

Zoe and Earl sat out the long-anticipated rainstorm inside the EMS truck. Fair crowds had scattered, taking refuge in the exhibit halls and barns. The premature dusk created by the heavy clouds brought the outdoor lights on earlier than usual, their bulbs creating starbursts and blurs in the rivulets streaking the truck's windshield and windows.

"What's the main event tonight?" Earl asked.

Zoe scanned the fair program they kept in the cab. "Some country music group."

"I suspect they're gonna be rained out."

"I don't know." She checked her watch. "It's only five o'clock. The show's not until seven. The rain might stop in time."

He grunted a response.

Zoe folded the program, stuffed it between her passenger seat and the console, and turned to gaze through the door window. The rain gave the fairgrounds a distorted funhouse mirror perspective, which matched her mood.

Diane Garland had been charged with theft by unlawful taking—the Pennsylvania equivalent of embezzlement. Her beloved 4-H leader. Proof once again that Zoe was a crappy judge of character.

She closed her eyes to block the image of Wayne taking Diane away. At least he hadn't handcuffed her. But it continued to play inside Zoe's eyelids. Diane had been ripping off the club for years. Vera Palmer had discovered her crimes. And now Vera was dead. Diane denied having anything to do with the homicide but what else would she say? Of course, she'd admit to a less serious crime to divert attention from the big one.

Zoe couldn't see Diane as a killer, but she never believed she'd steal from her kids either. No, Zoe as a character witness was the kiss of death.

Which brought her to Cody. Who killed him? Diane? The woman had scrambled to find a last-second replacement for him. It made no sense for her to murder the man the night before the show.

Unless that's what she counted on everyone believing. But why? Diane liked Cody.

Didn't she?

A sharp rap on the passenger window jarred Zoe out of her reverie. Even through the rain-smeared glass, she recognized Pete's face and opened the door. "I didn't think you'd make it here tonight."

His lopsided smile was fleeting and failed to crack through the tension on his face. "A little rain isn't gonna hurt me. Besides, it's letting up."

She looked around. He was right. The downpour had given way to drizzle, and the western sky lightened, even revealing a speck of blue. Zoe grabbed her ball cap from the dash, tugged it onto her head, and slid down from the seat. "You didn't change out of your uniform."

"No," he said. "Have you seen Baronick?"

"Earlier. I guess you heard he arrested Diane."

Pete gave a quick nod. "But have you seen him since then?"

Zoe studied Pete's face. He was in cop mode. Not merely the uniform. His stance. His expression. His laser-focused eyes scanning the area around him. "No," she said. "What's going on?"

He didn't answer. Instead he tipped his head in the direction of the fairgrounds' gate. "Here he comes now."

Wayne strode toward them wearing the same stoic expression as Pete. Two men on a mission. Wayne gave her a curt nod before facing Pete. "Have you seen him yet?"

"No. I just got here."

"Seen who?" Zoe demanded.

They exchanged a look. "We may have a break in Vera Palmer's homicide."

Him. Wayne had asked if Pete had seen *him.* "Someone other than Diane?" Zoe heard the hope in her own voice.

"Yeah." Pete gazed down the hill toward the midway.

Wayne reached over and slapped Pete's shoulder. "Let's go find our man."

Zoe's phone rang its generic jingle. The one not attached to any of her regular contacts. She slid it from her pocket but didn't check the screen. "What man?"

Wayne was already striding away. Pete looked at her. She could read his face enough to know he was debating the merits—or disadvantages—of revealing the identity of their suspect. "I don't think you know him. A guy by the name of Trent Crosby."

Before Zoe had a chance to process the name, Pete turned and followed Wayne.

Her phone continued to ring. The caller ID simply read "Pennsylvania." She swiped the green button.

"Zoe?" The male voice on the other end sounded scared.

"Yeah."

"This is Luke Holmes. Can you come over to the 4-H Barn? Now? I found something weird."

TWENTY-NINE

The midway rides sat silent and deserted due to the rain. But as the clouds gave way to patches of blue, fairgoers drifted from the exhibit halls. Amusement company employees removed dripping tarps from some of the games. Others rolled up canvas flaps or lifted steel panels that doubled as awnings. One by one, the games along the midway re-opened for business.

"I called the company's headquarters," Baronick said. "They told me Trent Crosby was assigned to run the balloon darts booth."

Pete stopped. "I think I met him."

Baronick stopped as well. "Oh?"

"The day I went looking for Merryn Schultz's son. I found him at that booth. Earl Kolter's boys too."

"What was your impression of him?"

Pete tried to recall what the guy looked like. Nondescript. Average height. Average weight. Brown hair, neither long nor short. No tats. No scars. "Nothing to send up any red flags."

"You mean your infamous gut didn't warn you about him?"

Pete glared at the detective. "Let's just find him."

But the booth where Pete had met Trent Crosby remained closed.

Baronick stood outside and knocked on the front counter, still wet from the rain. "Hello? Trent Crosby?"

When no one responded, Pete grabbed the zipper closure and opened it enough to peer inside. "He's not here."

Baronick turned his back to the booth and crossed his arms. "We'll wait."

Luke met Zoe at the entrance of the 4-H Barn, but she had to look twice to recognize him. "What the heck happened to you?"

"They buried me in the manure pile."

Which explained the brown slime matting his hair and covering his clothes. And explained the aroma. She would have asked why, except a memory of a similar rite of passage from long ago brought a smile. She'd been a spectator, not the victim, thank goodness. Luke hadn't been so lucky, but she suspected this wasn't the reason for his call. Or the look of fear in the kid's eyes.

He motioned to her. "I need you to see something."

She trailed him down the center aisle of the barn, past the stalls and tack trunks and chairs where kids and a few leaders rested after a long day. A few of them snickered at Luke's current condition.

He continued out the far door, the one facing the grandstand, and around to the side corner where the kids wheelbarrowed the dirty sawdust and manure, heaping it into a good-sized mound. Two older boys and a man Zoe recognized as one of the other leaders stood sentry.

Luke faced her, his expression grim. "Like I said, they buried me. These two idiots held me down." He gestured at the older boys. "And Mr. Weaver covered me up."

Weaver kept one hand on a manure fork, the other hand behind his back, and gave her a tight apologetic smile.

Zoe wanted to ask what Luke had done to deserve the honor, but from the expressions on each of their faces, she sensed the story went well beyond the prank.

Luke shot a glance at the mound before bringing his gaze back to her. "While I was wrestling around, trying to get loose, I hit my head on something hard." He nodded to the man, who brought his work-gloved hand from his back.

"This," Weaver said, holding out a tire iron, "was buried in there."

Luke squirmed. "And it looks like it's got blood on it."

"A lot of blood," Weaver added.

Zoe moved closer. What she'd first thought was a coating of rust did indeed appear to be something else entirely. She pictured the scene the previous night in the bus. Early this morning at autopsy. Multiple blunt-force trauma. The injuries to Cody's head and arms. Made by a heavy pipe of some sort, according to Franklin and Doc. She'd seen those injuries.

And the tire iron in Weaver's hand appeared a perfect match.

Another image floated to the surface of Zoe's swirling thoughts. A flat tire. Shane and Jack changing it. With a tire iron identical to this one.

She studied each of the male faces in front of her and suspected they might be thinking the same thing as she. "Do me a favor?"

No one spoke but all four nodded.

She pointed at the sentries. "Stay here and don't let anyone near the pile. Or the—" She almost labeled it as a murder weapon. "Or the tire iron." She looked at Luke. "Where's Diane's car?"

He seemed puzzled. "Same place it's been all week. No one moved it when she—left."

"Good." Zoe crooked a finger at him. "You come with me."

As they crossed the fairgrounds, she chanted a silent prayer. Please let Diane's tire iron still be in her trunk. Please let Diane's tire iron still be in her trunk.

The Ford Tempo sat in the same spot Diane had claimed from the start of the fair. Zoe tried the door half hoping to find it locked. But it swung open. She slid behind the wheel and started searching.

"What are you looking for?" Luke asked.

"The trunk release."

"There isn't one."

For a moment, the pressure behind her chest eased, until she realized if someone needed the keys to get into the trunk, and if the tire iron was indeed missing, that meant Diane was the only person who could have removed it.

Luke bent down and reached toward Zoe's feet. "The keys are under the mat."

"Oh." She lifted one foot as the boy fumbled with the mat and came up with a set of keys. She climbed out, snagged them from his hand, and headed for the rear of the car.

"Why do you want in the trunk?"

"I'm looking for something I really hope is still here." Zoe clicked the trunk open and lifted the lid. A tire, either the spare or the formerly flat one, perched atop a heap of horse blankets and gear, plastic bags from the grocery store filled with more plastic bags, and a couple of folding chairs. No tire iron. But Shane and Jack had taken the tire to be repaired. Stuff may have been moved around. Zoe reached in and hauled out the tire, which she propped against the back bumper. She leaned into the trunk. Shifted the chairs to one side. Squeezed the bags of bags in search of something solid. Raked through the blankets, halters, and lead ropes. Lifted, moved, and rearranged everything.

Everything except the tire iron...which was not there.

A half hour had passed and still no Trent Crosby. Pete leaned on the counter, trying to take some of the weight off his throbbing leg.

"You okay?" Baronick asked.

Pete glared at him. "The old war injury is making itself known." He scanned the post-rain crowd. "I don't think Crosby's coming back tonight."

"Maybe he spotted you in your uniform and decided to rabbit. I should have come alone."

"Yes, because you look so warm and fuzzy and unofficial in your suit and trench coat." However, Pete had to admit, Crosby could easily have seen them without them seeing him and opted to go anywhere but here.

"I'm done." Baronick took a step away from the booth.

"Now what?" Pete asked, more to himself than to the detective.

"Now you're going back to Vance Township to go through everything you have on Vera Palmer's death." Baronick shrugged from his trench coat as the sun burst out, raising steam from the damp pavement. "I'm going back to County to work on the Cody DeRosa case. As for Trent Crosby, we'll catch him. Either he'll show up for work tomorrow, or I'll put out a BOLO on him."

Pete's phone rang. "Any leads on DeRosa's killer?" he asked as he dug the phone from his pocket. Zoe's name and photo lit the screen.

"I've been making calls to his friends and neighbors out in Ohio. Still waiting to hear back from a few of them. The ones I've talked to haven't contributed much. Shane Tolland's still MIA as is Merryn Schultz. If I don't hear from either of them by later this evening, I'm gonna have the local news outlets post their photos and dub them persons of interest. That should flush them out of the woodwork."

Pete held up a finger and answered the phone. "I'm heading back to you now."

"Don't." Her voice carried a disquieting edge. "I need you to come to the 4-H Barn."

"What's going on?"

"I think we found the weapon used to kill Cody."

Pete looked at Baronick. "We'll be right there." He ended the call and changed directions.

"We'll be right where?" Baronick lengthened his stride to catch up.

Pete didn't reply, figuring the detective would find out soon enough. He spotted Zoe waving to him from the grandstand end of the barn, standing with four men. As he and Baronick drew closer, he could tell three of them were teenagers. All of them, including Zoe, looked solemn.

One of the teens, Merryn's son, looked—and smelled—like shit. Literally.

"What'd you find?" Pete asked Zoe.

She looked toward the other adult in the group who raised a tire iron. Pete listened to her tell about the manure burial and Luke's discovery. Baronick snapped on a pair of Nitrile gloves and took the chunk of metal from the man.

The detective sniffed it and wrinkled his nose.

"It's covered with horse manure," Pete said.

"And blood. Unfortunately, any conclusive evidence has been contaminated by the..." Baronick waved at the pile.

Zoe shoved her hands in her pockets. "Franklin would have to confirm it, but from what I saw of Cody's wounds in autopsy, it matches."

The detective nodded. "I agree."

Pete gazed toward the grandstand. "The killer came up through the grandstand seats, probably before anyone else was around." Pete pictured the as-yet faceless murderer crossing the paved road—the same one he and Zoe had taken to the tractor pulls a few nights ago—to where they currently stood. "He stopped here, shoved his murder weapon into the dung, then...what? Tried to blend into the crowd? While he had to be covered in blood?"

"Unless he changed clothes," Baronick said. His eyes narrowed in thought. "Or put on some kind of coveralls."

"The bus mechanics and drivers were all wearing coveralls," Zoe said. "He—" She winced. "He or she would have blended right in."

Pete caught the correction. "Zoe? Do you suspect someone in particular?"

She and Luke, who appeared on the verge of tears, exchanged a look. "I'm pretty sure that tire iron..." She tipped her head toward the thing in Baronick's hands. "...belongs to Diane Garland."

Zoe stood at the receptionist's desk at the county police station early Thursday morning, waiting on Pete's arrival. In all the confusion of the night before, Zoe had forgotten to ask Pete about Trent Crosby.

But Wayne arrived first. "What are you doing here?" he asked.

"Nice to see you too. I want to listen in when you question Diane."

"There's no need." He waved a folder at her. "I've already talked to your boss. Franklin gave me his report on the tire iron."

"And?"

"It's size and weight are consistent with the object used to bludgeon the victim. Because of where it was found, DNA analysis won't do us any good. Too many biologicals present. But he was able to type the blood found. It's a match to DeRosa."

The station door swung open, and Pete strode in. For a fleeting moment, a pleased smile crossed his face when he saw her, but it vanished into a scowl. "What are you doing here?"

She raised her hands in frustration. "Jeez, you guys sure know how to make a gal feel loved."

"There's no reason for you to take part in this interrogation," Wayne said. "And don't pull the 'I'm a deputy coroner' card."

His whiny mimic gave Zoe reasonable grounds for violence, but annoyingly, he was right. "I don't want to take part. I want to observe." She looked from Wayne to Pete, judging which one showed more inclination to see her way. But they stood shoulder to shoulder, both with arms crossed, unflinching cop expressions on their faces. "Diane won't even know I'm there. Heck, you guys won't know I'm there."

"Go back to the fair," Pete said.

She'd have stomped a foot except Wayne's impersonation still hung in her memory. She didn't want to give him added fodder. "Look. I know her. I might pick up on a micro-expression you guys miss."

Wayne raised an eyebrow. "Micro-expression?" He glanced at Pete. "She been watching spy shows on TV again?"

Pete grunted.

Her fingernails bit into her palms.

"She has a point though," Pete said.

"You just don't want her pissed off at you when she comes home from the fair in a couple of days."

"There is that."

She looked from one to the other wanting to smack both of them. But she kept her hands to herself and her mouth shut. They were caving, and she didn't want to change their minds.

Wayne held out his hand to the desk sergeant, who placed two passes in it. One for Pete and one for Zoe.

Did he already have it waiting for her? Had her bluster been for nothing? She accepted hers without asking.

They headed through the door leading to the interrogation rooms. Wayne elbowed her as she clipped her badge to her shirt. "You will stay in the observation room and you will stay quiet," he told her. "And Diane Garland will not know you're here."

A good plan. Except an officer and Diane approached from the other end of the hall.

"Zoe?" Diane called out. "What's going on? I was told I'd be arraigned and then released this morning." She searched each of their faces before settling on Zoe's. "And why aren't you at the fair? You're supposed to be judging the horseshow this morning."

"Mr. Weaver made some calls and got a judge from the Quarter Horse Association to come in for the day."

"Oh." A fraction of the tension in the woman's face drained away. "Good."

"As for the other thing, we have some new questions for you." Wayne nodded toward the interrogation room door.

Diane looked to Zoe, a million questions in her eyes. Questions Zoe didn't dare respond to. Pete opened a second door, caught Zoe's arm, and directed her through it into the darkened observation room.

She'd spent time here before, a silent witness to interviews, but rarely those involving friends.

Wayne took the chair directly across the small table from Diane and stated the date and time for the recording as well as listing each of their names. Pete claimed the other seat closer to the door. Zoe had a clear view of Diane and a profile view of Pete but could only see Wayne's back. He read the Miranda warning and concluded with, "Do you understand these rights?"

"Yes, of course." Diane rubbed her arms. "I've already admitted to taking money from the club. Did you talk to the extension agent about the kids' project books?"

"That isn't why we're here this morning." Wayne leaned back in his chair. "How long have you known Cody DeRosa?"

"Cody? I've known him since he was in 4-H. Twenty...no, twenty-five years at least."

"Had you stayed in touch with him since he moved to Ohio?"

"Sure. We exchanged Christmas cards. And I always saw him at Quarter Horse Congress every October. If he had time, we'd get together for lunch or dinner. Sometimes coffee."

"Did you like him?"

"Very much so. Why?"

Wayne shot a glance at Pete. "I understand DeRosa was quite the lady's man."

"Oh, heavens, yes." A trace of a smile crossed Diane's face. "He loved women. And he loved to flirt."

"Did he flirt with you?"

The smile vanished. "What? Good heavens, no. I'm old enough to · be his mother."

"Did that upset you? Did you wish he would pay more attention to you?"

She looked at Wayne as if he'd grown a second head. "Have you lost your mind? What's this all about?"

"I was wondering if his lack of attention to you—and his abundance of attention to younger women—might have driven you to a crime of passion."

"What?" Even in the artificial light, Zoe could see the color drain from Diane's face. "You—you couldn't possibly think I—killed Cody?"

"Did you?"

"*Hell no.*"

Zoe flinched. She couldn't ever recall hearing Diane Garland swear before.

Wayne opened the folder and removed a photo, which he slid in front of Diane. "Do you recognize that?"

She studied the picture. "It's a tire iron."

"Notice anything special about it?"

Zoe wanted to pound on the glass and scream. *Don't answer without your attorney present.* But she knew doing so would result in her immediate removal.

If Diane's expression was any indicator, she was thinking about needing an attorney too. She looked at Wayne then Pete and back. "It's a tire iron," she repeated, her voice level.

"Yes, it is. Don't you own one like it?"

"I imagine ninety percent of the population owns one like it."

"True. But I'm pretty sure if we asked ninety percent of the population to produce theirs, they could. Any idea where yours is?"

The remaining color drained from her face. She pressed her lips together in a tight, thin line.

Lawyer, Zoe thought, wishing she could send the message telepathically to Diane. *Lawyer, lawyer, lawyer.*

She did at least practice her right to remain silent.

"Okay," Wayne said. "If you don't want to talk, I'll tell you what I know. I know this particular tire iron is covered in blood. Cody DeRosa's blood. It matches the injuries he sustained during a vicious beating two nights ago. A beating that resulted in his death. A beating that might be considered a crime of passion. I also have witnesses who claim you have—or had—a tire iron like this one in your trunk. And guess what. Your tire iron is no longer there."

Zoe hated that she'd been the one who'd shared that tidbit of information with the cops.

The 4-H leader lowered her eyes. From Zoe's vantage point, she noticed Diane's folded hands, one thumb massaging the other. The room fell silent for what felt like an hour. When Diane lifted her head, her eyes glistened, but her jaw held a determined set. "I didn't kill Cody. That might well be my tire iron, but anyone who knows me can tell you I leave my car unlocked and the keys under the mat." She looked at Pete. "*You* know that."

Wayne turned to him. Pete shrugged. "She's right."

"I had a bad feeling when Cody was killed about who might have wanted him dead, but I didn't want to believe it." Diane kept her gaze on Pete. "And I didn't want to say anything, because I didn't want to ruin a man who's already had his life destroyed. Especially if he's actually innocent."

THIRTY

Pete held Diane's gaze, his mind racing ahead of her words and picturing the whiteboard back at his station. Shane Tolland. Merryn Schultz. Luke Holmes. None of them had a "life destroyed." However...

Baronick came forward, resting his arms on the table, forcing Diane to focus on him. "Give me a name."

She swallowed. "Jack Palmer."

If the look on his face was any indication, the detective clearly hadn't expected that answer.

Pete had. "Why," he asked, "would Jack want to kill DeRosa?"

Diane swiped a hand across her tear-streaked face. "Because Jack blames Cody for Cassidy's situation."

"What is Cassidy's 'situation?'" Pete kept his voice soft.

Diane inhaled a ragged breath, blew it out. "Jack and Vera had bought her a horse that turned out to be too much for her. Someone in the club suggested they send it to a trainer, and Cody was the best. They shipped the horse out to Ohio for what was supposed to be thirty days, but after a couple of weeks, Cody got back to them. The horse had some serious behavioral issues, and he felt it would take much longer than a month to make it safe for a young girl. If he could ever make it truly safe. So he made them a deal. He had another horse in his stable. Older. Quiet. 'Bombproof,' he called it. He waved the training fee on the first horse and offered to trade it for this kid-safe mare. I think Jack and Vera had to pay a good bit on top of the trade, but they wanted a good horse for Cassie, so they agreed."

Pete thought of the fat little horse he'd seen in the corral behind Jack's house.

"The mare turned out to be all Cody said it was, but it also turned out to be chronically lame. Navicular, according to the vet."

Pete intended to ask Zoe for a translation, but Baronick saved him the trouble. "What's that?"

"It's a degenerative disease of the navicular bones in the horse's front feet." Diane wiped her face again. "The mare would be sound for a while but whenever Cassie rode for any length of time, the horse would pull up lame. Over the next few months, the horse got worse. Cassie could never ride her. The vet bills were piling up. So Jack made the decision to have the horse nerve-blocked." Diane didn't wait for Baronick to ask. "It's exactly what it sounds like. An injection to stop the pain. Unfortunately, it also completely numbs the hoof." She shifted in the chair, her hands once again folded, but tightly now. "Think of when you have Novocain to have a cavity filled and you end up burning your mouth with hot soup or biting your lip because you can't feel it." She lowered her face.

"What happened?" Pete asked.

Diane took another deep breath. "Against the vet's orders, Cassidy took her mare out on a trail ride. They were on a hillside when the mare took a bad step and fell. With Cassie under her." Diane choked out a sob.

Wayne sat in silence.

Pete pictured the scene. A young girl severely injured doing what she loved. He thought of the unborn child he and his ex-wife had lost. The pain, which to this day bubbled up and nearly drove him to his knees. What if that child had lived? What if she—or he—had been on that horse? Under that horse?

Diane cleared her throat, breaking the silence and bringing Pete back to the present. "Jack and Vera were devastated," the 4-H leader said, her voice little more than a whisper. "They never left Cassidy's bedside those first few weeks. But for Jack, I think things only got worse once she was out of the woods. The hospital bills were staggering. He tried to sell the mare, but no one wants a lame horse. So he's stuck with feed and vet and blacksmithing bills on top of everything else."

Pete thought about the man he'd talked to. Whose home he'd been inside. Tired. Grief-stricken. Overwhelmed. But to brutally pummel someone to death? "I'm having a hard time picturing Jack Palmer as a killer."

"Under normal circumstances, you'd be right." Diane continued to rub one thumb with the other. "But...you see...Jack's an alcoholic. He was starting to get clean when he met Vera. She was his motivation for staying sober. And he did. At least I thought he did." Diane shook her head. "The last few weeks, I suspected he might be drinking again. His eyes were a little too red. He'd been...off. You know? But I chalked it up to the strain."

"The strain may have pushed him off the wagon," Pete said. He looked at Baronick, who was unusually quiet.

"That's what worried me. I didn't want to say anything in case I was wrong. But I know how angry he'd been when he heard Cody was going to be the judge at the fair." Diane unfolded her hands and placed them flat on the table. "And Jack helped change a flat tire for me the other day. He knew that tire iron was in my trunk."

Pete shot another look at the detective, who appeared buried in his own thoughts, and reached over to nudge him. When Baronick flinched and glared at him, Pete said, "Do you have anything else to ask?"

"No."

Pete decided he liked it less when Baronick was quiet than when he wouldn't shut up. After thanking Diane for her time and ushering her out of the room and back into the custody of the officer in the hallway, Pete stood over Baronick. "Well?"

He didn't move. "I blew it."

"What did you blow?"

He lifted his gaze to meet Pete's. "I should have seen this coming."

The door behind Pete opened and in the reflection of the mirror, he saw Zoe, but he kept his eyes on Baronick. "Why should you have seen it coming?"

He glanced past Pete to Zoe and back. "Because I've known Jack Palmer for years. He's been one of my PIs."

"Jack Palmer's a private investigator?" Zoe asked.

"Paid informant," Pete told her without breaking eye contact with Baronick.

"Yeah," the detective said to Pete. "I busted him when I was still in uniform."

"On what charges?"

"Drunk and disorderly. Simple assault. Possession of a very small quantity of marijuana. Penny ante stuff."

"Wait a minute. I ran him for priors. There were none."

"I know. I had the charges dropped and his record expunged."

Pete waited for the detective to continue.

"Jack had some connections to a narcotics ring we were after, and he really wanted to clean up his life. So he helped me take down the bad guys, and I helped him get into AA. That was about the time he met Vera. Ever since, he's been clean and sober, and he gives me tips on illegal activity when he becomes aware of it."

"Why the hell did you fail to mention this when his wife turned up dead?"

"For one thing, we've always kept his informant status confidential. For another, I still don't believe he had anything to do with Vera's homicide. I've never seen a man so crazy in love with his wife and child." Baronick looked down. "But I can believe he'd snap and take out the man he felt responsible for hurting either of them."

"Did you know about Cody DeRosa's connection to the daughter?"

"No. But I should have."

Pete braced his hands on his duty belt. "You're psychic now?"

Baronick raised his eyes to meet Pete's.

He reached over and slapped the detective on the shoulder. "We can't always predict the future, you know. I liked the guy too."

Baronick nodded. "I guess I need to drive out to his place. Wanna come with me?"

Pete wasn't about to remind the county detective that the Palmer residence was outside of Pete's jurisdiction. "You bet."

He turned toward the door.

And Zoe. The overhead lights shimmered off the tears welling in her eyes. "What's gonna happen to Cassidy now?"

Zoe struggled to accept Jack Palmer—the heartbroken man who'd helped her and Patsy catch a runaway pony a week ago—as a violent killer. While she walked out of the County PD with Pete and Wayne, another question surfaced in her muddy thoughts. "What about Trent Crosby?"

Pete stopped and faced her. "You sound like you know him."

She debated how much of the guy's connection to Luke she should share. "I've met him." When Pete gave her a look that demanded more, she added, "Earl's boys and Luke were hanging around his booth at the fair."

The answer seemed to satisfy Pete. "Stay clear of him. Tell the boys to avoid him too."

"Why?"

Pete looked after Wayne who'd kept walking. "I'll explain in detail later, but for now let's say he's a person of interest in Vera's death. And if you happen to see him, call me." He pressed a quick kiss to her forehead. "Gotta go."

Zoe watched him stride away and waited until he and Wayne drove out of the parking lot in their vehicles.

The term "person of interest" echoed in her brain all the way back to the fairgrounds. Luke's dad, the clean-cut carny guy who'd earned her respect and trust with his apparently sincere desire to do right by his son. The son he hadn't known he had until seven years ago.

Had she yet again trusted too easily? The parallel to her own situation wasn't hard to miss.

Zoe couldn't go toe-to-toe with her own brother, but she stormed into the fairgrounds, intent on giving Trent Crosby hell for his deception.

A pair of county police cruisers idling at the fair office distracted her from her mission. A semi-circle of onlookers, mostly farmers and exhibitors, created a perimeter around the vehicles. Zoe recognized one of them from the Pony Barn and approached him. "What's going on?"

"Someone robbed the office."

"Robbed? Was anyone hurt?"

"I don't think so. Apparently, the secretary came in this morning and found the door had been forced. Whoever it was busted her desk drawer lock and made off with the money box."

Technically, not robbed. Burglarized. Zoe stifled a grin at the idea that she'd been hanging around a cop long enough to understand the difference. But she decided against correcting the guy. "Any idea who did it?"

"Not a clue."

She thanked him, left the police to do their job, and headed down the hill to the midway.

Many of the concessions had yet to open to the sparse late-morning fair crowd. The aroma of onions, peppers, and sausages on a grill signaled lunch was imminent and set Zoe's stomach to growling. Ignoring the internal rumbling, she stormed through the midway, hoping to find Crosby at his post. Other carny hucksters called out as she passed, urging her to try her hand at their games. Ignoring them, she zeroed in on the booth she wanted.

But the canvas front was rolled down. She approached anyway. "Trent," she called. "You in there?" She rapped on the counter. "Trent?"

"He ain't here."

She spun and found another carny guy standing behind her, leering. "Any idea when he'll be back?"

"Nope. But I can take care of you if you want."

The leer combined with the guy's lewd tone gave Zoe a chill. "No thanks." She turned to walk away.

But he moved to block her. "It wouldn't be no trouble."

Zoe wasn't sure what he meant by "it" and had no interest in finding out. Over his shoulder, she spotted Merryn and Shane, hand in hand and both wearing sunglasses, strolling down the midway. Apparently, Shane had found a kindred spirit to take the sting out of Patsy's rejection. Whatever the relationship, Zoe had never before been so glad to see either of them. "Excuse me," she told the carny. "I see a couple friends I need to talk to."

Before he could cut her off again, she sidestepped and scurried away.

Merryn spotted Zoe's approach, released Shane's hand, and closed the distance between them. Zoe registered Merryn's slight shift in position, but the fist came forward too fast to block. The blow staggered Zoe, the pain searing from her left cheekbone into the core of her brain. She clutched her face and gaped at the crazy woman.

Shane stepped between them and placed a hand on Merryn's shoulder as if holding her back. "Jeez, woman. What the hell are you doin'?"

Merryn ignored him. "You." She jabbed a finger in Zoe's direction.

"You can't leave well enough alone, can you? What gives you the right to come between me and my boy?"

Zoe stuttered, stepping back in case Shane couldn't keep Merryn from taking another swing. "I—I didn't—"

"You're gonna try to tell me you had nothin' to do with Luke running off with that scumbag who claims to be his father?"

"I—what?" Zoe struggled to tamp down the throbbing pain and process Merryn's words. "Luke ran off? You mean Trent isn't...?"

Instead of throwing a second punch, Merryn dissolved into tears, which shocked Zoe even more than the punch.

Shane put an arm around Merryn's shoulders, and she slumped against him.

"Oh, Trent provided the sperm," she said, "but otherwise, he ain't no daddy to my boy."

Zoe struggled to process the rest of it. "Luke went with him? Where'd they go?"

"How the hell should I know? And if I did, I'd be dragging that boy's ass back home where it belongs."

Zoe studied the woman. The sunglasses. Shane, as scruffy as ever, comforting her. Zoe had her own experience with a self-involved mother, but Merryn made Kimberly look like mother-of-the-year material. "Maybe if you'd let Trent know he had a son—"

Merryn choked out a laugh. "Let him know? Why? So he could teach the kid how to be a loser? That man—and I use the term loosely— has never made an honest dollar in his life. The only reason he ain't in jail is because he's so good at making a clean getaway."

Zoe wanted to argue Trent's case. That maybe Luke wouldn't have felt the need to run off with his father if Merryn had allowed the two of them to see each other. But Merryn's words seeped into Zoe's brain, overwhelming the pain.

Merryn aimed a thumb over her shoulder. "Did you see them cop cars up by the office? Someone broke in and stole the cash box. Now who do you suppose might've done that?" She gave Zoe a knowing smirk. "I heard they hadn't made a run to the bank in a couple of days. Probably a pretty nice haul." Merryn tipped her head toward the closed game booth. "And now he's gone and taken my son with him." She moved closer to Zoe. Close enough that Zoe could smell the stale sweat on her clothes, the alcohol on her breath, and the anger radiating from her soul. "You may be right that I'm a crappy mother, but there's a damned good reason I never wanted my boy around that man."

A hollow space opened in Zoe's chest. Once again, she'd fallen prey to the same old story. Family. A child missing his father. The way she missed hers. The longing to fill a void. A void that could never be filled. Not in her case. But she'd hoped to fill it in Luke's. And in the attempt to put the broken pieces of a child's heart together again, she'd overlooked the fact that family was often the source of the heartbreak, not the solution.

THIRTY-ONE

Baronick's brake lights came on almost a quarter mile before the Palmer residence. Pete slowed. Shifted into park. Baronick stepped out of his vehicle and looked back at Pete, who did likewise and held up both hands in a question.

"Put on your emergency lights," Baronick called back to him. "We have livestock on the road."

Pete leaned in and flipped the switch for his red and blue beacons in case any traffic appeared on the lightly traveled residential road. Leaving his SUV, he approached the detective. "Livestock?"

Baronick gazed at the road ahead of them. "Livestock sounds plural. Is there a singular variation of the word?"

Pete followed his gaze to the small round horse looking forlorn in the middle of the pavement. He was pretty sure it was the same animal he'd seen in the corral behind Jack Palmer's house. "Yeah," Pete told Baronick. "Horse."

The detective grunted. "What's it doing there?"

"Why don't you ask it?" Without waiting for a smartass reply, Pete approached the mare, talking softly the way he'd seen Zoe speak to horses over the years. "Easy, girl." Diane Garland had said it was a mare, right? Plus, it wore a pink halter. "Easy there."

The horse made no attempt to escape capture. If anything, she seemed happy to see him.

Pete closed his fingers around the mare's halter and stroked her face. "Good girl."

Baronick came up behind him. "Look at you. Turning into quite the cowboy."

"I didn't exactly have to rope it."

"Zoe's rubbing off on you. She'll have you living out there on the farm in no time."

Pete hesitated, his hand resting on the wide space between the mare's eyes. "Maybe."

"I wonder where it belongs?"

"I'm pretty sure she's Jack's daughter's horse." Pete put some pressure on the pink halter and the mare willingly walked with him.

"Heel," Baronick said.

Pete wasn't about to explain that horses didn't respond to dog commands.

"I'll get my car and meet you at the Palmers' house."

Pete led the mare along the edge of the road, her hoofs slow-beating a rhythmic *clop, clop, clop* at his side. Maybe Zoe was rubbing off on him. Or maybe the small kid-safe horse was demonstrating her appeal in spite of her debilitating ailment.

Jack Palmer's house lay ahead. Pete heard a loud thumping coming from its direction followed by a man's voice.

"Jack? You in there? *Jack?*"

Pete broke into an uneven jog. The horse at his side did as well, her limp less noticeable than Pete's. Baronick in his unmarked sedan idled up behind him. Pete thought he heard the muffled rumble of another vehicle coming from the same direction as the shouting, but the detective's car drowned it out as he cruised past Pete and the horse.

They jogged clear of a clump of shrubbery, and the scene at the Palmer house came into full view. A man...the neighbor Pete had talked to on his first visit...stood pounding on Jack's closed garage door. The guy spun as Baronick wheeled into the driveway and waved frantically at the detective. The situation clicked in Pete's head. The garage door. The shouts. The muffled rumble.

He released the mare's halter and, ignoring the searing pain, broke into a pounding run. Ahead of him, Baronick was out of his car. The neighbor yelling and flailing. The hint of exhaust fumes on the stagnant, humid air.

Snippets of the neighbor's panicked words. "Can't get in...locked..."

Pete charged up the driveway, his heart pummeling the inside of his breastbone in beat with his tactical boots against the concrete. Were they too late?

Baronick flung open the trunk of his sedan, leaned in, and came out with a Monoshock battering ram. He looked up at Pete's approach and started toward the garage. "Jack—"

"I know," Pete said. "Hit it."

Baronick swung back. Heaved the ram at the door below the latch with a crashing thud. The space where two panels met dented but held. He swung again, making contact at the same spot. More damage, but the door refused to give. "Son of a bitch," he muttered.

On the third blow, both panels split. Pete stepped in, reaching through the gap. He fumbled to find the lock. Fingered it. And flipped the lever with a metallic squeal. He and Baronick bent down and heaved the crippled garage door open.

Inside, a faded brown minivan spewed clouds of exhaust. A figure slumped behind the wheel.

Pete pointed at the neighbor, shouted, "Call for an ambulance," and followed Baronick inside.

"Already did," the neighbor hollered after them.

Baronick rushed to the driver's door and yanked on the latch. It recoiled out of his fingers. He swore. "Who the hell locks their car when they're committing suicide?"

"Someone who's serious about making it stick." Pete rounded to the passenger side. Also locked. He reached to his duty belt, retrieved his ASP baton—the one with the glass-breaker ceramic pins on the end—and expanded it with a flick of his wrist. One quick strike punched through the safety glass, releasing a wave of alcohol-laden air to mingle with the exhaust fumes. Pete reached in and unlocked the door. Disregarding the glass pebbles covering the seat, he climbed in, pressed the fingers of one hand to Palmer's throat, and unlocked the driver's door with the other. "He's alive," Pete told Baronick. "Let's get him outta here."

Zoe wandered through the fairgrounds, barely aware of the pain in her cheek. Pete's words—*a person of interest in Vera's death*—mingled with Merryn's—*never made an honest dollar, a pretty nice haul, so good at making a clean getaway*—and replayed on a loop in her mind.

The sound of her name cut through her mental fog. She blinked and spotted Aidan and Ryan Kolter headed her way.

She faked a smile, which only reminded her of the impact from Merryn's fist. "Hi, guys."

Neither boy returned a smile, even a forced one. "Luke's gone," Aidan said.

"Yeah. I heard."

Ryan shoved his hands in his jeans pockets. "He ran away with that man from the balloon dart game."

Zoe studied the boys. Did they know who *that man* was? "Did Luke say anything to you about him? The balloon dart guy?"

They exchanged looks. They knew. And had probably been sworn to silence.

"He's Luke's dad," Zoe said, letting them off the hook.

"Yeah," Aidan said. "We didn't know that you knew."

"When did they leave?"

Aidan glanced at Ryan in another silent discussion of how much to reveal. "Early this morning. They'd been talking about it all week. But I didn't think they were serious. Just, you know, wouldn't it be cool if we did it?" He deepened his voice in what Zoe took as an impersonation of Luke. Or Trent.

"Then Trent tracked us down last night," Ryan said, "and told Luke to have his stuff ready to go at first light this morning."

Aidan shook his head. "I still didn't think he'd really do it. You know?"

"Yeah," Zoe said. "I know."

"What happened to your face?" Ryan asked, pointing at his own cheek.

"Nothing." She caught her lip between her teeth, thinking. If Earl's boys were privy to Luke's plans, maybe they knew even more than they'd already admitted. "I don't suppose Luke told you where they planned to go?"

Another exchanged glance. More silent sharing between brothers. "No," Aidan said, although it came out sounding like a question.

Ryan eyed his brother, clearly disapproving of his answer. He looked at Zoe. "Nobody told us. But we overheard them talking. I know exactly where they went."

* * *

While the paramedics ministered to Jack Palmer, the neighbor guy got a bucket of grain and a lead rope from the barn and managed to catch the mare. Pete left the ambulance crew to their rescue attempts and walked over to the man and horse.

"I was sure glad to see you," the neighbor said. "Chief Pete Adams, right?"

"Yes, sir." Pete shook his hand.

He must have suspected Pete didn't recall his name and tapped himself on the chest. "Miles Koskey."

"Mr. Koskey. Can you tell me what happened here?"

"You probably know as much as I do. I happened to look out and saw the horse was loose. I tried calling Jack to tell him but didn't get an answer. So I came outside and found the gate standing open. That's when I heard the car running in the garage and got a whiff of the fumes. I figured he must have turned the horse out to fend for herself before..."

Before Palmer took his own life. "Did you ever get the feeling that he might be suicidal? Did he ever say anything about it?"

"He never said anything. But I know things have gotten tough for him. Even before Vera..." Koskey's voice trailed off again. He clearly had an issue with death.

"How about since Vera died?"

"I haven't talked to him since then. Waved at him as he was coming and going. That's about it. I try to mind my own business, you know?"

Pete remembered. He also remembered Koskey was extremely observant for someone who minded his own business. "When was the last time you saw Mr. Palmer coming or going?"

"I saw him out feeding the horse this morning."

"But when was the last time he left the house?" Pete pointed down the road.

"Ah. Let's see. This is Thursday, right?" Koskey's eyes narrowed in thought. "I don't recall seeing him leave yesterday. I do know I saw his car leave on Tuesday. Early. And I saw headlights late that night. But I don't think he left again after that."

Late Tuesday.

After bludgeoning Cody DeRosa to death.

"Chief?" one of the paramedics called. "He's coming around."

Pete thanked Koskey and excused himself, moving to where Baronick was watching the ambulance crew work on Palmer.

His lips and cheeks still hinted at the cherry-red blush of carbon monoxide poisoning, but a healthy dose of oxygen had brought his coloring back toward normal. His eyes fluttered half open as he groaned.

"He's a lucky man," the other paramedic said. "I don't think he'd have lasted in there much longer."

Pete wasn't at all sure he'd use the word "lucky" to describe any aspect of Palmer's life.

Baronick dropped to one knee next to the patient. "Jack. It's me. Wayne."

Palmer's eyes shifted toward the detective, but he appeared to have trouble focusing. "Wayne? Baronick?" He slurred the last name and reached up to fumble the oxygen mask from his face. "I'm still alive?"

"Afraid so." Baronick took his hand. "Jack. Why'd you do it?"

Pete wasn't sure which "it" Baronick meant.

"My paperwork is all inside." Palmer sounded like his tongue was thick. "My insurance. My bank accounts. See that Cassie gets what's left of my money. 'Kay?"

"What Cassie needs is her dad," Baronick told him.

Pete wasn't sure if the choking sound Palmer made was a sarcastic retort or a result of being oxygen deprived.

"I thought—" Palmer sniffed. "I thought killing that bastard would make me feel better."

"Cody?" Baronick asked softly.

"Yeah. What happened to Cassie...was all his fault. He sold us that horse. When I told him the mare was lame, he wouldn't do anything about it. Said he'd told us to get it vet checked. As if we could afford that. He had the nerve to say, 'buyer beware.'" Palmer's laugh sounded more like a harsh cough. "Buyer shit outta luck is what he meant."

One of the medics placed the oxygen mask back over Palmer's face. "We need to get him to the hospital."

"Wait." He clawed the mask away again. "I gotta say this." His eyes wavered and settled on Baronick. "In the house. On my table. I wrote it all out. Everything." He turned his head, searching. And found Pete. "Chief. I didn't kill my wife. I know you prob'bly think I did 'cause I killed that rat bastard DeRosa. But I didn't kill Vera." Palmer raised a shaky finger and pointed at Pete. "You find who killed her. Please. Make them pay."

His arm dropped to his side like a chunk of lead. For a moment, Pete feared he'd taken his last breath. But the paramedic calmly replaced the oxygen mask, and Pete realized Jack had merely exhausted himself.

Baronick stood as the two paramedics moved their stretcher next to the patient. He and Pete helped lift Palmer onto it.

As soon as the ambulance wheeled out of the driveway, Pete slapped Baronick on the shoulder. "Let's go take a look at what he left on his kitchen table."

Pete had to admit, Palmer was thorough. And organized, unlike his wife's office. Life insurance policies. Bank account numbers. A sheet of paper with computer passwords. An empty Jack Daniels bottle.

And a suicide note.

In it, he spelled out how he'd started thinking about killing DeRosa from the moment he learned the man was going to be the horseshow judge at the fair. That was also the moment he fell off the wagon. He stated he'd hoped to surprise DeRosa and had avoided him the first few days of the fair, until coming face-to-face with him Monday.

I slugged him. It felt great. I'd actually started to reconsider my plan before that. But hitting him felt so good, I thought removing him from the face of this earth would feel even better. Unfortunately, I'd lost the element of surprise. So I called him. I apologized and told him Cassie was well enough to come to the fair and wanted to see him. To let him know she didn't blame him. I told him I was bringing her to the school bus demo derby so she could see some kids she knew. It was all a lie. Cassie will likely never be well enough to come to another fair. But he didn't know that and bought my story. We arranged to meet near the buses Tuesday afternoon. I told him Cassie had gotten tired and was sitting inside one of the buses. He believed me.

The note went on to tell the details of the murder, all of which Zoe and Franklin Marshall had already figured out.

The ink on the last two sentences was darker—Palmer must have pressed harder with the pen—and underlined. ***I did not kill my wife and don't know who did. Please find her killer and bring him to justice***.

Baronick slipped the paper into an evidence envelope. "I guess this solves the DeRosa case. One down. One to go." His phone rang, and he excused himself, walking away.

"Yeah." Pete said to the air and looked around at the house. The photos of a smiling little girl on a pony. Of a happy family on vacation at the beach. A family destroyed in bits and pieces. First, by an accident that may or may not have been prevented. Then, by someone drugging the mother and her subsequent death—maybe an accident, maybe not. And lastly, by a desperate and devastated father and a poor decision that would land him in prison for a very long time. Assuming he survived his own attempt on his life.

Pete couldn't do anything to put the pieces of the Palmer family back together again, but he could do one last thing for Jack. Find out who was responsible for his wife's death.

Pete's phone rang, jarring him from his thoughts. "Chief Adams."

"Pete," said the woman on the other end. "This is Sandy Giden at the Vance Motel."

THIRTY-TWO

As Zoe drove her old Chevy pickup along the sparsely traveled two-lane, Ryan's words echoed in her ears. "We heard Trent say they'd spend tonight at the Vance Motel before heading west in the morning."

She approached the weathered sign for the venerable establishment and slowed to make the turn into the lot. The other voice inside her head belonged to Pete, ordering her to stay away from Trent Crosby. She knew she should call Pete and tell him where she was and why. But he was busy with Jack Palmer. Besides, if Pete, Wayne, and a barrage of local and state police showed up, there was no telling what Trent would do. Luke might get caught in the middle. And Luke was Zoe's priority.

She would somehow get the boy out and then call Pete. That was her plan. It wasn't a good one, but it was all she had at the moment.

The motel's parking lot stood mostly vacant. A small SUV and a minivan claimed spaces directly across from the office. At the far end, a battered red Honda Civic nosed in toward the last room. The vehicles by the office probably belonged to employees. Zoe headed toward the Civic and backed her truck into a space across the lot, facing the room.

She cut the engine and thought she saw the curtains move in the window. Her truck's throaty rumble made a stealthy approach impossible, but Trent had never seen the Chevy. As far as he knew, she was simply another guest checking in.

She hoped.

She waited, giving whoever had looked out a chance to return to watching TV. Or catching up on father/son stuff. Satisfied that no eyes peered out at her, she slid down from the pickup's cab and closed the door as softly as possible. After a glance toward the office, she loped across the lot to room one. At the door, she paused and rethought her plan.

How was she going to get Luke out without letting Trent know she was aware of his theft? She needed a story to explain how she'd found them, why she was there, and why Luke should go with her rather than with his dad. She fingered her phone in her hip pocket. Calling Pete suddenly sounded like a much wiser idea.

Before she had a chance to pull out the phone, the motel room door swung open, and Trent Crosby loomed over her. Her brilliant plan and any words that went along with it jammed in her throat.

"Can I help you?" he asked, his tone anything but benevolent. "Zoe, isn't it?"

"Yeah," she managed to squeak out. Trying to sound innocuous, she added, "I'm looking for Luke."

The teen appeared in the room behind Trent. "Zoe?"

Trent braced an arm against the doorframe, blocking her from entering, although entering that room was the last thing Zoe wanted to do. "What do you want with him?"

"Just to talk." She winced at the quiver in her voice.

"Merryn send you?"

"No. Merryn has no idea where you are." That much was true.

Luke moved toward them. "Aidan told you."

She looked at the teen, wishing she could telepathically clue him in. "Actually, it was Ryan."

"Damn kids," Trent muttered. "Too nosy for their own good."

Zoe kept her eyes on Luke. "Can I talk to you?"

He glanced at his father and then back to her. "What about?"

Zoe could feel Trent's hot breath on the side of her face as she peered around him. "I wanna make sure you know what you're doing." She looked up at Trent, squaring her shoulders and forcing her voice to stay level. "If you can convince me you're leaving with your father on your own volition, I'll walk away and keep your whereabouts a secret from your mother."

A glance at Luke's expression told Zoe he bought her lie. Trent, however, did not.

But he smiled at her, a smile that chilled her blood, and dropped his arm. "Okay. Come in and talk."

"I'd prefer Luke and I talk out here."

Trent's hand closed around Zoe's arm like a vice. "And I'd prefer you didn't."

She yelped as he jerked her into the room and slammed the door but feared there was no one nearby to hear.

"Toby Jones is back."

"What? Who?" Pete ran the name around in his memory.

"Toby Jones," Sandy Giden repeated. "Oh, I know you said that wasn't his real name, but I can't remember what it was. And he's checked in with the same ID you said was fake. I know I said I wouldn't rent to him again because of the whiskey, but I thought I'd pretend I didn't know anything and then call you."

Pete knew who she was talking about the moment she'd mentioned Toby Jones not being the guy's real name.

Trent Crosby.

Baronick finished his call, and Pete snapped his fingers to catch his attention, waving him over. "When did he check in?" Pete asked.

"An hour ago or so," Sandy replied. "I meant to get in touch with you right away, but I had a couple of phone calls...business stuff I had to deal with. He's in the same room as before. Number one."

"Is he alone?"

"No. I made a point to look out the window after he left the office. I could see someone else in the passenger seat. Male. I think. Or a woman with short hair."

Baronick raised both hands, palms up, in a silent question. What?

Pete responded equally as silent, holding up one finger. Wait a minute. "You did the right thing," he told Sandy. "I'm on my way. Don't approach him. If he comes to the office, act like he's any other guest. Can you do that?"

She snorted a laugh. "I already did just by registering him."

"Good." Pete checked his watch. "I'll be there in fifteen minutes."

"What?" Baronick vocalized the question that had been on his face.

"Trent Crosby checked in at the Vance Motel about an hour ago."

A smug smile crossed the detective's face. "You don't say." He held up his phone. "That call I had? It seems someone broke into the fairgrounds' office and stole the cash box. They're still trying to figure out how much was in it, but their best estimate places the total in the thousands."

"Really? A burglary at the same time as our homicide suspect bugs out."

"Another coincidence?"

"Yeah."

In unison, they said, "I hate coincidences."

Pete slapped Baronick on the shoulder. "Let's go bust a thief and maybe a killer at the same time."

"Dad?" Luke's face registered his shock when Trent flung Zoe onto one of the double beds.

She hit so hard the springs screeched in protest, and she let her instincts kick in, rolling the same way she would if she'd been thrown from a horse. Her momentum carried her to the gap between the beds, where she slammed onto her knees and bounded to her feet.

"Dad," Luke repeated. Louder this time and without the question in his voice. "What are you doing?"

Trent aimed a finger at her. The anger in his eyes made her glad it wasn't a gun. "She's here to take you away from me. You don't want that, do you? You don't want to go back to that lunatic mother of yours."

"That's not why I'm here." Well, it was. Sort of. But the fact Trent had used Merryn as her reason for being there meant Luke had no idea about the theft.

The teen faced her. "I'm not going back. She's drinking and doing drugs again. Did you know that?"

"Yeah. I know."

"She's a lousy mother. She's only gonna drag me down with her."

Somehow, the words sounded like something he'd been spoon fed the last few days.

"I'm almost an adult. I'll be eighteen in two more months, and then I can go wherever I want. Live with whoever I want. Do whatever I want."

These words did sound like his. A kid eager to be a grownup.

Because life would be so much simpler then.

Zoe held Luke's gaze, intentionally avoiding Trent's. "Are you sure he's the one you want to live with though?"

"Shut up," Trent growled.

"He's my dad," Luke said, a plaintive note in his voice that tore at her heart. "This is our chance to make up for lost time."

"On the run? That's how you want to make up for lost time?"

Trent took a menacing step toward the bed separating them. "I said, shut up."

Zoe hoped Luke was paying attention. Gone was the easygoing smile, the earnest I-just-wanna-be-a-father-to-my-kid ploy.

"We won't be on the run," Luke said. "My mother won't bother to track me down. She'll probably end up busted and back in jail."

"It won't be your mother who'll be on your heels." Zoe shifted her gaze from Luke to Trent, putting on a brave façade. "Will it?"

Trent's eye twitched. Was she imagining it, or did he shift back a bit?

She could feel Luke's confused eyes on her, but she held Trent's gaze.

"What do you mean?" the teen asked her.

Zoe didn't answer. Didn't look away from Trent. Didn't even dare blink.

Luke turned to his father. "What does she mean? Dad?"

She weighed her words. She needed to get Luke out of there, but with Trent between them and the door, fueling his rage wasn't the way to do it. Softening her tone, she said, "They know you took the money." She didn't mention that "they" meant Merryn and Shane, neither of whom would likely talk to the police. Why hadn't she called Pete?

"But *they* don't know where to find me." Trent held her gaze. Determined. Angry. But the ferocity level had ratcheted down a notch. "I'm registered under a fake name with fake credentials. Trent Crosby..." He shrugged. "...is gone."

From the corner of her eye, Zoe noticed Luke's head swivel from Trent to her and back. "What money?"

Trent's eye twitched again, but he never looked away from her. "Ignore her, son. She doesn't know what she's talking about."

"Then why are you registered here under a fake name?" Luke

asked.

Smart kid. Zoe smiled in spite of her attempt at maintaining a poker face.

Which was a mistake.

Trent wheeled toward the kid with a backhanded slap that echoed like a gunshot in the small room. The blow spun Luke and sent him crashing into the ancient television set perched on a dresser. The screen shattered in an explosion of glass. The teen hit the floor, his knees thudding on the stained carpet.

Zoe registered blood on his face. But she also noticed the heavy shell of the television rocking, tilting, slanting toward the boy. She dived toward him. The jagged edges of what was left of the screen sliced her hands, her arms. But she ignored the pain. Shoved the heavy set, redirecting its fall. It smashed to the floor next to Luke. Zoe flung herself between him and the shards, wrapping him up in her arms, shielding him from the plastic and glass shrapnel.

The room fell silent, although her ears continued to ring as if a bomb had detonated. Once that too faded, all she heard was the rasp of her breath. Her arms, her face, stung from dozens of glass cuts. A moan, childlike and plaintive, rose from the boy in her arms, and she drew him back for a look at the damage.

A dozen or more small gashes speckled his cheeks and forehead, blood streaming. His eyes appeared fine. However, one larger shard the size of a paring knife blade remained impaled above his left eyebrow.

He lifted a hand toward his face, but Zoe grabbed it, stopping him. "Don't touch it."

Behind her, she heard Trent groan. "Oh my god. Son? Are you okay?"

She didn't release Luke but shot a look over her shoulder at his father, a look that she hoped told him exactly how much she despised him in that moment. Merryn was no gem by any means. But Zoe completely understood why she'd kept Luke shielded from this man. Why she'd been so determined to keep her son away from the midway. Why she'd been so furious at Zoe for allowing Luke to spend time with Trent.

He must have read the revulsion in her eyes, but instead of

walking away as she hoped, he took a step closer. "Luke? I'm so sorry. I promise it'll never happen again."

The boy trembled in Zoe's arms. He kept his head lowered, not looking at his father, but she didn't take her eyes off the man. "You're damned right it'll never happen again."

"I was upset. I'm sorry."

"Were you upset when you killed Vera Palmer too?" she asked.

"Huh?"

Luke lifted his face, choking a sob. "You killed Mrs. Palmer?"

"No," Trent said so firmly Zoe almost believed him.

Almost. "The police are looking for you. Not only because you stole the money from the fair office, but because they have you listed as a person of interest in Vera's death."

"I didn't." Trent sputtered, his face reddening.

Luke slumped, making no more effort to stop his tears. Zoe tightened her arms around him, careful of the glass sticking from his forehead. "You didn't what?" she asked, not caring about tact. There and then, with the boy crumpled and devastated, she knew nothing was going to keep her from walking him out of that room. Trent Crosby be damned. "You didn't steal the fair's money?"

"No. I mean, yeah. But—but—I didn't—I had nothing to do with—"

She shook her head, tuning him out and shifting her full attention to Luke. "Can you stand up?"

"Yeah."

Still holding him, she climbed to her feet, bringing the teen with her. "We're gonna walk out that door," she said to Luke, but the dare in her tone was for Trent's benefit. The look she shot at him said clearer than words—she would kill him if he tried to stop her. She wasn't sure how, but she would.

Trent swallowed. Nodded in understanding. And stepped out of her way.

She guided Luke across the stained carpet, acutely aware of Trent's position. Ready to take action if he made a move. At the door, Zoe reached for the knob, only then realizing how much blood she was losing too. With one sticky hand, she opened the door.

And came face-to-face with Pete.

THIRTY-THREE

Pete stood outside room one and raised his fist to knock when the door swung open. The sight of Zoe with slashed arms, blood everywhere, and Luke looking like he'd gone ten rounds with Freddy Krueger, stopped him cold. "What the hell?"

"We need an ambulance," she said, matter-of-factly.

Pete turned to Baronick who stood gape-mouthed behind him.

The detective gave a quick nod and pulled his phone from his pocket. "On it."

Pete ushered the wounded pair from the room. "What happened? Who did this?"

A glimpse of movement from inside answered part of his question and brought him back to his reason for being there. In one quick, practiced move, Pete released his Glock from his holster and brought it up, aimed at Trent Crosby. "Police. Let me see your hands."

Crosby complied, jerking both hands up so fast it might have been comical. If Zoe wasn't covered in blood. Some of which Pete was certain was hers.

"Don't shoot," Crosby said. "I'm not armed."

Pete edged into the room, his eyes taking a moment to adjust from the bright August sunlight to the dim interior. Baronick, sidearm drawn, appeared at Pete's side.

He took in the scene before him. Two beds, unslept in. A large duffel that looked like something Crosby had picked up at the Army Surplus store sat on one bed. A smaller overnight bag plastered with 4-H and horse stickers on the other.

The remnants of a television lay scattered in pieces across a full quarter of the room's floor.

"Put your hands on your head," Pete ordered. "And get down on your knees."

Crosby appeared as broken as the TV. He did as he was told.

Within ten minutes, an ambulance arrived along with two marked county police vehicles. By then, Pete had settled a handcuffed Crosby into the backseat of his Vance Township SUV and let him mull over his future.

Zoe stood at the ambulance's rear doors, pouring sterile saline onto her arms to wash away the blood. Her two colleagues worked on Luke inside, cleaning his facial cuts.

Pete crossed his arms. "I didn't realize Mon County EMS had gone self-serve."

She grinned up at him. "My injuries are superficial. The only reason they gave me the bottle of saline is because the blood was creeping Luke out."

"What about your shirt?"

From inside the ambulance, Luke yelped when one of the paramedics removed the shard of glass and quickly covered the cut with a sterile gauze square. "I think the blood on her shirt is mine," he said.

Zoe pinched the fabric and tugged it away from her skin. "Yep. It's yours, all right."

"Sorry."

She dismissed him with a wave. "Not your fault."

One of the paramedics took a closer look at the wound left by the formerly impaled glass. "That one's gonna need stitches."

"Is it gonna scar?" The kid sounded entirely too eager.

"Probably," Zoe said. "You'll look like a real badass."

"Cool."

Pete crooked a finger at her. "Can I talk to you a minute?"

"Sure."

He led her away from the ambulance to the edge of the parking lot, clear of the action, and reached up to gently thumb a red mark on her cheek. She winced, tipping her face away from his touch. "All kidding aside. Are you okay?"

Zoe held out her forearms and palms. The bleeding had stopped and none of the dozens of small cuts appeared to need stitches. "Like I said. Superficial."

"I'm not talking about that."

She gave him that slow sexy smile that made him want to take her far from places like this, far from danger, to someplace safe where there were only the two of them. Alone. "I'm better now," she said.

One of the county cops came out of Crosby's hotel room, holding up the Army Surplus duffel. "Found the money from the fairgrounds burglary."

Pete watched Baronick approach his officer to deal with the evidence. "What happened in there?" he asked Zoe.

She told him about returning to the fairgrounds, learning about the theft, and going to look for Crosby. Pete clenched his fists at her foolishness but kept quiet, letting her talk. She told him about Merryn and Shane showing up, apparently now a couple. And about Merryn slugging her.

"So Crosby didn't do that?" Pete pointed at the red mark on her cheek.

Zoe fingered the spot, wincing again. "No. And all things considered, I can't blame Merryn. I screwed up, encouraging Trent to be a dad to Luke."

"You meant well. How'd you end up here?"

"I ran into Earl's boys. They're the ones who told me Luke had run off with Trent and where they planned to stay tonight."

Pete gave her the best angry look he could muster. "Why didn't you call me?"

"I should have. I know. But I was hoping to get Luke out of there before you cops surrounded the place and freaked Trent out."

Pete made a point of eyeing her sliced-and-diced arms. "How'd that work out for you?"

"I know, I know. It was a bonehead move."

"Go on. What happened when you got here?"

She shared the rest of the story. Crosby throwing her across the room, backhanding the boy, and the resulting unfortunate assault with a deadly television set. "Your turn. You said Trent's a person of interest in Vera's death. He denied killing her to me, but seriously, what else would he say?"

"The night Vera died, Crosby was here. In that same room. Vera was here too. I found her phone and the heel from her shoe over there."

Pete gestured to the spot where Zoe's truck now sat. He looked toward his SUV. And Crosby in the backseat. "He either had something to do with her death or he knows about it."

"Then let's go ask him." Zoe started toward Pete's car before he had a chance to stop her.

He jogged and caught her arm. "You aren't going anywhere except to the hospital to get checked out."

She gave him a skeptical laugh. "I don't need to go to the hospital. And Trent and I already have a rapport."

"Yeah. I see that." Pete made a point of eyeing her cuts.

"I got these saving his son from having that monstrosity of a television set fall on him. Trent owes me."

Pete looked toward the ambulance. One of the medics slammed the passenger compartment door and headed around to climb behind the wheel. Movement at the end of the motel's drive drew his attention from the departing ambulance. His other township police vehicle rolled into the lot, Abby driving and Seth riding shotgun. "All right," Pete said. "But on two conditions."

Zoe cocked a hip. "What conditions?"

He held up one finger. "You keep quiet and let Baronick and me ask the questions."

She shrugged. Not a firm commitment. But even if she gave her word, Pete doubted she'd keep it.

He held up a second finger. "As soon as we're done, I'm taking you to the ER."

"I don't—" She shot a glance at her watch. "Crap. I'm supposed to be on call with Earl at the fairgrounds in five minutes."

"You're gonna be late."

"I gotta call him." She pulled out her phone. "Do not start without me."

Like her noncommittal agreement to keep quiet during questioning, Pete wasn't making any promises either.

Baronick had finished chatting with his officer and headed to Pete's vehicle. And Trent Crosby. Pete left Zoe to her call and joined the detective. They shared a knowing nod. Baronick opened the back door where Crosby sat, looking downtrodden and uncomfortable with his hands bound behind his back.

"You have the right to remain silent," Baronick began.

"I know my rights."

The detective finished Mirandizing him anyway and concluded with, "Do you understand these rights?"

"I told you I did." Crosby squirmed and winced, but didn't ask them to remove the cuffs.

"Tell us about last Thursday night," Pete said.

"Last Thursday?" Crosby made a face as if trying to remember. "Sorry. I don't recall anything about it."

"Let me help." Pete braced a hand on the doorframe and shifted toward the man in the rear of his car. "You checked in here. Same room. Under the name Toby Jones. Ring a bell?"

He squirmed again, but this time Pete suspected it wasn't his shoulders causing the discomfort. "Maybe."

"Why the fake name?"

Crosby glared at him. "You've met Merryn Schultz. I didn't want her knowing I was in the area."

"A reasonable answer." Pete didn't let on that he wasn't buying it. There would be time enough to get back to that later. "Tell me about Vera Palmer."

"Who?" Crosby asked smugly. The guy was a horrible liar.

"The woman you met here."

"I didn't meet any woman here. And definitely no one named Vera Palmer."

"What'd you do? Have drinks?"

Crosby stared straight ahead, his jaw set.

"Maybe you wanted to have some fun, and she wasn't as willing as you'd like. So you slipped something into her drink."

He brought his gaze to meet Pete's. "I never had drinks with her. And I sure didn't slip her a Mickey, if that's what you're suggesting."

"A Mickey, a roofie, whatever drug is your choice for getting what you want from a woman."

"What? No. I would never."

"Look. We know you were here. The motel owner IDed you. We know Vera Palmer was here. I found her phone and the heel that matches the shoe she wore when I found her body. Now are you honestly trying to tell us you had nothing to do with what happened to her?"

Crosby swallowed, his face paling. "Yes, that's exactly what I'm telling you."

Footsteps drew Pete's attention and he looked up to see Abby and Seth approaching. He also noticed Zoe had slipped up behind him and really was keeping quiet.

"Chief?" Abby said and gestured him toward them. "We have something you need to see."

Baronick gave Pete a nod. "I'll keep our friend company."

Abby and Seth led Pete back to their cruiser. "I was going through Vera's phone and found something interesting."

"A text?" Pete asked.

"No. That's why I hadn't noticed it before. I was searching texts and phone calls." Abby held Vera's phone in her hand and scrolled through the screen options before tapping it. She held it up for Pete.

A map appeared on the screen. "What am I looking at?"

"Vera Palmer had a tracker app installed on her phone."

"A what?"

"Like what parents use to see where their kids go. Only she wasn't tracking her kid. She was tracking her husband."

Pete looked at Abby. Her eyes gleamed with the kind of excitement young cops feel when they crack a big case. He took the phone from her and studied the path drawn on it.

"That's from last Thursday night."

"Vera wasn't checking texts on her phone at the restaurant," Pete mused out loud.

"Nope. She was checking on her husband. Tailing him without leaving her chair."

Pete zoomed in on the map for a better look at where Jack Palmer's wanderings had taken him. He'd told Pete he'd been at home all night.

He'd lied.

Pete stopped. Zoomed in more. "Is that what I think it is?"

Abby's excited grin grew. "Yeah. Jack Palmer was right here last Thursday."

"Good work, Officer Baronick." Pete turned to head back to his car and Crosby. "Come with me."

Abby's brother continued to stand guard over their prisoner. Zoe remained at Baronick's side, although she looked ready to explode. Behaving was hard on her.

Pete resumed his previous position, one hand braced on the doorframe, the other resting on his sidearm, except this time his fingers curled around Vera's phone. "Let's try this again, Mr. Crosby. Tell me about last Thursday night."

He glanced from Pete to Baronick and back. The worried furrow of his brow told Pete the man sensed something had changed in the last few minutes. "I already told you all I know. Yeah, I was here using a different name. But I had nothing to do with whatever happened to Vera Palmer."

"What about Jack Palmer?" Pete sensed more than saw Zoe's head snap around to look at him. Baronick's reaction was more subtle. But the downward shift in Crosby's posture was pronounced.

He didn't say anything for several long moments, but kept his head lowered, his shoulders slumped as if the weight of the truth had become too much to bear. Pete waited.

Crosby straightened. "Jack and I used to be friends. Before he met Vera and cleaned up his act. That night...last Thursday...he came to see me. He was already drunk, but didn't turn down my offer of whiskey. He was upset. To say the least. I'd heard about his daughter getting hurt but didn't know the whole story until then. And he told me the dude responsible for the accident was gonna be at the fair. Gonna be the judge or whatever. Jack couldn't stand it. Knowing this guy was walking around doing whatever he damned well pleased while Cassie was stuck in a wheelchair. Jack started ranting about wanting to kill the guy. I didn't believe him. At least not at first. I figured, you know, he was drunk. But he was also darker than I'd ever seen him."

Crosby grew quiet. His eyes focused on the seat back in front of him as if he was watching that night play out on an invisible movie screen.

After a few moments, he lowered his gaze. "By the time Jack left, he was blitzed. I told him he shouldn't drive, but he didn't listen. I went to the window to make sure he didn't fall in the parking lot. That's when I saw her."

"Vera?" Pete asked softly.

"Yeah. She was parked across from my room. I don't know how she knew he was here, but she looked pissed. Arms folded. Tapping her foot. You know. Angry-wife pissed."

Pete didn't like where this was headed. "What happened next?"

"Not much. Not really. I couldn't hear anything, but I could see she was reading him the riot act. He was yelling too. Arms flailing. Full-blown screaming match. Then he started to walk away. She grabbed him by the arm. Maybe she was like me. Not wanting him to drive in that condition. He tried to pull free. She wouldn't let go." Crosby took a breath. "And he shoved her. Not all that hard from what I could see. Just trying to get her off him. But she had those shoes on. The kind with high heels. I never could figure out how a woman could walk in those things. She must have twisted her ankle because she fell backwards. Whacked her head on her car. Hard."

"What did Jack do?"

"Nothing. I don't even think he realized she fell. He walked away. Got in his car and left."

"What did *you* do?"

"I opened the door of my room. Was gonna go out and make sure she was okay. But she got up. Dusted herself off. Got back in her car and drove away. She was fine. You gotta believe me."

No, he didn't have to. But he did.

Zoe cleared her throat. "Pete?"

He looked at her. "Yeah?"

"Vera had an epidural hematoma."

"Yeah?"

"Remember that actress, Natasha Richardson?"

He thought back. "She died in a skiing accident?"

"Sort of. She fell while skiing and refused medical treatment but died hours later. From an epidural hematoma."

Pete pictured the scene Crosby had described. It made sense. Everyone who knew Vera said she wouldn't have been drunk. Pete had found her face down in the brambles, but the injury had been to the back of her skull.

Received when she stumbled, broke her shoe, and hit the back of her head on her car.

From then on, she'd bled into her brain, become impaired, and eventually wandered across the Roadhouse's parking lot to die in the weeds.

Which left one thing nagging at him. "I believed Jack Palmer when he acted like he had no idea what happened to his wife. He lied about not seeing her that night."

"Maybe not," Crosby said.

Pete turned back to their fairgrounds thief. "What do you mean?"

"One of the main reasons Jack decided to quit drinking all those years ago? He started scaring himself." Crosby's gaze swept the group gathered around the car. "Jack suffered from blackouts."

THIRTY-FOUR

Zoe placed a call to Franklin to ask about Vera's toxicology report. He told her he'd just returned to his office from a traffic fatality and would check with the lab and get back to her. She used the pending call to help bargain her way into joining Pete and Wayne when they spoke to Jack Palmer. The rest of the deal involved her agreeing to let the ER docs check her out. But as she stood with the two cops outside Jack's hospital room, she suffered a pang of doubt.

Jack would survive his bout of carbon monoxide poisoning. The doctor called him lucky. Not the word Zoe would have used. He'd admitted to murdering Cody and would likely spend time in prison, although he presented an excellent case for a temporary insanity defense. His daughter had essentially lost both parents. And now he was about to learn that his wife's death had been his fault.

Jack's doctor spoke with them in hushed tones. "It's good you found him when you did. Five more minutes and he'd have suffered brain damage. Or worse. Psychologically, he's still in bad shape." The doctor looked from Pete to Wayne. "I don't suppose I can convince you fellows to put this off for a few weeks until he's in better condition?"

"Believe me," Pete said, "we're not looking forward to this. But it has to be done."

The doctor pursed his lips. "I'm going to be in there with you. I will cut you off if he becomes too agitated."

"Agreed."

Zoe trailed the men through the door. She remembered the first time she'd seen Jack, helping to catch the runaway pony. It felt like a lifetime ago. She also remembered when he'd received the news that Vera was dead. He'd reminded her of a deflated balloon. Now, in the hospital bed, his skin matched the white sheets. Tubing fed him oxygen and IV fluids. But he still seemed as flat and lifeless as the balloon. Eyes filled with sorrow and exhaustion looked up as they entered.

He'd wanted to die earlier today. Zoe couldn't help but think in some significant way, he had.

Wayne took the lead without any argument from Pete. "Hey, Jack."

His lips moved, forming Wayne's name, but if any sound came out, Zoe couldn't hear it.

"We need to ask you a few questions," Wayne said softly.

The doctor stepped forward. "But only if you feel up to it."

Jack looked from Wayne to Pete. "Vera?" he said in a whispery rasp.

With Jack focused on Pete, Wayne gestured. Go ahead.

"You said the last time you saw your wife was when she left to have dinner with her friends. Is that right?"

"Yes."

"And you were home alone all night last Thursday."

Jack gave a weak nod. "Yes."

"Are you sure about that?"

His eyes shifted slightly, thinking, before coming back to Pete. "Yes."

"I found Vera's phone."

"Oh?"

"Outside the Vance Motel."

Jack looked away, his forehead furrowed in thought. This time, he didn't come back to meet Pete's gaze.

"Do you have any idea what she was doing there?"

Jack shook his head.

Zoe studied him, searching for any hint of deception. She knew Pete was doing the same.

"Jack," Wayne said, "were you drinking that night?"

He snapped his gaze to meet Wayne's. Zoe spotted a glimmer of tears filling Jack's lower lids.

"No," he replied, but with an upturn at the end of the word, making it sound like a question.

Wayne tipped his head down and fixed him with a stern, paternal glare. "Jack?"

He closed his eyes. "Yes."

"How much?"

"I don't know."

Wayne looked at Pete who gave an almost imperceptible nod.

"Jack," Pete said, his voice still soft, but more commanding.

Jack opened his eyes, still gleaming with tears, and looked at Pete.

"Vera's phone had an app on it, set to track you. Did you know that?"

"No."

"It tracked you to the Vance Motel. To where Trent Crosby was staying. According to him, you paid him a visit. Had some more whiskey." Pete paused. "Made threats to kill Cody DeRosa." He paused again. "Do you remember any of that?"

"No."

"Are you saying it never happened?"

"No. I'm saying...I don't remember."

"Why do you think you don't remember?"

Zoe didn't think Jack could become any smaller, but he proved her wrong.

"I...have blackouts when I drink."

Pete and Wayne exchanged a look, but neither spoke.

Zoe's phone vibrated in her pocket. She pulled it out to find a text from Franklin.

The pause gave Jack time to process what had already been said. Realization—or partial realization at least—widened his eyes. "Vera was there? She saw me?"

"And you saw her."

The tears overflowed the bounds of Jack's eyes. "What happened?" From his tone, he already feared the worst.

"According to Trent, you and your wife had an argument in the parking lot as you were leaving. She tried to stop you. You pushed her. And she fell, hitting her head on the car."

"I—I would never hurt her. I loved her. I..." Jack choked.

The doctor raised a hand. "I think he's had enough."

Zoe edged closer to Pete, nudged him, and held up her phone. Wayne leaned in to read the message as well.

"We're about done," Pete told the doctor. He turned back to Jack.

"Trent said you didn't push her hard. But she was wearing heels and fell. You were already headed back to your car and probably didn't even see what happened."

"But you said she was drunk. Someone got her drunk. You said you found her body near Parson's. Not at the Vance Motel." The outburst seemed to suck every bit of energy Jack could muster, and by the end of it, Zoe had to read his lips to know what he said.

"That's what we thought," Wayne said. "But when she hit her head, she started bleeding into her brain. You were right when you said she'd never have gotten drunk. The lab work from her autopsy showed no drugs in her system and a blood alcohol level consistent with the one glass of wine consumed with dinner."

"Taking all the evidence into consideration, here's what I believe happened," Pete said. "After the incident at the Vance Motel, Vera drove back to Parson's. What the waitress interpreted as intoxication was actually the progressing effects of the subdural hematoma. In a daze, she left the restaurant, staggered across the parking lot and the road, and collapsed in the weeds where I found her."

"But it all started at the Vance Motel?"

"Afraid so."

Jack fell silent, his eyes shifting. Zoe could only imagine the horrors running through his mind. "If only..." he whispered. Then he covered his face with his hands and wept. "If only I hadn't been drunk—if I hadn't gone to see Trent—" His voice broke. "She'd still be alive. It's my fault. I killed my wife."

THIRTY-FIVE

"I now pronounce you husband and wife. Miguel, you may kiss your bride."

Zoe watched as Miguel Morales took Rose into his arms to a round of applause from the gathered friends and family.

This was the second time Zoe had stood up for her best friend, but it was no less sweet. She pictured Ted looking down on them, also smiling. He would be pleased to see Rose and their kids happy once again.

Even the weather cooperated with a clear and comfortably cool day, ideal for the outdoor wedding at Willow Creek County Park overlooking one of the area's premier fishing lakes. With the short notice, Rose hadn't been able to secure any of her first choices for the ceremony. Gazing across the sparkling water dotted with small fishing boats, Zoe decided the fallback plan had been serendipity.

Rose cleared her throat, snapping Zoe's attention back to her maid of honor duties. She returned Rose's bouquet—of roses—to her. Logan, on his guitar, strummed a lovely rendition of a song Zoe couldn't quite put a name to, but it seemed perfect for the occasion. Rose and Miguel led the recessional down the aisle between folding chairs provided by the fire department. Zoe moved to follow, pausing to take Pete's arm.

She wondered if it had been Miguel's idea to ask Pete to be his best man or if Sylvia and/or Rose influenced his choice.

Zoe didn't care. He looked more handsome than ever in a black suit with a charcoal shirt and tie that set off his salt-and-pepper hair. She'd had a hard time keeping her eyes off him and on the bride and groom.

Behind them, Allison brought up the rear, holding the hand of her new little stepsister. The two girls—one sixteen, the other six—had walked Rose down the aisle and had "given" her to be wed at the start of the ceremony.

White and gold streamers decorated the picnic pavilion only yards away. A breeze fluttered the table coverings and swayed the tissue-paper bells hanging from the rafters.

Pete leaned over to Zoe and whispered, "I'm going to help Bert." He strode away to wheel Rose's ailing and invalid mother from her spot in the front row to the reception.

The breeze coming off the lake raised goosebumps on Zoe's bare arms and ruffled her gauzy dress. After the heat of the prior weeks, she didn't mind the slight chill.

Sylvia appeared at her side. "It was lovely, don't you think?"

"Very." Zoe noticed a sheen of tears in the older woman's eyes. They didn't appear to be totally happy ones. "You know you'll always be Rose's family, right?"

Sylvia blew a raspberry. "Of course." She didn't sound so convinced.

Zoe slipped an arm around her shoulders. "Family isn't about blood, you know. It's about heart."

Sylvia gave her a squeeze. "You're absolutely right."

For several moments they watched the bride and groom greet their guests, which mostly consisted of Rose's friends and neighbors from Vance Township.

"Speaking of family," Sylvia said, "have you heard what will become of that little girl? The one whose father was arrested."

"Cassidy Palmer." Zoe's gaze settled on Miguel's daughter, happily romping around the pavilion with Allison in mock pursuit. "Children and Youth Services have taken over her case since Vera's gone and Jack's up on homicide charges."

"How sad."

"Diane Garland has applied to be her foster mom."

Sylvia looked up at Zoe. "The 4-H leader? I thought you said she'd embezzled from the club."

"Yes, but the members and their parents rallied around her. They refuse to press charges and are planning a series of fund-raisers to replace the money she took and maybe a little extra to help her out with her medical expenses."

"That's pretty generous of them."

Zoe rubbed her arms against the cool breeze and thought of her old 4-H leader's nervous habit of doing the same thing. "Diane has always gone above and beyond for her kids. The parents know that."

"What about that issue with the kids not being able to qualify for the district show?"

"Wayne Baronick spoke to the county extension agent and explained the situation. And apparently the state regulations are more lenient and don't require the project books be submitted until later in the year anyway. Everyone who qualified at the fair will get to show at district."

Sylvia grunted. "I guess that idiot detective has his moments."

Zoe bit her lip to keep from laughing. "Yeah. He does." She watched as Pete set the brakes on Bert's wheelchair, parking her at the end of the picnic table reserved for the bridal party and family. Patsy approached the frail old woman and knelt to talk to her.

"How's she doing?" Sylvia asked gesturing toward Patsy and Bert.

Since Sylvia had been chatting with Bert before the ceremony, Zoe assumed she meant Patsy. "She's okay. I think she liked Shane more than any of us realized. Their breakup hit her hard."

"He's a jackass," Sylvia muttered.

"You'll get no argument from me."

Pete caught Zoe's gaze and headed toward them without a hint of a limp.

"Shane and Merryn are an item now," Zoe said. "Even though Merryn's back in rehab."

"Where's that leave her son?"

Another breeze renewed Zoe's chill. "Luke is staying with friends." She looked over at Bert and Rose. "Like I did when Mother moved to Florida."

"He turns eighteen in two weeks," Pete added. "Legally, he'll be an adult."

"And I talked to him last week." Zoe smiled at the memory. "He's signing up for community college classes to be a veterinary technician." Luke Holmes was going to be okay. In spite of his parents.

"Are you cold?" Pete asked.

"A little. This dress would've been great if it was still in the nineties instead of the seventies."

He shrugged out of his suit jacket, paused to take something from its pocket, and draped it over Zoe's shoulders. "Better?"

Pete's body heat clung to the jacket's lining and warmed her on a much deeper level than mere fabric blocking the wind. "Much. Thanks."

He slipped both hands into his pants pockets.

"There's still a couple things I'd like to know," Zoe said. "You told me Vera had called Cody a couple days before her death. Why?"

"With them both dead, we'll never know for sure. But if I was to guess, I'd say Vera knew Jack was growing increasingly angry and unstable and wanted to warn Cody."

"Makes sense."

Sylvia ran a hand through her windswept curls. "What I want to know is why did Cody want to meet you that night at the fair."

Zoe pointed at her. "That's the other thing I want to know too."

Pete shook his head. "Something else we'll never have an answer for."

"But if you were to guess?" Zoe asked.

"I think you were partly right at the time when you said he wanted to report the assault. But it wasn't Shane who hit him. It was Jack. Maybe he even feared Jack would do exactly what he did."

Sylvia gazed across the lake. "Pete's suppositions were as close as we'll come to real answers. I guess that wraps everything up."

"Almost." Zoe glanced at Pete and grinned. "There's still the matter of Cassidy Palmer's horse."

Sylvia eyed her suspiciously. "Oh?"

"I'm taking her in."

"I thought the horse was lame."

"Only when ridden. She can live in blissful retirement at my place. And if Patsy decides she wants to show at the fair next year, Cassidy's mare can keep Windstar company." Zoe didn't say it, but she privately declared her horseshow days *over*.

"And if Cassidy ever wants to visit her horse, she'll know where to find her," Pete said.

The softness in Pete's tone when he spoke about the girl made Zoe fall in love with him all over again.

"Yeah. At Chambers Home for Old and Infirmed Equines."

"You got it."

The older woman chuckled. "Okay, you two. I'm going to help with the buffet table."

Pete hooked a finger at the knot in his tie and loosened it. "You're not supposed to work. You're one of the honored guests."

"I'm also part of the fire department's auxiliary, and we're the ones catering this shindig." She fluttered a hand at them and shuffled toward the pavilion.

Pete looked at Zoe. "I gather you've decided not to sell your horse."

She stiffened. "I...didn't realize you knew about that."

"About Cody DeRosa's proposition? Baronick told me."

Wayne. Of course. Big mouth. "He's worse than an old woman when it comes to spreading gossip."

"That's all it was? Gossip?"

Zoe thought back to...had it only been little more than a week ago? When for a brief moment, she'd contemplated accepting the offer.

Pete leaned closer until she felt his breath on her cheek. "I wouldn't have let you do it, you know."

Surprised, she shifted back so she could see his face. "I thought you'd be thrilled to have me get rid of Windstar. And the farm. Or as you call it, the money pit."

He stuffed his hands back in his pockets and gazed across the lake. "But then where would we live?"

Perplexed, Zoe opened her mouth but didn't know what to say.

Pete turned to face her, brought his hands from his pockets...and lowered to one knee.

"What are you...?"

From the direction of the pavilion, she heard a collective gasp.

Or maybe the gasp she heard was her own when a small burgundy velvet box appeared in his hands. He opened it to reveal a diamond ring.

"I asked you once before, and you didn't say yes. You told me to ask again. Well, here I am. And I'm asking. Zoe Chambers, will you do me the honor of marrying me?"

A million colliding thoughts rushed through her brain, clogging her throat and blurring her eyes. A million reasons why she wanted to say yes.

One choking reason why she couldn't.

"Get up," she whispered.

"No. Not until you say yes."

"Are you serious?"

He rolled his eyes. Looked toward the pavilion. Then back at her. "I wouldn't be down here on one knee getting grass stains on my only good suit trousers if I wasn't."

She sensed the silence from the wedding crowd. Twenty people holding their breaths. If she said no in front of everyone, Pete would be mortified. Humiliated. As would she. If she said yes for their sake and then took it back in private, the humiliation would simply be delayed.

Swallowing the lump in her throat, she dropped to her knees in the grass in front of him. And whispered, "There's something about me you don't know."

"I don't care. I know all I need to."

The right words, but she shook her head. "I should have told you before." Long before. Years before. "But..." But what? She was a coward who couldn't face her own truth. Denial had been her normal state of being for decades.

He must have read the agony in her face. "What is it? Whatever it is, it doesn't matter."

"Yes, it does. I know you want a family. Kids." She tried to swallow again, but her mouth had gone dry. "But I can't give you that. I—I can't have children."

He studied her. She felt his eyes burning into her soul. The soul she'd finally laid bare to him.

He rested one elbow on his knee. Reached up to cup her cheek with his other hand. "Look at me."

She lifted her eyes to meet his ice blue ones.

"I can live my life without kids. I can't live without you. Hell, you're always collecting strays anyway. Once we move onto your farm and you start boarding more horses, there will be kids all over the place."

The picture his words evoked brought a rush of heat to her face and choked a laugh from her throat.

"Zoe," he said, his voice raspy. "Marry me."

She ran the picture through her mind again. The two of them on the farm. Horses. Kids. Not their kids, but kids nonetheless. Her own words came back to her.

Family isn't about blood. It's about heart.

"Yes," Zoe whispered. Then louder for their audience. "Yes. I will marry you."

ANNETTE DASHOFY

USA Today bestselling author Annette Dashofy has spent her entire life in rural Pennsylvania surrounded by cattle and horses. When she wasn't roaming the family's farm or playing in the barn, she could be found reading or writing. After high school, she spent five years as an EMT on the local ambulance service, dealing with everything from drunks passing out on the sidewalk to mangled bodies in car accidents. These days, she, her husband, and their spoiled cat, Kensi, live on property that was once part of her grandfather's dairy.

**Books in the Zoe Chambers Mystery Series
by Annette Dashofy**

Henery Press Mystery Books

And finally, before you go...
Here are a few other mysteries
you might enjoy:

STAGING IS MURDER

Grace Topping

A Laura Bishop Mystery (#1)

Laura Bishop just nabbed her first decorating commission—staging a 19th-century mansion that hasn't been updated for decades. But when a body falls from a laundry chute and lands at Laura's feet, replacing flowered wallpaper becomes the least of her duties.

To clear her assistant of the murder and save her fledgling business, Laura's determined to find the killer. Turns out it's not as easy as renovating a manor home, especially with two handsome men complicating her mission: the police detective on the case and the real estate agent trying to save the manse from foreclosure.

Worse still, the meddling of a horoscope-guided friend, a determined grandmother, and the local funeral director could get them all killed before Laura props the first pillow.

Available at booksellers nationwide and online

Visit www.henerypress.com for details

BOARD STIFF

Kendel Lynn

An Elliott Lisbon Mystery (#1)

As director of the Ballantyne Foundation on Sea Pine Island, SC, Elliott Lisbon scratches her detective itch by performing discreet inquiries for Foundation donors. Usually nothing more serious than retrieving a pilfered Pomeranian. Until Jane Hatting, Ballantyne board chair, is accused of murder. The Ballantyne's reputation tanks, Jane's headed to a jail cell, and Elliott's sexy ex is the new lieutenant in town.

Armed with moxie and her Mini Coop, Elliott uncovers a trail of blackmail schemes, gambling debts, illicit affairs, and investment scams. But the deeper she digs to clear Jane's name, the guiltier Jane looks. The closer she gets to the truth, the more treacherous her investigation becomes. With victims piling up faster than shells at a clambake, Elliott realizes she's next on the killer's list.

Available at booksellers nationwide and online

Visit www.henerypress.com for details

ARTIFACT

Gigi Pandian

A Jaya Jones Treasure Hunt Mystery (#1)

Historian Jaya Jones discovers the secrets of a lost Indian treasure may be hidden in a Scottish legend from the days of the British Raj. But she's not the only one on the trail...

From San Francisco to London to the Highlands of Scotland, Jaya must evade a shadowy stalker as she follows hints from the hastily scrawled note of her dead lover to a remote archaeological dig. Helping her decipher the cryptic clues are her magician best friend, a devastatingly handsome art historian with something to hide, and a charming archaeologist running for his life.

Available at booksellers nationwide and online

Visit www.henerypress.com for details

MURDER AT THE PALACE

Margaret Dumas

A Movie Palace Mystery (#1)

Welcome to the Palace movie theater! Now Showing: Philandering husbands, ghostly sidekicks, and a murder or two.

When Nora Paige's movie-star husband leaves her for his latest co-star, she flees Hollywood to take refuge in San Francisco at the Palace, a historic movie theater that shows the classic films she loves. There she finds a band of misfit film buffs who care about movies (almost) as much as she does.

She also finds some shady financial dealings and the body of a murdered stranger. Oh, and then there's Trixie, the lively ghost of a 1930's usherette who appears only to Nora and has a lot to catch up on. With the help of her new ghostly friend, can Nora catch the killer before there's another murder at the Palace?

Available at booksellers nationwide and online

Visit www.henerypress.com for details